The little girl coul[...] His hair was matted and longer than hers, his body streaked with dirt. "Where are your clothes?" she demanded.

He reached up slowly to touch her fine, blond hair. It was as exciting as he had imagined. His little red tongue darted like a serpent's.

His fingers folded now like a bird's claw, now opening and closing spasmodically.

He saw her hand before him, got overly excited, and grasped it too quickly, his long nails digging into her dainty skin. She screamed . . .

Also in Arrow by Andrew Neiderman

Pin
Brainchild
Someone's Watching
Tender Loving Care

IMP

Andrew Neiderman

ARROW BOOKS

Arrow Books Ltd
62-65 Chandos Place, London WC2N 4NW

An imprint of Century Hutchinson Ltd

London Melbourne Sydney Auckland
Johannesburg and agencies throughout
the world

First published in Great Britain 1986

Printed and bound in Great Britain by
Anchor Brendon Limited, Tiptree, Essex

ISBN 0 09 942480 0

For Diane,
because it gets stronger
"as time goes by"

Preface

Old Cy Baum paused on his early evening jaunt. Usually, he covered the whole street, from his place all the way down to the turn leading into Centerville. There were ten other houses beside his on Wildwood Drive, but they were spaced far apart with woods and fields between them. This was still one of the quietest and prettiest secondary roads in the township. People guarded their clear land closely; there was little interest in giving any of it up to further home development. Cy liked it that way and hoped it would never change. In fact, he was disappointed when the O'Neils sold their parcel, opening it up to home construction, twenty years ago. Before that, there were only three houses here: his, the O'Neils', and the Oakses'.

All of his contemporaries on this road were dead. He was friendly enough with all their children; all except Mary Oaks. Widowed in her thirties, she was a tight-lipped, uncongenial sort wrapped up in her religious zealousness and her teenage daughter. The girl was pleasant enough, but always looked a little frightened. He imagined Mary Oaks had somehow poisoned her against him.

Two bats circling Mary Oaks' porch light were what stopped him. The sight of them froze him. He could tolerate most any animal, had hunted and trapped

1

almost every kind of game available in this part of the Catskills, but bats turned his stomach. He'd handled snakes, even kept one alive by his house, fed raccoons, let beaver live nearby; but bats were too much of nature gone bad.

He would have gone on, walked his distance as he had planned, ignored the bats, if it weren't for that godforsaken cry—that piercing, shrill scream unlike anything he had ever heard. It seemed a cross between something human and something wild. It drove him into the road, curled his toes, and arched his back like a cat.

Just as suddenly as he had heard it, he didn't. He listened hard, but it simply wasn't there. For a moment he wasn't sure he had actually heard it. He was sure that, whatever it was, it came from the Oakses' house. He wondered if he should go up and knock on the door to see if anything was wrong.

But the bats settled that question. They were still there.

He could stand anything but getting close to them . . . never. He satisfied his conscience by listening hard for a good minute. There were no more screams; just the sound of peepers and the rush of the stream that crossed under the road and went on to Brown's Pond.

So he walked on, now plodding as a man of seventy-five normally would, instead of as he usually walked. His remarkable energy had been sapped by the sight of the bats and the sound of that . . . whatever it was.

He was unhappy because there was no moon, too. It was darker than ever; it was a night for death. He could almost smell it. It spun him around and sent him trekking toward home, after only half completing his walk. His wife, Hilda, was surprised.

"You didn't go all the way tonight?"

"Tired," he said, but she knew it was more. He settled himself in the big, cushioned easy chair. He looked small in it, the cushions sucking him in. He had sat in it so many years, it was practically shaped and creased to the contours of his body, wrapping him in it like a body glove.

"You look like you've seen a ghost," she said.

"I think I heard one."

"What do you mean?"

"This scream. Terrible. Came from the Oakses', I'm sure."

"Did you see what it was?"

"Bats flying around the porch light."

"It wasn't them?"

"No, this was something different. I can't explain it," he said, and that made her even more curious and more afraid.

"Well, maybe I should call Mary."

He simply shook his head. He heard her go to the phone in the kitchen and speak in a low voice. After she hung up, she came back slowly.

"So?"

"Nothing wrong there."

"She said something else. I can see it in your face." His wife smirked. "Out with it."

"She said you probably heard the Devil inside you."

"Crazy as a loon. Gone haywire since Thomas was killed in that car with that woman."

"I pity her, pity them both. It has to be unpleasant for them, alone in that big house."

"We're alone."

"It's different. This house is half the size and we're old."

"Well, I don't care what she says. I heard something wild."

Hilda looked at him. For a moment she felt uneasy and embraced herself. It was as though something evil had slipped into their house, come in under the door, and brushed against her, leaving her chilled and trembling. Cy looked older than ever tonight, too. She had the terrible idea that Death was shopping, moving along their street, peering in at families, deciding.

Not yet, she asked, not yet.

Her silent prayer was answered. They lived on at relatively the same level of health for the next four years.

And then . . .

They discovered what Cy had heard that fateful night.

ONE

Faith put her homework down on the kitchen table and listened intently again. He was right beneath her, just under the floorboards by the sink. She had seen him crawl and climb over the old shelves built for the storage of canned fruit and pickles, so she knew he was capable of it. Sometimes, he writhed like a snake, which wasn't hard to understand. She imagined that down there he often saw snakes, and he had always been good at imitating things he saw.

He knew to be quiet; he knew what would happen to him if he weren't silent, if Mary were aroused and went down there. But even in his silence, he could communicate with her, Faith thought; and I can communicate with him better than Mary can, no matter what Mary thinks.

The floorboards in the Oakses' old house were no longer as tight as they once were. Surely, with his ear against them or his mouth to them, he could hear her and she could hear him. She did hear something now, a soft "s" sound so similar to a breeze penetrating the two-story wooden building that only she could tell the difference. He could even imitate the wind.

She was sure he had found a spot between the shelves, the wall, and the roof of the basement and had burrowed himself in comfortably so he could be part of what happened above. He had to be lonely and in need of others of his own kind, no matter what Mary said.

"I have seen his face," she had said, "and I can tell you he needs nothing but the darkness and other vermin."

It was on the tip of her tongue to say, "He's not vermin, he's . . . " But she was afraid and she wasn't completely sure. Mary was right about so many things, why couldn't she be right about this?

The rain began and splattered the windows like so many fingers strumming a tabletop. She heard the real wind this time. It turned on the house, penetrating the windows and doors, crawling through the walls, and emerging from every crack and crevice, tossing the curtains about, bringing them to life as mad dancing prints of white and gold. She heard the screen door opened roughly and slammed hard against the house. This looked like a summer ripper, not a spring storm. Through it all, she heard Mary come to the foot of the stairs. Mary's steps were distinct, her movements in the house always recognizable.

"Faith," she called, "check all the windows in the kitchen and get the screen door."

"All right," she replied. She thought she heard him groan. "It's all right," she whispered toward the floor. "Nothing bad. Just a little rainstorm." As if to add comfort to her words, she went by the sink and stood there a moment. Then she rushed around the room, checking the windows.

When she opened the back door to get to the screen door, the wind washed the rain over her, lifting her long, black hair from her shoulders and face. The drops were cool and refreshing. She didn't retreat at all and her thin white cotton blouse became drenched quickly. She welcomed the raindrops between her breasts and took a deep breath, inhaling the scent of freshly cut grass, pine trees, and darkness.

6

Realizing her purpose, she grabbed the screen door and brought it closed, locking it tightly with the latch. Then she stood behind it, gazing out like a prisoner behind bars, longing for the freedom that lay just beyond her reach. By the time she turned, her blouse clung to her; her hair, now soaked, hung in thick strands down the sides of her face, and her jeans had turned darker with the dampness. She was barefoot, so her feet were wet and her toes tingled with the coolness.

Mary was waiting in the kitchen, her hands on her hips, her thin face screwed tight by her frowning forehead, her pursed lips, and her small, molelike eyes. The paleness was blotched red near her temples and under her chin, which she held up so high and taut, that it strained the skin on her neck, drawing her Adam's apple into a knot. When she swallowed, it moved like a heavy thumb pressing and pushing its way to freedom. Something was trapped within her.

"Couldn't you move faster? Look at you. You're so stupid. You do such stupid things."

"It's raining hard."

"More reason to move faster. Go up and get into dry clothes before you catch cold."

She paused only for a moment and then rushed past Mary and obediently hurried up the stairs to her room. Once there, she closed the door as best she could. It was out of kilter and she could never really lock it. Mary wanted it that way.

"Closed doors are for people who do things they're ashamed of," she said.

Faith waited a moment. Mary wasn't coming back up. She was in the kitchen, probably making tea. But she wouldn't know he was right there beneath her; she wouldn't sense it the way I sense it, Faith thought.

She worked her buttons open, her fingers trembling just the way they always did whenever she undressed herself, and peeled the blouse off her. She tried not to

7

look at herself in the narrow mirror on her closet door, but she couldn't help it, even though Mary said it was sinful to feel so much pride in your own body.

When she unfastened her tight bra, her breasts exploded into their true fullness, the nipples already erecting because of the freedom and the coolness. She studied herself as she unfastened her jeans. They, too, were stuck to her skin. She slid out of them as quickly as she could, then folded and draped them over the shower curtain in the bathroom. Her panties weren't at all wet.

After she had wrung out her blouse and dropped it in the hamper, she began to wipe her body dry, studying herself with almost a stranger's curiosity. Her breasts had grown, her cleavage deepened. The curve at her waist was sharper, her stomach flatter and surely more inviting, although no one but Mary had ever seen it this way. The feelings rushed over her, as she expected they would when she looked at herself naked. She took her time massaging her bosom dry and then worked the towel down over her stomach in little circles, rubbing places that weren't even wet.

She listened. Mary was still downstairs, so she rolled the towel and brought it between her legs. Then, taking the ends in her hands, she pulled it up until it was snug against her crotch. She closed her eyes as she began the slow back-and-forth motion, gradually quickening it to keep pace with the heavy thumping of her heart. Her lips were slightly apart, her tongue touching them gently. That sweet, salty taste came to her. The rush of pleasure was so great she wanted to scream her delight, but she couldn't make a sound.

"FAITH!" Mary's voice broke the mood. She unraveled the towel quickly and pressed it so it wouldn't look creased. Mary could discover secrets in the smallest of clues; she could look beyond things and see their significance. Almost immediately, Faith paled with regret and guilt.

"Yes?" Her voice was too small, too revealing. She held her breath.

"What are you doing up there? You have homework, haven't you?"

"I'm just getting dry. Be right down."

"I'm making tea. Hurry up."

"OK."

She went back to her room and put on another pair of jeans and another bra. Then she picked out a pullover sweater and put it on as she walked down the stairs. Mary was seated at the kitchen table, sipping her tea and eating a cracker. She always nibbled at her food, Faith thought. She holds it in her fingers like a squirrel, afraid to take too big a bite.

"It's slowing up," Mary said.

"They say we're going to get summer weather earlier this year."

"Who's they?"

"My teacher did, Mr. Rush. He has that science club after school. They predict the weather and every morning their prediction is read over the public address system. You'd be surprised how many times they were right already this year."

"I'm glad to hear school's good for something besides meeting boys."

"I haven't met any boys," Faith said quickly.

"Didn't say you had." Mary stopped eating suddenly. "Why? You feeling guilty about something?"

"No."

Mary thought for a moment.

"That afternoon last Thursday, when you said you had to stay for extra help . . . "

"I did! You can call Mr. Feinberg and ask him. Five of us stayed!"

"We'll see how your marks reflect it. This is your senior year, you know. It's your last chance to do well."

"I'm doing well."

9

"Get yourself a cup of tea. The honey's on the counter," Mary said and went back to her cracker, chewing dreamily, that far-off look coming back over her quickly.

Faith moved obediently, pausing once to listen to the floorboards. Then she brought her cup to the table and drank quietly for a while. When she looked at Mary again, she saw that her mother was staring at her intently, making her feel very self-conscious about her every move.

"It's time to trim your hair again," she said.

"I didn't brush it; I just wiped it dry."

"Some downpour. Imagine forty days and forty nights of it."

"I was thinking," Faith said softly, "that it must be frightening to be alone in the dark when a storm like this starts."

"Frightening for who?"

"You know!"

"I don't know. How many times have I told you not to speak of him. We do what we must do."

"I can't help thinking about it."

"You've got to help it," Mary said, her eyes coming alive with the inner fire that brought Faith's nightmares to life. "When you stop helping it, you've been lost, too. Do you want that? Do you?"

"No."

"Then . . ."

"But I hear him crying more and more."

"When? That's not true. He doesn't need to cry. If he does, it's because he wants you to go to him, to be contaminated by him. He has no other reason. I told you, he would always get what he needs."

"You're just talking about the basic . . ."

"What . . . he . . . needs," Mary repeated and slapped the table. The cups jumped and Faith flinched. She looked down quickly. When Mary got like this, it could be bad. "I know what he needs. You think of us

10

and what's been done to us." She paused and tilted her head slightly. "I'm only doing what I've been told to do, aren't I? Aren't I?" she repeated.

"Yes."

"Now get back to your homework. It's late," she said and took the cups to the sink and cleared the table. Faith watched her out of the corner of her eye. When Mary was done, Faith looked at her again; then Mary left the kitchen to go into the living room to listen to one of her electric church programs. Faith waited until the radio was turned on. Then she looked to the floorboards.

He was there again; she was sure of it. She looked back through the doorway. Mary was occupied; it was safe now. She would be hypnotized by the sermons and would hear nothing else. Feeling more secure, Faith went to her knees. She crawled along the floor until she found the spot that was the most open. She pressed the palm of her hand against the crack and waited. There it was—the tingle, the feel of his breath; she was sure of it. She looked back at the doorway again. Still safe, she brought her face to the floor, her mouth to the crack, and blew her warm breath through it. She heard him sucking, taking her air like an infant taking his mother's milk. She did it again and then again. When she pulled back, she heard his disappointment, but she couldn't take too many chances. Mary would go wild if she merely suspected.

"Sorry," she whispered. "That's all for tonight."

She stood up, went back to her notebook, did her work, and then went through the living room to go up to bed. Mary was almost asleep in her chair, the radio playing soft organ music. Her eyes fluttered when she saw Faith looking at her.

"I'm tired," Faith said. "And I've finished my work."

"Good night, Dear," Mary said. "Don't worry. Everything will be all right. He gets what he needs."

11

"OK. Good night, Mom," she said and she went up to the sanctity of her own dreams.

To Mary the house had always been a challenge of one kind or another. Although she tried to repress her memories of the early days when she was young and her body was fuller and brighter, her voice lighter and softer, she couldn't help but recall the first time she had seen "The Oaks," as it was called by the family. Originally, it was a small farmhouse, its one luxury being the large, airy kitchen. But great grandfather Oaks was unable to make even a passable living from just farming. The land was too rocky; there was too much clay. So they took in a boarder one summer to help cover expenses. That proved successful and they took in two the following summer.

Additions were built. The porch was extended and new rooms were added. Before they finished, they had space for ten guests a season. As a small tourist house, The Oaks was more or less as successful as the hundreds of others that sprouted up throughout the Catskill resort area. The next generation of Oaks ran it that way until the early 1960s, when the tourist trade began to fall off. Rooms hardly ever used were eventually closed down. The house began to retreat into itself.

Thomas Oaks never had any interest in building a tourist business anyway. He made his living as an electrician and used only that part of the house that had been its original space. When Mary first saw "The Oaks" in the fall of that year she and Thomas met, she was taken by its brooding quality. She thought it was an impressive building, one of the largest in the area, and she was filled with ambitions to stir the giant structure back to its leviathan life.

Thomas hadn't actually proposed, but she was anticipating it. He had met her while he worked a job in Ellenville, a village ten miles away. She was only seventeen at the time, but she had taken care of her invalid mother for most of her mature life, and through that responsibility, developed an older, more settled viewpoint. There was nothing flighty or wasteful about her. Her parents had had her late in their lives and were in their fifties and sixties by the time she was seventeen. Because of her responsibilities at home, she was quite sheltered and innocent in comparison with other teenagers. Thomas, however, thought her to be some kind of a find—an untouched, natural beauty, virginal and capable. He was in his late twenties, had already done quite a bit of hell-raising, and had grown somewhat cynical of women. She restored his faith in the belief that he could find someone just like "good old Mom."

Mary had grown up in a very religious atmosphere. Prayer was a necessary and daily part of life. Because they were unable to get to the church easily, they created their own form of service in her house. The view of God that Mary's mother imbued in her was the view held by the early Puritans: God was angry because man was sinful. God punished man on earth for the things he did on earth. Therefore, as reverent as she was, because she was crippled, Mary's mother convinced Mary that God was punishing her for some past crime. "Man's accidents are God's purposes," her mother told her, and that was the way Mary saw the world.

In the beginning Thomas thought he could tolerate Mary's religious zeal. He even welcomed it as a wholesome element to be added to what he admittedly characterized as a wasteful, degenerate life. In many ways he saw Mary as a kind of medicine. She would cure him of his evil; she would be his saving grace. When she came into The Oaks she would bring with her all that was good and pure, and thus cast a fresh, clean paint over what had been dark, dingy, and lost.

He was attracted to her because of whatever con-

13

science he still possessed. Whenever he thought of his mother and what she had wanted for him, he felt guilty. Whenever he thought of his father and his grandfather and how hard they had worked to keep up "The Oaks," he felt guilty. Marrying Mary was his redemption. She was religious; she was untouched. She had stability. She could cook and sew and clean and keep him on the straight path. With her he could raise a good family and be a decent, respectable citizen. On top of all that, she was attractive and sexually mysterious to him, for she kept close guard on her body and her virginity. Because she wasn't obvious, he resorted to fantasy. He had gotten laid hundreds of times, but the picture he conjured of his wedding night went beyond anything he had ever experienced. For some reason, he imagined that making love to someone "decent" would be better. With her he would touch heights that were beyond the sexual ecstasies he had achieved.

Mary had just come off the death of her mother when she and Thomas first met. She wasn't interested in him simply because she found herself with so much free time to fill. There was something she recognized in Thomas—a dependence, a need. Mary was used to being needed, to providing something essential to someone else. Although Thomas was a strapping six feet two inches, with dark skin and deep brown eyes, Mary honed in on the little boy in him. He had recently lost his parents and was living alone in this enormous two-story house surrounded by beautiful, although unkempt, grounds.

Mary saw all of it—Thomas and his house and grounds—to be a great undertaking, a wonderful responsibility. It would quickly fill the great gaps in her world and give her life renewed meaning. Her father, a tired, melancholy man in his late sixties, was happy to see that his daughter would have a life laid out for her. He had viewed her as a burden now, terrified that something would happen to him before she was settled in either a career or a marriage. Thomas Oaks wasn't exactly the kind of a man he had envisioned for Mary, but he did make a decent living and she did appear very interested in him. He gave the marriage his blessing. As it was, he lived only a few more years.

It was inevitable that the wedding night would be a great disappointment for Thomas Oaks, no matter what happened. He had romanticized it beyond any resemblance to reality. He was going to open the doorway to sexual excitement for her, and in doing so, he would find an even greater excitement for himself. He would be gentle and loving; he would show her parts of herself that she never knew existed. They would make love many times, long into the night, and then fall into a blissful exhaustion. He must have gone over it and over it dozens of times before they were married. He was determined for his dream to be.

They had their church wedding and drove to the Poconos to a little motel near a large lake. He had scouted it a month beforehand, even choosing the room and the view he wanted. He located the restaurant in which he wanted them to have their first dinner. Everything was set as he had dreamed.

But that night was a disaster. He should have taken it for an omen. Mary was understandably modest, but he enjoyed that. He had bought a bottle of champagne, hoping it would relax her. However, when he got into bed beside her, she whimpered when he touched her. He coaxed her; he did all that he knew to warm and excite a woman, but she didn't loosen up; she didn't unclamp her legs.

"I can't," she told him. "Please. Don't make me."

"Don't be afraid," he said. He spoke as softly as he could. When he went to fondle her breasts, she pressed her upper arms tightly against his hands, making it impossible to move them over her body.

He stopped, lit a cigarette, and finished off the

champagne, while she curled up into the fetal position and remained silent, uninvolved. He put out his cigarette and tried again. This time he touched her only with his lips. Even the coldest woman he had been with reacted to that, but, when he got down to the small of her stomach, she nearly gouged out his eyes to keep him from prying her thighs apart with his face.

Finally, he grew angry. His coaxing turned into demanding. She tightened even more. In the end he actually had to attack her, subduing her screams by kissing her grossly on the mouth. She cried when he forced her legs apart. She fought him all the way. He wanted to give up, but every time he thought, how could he fail on his wedding night? His penetration of her was totally unsatisfactory. She didn't seem at all stimulated by it, so he did all the movement. When he finally came, it was more of a relief than orgiastic ecstasy.

Then she bled and there was a mess. He got dressed and went out to get another bottle. When he returned, she had everything straightened again, but she was asleep. He sat up in a chair by the bed, drinking away most of the night. After the morning light appeared, he got in beside her and collapsed into a restless sleep. Sometime in the afternoon, he awoke. She had gone out and gathered something for them to eat. He chastised her for that, telling her they were on a honeymoon and they would go to restaurants for every meal. Afterward, even though it was a nice day and they went on a lovely boat ride, he was sullen. He felt a deep sorrow, such as the kind one feels when he realizes he has made a terrible mistake, one that will cause him to lose money or time.

Despite the bad experience, he tried again the second night. She was just as resistant, so he skipped the softness and went right to the violence. While he was doing it this second time, he realized something: once he forced entry, even though she was tight and uncooperative, she was quiet. The whimpering stopped; the surface resistance ended. It was as though she wanted him to rape her, rather than make love to her. She wanted to be exonerated from any responsibility for it.

Afterward, like before, she was loving, considerate, and friendly. He eased into an amazement for the rest of the honeymoon. During the day, they were like any other newly married couple—enjoying the lake, going to restaurants, sightseeing. At night, when he approached her, she would resist until he became ruthlessly aggressive. She made him feel like a caveman.

"You make me feel guilty," he said. "Is that what you want?"

"I'm trying," she said. She started to cry, and once again he thought, maybe she is trying.

"How did you get this way? You never had any kind of a boyfriend?"

"I can't talk about it."

"Why?" She didn't answer. "You make it seem . . . dirty. It's natural; it's good. Isn't it good?" He waited. She looked as though she would answer. She did turn to him, but something stopped her; something made her shut her eyes and curl her fingers into fists. It was as though she were in great pain. He actually felt sorry for her and thought that, in time, he would free her of whatever it was that kept her from being emotionally free. It would be his great contribution to the marriage.

When they returned to The Oaks, she went at the domestic chores with a fanatical vigor. He couldn't believe how quickly she brought the house into order, making old things shine again. Neighbors complimented him for the way they were bringing the place back. And she was a great cook as well. He was especially pleased with the way she managed their finances, making his money stretch and accomplish things he didn't think possible.

Despite their strange love life, he believed she was devoted to him and to The Oaks. Every time he

17

questioned the wisdom of marrying her, something else in the house or something else she did for their lives made him feel proud and satisfied. It was true he found it easier to make love to her when he was drunk, but she didn't seem to mind it that way.

Even so, it came as a surprise to him when she announced one day that she was pregnant. He had almost come to believe she was incapable of that. In his imagination, he saw his semen shooting into some other part of her body. It had been like making love to a manikin. Suddenly, with her cheeks red, her eyes bright, she greeted him with the news. "We're going to have a baby!" He couldn't imagine what such a child would be like.

It wasn't until after Faith was born that Mary turned fanatical. The tendencies were there—the daily religious devotion, the hard, puritanical view of the world as a battleground between good and evil, the need for a continuous vigil against the Devil and the weaknesses in the human soul. In the beginning of their marriage, Thomas quietly accepted her criticism and complaining about his life-style. After all, she was supposed to serve as a brake on his downward slide.

But after Faith, Mary changed. She didn't criticize; she preached. She didn't complain; she ranted. The changes in her appearance reflected the radicalism of her beliefs. She went into the attic and found Grandma Oaks' high-collar blouses and long skirts. She wrapped her breasts in bras so tight she practically eliminated the appearance of a bosom. She stopped wearing the small amount of makeup he had asked her to wear, and she kept her once beautifully rich, long dark brown hair tied in a snug knot behind her head. The strands were pulled so taut they strained the skin at the top of her forehead and temples. It had the effect of giving her an habitual wide-eyed, wild look—the look of a woman in a frenzy.

Even their bizarre, one-sided lovemaking came to an end. She used her concern for the baby as her initial excuse, moving out of their bedroom and into Faith's room to be near her during the night. Her Biblical studies took up more and more of her time with the result that her concern for The Oaks slipped. Rooms once kept immaculate grew dingy and dusty again. She began to accept Thomas' original perimeters for the house, closing down rooms, no longer washing windows.

The light that she had brought into the large house faded. Ironically, the coming of the baby should have brought them more brightness and excitement. Instead, it sent Mary reeling into a mad retreat behind her prayers, her Biblical quotes, and her sexual inhibitions. Thomas Oaks was convinced that the giving of birth had had a traumatic effect on his wife. It had made her mad.

But it was difficult for him to complain to anyone about it. If he talked about her religious fanaticism, friends reminded him she was orthodox to begin with; he knew what he was getting. "And a little religion wouldn't do you no harm," they chided. He didn't want to talk about the death of their sex life. He wouldn't know where to begin, and he suffered from male false pride, seeing it all as somehow being his failure, not hers. After all, he had quite a reputation before he got married. His friends wouldn't understand.

Then there was the magnificent way she kept Faith. To begin with, the baby was beautiful. She had the face of a cherub with soft, rich-looking skin that could have easily won her a spot in baby commercials. Everyone who saw her remarked about her dazzling blue eyes. Even as an infant, the child had a way of gazing intently at people, making them feel self-conscious. "I swear," they would say, "that baby looks like she's thinking deep, grown-up thoughts."

19

Mary spent hours on her hair, washing it and curling it. She kept her little fingernails manicured. She worked days designing and constructing little outfits for her—uniquely bright, form-fitted dresses, blouses, and skirts that made other mothers envious.

And then there was all that time Mary gave toward teaching the child, talking to her, and training her. Faith was precocious. She was pretty and brilliant, speaking long sentences when other children her age were first forming words. She was at Mary's side continually, mimicking her work, listening, and learning.

Thomas was confused. He wanted to attack his wife for her extremism, but her results with Faith made him question even the things he saw. Gradually, he fell into a complacency and acceptance. He adjusted himself to one kind of life at home and one kind of life away. For the sake of the child, he even participated in some of Mary's religious sessions. Like a nineteenth-century nobleman, he left his estate for assignations with his various mistresses and then returned to his house and grounds and beautiful daughter.

The Oaks had once again returned to being a large, brooding building with dark rooms wrapped around an inner core of lit ones. At night, when Thomas drove up to the old house, he would see only the heart of it illuminated and he would think of small creatures like turtles and snails retreating into their shells. It left him with a sadness and a fear he couldn't verbalize.

Until one night when he came home from one of his "hot times" and parked his car. As he walked to the house, he saw Mary standing in the shadows on the porch, the yellow light barely silhouetting her in the corner. He stopped when she moved just a little to the left, dipping her face in the pale glow. Her skin looked sickly, but her eyes were on fire. She seemed to have grown out of the darkness. He stopped on the gravel drive and stared up at her, transfixed, stunned, numbed by her sudden appearance. How many times had she been there before when he returned?

"What is it?" he asked, ashamed at how his voice cracked. He cleared his throat quickly. She stepped further into the light.

"And death and hell delivered up the dead which were in them: and they were judged every man according to their works. And death and hell were cast into the lake of fire. This is the second death."

"No shit," he said and laughed. He felt protected by his laughter, but he couldn't face her off. It was easier to go into the house and up to his room, leaving her mumbling in the darkness behind him. But before he fell asleep, he saw her face in the porch light again and he promised himself that someday soon he would do something about her.

He never did.

And then it became too late.

Of all his sins, failure to act was his greatest.

Two

For so long he had known only darkness. The small amount of light that penetrated the boarded windows produced a hazy, dim illumination, outlining and silhouetting his whole world in a sandy gray that made everything dull and distorted. Even the creature that came down to him was shrouded in shadows. The small ceiling fixture she turned on seemed to concentrate the dark spots rather than eliminate them.

He could almost smell her as quickly as he could see her. He knew her scent better than he knew the features of her face. From the first day he could remember, she had been rough with him. There was never anything pleasant or soft in her voice, and she gave him no human comfort.

She provided him with food and the blankets and the box in which he slept. She brought down the pails of sand to replace any she took out from the square in which he littered. Long ago, through the inflicting of pain, she had taught him that this was the only area in which he could excrete.

His floor was made of stone and cement. The only soft spots were in his box with the blankets and in the sand, so he developed hard calluses on his feet, on his knees, and on his palms. In the beginning, he scratched and bumped himself often, developing sores and wounds. He never really cried aloud when that happened. Instead, he would utter a short yelp and sob within, his body shaking with the unhappiness. There was no one to appeal to, to seek sympathy from; so he licked his own wounds, stroked and rocked his body, and created a soft, monotone hum to quiet his fear and pain whenever he had any.

He had always had enough to eat and drink, although never in any great abundance. There was a time when the creature fed him. He remembered having to eat very quickly, swallowing almost as fast as she shoved the food at him. Now she merely left it by the box. A few times he had tried to use the spoon and the fork, but he found them too slow, for he was used to wolfing his food, to hovering over it like a rodent, scooping some of it in, chewing, looking about to be sure nothing threatened the remainder, scooping, chewing . . .

The creature wouldn't wait to watch him eat. He sensed early on that she wanted the least amount of contact with him as possible. He felt the same way toward her. If she didn't demand that he come to her, he would linger in the darkness, eyeing her like a field mouse in a hole, waiting for her to drop off the food and leave. Then he would scurry out quickly, before any other little animals could get there, and eat.

She wanted him to wear the diapers or the shorts, but he soiled them so often that she stopped changing him. The last one remained on him so long that it hung off in shreds before she removed it. Periodically, she would come down to wash him in the large basin she had left there for that purpose. He hated the baths, because the water was always so hot it nearly scorched him. She ran the water into the basin directly from the hot-water tank in the corner, mixing only a pail or two of cooler water with it. And she scrubbed him with that vicious vigor, suggesting she wanted to rub the skin off him. It was no use to wail or struggle.

If he did, she would squeeze his neck so hard, it would make his eyes pop; or she would smack him so sharply, it burned more than the hot water.

He always knew when she was coming because she flipped on the ceiling fixture first. She would never come down to him in the dark. As soon as the light went on, he would cover his eyes and scurry for a safe spot. Safe spots were the little caverns and openings he had found for himself. There was the area between the hot-water heater and the stone wall foundation; there was the tunnel he had found between the boxes and old furniture stored in the rear. Lately, he had been more inventive about safe places.

Stronger now, his hands more like claws, with his long fingernails and callused fingers and palms, he climbed up the fieldstone walls, inserting his toughened feet in slots and spaces, using the old stones like a ladder to work his way up to the rafters. Here, he would find places to embed himself between studs and corners, pressing his body into the roof or against the wall, so that he could balance and secure himself above the basement floor.

The first thing he learned when he did this was that he could hear and feel what was happening above him. Exploring the roof of the basement from this vantage point, he was able to discover places in the floorboards that were widely separated. Through them, he could see light and shadows and smell the scents of things that were fascinating and remarkable to him.

The good thing about the higher safe places was that they were really safer. The first time the creature came down to find him for his bath and he was up against the ceiling, she was unable to locate him for the longest time. He heard the great anger in her voice when she screamed, "WHERE ARE YOU, IMP!" He pressed himself as hard as he could against the wall and ceiling, instinctively making his body into the smallest target possible.

24

She began to pull boxes, furniture, and other things apart. Frustrated by her failure to find him, she took off the wide, thick leather strap she always wore when she came down to him and swung it about threateningly. "IMP," she called. "IMP, GET OVER HERE!" He hadn't heard the words often enough to really understand their meanings, but he read her gestures and the tone of her voice well enough to understand that she wanted him to come to her. He had seen her pour the pail of water into the tub and set up the hot-water hose. He knew what she was planning for him. So he resisted.

Furious, she went back upstairs and came down with a flashlight. The first time he saw that, he thought it was some kind of fire. He had seen fire in the furnace and she had burned him with a candle to show him that playing with fire was dangerous. He saw the beam moving over the wall, getting closer and closer to him. He was positive that when the light touched him, it would burn him the way the candle had. So just before it reached him, he screamed and came out of his safe place. Even so, she put the beam on him and he screamed in anticipation of the pain. She was at him instantly. As soon as she was able to reach up and take hold of him, she struck him with the belt. He cried and made his pleading sounds, but she was out to teach him a lesson.

She struck him until there were welts all along his thighs and his buttocks. Then she antagonized the pain immediately by forcing him into the hot tub. After she dried him and wrapped him in the towel, she put him in his box and stood over him threateningly. Again, it was only from her gestures and tone of voice that he understood she was warning him. He cowered and squeezed himself together, pulling his legs and arms in, folding himself and burying his head in his body, just as the little animals did when he trapped them in a corner of the basement. After he felt her heavy

25

shadow move off him and saw the cellar light go off, he unfolded.

There, safe in his darkness, he whimpered and hummed, comforting himself with the feel of his own arms around his torso, squeezing as hard as he could to subdue the pain. He listened to the buzz of motors and the sound of water traveling through pipes. He felt a spider crawl over his neck on its journey across his box. He pulled the blankets up over his legs, wrapping himself in his little cocoon, and fell asleep dreaming of field mice burrowing deeply into the coolness and safety of the stone walls.

Thereafter, whenever she came down to find him for some reason, she always brought her flashlight along. And when she called him, he came. The flashlight was too powerful. He believed it could even reach through things to find him. There was no safe place from the beam of light, so it was best to obey. After he came to her, he always curled up instinctively, expecting some blow or reprimand. Sometimes he whimpered for mercy; sometimes it worked and sometimes it didn't.

He hated looking directly into her face. There was a fire and an anger there that he felt strongly. But always when she washed him in the tub, it was difficult not to look closely at her. If he tried to turn away, she would grasp a handful of his hair and tug him around. Then he would have to face her, as she scrubbed his cheeks and ears.

Her eyes were always blazing. Although she was big, the biggest creature he had ever seen, she had small eyes—eyes that reminded him of the soft, furry creatures that lived in holes dug between the stone wall foundation and the cellar floor. Once he grabbed a small one and held it tightly in his hands. It struggled to escape and then, when it realized the futility, changed its look of fear into one of hate. It swung its head about, trying to seize the skin of his fingers into

26

its mouth. But he took hold of the top of its head and stopped that. He squeezed it so hard that red liquid emerged from its mouth. Finally, it stopped the struggle and fell over in his hand limply. He flung it into a corner to rot with other things.

She had this look of hate in her eyes, so he feared that one day she might bite him. Her teeth were small and her mouth twisted and turned, the lips squirming like worms. He had nightmares about that mouth. He saw it come down on his neck and shoulders; he felt the tongue pierce his skin.

He knew what it was to be bitten. The little furry creatures had nipped his legs and arms at times, especially when he was asleep. He'd wake with a start and slap out quickly. Often, he struck one hard enough to stop its movement and make it cold. He wished he could do the same to her.

She muttered sounds as she washed him. They had a rhythm to them that he began to recognize time after time. She'd stop in the middle sometimes and hold his head between her hands, while she looked up at the ceiling and muttered. When she dipped his head under the water, she held it down so hard and so long, he sensed a terrible danger. Then he would struggle as fiercely as he could, swinging and flinging his arms about wildly, until she relaxed the pressure. Once, when he did that, he scratched her and she beat him unmercifully, forgetting the rest of his bath.

He had gotten so he hated the sound of her, the feel of her, the scent of her. In the confines of his small world, there was nothing he feared and despised more. None of the small creatures threatened him. He was amused by them and even welcomed them, for they were company and amusement in a world of solitude and loneliness.

There was one thing that he did long for even more than food when he was hungry and water when he was thirsty. That was the other creature, the smaller creature. He hadn't seen her as much, but the few times he did, he instinctively recognized a warm, loving feeling between them. When she spoke, she spoke in soft, kind tones. The two times that she touched him when she was here, she touched him gently and affectionately. He wanted her to touch him more, to talk to him more, and to be with him more.

When he discovered that he could hear her and even feel her through the roof of the cellar, he was ecstatic. It filled his life with a terrific new pleasure. Sometimes he waited in his high safe spot for hours, just for a momentary sound, whether it be the sound of her footsteps or the sound of her voice.

For a long time he had been trying to attract her attention by blowing through the cracks in the roof. He was afraid that the bigger creature would hear him, so he was as careful as he could be about when he would do it. One day, the nicer creature realized it and blew back at him through the floor. He let her warm breath wash over his face like a kiss. Whenever she did it, he would turn his head, taking the air over as much of his head as he could. After she stopped, he would call to her with his tiny whimper or his own breath.

One day he discovered a board that would move just a little. There was enough of a space for him to squeeze a finger through it. She realized what he had done and put her hand over the opening to keep him from pushing too far up and revealing himself to Mary. That was when he touched her.

The feel of her skin sent an electricity of warmth through him. Never had he felt this ecstatic about anything. He got so excited about it that he pressed his face into the ceiling too hard and the wood scratched his skin. But he didn't mind the pain. The pleasure of her skin went beyond any pain. For this he would risk anything, everything. She let him touch her for as long as she could.

28

This became a ritual between them. He got so he could tell when it would happen. His natural clock kept him aware of time and events. If it were possible to do it at any other time, she would call to him softly. She didn't use the same word the big creature did. Instead of "Imp," she said, "Baby." He liked the sound of that much better, especially the way her voice traveled over the vowel and ended in the soft "e."

He had amazing hearing, his audio sense compensating for his diminished eyesight due to the darkness and grayness of his world. He could hear a rodent digging, a snake slithering, a fly buzzing across the basement. He got so he could distinguish between upstairs sounds. He knew the smaller creature's footsteps. The larger creature hit the floor with a sharper, harder step. He thought she was continuously angry.

But there were many upstairs sounds he didn't understand—the whistle of the teapot, the slamming of doors, the sounds of pots and pans, the frightening sound of churning motors in blenders and mixers. He liked the sound of music and recognized something soft and warm in much of it. Even the heavy organ music of Mary's religious programs was attractive to him. He moved along the wall, trying to get as close to the music as he could. There he would sit or hang for as long as the music was on. Sometimes he fell asleep to it; sometimes he simply went into a blissful trance. Whatever he did, he welcomed the sound as one of the few pleasures in an otherwise dismal existence.

Of course, he didn't know it as dismal. He knew it as his world, the world to which he had grown accustomed. In it there was little warmth and much hardness and roughness, unpleasant odors, confinement, and darkness. But all this made him harder and stronger, rather than weaker and puny.

His tiny body elongated into a wiry, muscular form. Like a monkey, he had gotten so he could grasp with

29

his feet as well as his hands, and swing and hang on rafters and pipes. He climbed everywhere—over the stone wall, across the ceiling, up the water heater, and around the boxes and old objects that were stored in the basement. Most of his day was spent exploring, fingering and tasting objects and things he had found. There was always something new: whether it be opening an old dresser drawer and then spending hours inspecting the contents, or working his hands over a machine, digging his fingers into openings, finding and removing loose parts.

These explorations, the excitement of the discoveries above, the experiences he had with little animals and small creatures, and the terror of dealing with the big creature were the events of his life. There wasn't much more, until the day he began to sense, with an ever-increasing intensity, that beyond the confines of the stone foundation lingered newer and even more wonderful discoveries. He began to think about it more.

And then, one day, purely by accident, while he was climbing over the stone foundation, he felt a rock loosen. He paused to inspect it with his "impish" curiosity and discovered that he could move it some more by pushing it from side to side. A tiny opening appeared, letting in the smallest amount of light. At first he was shocked and frightened by it. He pulled his hand away, expecting it to be burned or stung. When that didn't happen, he approached the rock cautiously again and jiggled the stone, until the hole grew wider and wider. Finally, it was wide enough for him to put his eye to it.

The sight filled him with life; he was like someone resurrected. Impatient with the strands of his long black hair that fell between his eyes and the hole, he tugged them away roughly and painfully. When he looked again, his gray, brooding face lit up with wonderment. The toughened, sandpaper skin of his wide, protruding forehead wrinkled with curiosity. His small, flat nose wiggled from side to side, as he widened the nostrils to gather up scents. His lips, pale and thin, opened and closed with a nervous rhythm. In his excitement, his prehensile fingers, with their long, sharp fingernails, dug into his own thighs.

The colors were the most exciting thing he had ever seen. There were the greens and the browns and off beyond them was something very blue and very soft. The pinhole view was enough to create a ravenous hunger for knowledge. Now, working as would a starving animal, he attacked the stones fiercely, pushing and pulling with all his strength. He was able to widen the opening only a trifle more. Disappointed, he sat back and moaned as he stared at it.

It was tormenting him; it was torture. He had to get a bigger view. He looked about helplessly and then retreated from the opening, as though he were going to sulk. He continued to stare in its direction, but his frustration was turning into anger—a vicious, nearly uncontrollable rage. He flung something at the wall. He gnawed his teeth. He rushed it and scratched at the rocks, until he was exhausted from the effort and the tips of his fingers began to bleed. Then he curled up to rest.

Just before he drifted off to sleep, something began to show itself in his mind. He saw his finger pressed into the opening, unable to go far or push the rocks further apart. But he understood that shoving it in there was the right kind of work. It was just that his finger was too soft and too short. His mind began to wander as fatigue took hold. But he was well along the way, for he realized that there had to be something else, something longer and stronger that he could shove into that hole and work back and forth, just the way he worked the rocks.

Something . . . something . . . he would find it; he knew he would, and that sense of optimism brought a smile to his face. It was one of the few times that happiness had emerged out of an idea. A warm feeling grew from the smile and lay over him like a soft blanket. He pulled the pleasure around him, curled his body tighter, and fell into a restful sleep.

He dreamed about the hole and the dream was so vivid, that as soon as he awoke, he pursued the task again, this time knowing exactly what to do. There was a piece of half-inch pipe behind the water heater. He didn't know what it was; he knew only that he could do the right work with it.

He rushed back to the hole and shoved it as far in as he could. Then he leaned back and pushed forward, leaned back and pushed forward, doing it continually until the whole fieldstone broke loose. When he pressured that, it caused another stone to loosen and another. Carefully, he pulled the stones toward him. The lime mortar around them gave, but held other stones from collapsing.

With every stone he removed, another fascinating piece of the world outside was revealed. The large soft blue behind the green and brown things had turned darker. He saw tiny silver speckles all over the blue background. Each time he removed a stone, he sat and stared at the new sights. What a wonder. His heart began beating fast and hard. He put his hand against his chest to quiet it, but it would not stop. It annoyed him, but he didn't have time for it now. There was too much to see; too much left for him to do.

He worked faster, tugging and chipping at the stones, until the hole was as large as him. When he realized that, he stopped; but he was too frightened to do anything else. A long time passed. The blue turned almost as dark as his basement world, but those little specks of light grew brighter. He was intrigued by them and wondered if he could touch them.

Finally, his curiosity overcame his fear and he

moved forward into the hole. The first thing that struck him was the scents—there were so many different and interesting ones. Right before him, the earth was soft. It felt different from the sand in his box and it had a more pleasant odor. He didn't care for the taste, but he liked the cool feel of it. Then there were all those green things coming out of it. Some of them ripped easily. They tasted funny, but tolerable.

He moved further out until his entire body was nearly through the hole. The darkness around him wasn't prohibiting for him. His eyes were used to it and, in fact, he favored it. He curled up outside the hole, listening to, feeling, and smelling all that was around him. Without having to go more than a foot or so from the house, he had found enough to interest him for hours. He couldn't taste and touch enough. And every few minutes, he had to look up at those silver specks and stare at them, until his neck ached.

Suddenly, he heard the most frightening sound of his life and looked to his left. He couldn't see the road, but two large flashlights were flying through the darkness, roaring down toward him. Instantly, he cried out and rushed back through the hole. He hurried over the floor to his box and curled up under the blanket as quickly as he could. There he remained, shaking and whimpering, expecting whatever it was to come after him through the hole.

But nothing happened; nothing happened for the longest time and it was very quiet again. His heartbeat slowed and he felt himself gain confidence. He sat up, listened, watched the hole, and then slowly crawled back to it. He peered out timidly, waiting, but he heard nothing threatening, and all those scents and sights called back to him. He went through the hole again.

This time he moved a few feet further. He found and explored a bush. He went a few feet further than that and then turned around. It was then that he saw the house, saw the lit windows, saw the immensity of it. The sight frightened him, but he held his ground. He listened hard. He could hear the small creature; he was sure of it. His mind began to work. This that he saw was what was always above him, what he climbed to hear. What did that mean?

He moved a little further away, over the cool green blanket of soft earth, until he could see even more of the lit window. He heard the small creature's voice again. It sounded so close. Then the most wonderful thing of all happened—she appeared in the window, standing there looking out at this wonderful place. Did she see him? What if she did? Would she tell the big creature?

Instinctively, he knew that would be bad. The big creature wouldn't want him out here. There were so many more places to hide. He could move faster than she could and she would never be able to catch him to put him in the hot bath. She mustn't know; she mustn't know what he had done to the wall. He would have to put the stones back when he went back in. He understood that, because he knew it was something he had to do to protect himself.

The smaller, warmer creature moved away from the window. He longed to see her again, but she was gone. He waited and listened to the many strange sounds. Some frightened him; some intrigued him. He looked beyond the fields into the darkness where he could see the lit windows of another house. He wondered if there were other small, warm creatures in those windows, like there was here. It was something to think about; something maybe even to go to see. For now, though, he was afraid.

He scurried back to the hole, took one more look at this wonderful new place, and disappeared within the basement. A moment later, the rocks began to fall into place. Although the mortar was gone, the rocks fit like pieces of a jigsaw puzzle and he had a great sense of configuration. He enjoyed working the stones tightly and perfectly against each other, until there was barely any visible difference from the way they were before he had discovered the pinhole.

When he was finished, he went back to his box and sat there with his blanket wrapped around him, thinking. He catalogued all the sounds and scents he had just experienced. He reviewed the structures—the trees silhouetted against the dark sky, the bushes around the house, the tall grass that covered the long fields, making them look like large, dark bodies of water.

And then he thought about the window again and the small, warm creature captured in its light. Because it was lighter around her, she looked different. She looked even warmer. He was anxious to touch her again and feel her breath.

There were so many things out there; so many more things to do. He couldn't wait until he would do it again. Again, through instinct, he sensed that it would be safer to go out there when there was less light, when the blue was darker and those silver specks appeared. The big creature wouldn't see him then and he would be in the biggest safe place of all.

His happiness made him make a new sound. He didn't know what it was, but he liked it and did it again. He did it until he grew tired of it. Now, when he looked around his basement world, he was bored. This was nothing compared to what he had just seen. In fact, he was intolerant of it and couldn't wait until he had his next opportunity to take the rocks out and go through the hole.

It took all the self-discipline he could muster to wait, but he had the clever patience of a cat on a hunt. He had often sat for hours watching a field mouse emerge from a hole. He studied the way it sniffed the air and listened for danger. The creature came out very slowly, taking a step and freezing its body, taking a step and sniffing. He didn't move either, learning early on that when he made the slightest gesture, the rodent would scamper back into the safety of its hole. But, if he were quiet and still, the mouse would come forward, almost right up to him. Then he could pounce on it if he wanted.

It was only a game, but it taught him things—things that would be of great benefit to him later on. He couldn't verbalize it, but he understood the power of timing. He had the speed of a snake, the caution of a mouse, the sensitivity of a bat, and the sleekness of a cat.

Because of his kinship with the animal world, he felt an affinity for the wildness outside. The darkness beyond the stones called to him with a voice he wouldn't resist. All that was primeval in him lingered out there in the bushes and trees. He was anxious to join it and become one with the new night.

Seven-year-old Billy O'Neil slid off his bed quietly and slowly. When his feet touched the carpet, he turned and listened. Downstairs, the television program ran on with its canned laughter and abrupt and loud commercials. He had gotten so he didn't hear it anymore when he went into his room to sleep. Even his mother's and father's and his big brother Bobby's laughter didn't disturb him. He wove those sounds in with the drone of the television.

Because the set was on so loud, none of them heard Captain barking. He had just told his father about it today; how Captain barked and barked the night before, how he had gone to the window in his room and looked out back and saw Captain standing there barking out at something in the field. He told his father it must be something Captain was afraid of, because he didn't go near it; he just barked at it. His father said Captain was too stupid to be afraid of anything. What about the porcupine last summer? Did you forget all those quills in his snoot? Billy thought that made sense, but if Captain wasn't afraid of something out there, why did he just bark at it?

"I don't know," his father finally said, impatient with the constant questioning. "I never wanted the mutt to start with. Your mother was the one who fell in love with him. Anyway, what's the difference what he's barking at? That dog would bark at his own shadow." His father liked his own joke and went off laughing about it.

But to Billy there was a difference and that difference was a mystery. He went to the window and looked out. The half-moon cast enough illumination over the field for him to make out familiar shapes— bushes, small trees, the old garbage can he used for slingshot practice, the half a treehouse he and Bobby were forever building, even the path that led to Mrs. Oaks' property down the road. And there was Captain, standing at the edge of their cleared backyard, growling and barking, growling and barking.

Billy opened the window screen and stuck his head out.

"CAPTAIN," he yelled, "CAPTAIN."

The four-year-old cross between a collie and a police dog turned and looked up at him, wagging its tail almost immediately.

"WHAT IS IT, HUH? WHAT? A BEAR? A WOLF?"

The dog looked at him a moment longer and then turned and began to growl again. Billy studied the field and squinted to get a clearer, closer view. Something was out there in the brush. He could see the wild vegetation moving gently and he could almost hear the branches separating. Something was definitely . . .

His eyes widened and his mouth opened. He nearly leaned too far out of his window and had to tighten his grip on the sill. Then he pulled himself back and turned around in confusion, knowing instinctively that no one would believe him. They'll just have to go out and see for themselves, he thought; they'll just have to.

He ran out of his room and down the stairs. No one looked away from the set, until he was in the room screaming.

"I SAW IT! I SAW IT!"

"What?" his father turned halfway from the set, drawn to the program, yet pulled by Billy's outburst.

"Calm down, Billy," Cindy O'Neil said. She wore that habitual half smile that made it seem as though she took few things seriously in her life. It, plus her custard-smooth skin and dancing blue eyes, gave her a very youthful appearance. Dick O'Neil was often kidded about his marrying a child bride, even though only three years separated them. "Now, what is it?"

"Just like in the movies," Billy said in a dramatic, loud whisper. "Just like . . . E.T."

"Oh shit," Bobby said.

"Bobby! Now Billy, what are you talking about? We're watching a show, one of your father's favorites."

"I saw it. I saw it. Captain was barking again and . . ."

"Oh, not that damn dog," Dick said. He turned back to the television program and tried to ignore the interruption.

"What about the dog?" Cindy asked.

"He was barking, so I got out of bed and looked out my window."

"So?"

"There it was."

Dick O'Neil turned to look at his wife and shake his head.

"What, Billy? We still don't understand."

"He must've had a dream," Dick offered without looking back at them.

"Lucky he didn't piss in his bed," Bobby said.

"Bobby! Dick, will you speak to him."

Dick O'Neil, frustrated and annoyed, spun around on the couch. Bobby flinched, expecting his father to strike him. He knew his father had a hairpin temper that reflected only two degrees of anger: mad and very mad. Often he didn't distinguish much between the seriousness of things, either. He could come crashing down on him or his little brother for the simplest of offenses.

Although Bobby was six feet one and a high school senior, he was no match for his father, a two hundred and forty pound, six feet four inch construction worker. It still took Bobby two hands to lift what his father lifted with one. Bobby spent his summers working with him on jobs. From time to time he did some independent contracting and the two of them would work on weekends during the spring and the fall. Presently they were working weekends for Robert Miller, the newest neighbor on Wildwood Drive, building a deck on the rear of the house.

"Do you have to contribute to this problem?"

Bobby turned away quickly and pretended to be interested in the television program again.

"Now Billy," Cindy said, reaching forward and taking her small son's hand into hers, "speak calmly, slowly, and tell me what you saw."

Billy looked up at Bobby's hurt expression and his father's red, angry face. The laughter on the television program suddenly made him feel sick.

"Nothing," he said. "Captain was barking again and I looked out the window."

"I told you," his father said slowly, making his great effort to control himself obvious, "it can't be anything. Maybe it's another porcupine and that dog smartened up since last summer, that's all."

"That's probably it," his mother said. "Is he still barking?"

"No."

"So, it went away, right?" She waited. Billy looked down at the floor. He wanted to blurt it out, to say he knew they were wrong and what he saw was more exciting than their television program. He had seen the real thing! But, his mother's tone of voice put an end to it. He felt himself settle into resignation. "Right?" she repeated, putting her hand under his chin to lift his face.

"Right."

"Good. Now why don't you try to go back to sleep. Tomorrow, I'll take a walk out there with you and we'll see if there's anything there, OK?"

"It won't be there in the daytime," Billy said. He felt confident that what he had seen was a thing of the night.

"We'll see." She pulled him to her and gave him a kiss. "You want me to come up with you and see you into bed?"

He shook his head. Bobby smirked at him and his father was completely involved in his show. Billy retreated slowly. Before he reached the stairs, he heard his mother ask a question about the television program.

"How do I know?" his father replied. "I couldn't hear half of it with all this damn nonsense. We oughta bring that animal up to the pound."

"We will not. That's a terrible idea. You know what they do to them there."

"It'll happen anyway. He's about the dumbest dog I've seen."

Billy ran up the steps. He rushed into his room and looked out the window again. Captain wasn't barking anymore, but he was sitting and staring out toward the field. Billy studied and studied the backyard, waiting for another sighting. It didn't come and he grew tired.

He crawled back into his bed and lay there a while

with his eyes opened, thinking. It could be true, he thought; it could really be and only he knew it. Maybe he wouldn't tell them again. The kids in *E.T.* didn't tell. That's it. He'd keep it a secret and tomorrow he would try to figure out a way to be there the next time Captain barked and it appeared.

He went to sleep dreaming of fingers of light.

THREE

Since it was Tuesday, Faith decided to get off the school bus in Centerville and walk the rest of the way home. It was a perfect day to do it, because Mary wouldn't be home for hours. She was on one of her charity missions, helping to distribute food to the poor and the helpless on the western end of the county, so she wouldn't be home until just before supper. Faith was to make it, but she had plenty of time to do that.

Although she didn't want to admit it to herself, she was getting off so she could stop at Frank's Auto Dump and see the car again. She was drawn to it by a mixture of love and hate. It held a fascination for her that she couldn't ignore.

Bobby O'Neil, pretending to trip her, stuck his foot out as she got up to walk by. He smiled up at her when she stepped over him.

"Hey, where are you going?" he asked.

"Town," she said.

"How long?"

"Why?"

"If my father's home, maybe he'll give me the truck and I'll come down to pick you up. We can go for a ride," he added, his smile widening. This was the first year they had any classes together and actually the

42

first year she said more than two words to him. She knew the girls he went with—girls like Merle Becker and Susan Lane. They didn't believe in relationships; they believed in "good times." In many ways she envied their freedom. Conscience was a burden, and morality sometimes felt like walking with an extra weight on your back. But Mary had poisoned her against such girls and made her see that being friendly with them usually resulted in being like them.

"They change you faster than you can change them. That's why it's better not to even associate with them. 'Let us keep the feast, not with old leaven, neither with the leaven of malice and wickedness; but with the unleavened bread of sincerity and truth.' "

Even so, she stood there considering Bobby's invitation for a moment. He was a handsome boy. She had been admiring him for years. Now, when she saw him across the field sometimes, working shirtless, his upper body gleaming in the sun, the muscularity sharp and smooth, she felt herself stirred. The longing was there. How did Mary keep it down, keep even the hint of its appearance away?

"No," she said. "I don't know how long I'll be." She hurried out of the bus before he could say anything that would change her mind. Willie Rosen, the driver, smiled at her, too, as she passed him. He always looked so intently at her when she stepped on the bus in the morning; and twice, when she was the only one left on the run, because the Cooper kids who lived two houses down were sick or playing hooky, she felt uneasy being alone with him. He talked to her and smiled at her and moved his body in suggestive ways. She was going to tell Mary about him, but she was afraid that somehow she would find fault with her for it.

"A man wouldn't get interested in a woman, unless a woman gave him some reason to," she said. "Of course, that doesn't excuse the man, but it doesn't

43

excuse the woman, either." Faith understood that this logic made it easier for Mary to go on.

"Want me to wait for you, Faith?" Willie asked and laughed. She didn't turn back. After the bus pulled away, she started slowly behind it.

She walked slowly with her head down. She was long legged and Mary made her wear those ankle-length dresses to school. The material rustled with each step, an almost indistinguishable whisper of cotton that made for a continuous and monotonous sound track. She held her books against her stomach and looked up only occasionally. Sometimes, she even closed her eyes.

Wildwood Drive was a little more than two miles from Centerville, a hamlet in the Town of Fallsburg, in Sullivan County, New York. The area, which had once catered mainly to city tourists, had lost most of its bungalow colonies and small hotels to changing times. Economically depressed and forlorn, some of the buildings actually sagged and leaned. Empty store-fronts reflected half-empty streets with little traffic in the winter, spring, and fall. There was still some activity in the summer, but it was nothing like it used to be.

Overgrown fields swallowed up the small bungalow units and the grounds of the little hotels. It was as though the earth was reclaiming what had been taken. Cracked and broken swimming pools, tennis courts, handball courts, and the like were literally being bull-dozed out of existence by weeds and vigorous wild vegetation.

For Faith the walk back to Wildwood was very solitary. Few houses had been built where bungalows and tourist houses once stood. The unmanaged land came back, the forest creeping toward the road, the bushes joining in a chain that threatened to reach across the very macadam. Once in the spring, and once or twice in the summer, the town sent a tractor and a mower down the road to cut back the overgrowth, but, for now, that had yet to be done.

As she drew closer to Frank's Auto Dump and the car, the images and the memories became more vivid. Today she remembered him at a time when she was a very little girl. She recalled him coming home from work and sweeping her up into his arms, pressing her tightly to his body. She would inhale all the scents, the manly odors of sweat and cigarettes, and often the strong scent of whiskey or beer.

He held her close to him even when Mary greeted him with anger and criticism. She would bury her face in his shirt and try not to hear the shouting. Sometimes he put her right down; sometimes he squeezed her tighter. Once he squeezed her so hard, she cried out in pain and fear. Mary made a big thing of that.

Whenever she tried to remember his face now, she would draw up different images. That was Mary's doing; she wanted her to see the Devil whenever she thought of him: eyes on fire, smile sardonic, his lips curling "even when he looks at you!" Mary never failed to use him as a lesson. "He surrendered to lust; he took it into his veins and it killed him as it will all bad people. 'Beware lest any man spoil you through philosophy and vain deceit, after the tradition of men, after the rudiments of the world, and not after Christ.'"

But Faith couldn't help but recall the visual details. She had gotten to know them too well, to know every crease and wrinkle, to know every little blemish, every hair. How many times had she run her forefinger over that small scar on his chin and pressed her fingertips in between his lips. She remembered the way his eyebrows thickened as they reached the bridge of his nose, the way his cheekbones pressed upward, cutting his face with stonelike sharpness.

45

She didn't want to think of him as evil, but how could she deny it? Look at what he had done; look at the sins he had committed. Mary wasn't wrong about that. And the evil that was in him could have been passed on to her. Mary was right. Mary had power. Sometimes she believed Mary did get special help from God and that Mary was one of God's agents on earth. She had been selected, just as she claimed. There were things she knew; things she could do that others didn't know and couldn't do. It had to mean something.

She looked up. She was at Frank's Auto Dump, a large field beside Frank Stratton's house. The wrecked cars and trucks were kept for parts. A good part of the field was overgrown here, too, but here it was appreciated, because it hid the offensive-looking vehicles from the public. There wasn't any logic to how the wrecks were piled and stored, but Frank knew where to look for models and parts. She knew where to go in the field, because she had gone there so many times before. Of course, Mary didn't know she did. It would be terrible if she found out.

She turned into the dump and walked past the pile of trucks, the battered small autos, the rows of parts and tires and oil drums. As usual, there was no one around, and even if there were, no one would bother her. Frank knew what she came to see and he told anyone else who worked there.

In a moment it was there before her, the wheels stripped off, the axles up on cement blocks, the rear door on this side gone, the windshield smashed in, and the roof battered down so far, it hung in jagged creases within the automobile. Interestingly enough, the dashboard was still in good shape, except where the radio had been ripped out. The seats were torn and rotted in places, but she liked getting into the car, sitting behind the steering wheel, and thinking.

In this car, one summer night, her father and a woman he had been seeing missed a turn on Olympic

Hill, a steep hill just outside of Centerville. They went over the edge and bounced a half mile down before resting on the bottom. Their bodies were broken and bleeding, yet they were found on top of one another, clinging to one another in a last, desperate gasp of love and protection. At least, that was the way she liked to think of it. Mary said they were married by the Devil, so they could spend their honeymoon in Hell.

Mary refused to make a funeral. She removed everything that she could that was associated with him, burned some of it, and gave some of it to charities, hoping that nothing was contaminated, for to Mary, evil was a disease—something that could be spread and caught like a cold, something that had to be cured with faith. She wouldn't tolerate his picture or his jewelry, nothing that in any way reminded them of his existence in their house. That was why Faith came to this car so often, for it had been his car, and it was a tangible reminder of what he was and who he had been.

She had good memories of riding in this car. She could remember when they had first gotten it, how proud he was of it, polishing and cleaning it so much. She remembered how much it angered him that Mary wouldn't go for rides unless they had a destination. "Rides for the sake for riding is wasteful and anything that is wasteful, is sinful," she said.

When she sat in this car, she could sense his presence and remember him even more vividly. She could almost hear his laugh, his singing, his soft voice, even his shouting. She could almost smell him again, although she had to admit to herself that was a little too farfetched. It was sinful to do this, she knew; but there was some mystical pleasure for her when she sat in this car, the place where he had been when he was last alive. She could touch things he last touched. Through this car, she could reach him. In it she held her own, private séance.

Was it the Devil who drew her here, who tempted her to remember her father? The possibility was so vivid to her that she often looked about, half expecting the fallen angel, Mary had drawn so clearly for her, to be standing next to one of the wrecks watching her and smiling. Once, she thought she did see him and her heart skipped a beat. She broke out into a terribly cold sweat and for a few moments she could hardly move. Trembling, she got out of the car as quickly as she could and ran off. It took weeks before she was able to come back again, and when she did, she was even more cautious, more tentative.

It was like the beginning when she first decided to do it. Nothing she had done until then had been as terrifying for her. All the while, she could hear Mary's chastising voice and see her angry face. It haunted her so intensely that night, that twice she got up from her bed to go to Mary's room and confess. If it were the Devil who brought her there, Mary could save her, she thought.

But she was too frightened to tell her, and she didn't want to end it. Maybe it was wicked; maybe it wasn't. Whatever the case, she couldn't resist, and, anyway, she told herself, she was there remembering only the good things about him. She didn't think of him as drunk and lustful; she didn't recall the violence and the hate. She thought about the earlier days, when he looked young and healthy and there was always a great deal of laughter for them. Surely, this couldn't be sinful, and she had her wits about her enough to resist any suggestions the Devil might make.

Then there were the times when she came here simply because she felt terribly alone and had no one to talk to. Sitting there behind the steering wheel, she could talk to her father and imagine his responses. Sometimes she simply cried. Sometimes she sat and felt nothing but disappointment. Those were the saddest of times and the most frightening; for despite what

Mary had taught her and made her believe, she thought, if she lost her father completely, she would have only Mary and what Mary and she had done. That was too much to face alone, no matter what Mary said about her voices and her visions.

And deep down inside, she had the nagging feeling that it was all terrible, even if God wanted it. The feeling was growing stronger and stronger, growing as he grew in the basement and clawed away at the ceiling. The same kind of clawing was taking place within her. It was as though they were prisoners of the same madness, hungering for the same kind of freedom.

This thought frightened her, because it made her think that Mary might be right when she said, "Beware of him. He can infect you, even easier than he would infect others if he were free; for you share the same blood."

Hearing Mary's words in her mind made her shudder. When she lifted her hands from the steering wheel, she saw that the palms were damp and red. She had been holding on so tightly the whole time she sat there. She wiped them on her skirt and got out, looking back only once before leaving the dump. Now the car looked small and insignificant, even a bit comical, with its twisted metal and shattered windows. She questioned why she should feel any mystery about it, but she also knew that the feelings that brought her here would return and she would sit inside it again.

The sound of Bobby O'Neil's pickup truck pulling up behind her filled Faith with a combination of fear and excitement. Her heart began to pound; her face flushed. She walked on, pretending not to notice his slowing the vehicle to a crawl to follow along with her. Finally, she turned and he smiled out at her. He looked older and more mature sitting behind the steering wheel in the dark blue truck cab. For a moment she

49

thought of her father again, his shoulders pulled back wide and high, his smile framed in the windshield.

Bobby drove the truck beside her, leaned over to open the passenger door, and looked out at her. The sunlight was just behind him now, and the glare made her squint.

"I was looking for you," he said. "Where were you? I gave up and started back."

"I told you not to."

"Yeah, well I did. Come on, get in."

"I wanna walk."

"Walk? Why?"

"I just like to, that's all," she said and started away. He watched her walk before him and studied the long lines of her body, the way her hair lay softly on her shoulders, and the almost imperceptible movement of her hips within the loose, long skirt. Instead of giving up, he left the truck in low gear and crawled along behind her, the passenger door still opened. When she stopped, he stopped.

"What are you doing?"

"Just waiting for you to change your mind."

"I didn't tell you to come get me."

"Yeah, but I already did, so we can't let it go to waste."

She turned away again and walked on. He drove the truck forward, just as slowly and just as far. A car going in the opposite direction slowed down when it came to them and the driver studied the scene, a wry smile on his face. Faith imagined he saw it as some kind of lovers' quarrel and thought that she had jumped out of the truck.

"Damn it, Bobby O'Neil," she said, spinning around. He brought the truck to a stop again. He was still smiling widely, his eyes bright with mischief. She had to smile, too, but she looked away to do so. Then she thought, what difference would it make if I rode with him? Mary wasn't home yet; she wouldn't know. She ran to the truck impulsively and stepped in. "You're embarrassing me," she said. "That's why I'm giving in."

"Close the door. I don't wantcha to fall out now that I gotcha."

There was something very attractive about his smile, she thought, and it wasn't only his straight, white teeth. It was in his eyes, in the laughter, and sexual excitement that lay just behind them. It was that little expression of knowledge, that challenging enticement that she had seen in her erotic dreams. For her there was a danger here, and that danger quickened her heartbeat and sent a tingling up the inside of her thighs. She tugged her skirt tightly around herself after she closed the truck door. He didn't start off immediately; he simply sat there smiling like someone realizing an accomplishment or a prize.

"Well?"

"Why are you so nasty?"

"I'm not nasty."

"You're not the friendliest person I've ever met."

"I don't like being tricked," she said, but her voice already indicated some retreat. She didn't like being thought of as unfriendly and nasty, and she wasn't sure she wanted to be nasty to him anyway.

"It's not really a trick. It's just my way of trying to get to know you," he said, making it sound like a sincerely simple explanation. She turned and stared at him for a moment, her eyes small and suspicious. His smile began to melt.

"Why?"

"Because . . . because we're neighbors for so long and we've never really been friends."

"Why did you decide to become friends now?"

"Boy, you're tough."

"Why?" she insisted. His smile returned.

"Because I think you're pretty," he offered. The honesty of the statement threw her into a blush and left her momentarily speechless. All at once she had the urge to open the door and jump out so she could run away; and yet, at the same time, she felt like smiling, like moving closer to him, like getting to know him. He sensed her indecision and spoke quickly.

"It wasn't easy for me to tell you that so fast, but you wouldn't give me the chance to lay any ground-work. I'm not a fast-talker, believe me. When you act like this, I don't know what else to do but speak the truth. I'm not giving you a line," he added.

"I'll bet," she said, but she believed him. She turned away to hide her pleasure.

"You'd lose," he said and started up the road, almost as slowly as before. It was obvious that he wanted to prolong the ride.

"How come you keep to yourself so much?" he asked.

"What do you mean?"

"I never see you at any of the parties."

"So? Those parties are stupid. There aren't too many people around here I care to know anyway," she added defensively. She didn't want to tell him her mother forbade her to go to school parties.

"Yeah, I know what you mean, but still . . ."

"Besides, I'm serious about my life. I want to do something with it."

"Really?" he asked, as though he had never met anyone serious before. "What do you want to do?"

"I don't know yet. Maybe . . . maybe be a doctor."

"Wow. I'm not even sure I'm going to college. My father thinks I should stay and work with him. He says I'll learn more and make more faster."

"He's wrong," she said. Her definite tone of voice annoyed him, but he didn't show it.

"Well, he doesn't do too badly. If he wanted to work more, he'd make a lot more."

"That's just it—he's lazy. Like most people around here."

"Why are you so down on the people around here? Your father was from here, wasn't he?" This time he couldn't hide his unhappiness. She didn't reply. "My father says your father was a good worker."

"I don't like talking about him," she said. He looked at her. There was a heavy silence between them for a few moments.

"Getting nice now, isn't it?" he asked, hoping the conversational change would bring back whatever it was he first felt when he saw her walking along the roadway. "Took my little brother fishing on Brown's Pond last weekend. We put a rowboat on it, you know."

"Why do you call it a pond? It's a mile-long lake, isn't it?"

"I don't know. My father always called it a pond. I guess to him it's too small to be a lake. Does your mother call it a lake?" he asked timidly. He didn't like bringing up her mother; he had heard too many stories about her. His mother thought Mary Oaks was "wack-o." If she knew he was interested in Faith Oaks, she'd bawl him out for it. "The less we have to do with those neighbors, the better," she always said.

"She calls it a . . . a pond, too," Faith confessed. "But I call it a lake."

"All right," he said, nodding and tapping the steering wheel as though he had come to a major decision. "From now on, I'm going to call it a lake, too."

She looked at him with a terribly serious expression on her face and then, she broke into a laugh. It was a short, soft laugh, which he thought was kind of cute. He liked the way she looked sideways at him, giving him what he thought was a very sexy look. He had suspicions about private girls like Faith: they harbored greater frustrations. He didn't tell any of his friends about it, though, and he especially didn't tell them of his interest in Faith Oaks. They thought she was too weird.

"Say," he said, "why don't you and I go rowing tonight? It's going to be a warm night. It'll be fun."

"Oh, I can't," she said quickly. "I've got to study."

"Me too, but we can't study all night. It's good to take breaks. Your mind works better."

"Who told you that?"

"Mr. Pellerman. He oughta know; he's a genius."

"Well my mind works fine without breaks."

"I'll call you later. Maybe you'll change your mind."

"No, I don't want you to call!"

He looked at her. She seemed genuinely terrified.

"Well, what's the harm in that?"

"I know I won't be able to go."

"You mean your mother won't let you go?" She didn't respond. They drove on in silence for a while. "Can't you sneak out somehow?"

She thought about it. There was a way she could sneak out. She could wait until her mother got involved in her Bible programs and then tell her she was going up to bed. She could go out her window and down the old metal fire escape Grandpa Oaks had built when they had increased their intake of tourists forty years ago. It was old and rusty, but she had been out on it before. There was no danger if she were careful.

"It wouldn't be right."

"But you could do it. I know you can," he said smiling. "We'd have a good time. It's beautiful out there at night. Let's do it," he added, his voice filled with a childlike excitement that infected her.

"I don't know," she said. Even that statement seemed sinful.

"How's nine o'clock sound? I'll wait for you by the path behind your house."

"How do you know about that path to the lake?"

"I've been around. Don't forget, I grew up here, too."

He pulled into her driveway and started up toward "The Oaks." Even though there was at least another good hour before her mother would be home, she was very nervous about it.

"Stop here," she said. "Please!"

"Sure."

"Thanks for the ride," she said and opened the door quickly.

"Nine o'clock," he called after her. She didn't turn around. "I'll really be disappointed if you don't show. So will you," he added.

She smiled, but she didn't turn around for him to see. He watched her hurry up the drive toward the big, dull-looking house. Even now, in daylight, it looked dark and sad to him. He didn't like going near it. When he was younger, he was afraid to go close to it. His mother's description of Mary Oaks frightened him. Once, when she was mad at him for wandering too far from their house, she told him that Mary Oaks could have gotten him and made him do some terrible religious ritual. From what he had seen of her, he believed it. She reminded him of some kind of wild bird, a mad vulture. It was hard to believe that Faith was really her daughter. But his father told him that once Mary was a pretty woman.

"Before she got so wrapped up in hellfire and brimstone. It changed her, like something inside her sucking the life out of her. I always felt sorry for Tom," he had said.

When Faith disappeared from sight, Bobby backed the truck out and started away. He wondered if she would be there at nine o'clock. She had been so frightened. Maybe it was wrong of him to tempt her into it. If she got caught, it would be his fault. Then he considered the possibility of getting caught with her down at the lake. What if Mary Oaks followed them in the dark? He shuddered. This whole thing might have been a terrible mistake. Faith was quite different from other girls her age and she did act strange at times. If there were some kind of scene, his parents would get mad and Mary Oaks . . .

This is stupid, he thought. It's stupid to be afraid of some crazy, skinny woman. Just to emphasize the point and support his own courage, he gunned the engine and spun around the turn in their driveway, sending gravel flying up behind him. Then he concentrated his thoughts on Faith and the way her body moved under that long, loose skirt. He thought of the smooth lines of her neck and he thought of her undiscovered breasts lying softly and fully beneath that silly, out-of-fashion high-necked blouse.

It drove all hesitation from him. He'd be there at nine o'clock, waiting and hoping.

Cy Baum stepped out on his side porch. He had just sent his son and granddaughter out to see the rabbit he had gotten for her. He had kept it as a surprise until after supper, telling her he had named it "Buttons," just as she had always wanted.

He started to loosen his belt to give his full stomach some relief, but paused instead. He could tell from the way Arnold was leaning over and embracing Gina that something was wrong. After a moment, the four-year-old girl's shoulders shuddered and Arnie squatted beside her to comfort her.

"What's wrong?" Cy called. His granddaughter broke from her father and ran toward him, the tears streaming freely down her cheeks now.

"Oh Papa, he's gone! Someone opened the cage and let him out!"

"What?" He took her into his long, brown-speckled hands and held her against his leg. "What's she talking about, Arnie?"

His son came toward him, his arms out, palms

turned upward as usual, looking stupid and helpless. Here he was, forty-three years old, earning more income yearly than Cy had seen in ten years of work, and yet, he could not handle the simplest problems. For Cy it was as though his youngest son had skipped a whole area of development and somehow gone off to college to graduate with honors. Now he was a chemical engineer living in White Plains; a father with three kids, two of whom were spoiled rotten by his wife, Bea. Cy thought it was characteristic of the newer generations that his daughter-in-law couldn't boil water, needed a cleaning lady four times a week, and a mother's helper as much as possible. Yet, she was a pretty woman, too pretty for Arnie, who he thought was homely. Cy's two older boys were much better looking, but their wives weren't half as pretty as Arnie's. There was no logic to it, he thought.

Cy usually kept these thoughts to himself, but Hilda was angry today, because Bea hadn't driven up with Arnie and Gina. When Hilda wanted to know why, Arnie said she was too exhausted. Then Hilda, in that dry, sarcastic way of hers Cy loved so much, asked, from what? Arnie then listed Bea's life—her charity work at the hospital, the tennis league, her shopping at the mall, and her woman's club theater parties.

"Well, things must be a little easier for her this year with Teddy and Sammy at school."

"They are," Arnie said, "but Gina's a full-time job."

"You still have the mother's helper, don't you?" Hilda pursued. Cy loved to watch this—her gentle demolishment of Arnold. He hemmed and hawed. Yes, but the woman's been unreliable, sick often, etc. And then they didn't have her on weekends anymore. "What happened?"

"She just couldn't do it and it's been difficult getting someone else we can trust."

"It's very hard living in today's world," Cy finally

said. Hilda and he looked at each other a moment and then both broke out in laughter. That was when Arnie took Gina out to look at her pet rabbit. Cy had gotten it two weeks ago in anticipation of their visit.

"So?" he asked.

"I don't know, Pop. The cage door's open and the rabbit's gone."

"Open? What do you mean, open?"

"Go look."

"Come, Gina, let's look again. Look with Papa," he said and he took her tiny hand into his. She wiped her face with a clenched fist and sobbed silently as they walked back to the cage. Arnold followed closely behind.

Although he had Cy's frame and height, his physical appearance reflected his inner softness. He was at least twenty-five pounds overweight, most of it hanging on his waist and stomach. His face was bloated and his features were swollen—his lips thicker, his nose wider, and his chin closer to his neck. Also, he had taken after Hilda's side when it came to hairline. His had already retreated considerably and his light brown hair, speckled with gray, had thinned to the point where his scalp was visible in many spots. In truth, instead of looking like the affluent, upper-middle-class man he was, he looked like someone who had recently recovered from a very serious illness. Cy was sorry that Arnie had grown up during the time when their farming enterprises were no longer profitable. Perhaps if he had worked harder, he'd be stronger now in many ways, Cy thought.

"Damned if you ain't right," Cy said. He held the small cage door out and studied the latch. "No rabbit or fox could've opened this like that."

"What do you think, Pop?"

"I think some little bastard on this street came by last night and either stole the bunny or let it loose," he said and looked around the lawn as though he expected the rabbit might still be there.

"Should we look for it, Papa?" Gina asked.

"No, I don't think we have much of a chance of finding it. Don't worry, though. I'll get another one today."

"But I liked the name, Buttons."

"We'll call the new one Buttons, too," Arnie offered.

"If it's a new one, you can't call it Buttons," she said, grimacing at her father. Cy liked that. This one had some spunk and took after him, he thought.

"We'll call it Buttons II, get it. Buttons with a two after it."

"No," Cy said. "This time we'll let Gina pick out the name. OK, Gina?" His granddaughter nodded and embraced him tightly.

"You been having trouble like this, Pop?" Arnie asked.

"Naw, this is the first thing like this. I mean, I had raccoons steal stuff, break into the garage and the like, but nothing like this."

"Got any ideas?"

"I don't know. There are a few kids on the street now. Hardly any of 'em come down this way, though. Those Cooper kids one house past us are hell raisers. Coulda been them."

"Want me to go over there and take a look?"

"Hell no. We don't need no arguments. Come on," he said, "we'll take a ride up to Willie Cotter's place and see if he's got another rabbit for us."

"Maybe we can take it home, too. Can we, Daddy? Can we?"

"I don't think so, Sweetie. We don't have any place for it."

"You've got a helluva backyard down there," Cy said.

"Yeah, but you know how Bea feels about animals, Pop."

"Yeah, I know," he said sadly. "We'll keep it here, Gina, and that way your father will visit more, eh?" He winked at his granddaughter and she smiled up at him. She's a smart one, he thought; she's on to him already.

"Arnold," Hilda called from the porch, "Bea was just on the phone. She said you forgot about the Robinsons' affair tonight."

"Oh damn."

"Said you'd better start back immediately."

"But Daddy," Gina said, "we gotta go with Papa and get another rabbit."

"We can't, honey. We'll do it next time."

Gina began to cry again, this time clinging to Cy's pants.

"Why don't you leave her here with us for a few days, Arnie?" Cy asked. Gina paused and held her breath in anticipation.

"I can't do that, Pop. We didn't bring any of her stuff."

"We got what she'll need and we'll get whatever else she needs."

"Her clothes, her underwear, socks . . ."

"I'll buy her a new outfit and some underwear and socks," Cy said and stroked his granddaughter's long blond hair. She turned her cherry vanilla face up to him hopefully. She has the best of Bea's features, Cy thought—the little upturned nose, the ice-blue eyes, the small mouth that tucked in just a little at the corners, making for a cute smile, and the same soft blond hair that looked so rich and healthy, she could model for shampoo commercials.

"I don't know, Pop. Bea might . . ."

"Bea'll be happy. You won't need that unreliable mother's helper for a few days."

"Please, Daddy, please."

"Well . . . all right," he said. "I'll be back up on Thursday. I'll come after work."

"Why don't you wait until next weekend? Bea could come up with you and you could make a day of it. She hasn't been here for a while."

"I'll see, Pop," he said.

"Go and tell Grandma you're staying," Cy said. His granddaughter shot off instantly, her little legs wobbling with her enthusiasm. He had to laugh.

"You're sure she's not going to be a problem for Mom?"

"Well, son, your mother brought up three of you, kept this house, helped me in the fields often when we had the farm going, and even took a side job for a time when we had those bad days." Arnold knew he was referring to the time he had gotten hurt on one of his carpentry jobs. "You were already fifteen then, but there was still a lot to do."

"I know what you mean, Pop, but she might be tired by now. She's no kid."

"What your generation doesn't understand, Arnie, is that often, work, good work, makes you stronger and happier. There's all kinds of pleasures and all kinds of reasons to be alive."

"OK, Pop, OK. I was just asking."

Cy nodded. He looked back at the disturbed rabbit cage and shook his head.

That night he took his granddaughter to his friend's farm up in Neversink. Willie Cotter was more than eager to get rid of another rabbit. Gina named it Silver Bell, because it was the color of silver and it had a head she said was shaped like a bell. They put it in the cage and she spent all her time with it, up to when she had to go into the house to eat and to sleep.

She was the first up in the morning, eager to give her new rabbit breakfast. Hilda prepared something and the two of them went out to feed it. Cy was in the bathroom shaving when he heard his wife's scream.

He nearly cut his chin. He went to the window and opened it quickly.

"What is it?"

"There," Hilda said. She pointed to the opened cage and then to the right. This rabbit had been freed, too, only this one lay nearby, dead. When he came downstairs and looked at it in amazement, he discovered that its neck had been broken.

"Why?" Hilda asked him. He looked down at the pathetic animal and shook his head. When he turned to her, his face was gray and his eyes were dark. She couldn't remember when he had had such a look of sickly fear.

"This ain't no prank," he said. "This is evil."

He picked up his distraught granddaughter and the three of them headed back into the house, a heavy silence now covering the morning. Inside, he kissed away Gina's tears.

"We'll get another one," he said, "only this time we'll keep it in the basement. Willie Cotter's going to think we're having stew every night," he told Hilda. She laughed and that broke their dark mood for the rest of the day.

But toward evening, Cy thought again about the dead rabbit and the opened cage. He went out and buried the animal and then inspected the cage door. The latch worked perfectly; there was no way the rabbits could have gotten themselves out. He looked to the right and thought about the Cooper kids. He didn't know them that well, but he couldn't imagine them doing something this vicious and this senseless.

The sun was going down quickly. By now its rays were well dissipated by the trees, as it sunk on the horizon. Long shadows were cast as always, but somehow they looked longer and darker this evening. He noted how quiet the birds were and how still everything suddenly seemed. A chill passed through him and he spun around quickly to look the other way. It was as though he had sensed something behind him, something out there where the bushes grew heavy and the grass was tall and thick. For the first time in all the years he had lived here, he was afraid of something on his own land, something that moved in the darkness and watched him unseen.

He felt his heartbeat quicken; he felt the cold sweat break out on the back of his neck and he headed for the house. He couldn't explain why, but he felt it was terribly important that his wife and his granddaughter not come out here when nighttime fell.

FOUR

He was out again. Each time had been more exciting than the last, and each time he had been more anxious to start. He was leaving earlier and earlier, realizing that once the big creature fed him and went upstairs, she didn't return and he was free to do what he wanted.

Tonight the sun was not quite gone and the added illumination changed the face of much of what he had previously seen. Colors were richer; the leaves were transparent and dazzling. Those that he could reach sparkled like jewels in his fingers. He tasted them and inspected them with a scientific curiosity, tracing the veins, studying the shapes and textures.

The first time he touched a tree, he half expected it to move. He thought it was some kind of big animal. The large maple just outside his hole loomed above the house; its branches stretched like long, bony arms. He could think only of spiders, for the leaves of the maple formed a green web. It took him a moment to understand that it was the wind that moved them and not the tree moving itself. He sat directly under it and, without touching the trunk, looked straight up. When the branches dipped downward, he scurried away, terrified that the tree was going to seize him.

It didn't and he understood that it didn't have that kind of power. When he explored it further, he saw that the bark was rough, but he could peel some of it off. He didn't like the bitter taste, but he liked the strong, solid feel of the trunk. He embraced it, inhaled the scent of it, and felt a sense of security and confidence because of it.

Overcoming his fear of trees, he was able to venture into the woods behind the house and even begin to pull himself up on smaller trees with lower branches. For him the branches were like the pipes in the basement that ran along the ceiling. He could raise himself gracefully onto them and place himself securely in the nooks where the branches and the trunk joined. As he grew less fearful, he climbed higher, discovering that the added height enabled him to see further and learn more about his surroundings.

It had been during one of these early climbs that he saw Cy Baum's farmhouse. The lighted windows attracted him to it. He recalled his first night outside and his thought that there might be another nice creature within this house. From this height, he understood the distance and how to approach it.

There was a time when The Oaks had some of the most beautiful grounds in the area. The flats on the south side were cleared, plowed, and groomed neatly by Great Grandfather and Grandfather Oaks, both fastidious farmers who took almost as much pride in the appearance of their farm as the produce they could glean from it. A little more than a half a mile from the rear of the house, the forest was left relatively untouched, for it grew on a rocky hillside unsuitable for farming. When the house had been mainly heated by fireplace and wood stove, the forest was a source of fuel; but since then, the woods had thickened and deepened, the saplings creeping up on what was once cleared, gently rolling grounds.

Long unused, the south-side fields became overgrown with thin, hardwood trees, tall grass, and bushes. The once well-fertilized earth provided a rich environment for weeds, wild berry bushes, and crab grasses. In the spring and the summer, it thickened into a sea of yellow, white, and dull green. On hot summer days there seemed to be a continuous circle of mad insects hovering above. Gradually, it became a safe thoroughfare for rabbits, skunks, woodchucks, field snakes, and the like that enjoyed the cool pathways and the security of overgrown foliage.

At the end of the south-side field, there was an old corral fence to mark the boundary between the Oaks property and the Baum property. Much of the fence had degenerated and crumpled, but, since neither family cared much about farming anymore, there was little concern. Cy Baum could look out and try to remember the once rich cornfields, the odor of newly turned soil, the sounds of tractors and men; but, looking at what was there now, it was difficult for him to picture the land as it was.

The forest that grew behind Cy Baum's house and the back of The Oaks formed a natural barrier on the north side between The Oaks and the O'Neil property. The same forest extended back to and around Brown's Pond. It continued on for a few miles, until it reached one of the main highways on the other side of Centerville.

Despite its relative proximity to well-developed areas, the wild and now untouched territory supported a population of wildlife matched in few other areas of the Catskills. All of the families on Wildwood Drive had their land posted, but during big game season, much of it was trespassed upon, especially from the west end. Brown's Pond attracted white-tailed deer, bear, fox, and bobcats. Because of its distance from the highways and because of the thickness of the forest, the large pond was as close to its natural state as it could be.

Before the "imp" climbed the trees, he had no concept of all this. Even so, the distance and the difficulty of traveling through the wild land made no impression on him. He was driven only by what pleased and attracted him. His acute sense of smell and hearing, his nocturnal eyesight, and his hardened, callused body made it possible for him to move like a wild creature anyway. He traveled in a half-crawl, half fast-walk; but even when he stood up completely, he rarely stood straight. For him it was instinctively safer to keep his shoulders slightly turned down, his head poised stiffly, so he could look quickly from side to side and listen to all the sounds around him.

There was some distortion in the shape of his short arms. They were thick at the wrists and then slim and wiry to the shoulders. Because of his poor posture, his shoulders were curved forward. Although his upper body bone structure was well outlined, his torso was wide for his height, this wideness exaggerated by the shortness of his legs.

All in all, though, his body was an asset to him in the wilderness. He fit under bushes and between small openings. He moved with a natural grace over rocks and stumps, and he had the strength to climb and swing whenever he had to. Now, in the wide open spaces, where he could exercise his muscularity, he quickly developed wind and endurance, taking an animal pleasure in his quickened heartbeat, the pounding of his blood, the straining of his sinews, and the challenge of the travel.

Used to the necessity of moving silently, he slipped in and out of shadows, as though he were kin to the night. Often he would come upon other wild creatures, surprising them with his sudden appearance. Once, he nearly fell over an unsuspecting woodchuck. The animals fled to safe distances and studied him. They neither welcomed nor attacked him. He was simply another part of the forest, something that had just emerged, but seemed to have been there as long as they.

He was interested in every animal he saw, but they were all much harder to capture than the mice in the basement; so when he first went to Cy Baum's house and saw the rabbit in the cage, he became terribly excited. It took him only a few moments to understand that the rabbit was trapped. He thought about himself, trapped in the basement. There was something he sensed in the rabbit's eyes, when it looked out at him, that made him feel sorry for it. He wanted to hold it and hum his soothing sounds.

He knew immediately why he couldn't simply open the door to release it. Mechanical things had always been one of his few distractions in the basement. He loved taking them apart and fingering the little screws and hasps. So it was with little difficulty that he released the rabbit. As soon as he opened the cage, however, it hopped out. When he went to grab it, it skipped away from him quickly and disappeared within the bushes. He went into them to find it, but the rabbit was too quick and too frightened.

The next night, when he returned to the Baum farmhouse and found another rabbit in the cage, he was more careful when he opened the door. This time he grabbed it before it got to the opening and he held it tightly in his arms. It struggled to get free and he squeezed it tighter and tighter until, unknowingly, he snapped its neck. It turned still like the mouse in the cellar, so he threw it down and ran off in disappointment again.

Tonight, though, after he had climbed his tree and looked out at a more lit-up world, something else attracted him to the Baum farm. He turned his head sideways to catch the full meaning of the sound. His dark brown eyes widened with curiosity, and he sniffed the air instinctively to tie a scent in with the noise that seemed musical to him. He looked to it with greater and greater interest, recognizing something warm and similar in its origin. He was like an extra

68

terrestrial who had discovered the possible existence of his own kind. He strained to hear more. When it came, he scurried down the tree excitedly, determined to go back to the place of the rabbits.

With radar accuracy, he honed in on the sound and its origin. He scampered through the fields in a direct line to it. Nothing that appeared in his path could hold his interest. He was drawn magnetically, vaguely remembering that he, too, had made a similar sound, although not as softly or as sweetly.

He stopped at the broken fence and went to his hands and knees. Crawling carefully, he moved through the heavy bushes, until he was almost to the cleared portion of the field by the Baum farmhouse. There he stopped and parted the tall grass so he could look out clearly. What he saw fascinated him and filled him with such longing and pleasure, he had difficulty containing himself. But he understood that he must be still and he must go unseen; for the creature that stood next to the little one was as big as the one back at his home, and, even though he looked different, he could be as dangerous.

The little one was laughing. She held the rabbit close to her with a leash tied to its collar. When the rabbit hopped off, she followed behind, laughing and shrieking with delight. It was that sound that had drawn him here. He saw that the big creature laughed, too. That confused him and for a few moments, he sat there, his head tilted, studying them. Then he focused in only on the little one.

Her golden hair looked delicious. He tried to imagine the taste of it. He wondered about its feel and its scent. The little one's face looked so warm and alive. He thought about her rosy cheeks, the softness of her little legs, and the pleasure of her tiny voice. He could even imagine a warmth to her. He wanted so much to touch her and squeeze her and nibble gently on her that he began to whimper ever so slightly. He caught himself doing it and stopped, but the big creature had already turned to look in his direction.

He backed deeper into the bush. The big creature took a few steps toward him and paused, still looking his way. The imp was silent, one with the earth. He didn't blink; he barely breathed. The little one's laughter continued, so the big creature turned back to her. But he put his hand on her head and knelt down to her size to speak very softly to her. She nodded her head and pulled the rabbit to herself, until she could take it into her arms. It seemed easy for her to do so, and the rabbit didn't get still.

The big creature looked back once more and then the two of them went into the house. He waited, but they didn't come out. It grew darker and darker. He ventured closer to the house and listened for her sounds, but he couldn't hear them. He heard older, harder voices and some music, too. He wished he could call out, make some noise that would bring the little one back, but he didn't know anything to call and he was afraid of the big creature.

After a while longer, he retreated. He moved back through the fields slowly, carrying deep disappointment and sadness. He could think of nothing but the little one. Every once in a while on his return journey, he would stop and listen hopefully to the sounds of the night; but her sounds weren't there. For him the night had suddenly turned empty and too dark.

When he reached the house, he paused and looked back over the fields. He whimpered once and crawled through his hole. Inside, the rocks felt heavier as he put them back. When that was done, he went to his box. He was tired and his sadness made him more sleepy. For a while he thought of the little one and hummed his sounds. He knew he would go back until he could get close enough to the little one so he could touch her. He thought that if he grabbed her quickly like he grabbed the rabbit, he could keep her from leaving him. He would hold her even tighter than he held the rabbit, and if that made her cold and still, he wouldn't throw her down. He would bring her back here with him so he could always touch her.

These thoughts pleased him. He curled up in his box, put his fingers close to his lips, inhaled the odors of the outside world that were on his hands, and fell asleep dreaming of the long, gold hair, the soft, sweet face, and the sound of laughter.

The first time Faith sensed an emptiness in the basement, she felt panic. He could have died down there, she thought, and we wouldn't know until Mary actually sought him for a bath or one of her "lessons." Tonight, just like any other night, Mary had gone down to leave him his supper. She then came up, locking the door behind her, as usual; but, unlike some other nights, when Faith went to the floor and called to him, there was no response. She wanted to ask Mary about it, but she didn't know how. What would she say, I've been communicating with him through the kitchen floor and tonight he doesn't respond? Mary would go wild if she knew that, and tonight she was already hyper enough as it was.

Mary had returned invigorated from her church mission. She talked about the "voices" and how good she felt helping the poor. It reinforced her belief about her purpose in life.

"They looked up to me with such loving eyes," she said. "I was like a returning angel. One old lady kissed my hand. When I stroked her hair, I felt a power traveling through me and into her. Something must have happened because she grew stronger, happier, lovelier."

She paused to see how Faith was listening. Faith was attentive, but, as always, it was more because of fear than of interest.

"You should come along with me sometimes. You should see what it is to do this good work."

"I can't. School . . ."

"I know, I know. But when school ends, that's when you should go."

She went on talking about the people she had touched and the things she had said to them. She described a momentary vision she had had when it was all over. Clouds had parted and a bright light had appeared. Only she saw it, but that was because it was meant only for her eyes.

After dinner, Mary left Faith to wash the dishes and Faith tried to reach him, as always. There was no response, no matter how intently she tried. She even tapped the floor, risking Mary's hearing her. That was when she envisioned him dying or sick. She wondered why Mary, who had such compassion for the sick and the poor, couldn't have any compassion for him; for despite what he was spiritually, he was still an infant, wasn't he?

She couldn't discuss it. Mary would get very angry if she mentioned him tonight; but maybe she could come up with something that would make Mary think of him in a roundabout way. She began to think of ideas, when Mary did come charging back into the kitchen in a rage. She had gone into Faith's notebook and found her failing papers.

She slammed the notebook down on the table and held the papers up before her. Her eyes were wild and her thin, narrow face was pulled so tight with anger, it sharpened her bone structure even more, making her look like a living skeleton. Under the kitchen's bright ceiling fixture, the shadows below Mary's eyes darkened. She appeared about as frightening as she could. Faith stepped back, embracing herself. She knew what Mary's tantrums could bring.

"This is the result of your extra help! This is why

you stayed after school? Liar. Liar." She grasped the notebook and lunged forward. Faith held her arms up in front of her face and Mary brought the notebook down on them sharply. The whacks didn't sting as much as they frightened. Faith went to sidestep her and Mary seized her hair. That hurt, so she cried out in pain and went to her knees, pleading for an end to it.

"I did stay after. I did."

"How could you fail then? How could you fail?"

"He tested us on something different. Let go." She struggled to get Mary to release her grip. Instead, Mary went to her knees beside her, bringing her violent face close.

"You're lying to me. Your marks have been getting worse and worse. That means something. Don't think I don't know what it means. I know," she said, widening her eyes even more. She paused. Her breath was hot and heavy against Faith's face. Faith closed her eyes and prayed it would end, but Mary kept her position and kept her grip on her hair. The next thing she said came more in a whisper. "You're touching yourself." Faith opened her eyes. "You're lusting." Faith shook her head. How could she know? "The Devil's in your hands, making you do it."

"No," she said, but her voice was so weak it was as good as a confession.

"You're letting Him distract you; you're letting Him defeat you."

"No." She spoke louder and stronger this time. Mary studied her face. Faith didn't look away. She told herself she had to meet those eyes.

"Have you been with a man?"

"No, never."

"You think about it."

"No."

"Why did you fail these tests?" There was some retreat in her voice. Faith was hopeful.

"I just didn't understand it. He's going to explain it again. Most of the class failed. You'll see. I'll do better."

Mary's grip lessened. Her eyes took on that far-off look that indicated to Faith that Mary was no longer concentrating on anything specific. She would merely begin to preach now. That was tolerable; she could turn her off and think of other things.

"Know ye not that the unrighteous shall not inherit the kingdom of God?" Mary said and released her hold on Faith's hair. But she put her hands on her shoulders and made her stand with her. "Be not deceived: neither fornicators, nor idolaters, nor adulterers, nor effeminate, nor abusers of themselves with mankind, nor thieves, nor covetous, nor drunkards, nor revilers, nor extortioners shall inherit the kingdom of God."

Faith nodded, her tears ending. Mary seemed placated by Faith's look of agreement and gratitude. She backed away and looked at the notebook again.

"I want a letter from this teacher telling me you were there working with him after school."

"But that's embarrassing. Why must everyone know you don't trust me?"

"Because I can't trust you."

"Why?" Faith demanded. She surprised herself with her aggressiveness.

"Never forget you are your father's daughter," Mary said. Her eyes got smaller, sadder.

"But I'm your daughter, too."

"Know ye not that he who is joined to a harlot is one body?" she said and turned away from her. Her shoulders sagged as she left the kitchen. Faith watched her go and then sat at the table, her head in her hands. She wanted to cry, but the tears wouldn't come. Suddenly, she felt very tired and alone. After she completed the dishes, she decided to go up to bed. She paused in the living room doorway. Mary was sitting in her easy chair, staring at nothing.

"I'm tired and I don't have any work tonight, so I'm going to sleep early."

Mary looked at her and nodded. She looked stunned, on the border between the past and the present, and on the verge of drifting onto some mental avenue that would take her away for hours. It was almost a catatonic state. Faith was familiar with it, and tonight she was grateful for it. She hurried up to her room and closed the door as far as she could. Then she put on her light by her bed and sat thinking.

Never had she touched herself when Mary was anywhere nearby. She didn't even think about it in Mary's presence, for fear that Mary would read her thoughts or see the temptation in her face. How did she know to ask that? Could she see through the walls? All her life, Faith had believed that Mary had some special spiritual gifts. Didn't this prove it?

Perhaps she was only guessing, Faith thought. Maybe she was simply assuming. That could be. She could be remembering her own youth. All the girls did what she did; it was natural. Mary didn't know anything specific. She knew that Faith was a normal girl and would have normal feelings.

But was she a normal girl? she wondered. Did she have normal feelings? How could she measure them? She knew only what she had read secretly in the library at school. She couldn't compare notes with other girls; none of them cared to be friendly with her. Maybe that was her fault as much as it was theirs; but nevertheless, it was still true—she had no one to confide in, to be intimate with, to call a friend.

When she heard Mary's religious music start, she got up to get undressed for bed. It was then that she remembered Bobby O'Neil and his invitation to go rowing at the lake. The whole idea now seemed more frightening than ever; and yet, she wished she could do it just to prove to herself that she was a normal girl.

Because of what Mary had said to her, she avoided

looking directly at herself in the mirror when she undressed. She put on her heavy cotton nightgown quickly, went to the bathroom to brush her teeth, and then returned to her bedroom intending to go right to sleep. She had a deep, sick feeling in the pit of her stomach and thought that only sleep would end it. But the moment she turned off the light and put her head on the pillow, her mind reeled with images and thoughts. The whole day came back at her.

She saw herself in her father's wrecked car; she imagined the Devil hiding behind another car, watching her and smiling. She thought about Bobby O'Neil's sexy eyes and remembered the warm excitement in his voice. She saw Mary in a rage, felt her blows, and heard her whisper, "You're touching yourself."

In replay, the words practically burned her. She pulled her hands away from her body and lay there in fear of herself. She grew clammy and hot. It was going to be harder than she thought to go to sleep. She began to toss and turn. It was then that she heard the first pebble hit her bedroom window.

Bobby had hoped that she would meet him, but he didn't actually expect it. When she didn't appear, he was frustrated. Then he became angry and, finally, he got brazen. It took courage to approach The Oaks. The house loomed above him, the windows of the dark rooms catching the moonlight and making it seem as though the building were alive with Halloween eyes watching him. He didn't know what he was going to do when he got closer. He certainly didn't intend to go calling on her. Just the thought of walking up to that big, heavy oak front door was enough to send shivers down his spine. As though to punctuate his fear, two bats flew out of the eaves and dove in his direction.

He was about to retreat when he lucked out. He had no idea which room was Faith's. But suddenly, lights went on and he saw her through the window. He saw

76

her start to take off her blouse. Then she disappeared from sight. When she reappeared, she was wearing a nightgown. A moment later, her lights went out. He stood there a little confused. Why would she go to bed so early? Had she gone to bed or simply gotten into a nightgown and then gone to some other part of the house?

The only way to find out was to draw her attention, so he felt about for small pebbles and tried throwing them gently against her second-story windowpane. When that didn't seem to work, he considered the fire escape. There was a small landing right by her window, but he wondered if the metal was too old and rusted to hold him.

What was he doing, risking all this? he wondered. Was she worth it? What if he got hurt? How could he explain any of it? His father would kill him, if he didn't kill himself on this old metal ladder. Nevertheless, he went forward. But before he had climbed two rungs, he heard her window open. He stood completely still and waited.

"Who is it?" she called in a loud whisper. That nearly made him laugh aloud. Who did she think it was? How many boys proposed a date with her tonight?

"It's Romeo," he said. She looked down through the landing grate.

"Go away."

"Hey, that's not what Juliet said."

"I'm not Juliet."

"Well, what are you doing? You're certainly not studying."

"I'm . . . I'm not feeling that well, so I'm going to sleep early. I told you I wasn't going to be there," she added.

"Not in so many words, you didn't."

"Well, I'm telling you now. Go away."

"That's not very friendly."

77

"I don't feel like being friendly tonight."

"How about tomorrow night?"

"No."

"The night after that?"

"Never."

"That's what I thought." He continued to climb the ladder.

"What are you doing?"

"Risking my life to meet you. What else?"

She looked behind her. Mary's music was still loud, but her program wouldn't last that much longer. If she came up the stairway and found him here . . . especially after the incident downstairs!

"Please, go home."

He was nearly to her landing. She debated closing the window and getting into bed. Then if Mary discovered him, Faith could claim she didn't know he was there. Of course, the chances were that Mary wouldn't believe that and then Bobby would get into a great deal of trouble.

"You know, this isn't a bad spot," he said when he reached the landing. "I mean, there's a view from here."

"There's nothing to see out there."

"I wouldn't say that. So," he said, turning to her and seating himself comfortably on the metal landing, "what's wrong with you?"

"I've got a headache."

"Did you try aspirin?"

"We don't use medicine, unless it's absolutely necessary."

"Really? Why's that?"

"Mary . . . my mother believes that the body gets sick only when the soul is sick."

"Heavy idea. You believe that, too?"

"I don't know. She's right about most things," she said, and realized for the first time that she was leaning on the windowsill, that she was dressed only in her nightgown, and that Bobby O'Neil was sitting on her fire escape landing only inches away from her. She had never been this close to a boy while she wore so little. She knew that her breasts were visibly outlined beneath the garment. That knowledge stiffened her nipples quickly and sent a warm flush over her face and down her neck. She pulled back slightly so she was more hidden and then folded her arms across her bosom. He seemed very nonchalant, though, looking out at the fields and the sky.

"Well, do whatever makes you happy, I say," he said, turning back to her. With the moonlight behind him, his face was mostly in shadow, though she thought she could see that playful smile around his eyes.

"What are you doing here? What do you want?"

"Huh?"

"Why did you come to my house?"

"I told you. It's a beautiful night. We should go rowing."

"I don't want to go rowing. I can't go rowing."

"Too bad." He tilted his head to look past her into the room. "Where's your mother?"

"She's coming up any moment and if she finds you out here, she's going to be very mad."

"What will she do?" There was a tone of sincere interest.

"She'll . . . she'll call your parents for one thing and then . . ." Faith looked down. "She'll punish me."

"She will? Just for talking to me?"

"This isn't just talking. You're on my fire escape. By my bedroom!"

"So what? I'm not in your bedroom, am I?"

"What?" That idea never occurred to her, but now that he had brought it up, it seemed the most frightening, and yet exciting, thing she had ever heard. What if he did come in? All he would have to do is climb through the window and she would have a man in her room.

"Of course, if you came out, we could go rowing and she wouldn't have to know anything."

"She'd know. You don't know her. Can't you go away?" she said, but there was something weak about her voice, some added tone she barely recognized. She wasn't aggressive in her demand; she was gentle. She wanted him to go and yet . . . she didn't.

"I'll go if you promise to come out tomorrow night."

"I can't. I told you."

"Doesn't sound like you have much fun."

"That's not your concern," she said, this time clearly showing her anger. He looked into her room again and she listened hard for any sign of Mary.

"This is a big house. How much of it do you actually use?"

"Why?"

"Just curious."

"You're just stalling."

"Must be hard to keep it clean," he said, ignoring her. "Takes up a lot of your time, huh?"

"Yes."

"I'll tell you something," he said folding his legs into a Yoga position, "it wasn't easy for me to come over here. My mother's on my back, too."

"Really?" That interested her. How did he get along with his parents?

"Yeah. My little brother's got everybody crazy about this place."

"What place?"

"Around my house. You know," he said, gesturing with both hands. "The whole area."

"Why?"

"He says he saw E.T. out there."

"E.T.?"

"E.T., E.T. You know, the movie."

"Oh."

He studied her face for a moment. In the moonlight she was even prettier. He could see part of her collarbone through the slightly opened nightgown. Her skin glittered, the soft lines of her neck teasing him as they disappeared within her garment. It would be so wonderful, he thought, to lean in and kiss her.

"You act like you never saw the movie."

"So?"

"You didn't?" He tilted his head with suspicion. "What was the last movie you saw?"

"I don't remember. What's the difference?"

"I bet you haven't been to the movies in years. Have you?"

"I've got to go to sleep. You've got to go away. Don't you understand? You'll get us both in trouble."

"I can get the truck tomorrow. You want to go to school with me?"

"No."

"How about coming home with me? I'll wait for you."

"I can't. Please."

"She won't let you do anything. Is that it? Christ, you're seventeen. You're a senior. You're . . . "

"Don't say 'Christ.' Don't take the Lord's name in vain."

"Huh?"

"It's a sin."

"Everybody does it."

"I don't."

He looked directly at her and sensed her seriousness. There was much debate in him then. Was this girl as wacky as most thought? What had brought him here? He returned to the belief that she was a "find," and he couldn't deny how much he was attracted to her.

"All right. I'll never say it again and you'll be the

one who stopped me. If you promise to meet me here again tomorrow night," he added.

"No."

"I'm not even talking about going rowing. Just meet me here at your window."

"No."

"I'll come anyway."

She thought she heard something in the hallway outside her room, so she turned around quickly. Her movement scared him and he started for the ladder. She stood perfectly still, though, listening and waiting at the window. Since she didn't retreat, he didn't. He inched back to his spot, taking advantage of the opportunity to get even closer to her.

"What's that music?"

"Shh."

"It sounds like . . . "

"My mother is listening to her Bible programs."

"Good. So she won't listen to us." He leaned forward, touching the windowsill. "Um, something smells good in here. What is it?"

"A body lotion I use." He closed his eyes and inhaled hard. She nearly laughed at his exaggerated look of pleasure.

"Smells like . . . "

"Roses."

"Roses?" He backed away and held his arms out dramatically. "What's in a name? A rose by any other name would smell as sweet. That's from . . . "

"I know. Romeo and Juliet."

"You probably laughed before when I said that, but I felt like Romeo, and you're as pretty as Juliet could ever be."

"Don't say things like that."

"Why not?"

"It's . . . dishonest."

"No it's not. It's what I feel."

She looked at him there on the landing. He didn't

82

look evil; he looked sweet and loving. He didn't look like Temptation; he looked like Promise. Was all romance the work of the Devil? Mary couldn't be right about this. Just because her love went sour . . .

Then she heard the music go off.

"Quickly, go, she's coming up!"

"OK, OK, but will you meet me here tomorrow night? Will you?" She hesitated to close the window. When she raised her hands to it, her breasts fell free. The cool sense of her nudity beneath the thin garment quickened her heartbeat.

"Yes," she said and brought the window down between them. My God, she thought, what have I done? She didn't have time to think about it, because it wasn't more than a few seconds later that Mary came up. Faith heard her pause at her doorway. She held her breath and watched the small opening, but Mary didn't look in. When she moved on, Faith released her breath. She had had visions of Mary coming into the room and looking out the window to spot him.

But he was gone safely. She went back to the window and looked into the darkness. She thought she caught his shadow in the moonlight. Was he looking up at her? She hoped he was. And then she wondered, what part of her hoped he was? Was it good or was it the evil Mary always warned her would someday come forward and doom her to the same hell her father had found?

She wasn't sure, but she knew she would have to know. She went to sleep dreaming about Romeo and Juliet.

FIVE

Billy O'Neil stepped out of the house as innocently as he could. His father had gone into the living room to read the papers, Bobby had gone upstairs to do his homework, and his mother was at the sink rinsing the dishes. Even so, he hadn't quite closed the back door behind him when his mother yelled out, "Don't go too far, Billy. You've got to take a bath and have your hair washed tonight." He didn't answer her. That way, he thought, he could claim he didn't hear her.

Captain was waiting lethargically next to his doghouse. The unusually hot spring day left the animal tired and uncomfortable. He lay on his stomach, his tongue drooped to the side, his eyes hardly opened. His tail barely wagged when he caught sight of his little master, but one could almost read hope in the dog's face—hope that Billy had no plans for any real activity.

When Billy called to him, the dog pretended as though he hadn't heard the first command. He looked to the side, taking false interest in the flies that flew in circles around the roof of the doghouse. But Billy raised his voice and slapped the side of his own leg to emphasize obedience. Reluctantly, Captain got to his feet, his tail wagging faster and harder now, and went to Billy's side. The little boy knelt so they were head to head. He put his arm around Captain's neck and brought his mouth close to the dog's ear.

"We're going exploring," he whispered, looking back once at the back door of the house. "We're going out there to find the E.T. Don't be afraid," he added. "He won't hurt us."

Without any further hesitation, Billy stood up and headed for the path through the fields. All day in school he had been thinking about this. He had been tempted many times to tell his friends about it, but he had resisted the urge, remembering how important it was for the kids in the movie that they keep their secret. He thought he would go down the pathway to the start of the woods and then circle to The Oaks. If in doing that he failed to find him, he would go straight out to the road and walk home that way. It would be a faster return and he could do the whole circle before his mother noticed he was gone.

Before he reached the entrance to the pathway, he picked up a long stick to beat away bushes and poke into the tall grass. Captain looked back longingly at the shady spot near his doghouse, but Billy's voice took the pause out of him and he followed along at the little boy's heels.

Besides the heat, the dog instinctively sensed an early warning. Images of what he had smelled, seen, and heard the last few nights returned. Together they produced a tiny gnawing in the base of his stomach. The message it sent to his brain wasn't yet shrill. It was more like an annoying buzz. The further they ventured into the bush, the more intense it became. His physical reactions were automatic: his head rose and his ears opened to react like sonar, distinguishing and reading every sound it could; his drooping, heavy eyelids snapped back and his eyes brightened with a sharpness of vision that turned him into a scanning device, penetrating every shadow, following every movement; his muscles tightened and he walked with stiffer, sharper steps.

As he went along, a practically inaudible growl began to roll over Captain's tongue. Billy might have heard it, or seen some of the changes in his dog, if he had paid any attention to the animal; but his interest was directed solely on the fields before him. He had imagined all sorts of scenarios and expected at least one of them would take place. Nothing detracted from his purpose. Dressed in a polo shirt, a pair of shorts, and sneakers, he didn't even recognize the heavy humidity and unusually high temperature for this time of the year. Reality was the least of his concerns. The twilight created a world that seemed fantastic anyway.

Because of what he thought he had seen out here, all of the familiar ground had been changed for him. The maple and oak trees that were scattered throughout the fields looked like twisted, sleeping creatures just waiting for night to fall so they could come to life. The boundary between the tall grass and the now darkened forest seemed ominous. He decided he would skirt it in making his circle, but he would not penetrate the heavy shadows that thickened and climbed around the trees. Some of the bushes in the field were taller than he was. When he looked back down the pathway, they appeared to be closing in around him. He was being swallowed into another world—a world peopled by every fantastic thing he had ever seen in cartoons and in movies.

It was his imagination, however, that drove him forward and kept fear at bay. It was as though he had the power to create through his dreams. Anything unpleasant could be destroyed by popping it out of his mind. He could turn the bushes into a friendly army or a defeated one. With his stick, he could slap down monsters. All that was evil fled his path. But his imaginary E.T. would recognize that he was an ally and would come forward.

86

Captain's first loud growl brought Billy back to reality and made him pause. He had gone nearly three-quarters of the way, cut in close to The Oaks, pried bushes apart, slapped at the tall grasses, charged into openings, and found nothing. Now, he held his stick high, like a lance, and, without moving a muscle, he listened as hard as he could.

At first, he heard nothing. He stepped back to Captain and slowly knelt beside him again. When he embraced the dog's neck, he was surprised at the animal's tightness. He was as hard as a statue. The growl vibrated through his entire body. Captain pulled his lips back tightly over his now clenched teeth.

"What is it?" Billy whispered. The dog ignored him. Billy tried to follow Captain's pathway of vision to see what he saw. As far as he could tell, there was nothing there but the bushes and the weeds. He listened intently again, but the dog's growl drowned out everything. "Shh," he commanded. Captain only intensified his sound of anger.

Billy stood up and strained to see beyond the overgrowth. Then he continued moving forward. Captain did not want to follow. There was a tiny clearing ahead of them in the path where the bushes and weeds separated into an X shape—one part going back to his house, one part going toward The Oaks, and the others going deeper into the field.

"Come on," Billy commanded, but his dog did not move. Billy considered the path before him again. Then he looked back at Captain. This time the dog took a few steps forward and then barked. "Quiet," Billy said. He went further forward and extended his stick, until he touched the bushes directly in front of him. He separated them gently and peered within.

"Hello," he said. "If you're in there, don't be afraid. I won't tell anyone about you."

He waited. There was nothing now but the sound of the dog's low-toned, but continuous, growl. He hesitated and then went further ahead. The moment he did so, Captain barked louder and harder. Billy's heart began beating faster because of the excitement, and now, the early sensations of fear. It suddenly occurred to him that perhaps his theory was wrong, that this wasn't another E.T., that his parents and his brother might be right. Deep in the bush, night falling faster, shadows moving almost in a liquid fashion around him, casting darkness everywhere, he realized that he might very well have placed himself in some sort of danger.

He looked back toward his house; he could barely see the upper level and roof. When he turned to the other direction, however, he noted that The Oaks was in clearer view. For the first time, he realized just how close he was to it and how dark and frightening it was. In fact, it looked like it moved toward him. Actually, it wasn't the house so much as it was its shadows that stretched over the field, thickening the darkness. All the stories he had heard about the house and the Oaks family came back to him. He remembered his mother's warnings. The early sensations of fear grew stronger and he considered a quick retreat.

It was then that he heard the bushes separating. Captain heard it too and it set him into a series of sharp, shrill barks. As he barked, he backed away slowly. Billy stepped to the left of the bush he had separated, but his little legs felt weak and wobbly, and he wasn't sure he could just turn and run off. A clammy, cold feeling ran down his back when he realized that the noise was still there and that something was coming toward him. He held his breath, raised his stick defensively, and then . . . he saw it.

He didn't know the boy existed, so he didn't have any intention of confronting him. He had known about the dog, having heard it and seen it, but he didn't like it, and he didn't want to be near it. When he came upon some day-old field mice huddled together in a pink mound, their eyes still sewn closed, their furless bodies intertwined in a web of security, he paused to study them, prying them apart and holding them gently, but firmly, in his palms. He was intrigued with their nervous, almost somnambulistic movement, and he didn't pay much attention to the sounds coming from the right. By the time he heard the dog's growl, it and the boy were only a few feet from him.

He placed the field mice back in their nest and listened. It was then that he heard the boy speak and saw the bushes being parted. He couldn't help his physical reactions. This was the first time he had been discovered on the outside and all he could think about was the big creature and her strap. There would be punishment, terrible punishment.

Once again, he had come out of the basement before it was totally dark. Anxious to make his journey around to see the little girl, he had barely waited for the big creature to go back upstairs after feeding him. He gobbled down his food, scooping it and shoving it into his mouth carelessly. Much of it was wasted. He knew that if the big creature found it scattered about, she would be enraged, so he had to take time to hide it and dispose of it anyway.

Then he opened his hole in the wall and escaped into the early twilight. He followed the path up toward the woods and came upon the mice. He imagined that they and things like them were along the path the night before, but it was only because of the added light that he was able to see them. He had a strange reaction to more light—at first it frightened instead of pleased him. More intense illumination changed his world. Comfortable with shadows and dark shapes, he felt threatened and intimidated by visible details. This outside world seemed more foreboding, more challenging.

Because of this added nervousness and fear, because of the dog, and because of the suddenness of being discovered, he reacted like a caged animal. The moment the boy came into view through the bushes, he hissed and folded his body into a spring of muscles, long fingernails, and teeth. Squatting so compactly, he looked even more deformed.

Billy didn't retreat or pull his stick away. For a few moments, all he could do was stare at the imp. This wasn't the E.T. Billy had envisioned, but that didn't mean it wasn't something extra terrestrial. What else could it be? Perched down in the bushes, its hair long and stringy down around its shoulders, its eyes big and wild, its arms long like a monkey's, naked with the face of a human, but the look of something else, it had to be something from another world. And he had discovered it, just as he had planned!

Captain was growling and barking louder and harder now; but, seeing that Billy wasn't backing away, the dog stopped his retreat and inched a few feet forward. The imp saw the way the dog flashed its teeth, and he did the same. He even tried to imitate the growl.

"Hi," Billy said. "Don't be afraid. We can be friends." He turned on Captain. "Quiet, Captain. Shut up. Quiet," he commanded, but the dog didn't obey. The imp shifted his weight from one foot to the other. He considered flight back to the basement, but, before he could make the move, Billy came toward him. He extended his hand slowly, with the intention to show him friendliness and perhaps lead him out of the bush. Billy felt sure that once Captain saw the imp take his hand, the dog would stop growling and barking at him.

For the imp, the oncoming hand and arm, reinforced with the continuous sound track of the angry dog, was one of the most frightening things he had seen. Billy still held the stick straight out with his other hand to keep the bushes apart, but from the imp's perspective, it looked like a weapon about to be launched against him. True, the boy's voice was soft and his face was bright, but he had seen the big creature's face like that and heard her voice as soft, just before she inflicted some kind of pain on him.

When the boy's hand was just inches from his face, the imp reacted. Both his arms shot out, his hands cupped like claws. He clamped down on Billy's arm just above the elbow. It happened so quickly, Billy barely acknowledged the pain. The imp's sharp, hard fingernails pierced Billy's skin as though it were tissue paper. Polka dots of blood appeared instantly. Shocked, Billy started to pull his arm back; but the imp didn't release his grip, and his tiny knifelike fingernails continued to cut and slice down Billy's arm, peeling the skin back, drawing lines of blood down to and over the elbow on both sides.

Billy screamed and held his arm up and away. The sight of his own blood now tracing little streams over his forearm drove him into a greater panic. For a moment he was unable to move. Captain lunged forward until he was at his side, snapping wildly into the bush. The imp, almost as frightened by what he had done himself as he was of the dog, fled through the undergrowth, tearing a new path in the tall grass.

Captain started to chase in after him, but stopped when the imp was out of sight, deep into the field. Billy, screaming and crying, ran back toward his house, also disregarding the beaten path and charging through bushes. Branches sliced freely at his exposed legs, creating tiny red line drawings over his calves and knees, but he had no realization of it. The dog barked wildly at the tall grass, until it tired of the effort and retreated, carrying a heavy motorlike growl in the bottom of its stomach.

Billy was only a few feet from his house by the time Cindy O'Neil was out the back door. By then, the ten small streams of blood had turned the little boy's arm into a red sleeve, making it appear far worse than it was. Cindy began to scream hysterically. Dick O'Neil, followed by Bobby, came charging around from the front of the house, where they had been repairing a screen door.

"WHAT IS IT? WHAT HAPPENED?" Cindy embraced Billy, took his hand, and held his arm up before her. The little boy couldn't speak. His eyes were locked in a glazed look of terror. Cindy seemed incapable of doing any more than screaming questions at him, so Dick O'Neil scooped up his son and carried him quickly to the house. Bobby followed his mother inside, trying to calm her. He looked back once to see Captain standing there, his tongue out, his face in a wry smile. If animals could look frightened, this one did.

When they cleaned Billy's arm in the bathroom, they saw the ten tiny but deep punctures. Tears continued to stream down the little boy's face, but he wouldn't speak. Calmer now, Cindy O'Neil knelt beside her son and tried, in a soothing voice, to discover what had happened. Bobby remained in the doorway, watching his parents question his little brother.

"It . . . grabbed me," he finally said, spacing the words between sobs.

"What grabbed you? Oh Dick, do you think it could have been something rabid? With that second dog in the county reported . . . "

"Just take it easy, willya, Cindy. This wasn't done by any dog."

"Captain," Billy said, nodding his head and swallowing hard to get out more words, "saw . . . it first."

"That damn dog," Dick said. "Must've trapped a raccoon. Shit," he added and turned to Bobby, who quickly nodded in agreement.

"We've got to take him to the hospital and get him a tetanus shot," Cindy said. At the suggestion of that, Billy began to cry harder. In his garbled words, he tried to tell them that it wasn't a raccoon, but they were no longer listening. Cindy wrapped a wet towel around his arm and then Dick carried him out to the car. He tried protesting again, telling them it wasn't an animal, it was an E.T., but Cindy only embraced him harder and Dick O'Neil drove faster.

Fortunately, the Community General Hospital was only fifteen minutes away via a back road that took them out to a main highway. There was a lull in the emergency room when they arrived, so the doctor on call took them right into an examination room. By this time, Billy, who was more frightened of being taken to the hospital than by what had just happened to him, sat subdued, his sobs more like hiccups, his eyes watery and red. He sat on the table, practically unable to keep himself up.

Cindy held him, while the young intern, a man with curly red hair and a freckled face, unwrapped the towel. Dick O'Neil scowled, obviously thinking this man was too young to be a real doctor; but the intern went about his business undaunted. He smiled and spoke soothingly, trying to make everything seem insignificant and silly. Billy did begin to relax a little.

"So what happened, Buddy?" the doctor asked. Billy looked helplessly toward his parents. Dick O'Neil stepped forward, his face reflecting more of a look of anger than concern.

"I think our family dog led him to a raccoon."

Billy started to shake his head, but the doctor mistook that to mean he was being apologetic.

"Oh, attacked by a wild animal, eh? Yeah, you must've stuck this arm somewhere you shouldn't, huh, great white hunter?" He began cleaning the wounds. "He was scratched all right. Can't say I ever saw a raccoon's work, but I imagine this is it."

"I've seen them do jobs on dogs," Dick said. "He was lucky."

"It wasn't a raccoon," Billy said.

"What's that, little Buddy?" the doctor asked, as he applied the antiseptic.

"It wasn't a raccoon. It was an E.T.," Billy said.

"E.T.?" The doctor turned to Cindy.

"Oh, he's been talking about seeing E.T. He saw the film twice."

"Uh huh. Well, as I recall," the doctor said, "E.T. was not a dangerous or unfriendly creature, right?"

"He's right, Billy," Cindy said. Billy looked at both of them. He wanted to say this wasn't the same E.T., but it was still something not from this world. He didn't, though, because he could see from both their smiles that they wouldn't listen to him.

"It was a raccoon," Dick O'Neil said with more definiteness than ever. "They can look like little children, but they're dangerous as hell when they're threatened."

"I believe that," the intern said. He began to bandage Billy's arm. By the time he was finished, Billy was very tired. He was almost unaware of the tetanus shot, but, when it came, he began crying again. That and all that had happened to him left him totally exhausted. Soon after they got him back into the car and headed home, he was fast asleep.

Dick O'Neil carried his little boy up to bed, where Cindy undressed him and covered him. They stood by his side looking down at his now relaxed, soft face. Cindy kissed his forehead, brushed some hair off his temples, and left him to sleep. Downstairs, Bobby stood anxiously in the living room.

"Oh boy," Cindy said, "can you believe this?"

"Maybe we should go out with a shotgun tomorrow, Dad," Bobby said. Dick O'Neil grimaced.

"For what? What are you going to do—shoot all the raccoons back in the bush and the woods? You'd be there forever. Naw, we just got to keep the kid from wandering off by himself."

"I don't think he'll do it again," Cindy said.

94

"I bet Captain was some help," Bobby said.

"Some help? That dumb dog probably riled up the coon and drove him into Billy. I want him tied up from now on, hear? You go out there and do that right now," Dick commanded. "That dog's as dumb as they can come."

"It could have scratched his face, God forbid his eyes," Cindy said, just realizing what might have happened.

"Nature can be wild. The coon was probably more frightened of him than he was of it. The dog drove it into a frenzy and then it attacked Billy. That's what must have happened," Dick said. Blaming it on the dog made some sense. It was practically the only thing he could think of that made sense.

"Go on, Bobby," Cindy said. "Do what your father says and tie up Captain."

"OK."

When he went out back, he found the dog lying by his doghouse. The animal looked up at him gratefully, when Bobby knelt beside him and stroked his head. The dog's sad eyes made Bobby think it felt responsible for what had happened. He wondered if it could have that kind of awareness.

"What did you guys do, huh? Now you're going to have to stay close to the house. No more wandering through the fields," he said and hooked the chain to the dog's collar. The animal didn't seem unhappy about it. "I almost think you'd rather have it this way, huh Captain?" The dog wagged its tail and then looked out at the darkness. When it did that, it whimpered and then growled.

"Think it's still there?" Bobby said. He studied the darkness himself. Then he looked back at his house and thought about his father's anger. "Well, maybe you and I will go out there when Dad's not home. I'll bring a shotgun. Can't hurt knocking one or two of them off, can it? And maybe we'll get the one that hurt

Billy, huh? We'd all sleep better, wouldn't we, Captain?" he said and he stroked the animal again.

The dog looked up at him and then turned to the darkness again. The dog seemed drawn to it, as though it expected whatever it was to come back. That brought a tingle of fear to Bobby O'Neil. He couldn't help but think of his brother's bloody little arm.

"Damn," he said and started back to the house, looking behind and around himself as he walked. He was almost to the door when he remembered he was supposed to have met Faith Oaks on her fire escape landing a little more than two hours ago. Now it was too late. That added frustration and disappointment to his feelings of fear and anger. Like his parents, he found it very hard to fall asleep that night.

To Faith it seemed as though the night sky was ablaze with stars. She was sure it had been this way before, but never had she been so aware of it. There was something about the combination of the warm evening and her anticipation that made her sensitive to every sight and sound. Her body had come alive and she was filled with the excitement of expectation. There was a flush in her cheeks and a quickness in her eyes. She felt as though her face was absorbing the moonlight, turning her into a citizen of the night, pumping her veins full of the electricity of the constellations.

Sitting there on the windowsill, her back against the frame, the warm evening breeze penetrating her nightgown and caressing her softness, she felt light enough to float. When she closed her eyes, she caught the scents of grass and earth. She thought she heard the sound of a car horn far off and away, coming and going like a call, urging her to let go of herself.

She thought she didn't want this. All day long she had fought it, fought the desire to talk to Bobby, to look at him, and to have him look at her. Last night's

96

visit passed like a dream. Keeping the memory thin and ephemeral, she was able to avoid the guilt; but tonight, sitting here like this, watching for him, thinking about him, she could no longer deny that for which she hoped.

She studied the shadows below, waiting for some movement, something that would send chills up her spine and bring back the exquisite sense of danger she had felt when he was here. When he didn't come, she was disappointed. As more time passed and it became obvious to her that he probably wasn't going to show, her disappointment turned to anger, first at herself, and then at him. She chastised herself for wanting him, for succumbing to her sinful desires. Why did she want him to come? What did she expect would happen? What did she want to happen?

She couldn't help but recall the way he had said, "I'm not in your bedroom." As a result, she fantasized it. When she let herself imagine it, she saw him on the landing; she saw him talking softly to her until she let him come through the window. Where would they go but to her bed to embrace passionately? Just before she gave herself to him in her fantasy, she forced herself back to reality. It was like dreaming of falling from a tall building and then waking up before you hit the ground. She snapped to with the same abruptness.

She got up from the windowsill and brought the window down, but she did it too vehemently and as a result, the sound was loud enough to attract Mary's attention. Just as Faith got into her bed, Mary was at her door, coming from her own bedroom.

"What is it?"

"Nothing. I had my window open, because it was so hot, but the bugs started coming in."

"Bugs?" Mary walked to the window. "Why is your screen up?" Faith hesitated. Leaving the screen up was a mistake. How would she explain it? "Have you been going out on this landing?"

"Yes," she said weakly. Mary opened the window and closed the screen.

"I don't know where your brains are sometimes. Why didn't you simply close the screen?"

"I don't know. I didn't think of it," she said quickly. It wasn't a good answer, but she couldn't think of anything else. Mary looked about suspiciously. Faith held her breath, expecting that somehow her mother would know everything.

"You shouldn't go out on the landing. I'm not sure it's safe."

"It didn't feel shaky or anything."

"Nevertheless, I wouldn't do it."

"OK," she said, hoping that would end it. Mary turned back to the window. By the way she stood there staring down, Faith thought she might have spotted Bobby O'Neil.

"This heat does make it hard to sleep," Mary said, but she said it with unusual softness. There was no hint of anger in her voice; it was more like sadness. Faith opened her eyes wider and looked at her. Mary turned away from the window, embracing herself as though she were in pain. "He was killed on a night like this," she said. Faith held her breath. Mary rarely mentioned him and almost never reminisced. She didn't look at her when she spoke. It was as if she were talking to another part of herself. "I knew he was dead the moment I saw the police car drive up, and I thought, 'And the fruits that thy soul lusted after are departed from thee, and all things which were dainty and goodly are departed from thee, and thou shall find them no more at all.' "

Faith sat up slowly and embraced her knees. Mary was at the foot of her bed now and the invading moonlight turned her into a chalky statue. Her hair was down and the strands lay flat over her shoulders. There was a long moment of silence, during which neither of them moved. Faith felt as though they were both captured in an eerie painting that might very well be entitled, "While Death Slipped In Between Them." She felt a cold chill and shivered silently. Mary turned toward her slowly, her hands now clasped together and held just below her bosom.

"I remember when they came to the door to tell me. They tried to hide their smiles, but I could see what they thought, knowing where he had been and what he had been doing. They thought I would fall apart like some weak-faced, clinging vine of a woman who had tied herself to the whims and the promises of a man," she said, her voice harder, sharper.

"But shouldn't you mourn for a sinner, too?" Faith asked. She was surprised herself that she had thought of the question.

"One who shows signs of repentance, yes; but he was so steeped in his lust that I knew he was beyond redemption. He was the Devil's own, and when he became that, what was his, was not mine," she added. Even in the cool moonlight, Mary's face turned hot with passion. She came around to the side of the bed, her hand trailing along the blanket, until it reached Faith's leg.

"They come to you on nights like this," she said in barely more than a whisper. "They know you're weak and vulnerable; they know you're lonely and afraid. You yearn for their affections, for their softness, for their strength. They talk away your resistance and you open yourself to their lusting. They spend themselves in you. Their seed is so hot it burns into your very soul and, when they withdraw, you have been contaminated with their evil."

Mary brought her face close to Faith's and Faith couldn't keep her heart from beating hard. She was certain that Mary's fingers felt her quickened pulse.

"Promise me you'll be honest," Mary said. "Promise."

"I promise."

"Good," she said and relaxed her grip on Faith's leg. "Good." Faith lay back slowly. Mary turned as though in a trance. She paused when she looked at the window and then continued on out of the room, moving like a shadow, as silent as a silk curtain lifted in the breeze.

Faith released her breath, but she was afraid to move. She lay there, cover pulled to her neck, listening. She felt if she heard Bobby O'Neil's footsteps on the fire escape, she would scream. When she closed her eyes, she did hear herself screaming. But that was a long time ago, the memory resurrected by Mary's remembrance of that fateful night.

She remembered how her father had come home drunk and angry. She had seen him drunk before, but never as angry. His eyes were blazing just as Mary said they would be when the Devil took hold of him. When he looked at her, he seemed not to see her. His hair was wild and his shirt sleeves were rolled up, the shirt unbuttoned nearly all the way. Even standing six feet or so away from him, she could smell the whiskey. It was as though he had bathed in it. His face was red. Later, Mary would say the "fires of perdition" burned within him. He did act as if he were in some kind of pain; he couldn't stand still.

When he came through the door, he spun around. The door flew open; he nearly tore it off its hinges. Luckily, neither she nor her mother were standing nearby. Mary was in the kitchen. She heard him scream, "Mary, you bitch. Where are you?" But she didn't come forward. Faith wanted to say something to him, get him to calm down, but she couldn't get herself to make a sound. She could only stare at him, and he was completely disinterested in her. He went on into the kitchen, his hands clenched into fists. She wanted to follow, but she didn't. She waited on the couch in the living room.

He didn't yell at Mary when he went into the kitchen. Faith could barely hear his voice. He spoke in a low tone that sounded almost soothing. She remembered being confused by that. What was he asking her? It didn't sound like an argument, but Mary came running out of the kitchen shortly after and fled up the stairs. He followed. Faith went to the doorway of the living room just as he went by. She would never forget the look on his face—he didn't appear angry or wild; he looked hurt, in despair, in pain. At that moment she actually felt sorry for him. Once again, she tried to speak to him, but he was on the stairway and up before she uttered a sound.

She heard him force his way into the bedroom. Mary had locked the door. She heard their voices raised now. Mary was calling him her usual names, only this time he wasn't taking it quietly. When Faith heard the slap and the scuffling, she went to the foot of the stairs. She heard Mary's screams, shrill and sharp, piercing the walls. She covered her ears, but that didn't block it out, so she began to scream herself. She formed a bizarre chorus, an audience gone berserk, in sympathy, standing at the foot of the stairs, the tears streaming down her face, her fingernails digging into her scalp.

She embraced herself and sat on the step, until the screaming and the fighting stopped. Afterward, she went back to the living room and curled up on the couch. Later that night, Mary came to her. Her face was swollen from his blows, her lips were bruised. She took Faith's hand and made her kneel beside her on the floor. Upstairs, satiated, in a drunken stupor, he slept.

"Pray with me," Mary whispered. "Pray that we be saved, for the Devil is in this house and he has taken me unto him and violated me." As though to demonstrate what had happened, she clutched at her own breasts and grimaced in pain. Faith was terrified. She looked up obediently when Mary turned her eyes to the ceiling. "Pray. Pray that the Lord brings down his sword of righteousness and delivers us from evil. Pray."

She prayed. She repeated Mary's words and when she was finished, she went upstairs to sleep, leaving Mary in the living room, holding a night-long vigil.

Two nights later, the police came to tell them he was dead; killed with the woman in the car. When they left, Mary turned to her, her eyes lit with religious ecstasy.

"But these, as natural brute beasts, made to be taken and destroyed, speak evil of the things that they understand not; and shall utterly perish in their own corruption."

She walked off in a trance, fixated on her memorized scripture. Faith couldn't believe it all had happened and couldn't help feeling partly responsible. Hadn't she prayed with her, asking for this very thing? But if Mary had such power that God listened to her, then, Faith thought, Mary must be right in what she did and said.

She hid her pregnancy from the world . . . wearing the tight girdles, remaining within the house during the last two months, and giving birth like a beast, squatting in the basement, screaming like a wild animal. The first time Faith saw the baby, she thought Mary was right—he was so bloody and ugly with the face of a rat. Faith fled from the scene and remained in her room trembling, nearly hysterical, until Mary came to her to tell her God had spoken to her and they would do what He had told her to do.

Faith was stunned, hypnotized by the events. She let herself be led down to the basement again, where she knelt with Mary before the infant in the box. Three lit candles in holders were placed around it. It was the only light Mary wanted. She had the cup of wine and the wafers, and the large silver cross, which she

102

clutched in her hand like a weapon. For a while she just held it over the infant. Faith didn't make a sound. The whole time she waited, half expecting some magical thing, perhaps a light, to come from the cross and cover the child.

When Mary made her clutch the cross, she thought it was hot in her hand. Mary prayed silently and then she told her what they must do.

"We mustn't kill it. That's what the Devil would want us to do, to commit murder; but we mustn't let it be seen. We mustn't let it grow in the open, where it could contaminate and spread his evil. No one must know that he's here and you must never come down here, unless I tell you first."

The baby began to cry. Faith turned to it. This was the product of evil, the Devil's work, yet he looked so helpless, so soft, and good. She wanted to ask Mary if she was sure, but she didn't have the courage. Nevertheless, Mary could see the thought in her face.

"Stay away from him. He can tempt you to the flood. One day, you will see, he will speak just like the serpent in paradise. We must be ready. It's the greatest test of all. Do you understand?"

Faith nodded. She watched Mary lift the baby from the box and give it her breast.

"Until the Lord wants it otherwise," she said and she prayed as the infant sucked.

Afterward, they did the ritual with the wine and the wafer, swearing their secrecy, promising God what Mary said He had demanded they promise. There in the candlelight, the shadows pressed against the old fieldstone walls, the darkness draped around them like a shroud, they looked down at the sleeping infant. Something within her wanted her to think of him as her brother, wanted her to lift him out of the box and hold him close to her. But Mary's power was too great. Faith could feel her force radiating beside her. She dared not reach out to touch him; she hesitated even to

103

look closely at him. Consequently, she couldn't remember his facial features and imagined him the way Mary had described him.

She would often think about him down there, and, when she heard his cries, she would again feel the urge to think of him as her brother. But simply thinking about touching that basement door handle was frightening. Mary, sensing the temptation for Faith, installed another lock on the door. She practically forbade any mention of him and refused to acknowledge any references to him. For all intents and purposes, he didn't exist. Sometimes Faith questioned it herself, hoping that it had all been a terrible nightmare. If she did make any mention of him or try to get Mary to talk about him, Mary would tell her it was the Devil's way of tempting her.

Tonight, as she lay there in the dark thinking about Bobby O'Neil, she wondered if Mary's warnings weren't God's. It was a warm night; she longed for his affection and softness. She was lonely and afraid. She wanted him to come. She trembled, both from her own longing and her own fear. Unable to deal with it any longer, she got up quietly and closed the window softly, locking it shut.

When she got back into bed, she wished for the morning and the chance to bathe her face in sunlight. That made her think of him in the basement below, hovering alone in the darkness, waiting for the sound of her footsteps and the feel of her breath through the cracks in the floor. Had he already become the serpent? Was he tempting her to evil? The thought frightened her. Perhaps she had better stop communicating with him, before it was too late. She promised herself she would try, but the promise wasn't enough. She had to get out of bed and kneel on the floor to pray for God's forgiveness.

Still, she was unable to fall asleep. She had the feeling she had betrayed someone. Who? Not Mary.

104

Certainly not her father or the baby. Could she have somehow betrayed herself? That thought lingered with her, until sleep mercifully rescued her from the conflict raging within.

After he slipped back through the hole, he could barely lift the rocks to return them to their proper places. That was how frightened he was. While he worked, he whimpered like a frightened puppy. As soon as he finished, he scampered back to his box, where he clutched himself and hummed his sound and rocked back and forth. But nothing seemed to help. Never before had he felt so cold and alone. He looked for something to clutch, something to cling to for sympathy and comfort; but there was nothing, nothing but the sounds of the water running through the pipes above him and the creaks in the ceiling.

When he heard the large creature's footsteps, he got very quiet and very still. He listened as hard as he could to determine whether or not she was headed down to beat him. He imagined she had found out he had been outside and she had learned what he had done. But her sounds went off in another direction, so he released the nervous grip he had on the sides of his box and relaxed. He grew calm enough to think about what had just happened.

With the fear subsiding, his curiosity grew stronger. He thought about the look on the boy's face when he had grabbed him and scratched him. The boy's pain and fear had been so vivid, it had driven fear into him, but now he felt different. He was regaining his confidence, but along with it came a new sense of power. He could make someone else, someone bigger, scream and cry. True, he had been afraid of the dog and had run from it as well, but what if the dog hadn't been there? There was no dog where the little girl was, only rabbits, and rabbits didn't scare him.

He stopped sobbing. His breathing became regular

105

again and he stretched his body out with more assurance. The box had become too small for him some time ago. He could no longer straighten out his body completely. Even so, he could loosen and unfold himself enough to be more comfortable.

He was sorry now that he hadn't been able to go to look at the little girl. It was what he had been waiting for all day. He felt his frustration turn into anger. Searching for a way to express it, he recalled the sounds made by the dog. He had tried to imitate them out there, but the boy had interrupted him. Now, he tried it again: he imitated the growl and even tried the bark.

When he made that noise, it came out so loud and sharp and accurate that it frightened him and he curled up in his box again quickly. He actually looked about to see whether or not the dog was in the basement with him. After a moment he realized he had done it successfully. He unfolded his body, started the growl, and experimented with short, low barks. It began to amuse him. He barked faster and louder and scurried across the basement floor pretending to chase away invaders like the boy and the dog. In his imagination it worked.

When he grew tired of it, he went back to his box and thought about the outside world. He was eager to get back into it, but he didn't have the courage to do that now. Besides, by now the world had grown very dark and the little girl would be in the other big house. He wondered if there were a way to get into the bottom of that house, just as he had gotten out of and into this house. He couldn't recall if there were any rocks to pull, but it occurred to him that there might be and that he should look for them when he went back there.

Still embracing himself, he closed his eyes and from his bank of new and exciting images, drew out the picture of the little girl. He heard her laughter and saw her smile. He saw the way her hair floated over her shoulders and bounced gently when she ran. He heard her giggle and dreamed of that sound. He wished that he could make it, but all his attempts failed. They lacked the softness and the happiness. He wanted her to teach him that sound most of all.

As he lay there creating these pictures, he drew sleep over himself like a warm blanket. His body seemed to sink into a cool, numbing liquid. He whimpered a little, turned, and twisted himself into a more comfortable position, sniffed the air to be sure he was safe within his dark sanctuary, and closed his eyes even tighter. Soon his embrace of himself lessened, his body became limp, and he sank completely into his own inner world. The field mice that scurried around his box ignored him. The spiders in the corners of the walls and ceiling harvested their day's catch, and the beams of the house creaked with the slight, almost imperceptible shifting of the structure. Then, all was quiet. The footsteps above him seemed to rise in the air, as Mary returned to her own darkness.

All three of them slept; each with his private dreams, each anticipating a new day unlike any that had come before.

Six

Faith was ambiguous about Bobby O'Neil. On the one hand, she hoped he had decided not to have anything to do with her. With that much less to worry about, her life would be simpler. Yet, as she walked through the corridors at school that morning, she couldn't prevent the feelings of excitement that came with her expectations of his approaching her. He hadn't been on the school bus, and she didn't see him during home-room period, nor did she see him when she passed to her first period class. The thought occurred to her that something might have happened to him and that was why he never appeared on her fire escape landing as he had promised.

In her mind, things didn't just "happen" to people. If he had an accident or was very sick, it could be because his coming to her at night had been something evil and God had punished him, as Mary said God always would. And then there was the nagging fear in the back of her mind that Mary had discovered his visit, even though she hadn't come right out and said so. Then using her powers of prayer, as she had done many times before, she had caused something to happen to Bobby O'Neil.

The Fallsburg Central Schools bused its students in from seven hamlets, Centerville being one of the biggest. Since the year-round population of the entire township was only nine thousand, the school population rarely went above twelve hundred, K–12. In so small a school system, students were well aware of one another. Faith's few speaking acquaintances were loners like herself. In all the years she had gone to school, she had never had a friend over to her house or been permitted to go to one of theirs. She never went to a school party nor got invited to a private one. Most of the students considered her a loser and had little or no contact with her. She sat alone at the tables in the cafeteria, even when there were others at the table, and rarely did anyone acknowledge her or she anyone, for that matter.

On this particular day, however, she paid real attention to some of the conversations going on in the halls and in the classrooms, hoping to learn anything about Bobby O'Neil, if there was anything to learn. Apparently there wasn't. No one mentioned his name and none of the boys that she knew were friendly with him looked concerned about anything. Finally concentrating on her work, she put it all out of her mind. During lunch, she sat at a corner table, eating very mechanically and looking lost in a daze. She didn't even realize Bobby had come up beside her, until he took the seat next to hers. She turned in surprise and saw him smiling widely.

"Hi."

For a moment she didn't respond, but her face must have revealed some happiness, because his eyes brightened even more. She corrected herself immediately and turned back to her food. He slid his tray close to hers and began opening a milk container.

"Sorry I wasn't on your balcony last night," he said.

"It's not a balcony. It's a fire escape and I told you not to come."

"That wasn't why I didn't come."

She didn't turn completely around, but she permit-

109

ted herself to tilt her head just enough to catch the laughter in his eyes. She envied the lightness he expressed, the happy-go-lucky manner. What did it feel like not being dominated by heavy thoughts, by serious questions about life and morality and God? Her mother made her feel that other young people her age were loose because of their poor upbringing, but she couldn't harden her heart against Bobby O'Neil, not with his face as soft as it was, not with his eyes as warm as his were, and not with a voice as sincere as his sounded.

"Don't you want to know why I didn't come?"

"Since I didn't ask you to come, I don't expect you have to tell me why you didn't," she said. She regretted how harsh she sounded. Fearful he might just pick up his tray and go, she added, "But I imagine your mother found out and told you not to."

He laughed. Some of the kids at a nearby table stopped talking and looked their way. Bobby nodded at them and most of them smiled. She didn't like their "cat-ate-the-mouse" grins. They made her feel self-conscious. Was she being made a fool? The thought panicked her and she looked around the lunchroom quickly. It did seem like most of the students were looking her way. Was all this some kind of a joke, something Bobby O'Neil and a few of his friends cooked up for laughs?

That had happened to her before—like the time Barry Weintraub asked her to the Junior Prom. Of course, she turned him down immediately, but some of the girls in her classes, girls who hardly ever spoke to her, approached her under the guise of trying to talk her into going. "He's such a nice guy," they said. "He really likes you," they said. She didn't argue with them, but he asked her again, this time in a very dramatically staged manner, after school, while the buses were loading. They had quite an audience.

After she got onto the bus, a group of kids went into a chant: "Faith said no; she won't go. Faith said no; she won't go." For a while that afternoon, the whole bus load of students was chanting it, raising their voices even louder when the bus approached Centerville. She closed her ears to them the way Mary had taught her. While they chanted, she quietly recited the Lord's Prayer. Willie Rosen obviously thought the whole thing was funny, because he didn't turn around and get the kids to stop. He heard her reciting though. She remembered the look on his face—this quizzical and then almost frightened expression when he realized what she was saying.

After a while, like most everything else the kids did or said in relation to her, it passed. She wasn't enough to hold their attention for long periods.

"No," Bobby said, snapping her out of her memory, "that wasn't it." His expression changed, the smile quickly fading. When he looked down and poked at his food, she had real interest.

"Something happened?"

"To my little brother. You know Billy. He's always getting himself into something."

"What happened?"

"He messed with a raccoon and got his arm badly scratched up. We had to take him to the hospital and by the time we got back, it was pretty late."

"Oh. A raccoon?"

"Yeah. My father thinks it was my dog's fault. He thinks Captain led Billy to it. I'm supposed to keep him tied up all the time now."

"That's too bad. I'm sorry. I've seen raccoons, but I've never thought about them scratching me."

"Me neither. I asked Mr. Hoffman about it and he thought it was very unusual. He said that coon must have really been trapped."

"Well what does Billy say about it?"

111

"Forget about what he says," Bobby said. "He's got some imagination. My mother doesn't want to take him to the movies anymore. Whatever he sees on the screen, he thinks he sees in our backyard. And yours, too," he added.

"Oh."

"He's probably covering up for doing something wrong anyway. My father doesn't like our dog and he's always after Billy about him. You don't have a pet, do you?"

"No," she said. She said it so quickly that he looked at her askance.

"Your mother doesn't like animals?"

"It's not that. We don't have the time for such things."

"Yeah, I know what you mean," he said, but she didn't think he did. They were both quiet for a while. Danny Rosenbloom and Carole Shatsky stopped at the table to say hello to him. They talked about a math test they were having tomorrow and then Carole looked at Faith as though she had just noticed she was there.

"How's it going?" she asked. For a few seconds, Faith was unable to respond. She had always admired Carole Shatsky from afar, envious of her chic and her popularity with other girls. She seemed more mature than the rest of them, and although she was never very friendly with Faith, she was never blatantly unfriendly either.

"OK," Faith finally replied. Carole smiled warmly and then she and Danny moved on. The whole encounter, as short as it was and as insignificant as it would appear to anyone else, left her with a warm feeling. Because of that, she wasn't as adamantly negative as she thought she should have been when Bobby talked about their meeting again at night.

"You can't come up again," she said. "My mother . . . my mother is suspicious, I think."

"She heard me there the other night?"

112

"No, I don't think so."

"Then how could she . . . I mean, why would she be suspicious?"

"You don't know my mother," Faith said and thought she had said enough. She started to put her things together to get up and go.

"You could come down then."

"What?"

"I'll be at your house waiting. What time does your mother usually go to sleep?" She simply stared at him. "From the way you were talking the other night, I gathered she goes to bed relatively early. Right?"

"Right after her programs."

"You mean that religious stuff I heard?"

"Yes," she said sharply, her eyes smaller.

"So I'll be at your house by nine. You come down the fire escape and we'll go to the lake or pond or whatever you want to call it."

"No, I couldn't."

"Sure you can. It'll be easy."

"No," she repeated, now feeling frightened. She got up.

"If you don't come down, I'll come up."

"You better not."

He took her hand, literally holding her to the table. She was too embarrassed to pull away, but the feel of his hand firmly around hers brought her an unexpected pleasurable sensation—it started as a chill, but quickly turned into a warm flush. She looked about to see if any of the other students were watching, but now everyone else seemed totally involved in their own conversations.

"Try it just once," he said. "We'll have fun. You'll see."

"No," she said shaking her head weakly. "I couldn't."

"You can."

She slipped her hand free and started away.

"I'll whistle," he called, but she didn't look back at him until she was at the door. He was eating quickly and reading his math textbook, acting as though nothing much had just happened. For her it was like the opening of another world. She trembled from both fear and excitement, squeezing her books closely against her body for security.

All through the remainder of the day, she thought of nothing else but the way he had grasped her hand and the proposal he had made. She found herself seriously considering it. Did she dare? Mary would go to sleep early as usual, right after her programs. Faith would say goodnight to her and then . . . she would dress quickly and quietly and sneak out of the window. She imagined that every squeak of the fire escape would make her heart beat like crazy.

And what if she got down safely and undetected? Would she go off with him alone in the darkness? Would she get into his rowboat and look up at the stars? Would she let him take her hand again? Would she want him to touch her in places she was afraid to touch herself? Nothing seemed more frightening and all at once more exciting. The debate raged on within her.

When school ended, he was waiting out in the parking lot. He had his father's pickup truck, which explained why he wasn't on the bus in the morning. She pretended she didn't see him, but he called out to her and gestured. Some of the other girls looked at her enviously. She considered the bus, Willie Rosen sitting there, grinning out at her, the other kids filing on. Her heart beat so quickly she thought she was going to faint, and her hands were so weak they could barely grip her books. She hesitated. Bobby stood there smiling, his hands on his hips. With some of his wavy light brown hair lying across his forehead, and with his broad, thick shoulders pulled back, he reminded her of her father—strong and alive with masculine energy, exciting and dangerous, like Prometheus, unafraid of flaunting in the face of the gods. Taking what seemed to her like the biggest steps of her life, she started in his direction.

Without another word, as if he were afraid that speaking would frighten her off like a doe, he opened the truck door for her. She got in quickly and he hurried around to his side.

"You've got to let me out where the bus would," she said before he started the engine, "so my mother doesn't know."

"Sure. I'm not going to get you into trouble." He smiled. Too arrogantly, she thought, but she wanted so much to believe him.

All the way home he talked about Brown's Pond and the rowboat and what it was like to be out there at night "when the stars make you bend your head back until your neck hurts."

"You feel like you could fall off the earth," he said. She thought he talked like a little boy, but he did make obvious things, things she had always taken for granted, seem like special things. In fact, he talked all the way home, never once pausing to let her say anything. She was grateful for that. As long as he talked, she didn't think about being in the truck on an afternoon when Mary was waiting at the house. She didn't think about the dangers.

He deliberately rode right behind the bus, so they would arrive at the same time the bus did. She got out at her usual spot, which was far enough from the house so Mary couldn't see. She was just going to say thanks and close the door, but, when she turned around and saw him sitting there looking so admiringly at her, she paused. The silence was exciting. She was sexually stimulated by it, and it brought heat into her cheeks and wetness to her lips.

"See," he said. "I told you I wouldn't get you into trouble. You can trust me."

Mary's words began to haunt her: "They know you're weak and vulnerable; they know you're lonely and afraid. You yearn for their affections, for their softness, for their strength. They talk away your resistance and you open yourself to their lustings . . ."

No, she screamed back at her thoughts, no, it's not true.

"I'll whistle," he said. She closed the door and started away. He leaned out the side window. "I'll whistle. Will you come? Will you?"

She spun around and stared at him, her eyes small, her lungs frozen. The whole world seemed to stop, every sound dying. It was as though she were suddenly deaf. She could only feel her own heartbeat, her own blood pulsating through her veins.

"Maybe," she whispered. "Yes." she added quickly, loud enough for him to hear, and then she turned and ran as hard as she could to the house, as if it would give her the sanctuary she needed, sanctuary from herself.

This time he waited until it was darker, and this time he didn't stop for anything. He saw little animals scurry away; he heard interesting and curious sounds. He smelled odors that attracted him and touched leaves and soft things he wanted to explore; but each time he fought off the temptation, for tonight he would not make the same mistake. His mind was set on one thing and one thing only—the little girl with the beautiful hair and the happy sounds.

When he reached Cy Baum's house, he waited in the bushes at approximately the same place from where he had first seen the little girl. There was no one outside and no indication that anyone was coming outside. This disappointment, on top of what had happened the night before, was more than he could tolerate. He was determined to see her again.

Cautiously, he emerged from the protection of the bushes, and taking care to remain within the shadows, he made his way across the lawn, crawling with his palms down, his feet arched so that his knees stayed inches above the ground. The calves of his legs had grown hard and round from this movement, as had the deltoid muscles in his shoulders. It gave him a knobby-like appearance, but he had yet to see a clear and full reflection of himself. He slowed as he drew closer to the house. The windows on this side were lit and occasionally he saw a shadow move across them. He heard the familiar sounds of a radio and decided to move to the windows that were closer to it.

At the house, he crouched beside the cement wall. There were no rocks here, nothing to pull out, no way to create a hole so he could enter. All of the windows were much too high for him to reach and look through. It was all so frustrating, so he decided to continue around the house.

There was a small porch in the rear. He paused by the railings and studied some of the things that were on it—empty bottles placed in a soda case, two folding chairs, a neatly rolled garden hose, and a small tricycle. The little bike interested him. He slid through the bars in the wooden grate and cautiously approached the tricycle. Then he explored all of it with his fingers, tracing the frame back from the handlebars to the rear wheels, running his palm over the soft, vinyl seat, gripping the chrome bars, and pressing down on the pedals. When he did that, the front wheel turned and he was frightened by the bike's forward motion.

He retreated a few feet to think about it. What could it be? Was it alive? Was it another kind of small animal? He leaned forward and touched one of the rear wheels. Nothing happened until he pushed on it. The bike moved forward again, only this time it continued its motion until it crashed into the soda case filled with empty bottles. Their rattling sent him scurrying off the porch and around to the other side of the house, where he waited anxiously in the shadows. He remained crouched on all fours, ready to rush into the bushes again. He listened, but no one appeared.

He was about to return to the porch, when he noticed the basement entrance way. He crawled to it and looked down the cement stairway that led to the basement door. He looked up at the house and then down at the door, his mind putting images and relationships together in lightning fashion. This was a different kind of hole in the wall, he thought, and he began to descend.

At the door he struggled for understanding. Simply sticking his fingers between it and the wall did not provide the opening he needed, no matter how hard he pulled. Holding the door out from the jamb, he stood up and traced his fingers upward. This took him to the doorknob, which he seized roughly. Tugging on it did no better than tugging on the door itself. He was about to give up completely when he inadvertently turned the knob. Something clicked and the door opened so quickly toward him that he fell backward on the cement steps.

The door started to close again, but he rose fast to crawl through this giant hole that it made. It was pitch dark inside, as dark as his own place, he thought. For a few moments he simply sat there on the cement floor, listening and looking about. Sounds from above intrigued him. He had ears that were especially attuned to them. Looking at the dark ceiling above him, more with his ears than his eyes, he followed footsteps across the house from one room to the next. He knew that these footsteps were not the girl's, because they were too heavy; but he sat there patiently, longing to hear her walk, to locate her in the black emptiness above.

He didn't, and he was about to give up on the idea when he heard something breathing just a few feet to his right. He studied the darkness, his nocturnal eyes distinguishing shapes, until he saw it. It had been crouched quietly there, hiding behind a beam. He smiled to himself. It was another one, only this one was different, because he had seen how much joy it had brought to the little girl. He had to be more careful about it, more gentle. After all, it was something she liked; something that was hers.

When he moved toward the rabbit, it instinctively went behind the beam again, crouching down against it for protection. He wanted to do something to make it unafraid, but he didn't know what to do. He thought about the things he did to make himself unafraid. It gave him an idea—he took the rabbit into his arms and held it against his naked body. The fur felt soft and warm, and he even enjoyed the little nervous movements against his chest and stomach. Then, this time taking great care not to crush it to death, he held it securely and began his soothing hum.

He could feel the rabbit's quickened heartbeat, but, as he sat there rocking and stroking it, he was sure that the heartbeat slowed and the rabbit became more comfortable. This encouraged him. If the rabbit liked him, the little girl would like him. Then he thought that, as long as he had the rabbit, he had a chance of having the little girl with him. It was a good idea; something that made sense in an otherwise frustrating experience.

He started to take the rabbit with him, but found it had been tied to the beam. This annoyed him. He tugged on the leash, but it didn't give. He put the rabbit down and pulled on the leash with both his hands, yet it didn't come loose from the beam. He traced it back to the beam, but he had no understanding of knots. To him the leash was a permanent part of the beam now. He thought about pulling it away from the rabbit, but when he attempted that, the rabbit simply slid along the cement floor. There was only one thing to do.

He brought the leash to his mouth and bit down on it as hard as he could. His teeth barely dented it, but he bit down again and again, tugging and pulling while doing so. Finally, he felt the leash begin to part. He took a chunk of it into his mouth and chewed wildly. The taste wasn't that unpleasant to him, so he kept it up until the small tear grew larger. When he broke through completely, he took the rabbit into his arms again.

Now that he had succeeded, he wondered what he should do. Should he just wait here with the rabbit until she came? He couldn't go out with it and wait. She wouldn't see him in the dark. So he remained there, holding the rabbit and listening to the sounds above. Twice, he thought he heard her footsteps and got excited. Once, he was positive he heard her voice, but it didn't last long and when it was gone, he thought it might be forever. He grew tired of the waiting and understood that he would have to give up and come back another time.

But what about the rabbit? He couldn't leave it here now, especially since he had broken its leash in half. It might run away and be gone into the bushes like other rabbits. Why couldn't he take it with him and hide it somewhere? Tomorrow night, when he returned, he would bring the rabbit with him. The little girl would see it and she would come to him.

All these ideas were born in his mind quickly, flashing through in images that resembled previews of coming attractions in a movie theater. The imagery was so strong and so vivid that he thought it had to be right. Clutching the rabbit to himself tightly, but still taking great care not to crush it, he started for the basement door. Just as he reached it, there was the sound of the upstairs door opening.

The light from the house above threw him into a panic. He rushed for the nearest deep shadow and pressed himself against the wall. In his excitement, he relaxed his hold on the rabbit and it hopped out of his arms. It moved quickly toward the light, dragging the torn leash behind it. He started after it, but the voices drove him back.

"No, Gina," Hilda Baum said, "it's too late. You can't go down now."

"But I want to say goodnight, Grandma."

"You said goodnight, Gina. Now it's time for you to go to sleep. The rabbit's asleep anyway," she said. As though the rabbit wanted to appeal for their help, he moved further toward the stairway and the illuminated section of the basement.

"Come on, Honey," Cy Baum called from behind them, "there'll be plenty of time to play with the rabbit tomorrow. You don't want your grandma to get mad at me for buying it, do you?"

"Don't mention that," Hilda said.

The door was closed and darkness quickly returned. He waited until he was certain and then he shot forward. The rabbit tried to get behind some furniture, but he thrust his hand out and scooped it up in midair. Then, without further hesitation, he rushed back to the basement door. Just as he had learned to close his own hole in the wall to keep from being discovered back at home, he closed this bigger hole. The door clicked shut behind him. He waited a moment and then scampered up the steps. He went around the back of the house again, following the same path he had taken to discover the basement entrance.

When he was in the bushes, he felt safe and lightened his grip on the rabbit. It tried to slide out from under his arms, but he worked his fingers in under its collar and it was unable to drop off. He was more than halfway home when it occurred to him that he still had to find a place for it. He couldn't bring it into the basement with him, because the big creature was sure to find it and know he was getting outside. What would he do?

He quickly reviewed the kinds of hiding places he had seen during his travels—holes in the ground, small gullies between rocks, a pile of sticks—none seemed good enough. If he put the rabbit in any of those places, it would get away. Sitting there in the bushes, thinking about his problem, he looked out at The Oaks. One of the garbage cans at the side of the house had been turned over by skunks. They had satisfied their hunger and gone on, but the containers looked very promising to him. What a perfect place to hide the rabbit!

He rushed to them. Uprighting one of the cans, he dropped the rabbit into it and then placed the cover back on top. He waited a few moments to be sure that the rabbit was secure and then headed for his hole in the wall. The night's adventure had not been what he had hoped it would be; but sitting inside his basement, he could think about her rabbit safely contained just outside his wall. In a way he had a part of her near him.

Tomorrow night, he would go out a little earlier, take the rabbit with him, and then, holding it by the remainder of the leash the way she had held it, he would show it to her and get her to come to him. He had no idea what he would do after that, but somehow he felt that whatever followed would be the most delightful thing he had ever done. Now that the rabbit was in his possession, he had real hope. Whatever he wanted to happen would happen. It was almost as simple as chewing through a leash!

* * *

Faith heard the garbage cans turn over and imagined it was a skunk tugging on a garbage bag until the can toppled. She had seen skunks do that before. In the morning she would go out there and straighten things, but for now, her elbows on the windowsill, she leaned out to study the night sky, which seemed brighter and more filled with stars than ever. The moon was almost too brilliant to look at. She closed her eyes and inhaled the night air, as though a bed of roses were planted right beneath her window. Everything was richer and deeper. She had a difficult time containing herself and keeping herself calm enough that Mary wouldn't detect anything different about her, even though there was. She had been rebellious; she had ridden in his truck; and she had had the audacity to tell him she would meet him.

Afterward, when she had entered the house, she had gone right to her room, claiming she had a "load of homework." Mary didn't question it, because Faith had done that before, especially when she wanted to avoid Mary's inquisitions: her questions about the other kids, the things teachers might have said, and her relationships with boys. Up to now, there really hadn't been any; but, nevertheless, Mary pursued, Mary inquired, as though she had been waiting for just this very thing—an opportunity to pounce on her and demonstrate that her theory was right: Faith was in continuous danger of inheriting her father's evil strain.

"You've got to be wary; you've got to be on guard. It comes in a flash and dooms your soul for eternity."

For as long as Faith could remember, Mary had recited these lines or similar ones. They practically formed a chant. And now . . . now it might very well be coming true. She could feel it; she was on the brink of something. The recklessness and the defiance were symptoms. She knew that, but for some reason she wasn't as afraid as she thought she should be.

Earlier, when she had gone down to the kitchen to set the table, she was so involved in these thoughts, that she nearly forgot about reaching the baby through the floor. Then she realized that he wasn't making the usual effort to reach her. Mary had gone upstairs, so Faith felt safe going to her knees and blowing through the crack. She waited, but he didn't blow back or push his finger into the opening. She blew again and then put her ear to it to listen. The silence was puzzling, but the sound of Mary's footsteps on the stairway ended her investigation.

She couldn't help thinking about him, though. Right after Mary said grace, she took a chance.

"If you haven't fed him yet, I'd be glad to go down."

Mary held her spoonful of soup in the air. Her eyes widened and her lips tightened, causing a whiteness at the corners of her mouth. Faith looked down quickly, immediately regretting her offer. What was happening to her? Why was she suddenly so brazen? She felt as though she had uttered a blasphemy.

"Fed? Fed who?"

"I just thought . . . " She shrugged. "I just wanted to help you."

"This is how you would help me? To remind me, to continually keep the image of that . . . that dwarf before me, to torment me with the reality of what's down there, of what your father did to us?"

"I'm sorry," she said. She tried to look as repentant as she could. It worked, because Mary's face softened. She ate her soup and let the silence mend the wound.

"I've already fed him," Mary said. Faith didn't openly acknowledge it, but she felt relief. That meant he was all right. Too many nights she had dreamed of his dying down there in the darkness; of Mary discovering the body and carrying it out under the cover of night to bury the little thing in an unmarked grave,

124

somewhere in the fields behind the house, keeping it a secret even from her. In fact, and this new thought made her flush with fear, that might have already happened. Maybe Mary was lying when she said she had already fed him. Maybe she brought food down to no one tonight. She made a mental note to increase her effort to contact him tomorrow and if she couldn't . . . she would do something . . . maybe steal Mary's key and sneak down.

Mary stopped eating again and stared at her. Faith tried to ignore it, but Mary's gaze was too intense. She had to look up.

"Are you thinking about him more and more?"

"No," Faith said quickly.

"You must tell me if you are. You must tell me if he's on your mind, in your thoughts."

"He's not," Faith said. "But what will we do when he gets too big and too old to stay down there?"

"God will tell us what to do," Mary said, her voice quickly turning soft and pleasant. She smiled and reached across the table for the butter dish. "He always does, doesn't He?"

"Yes. I was just wondering if He had said anything lately." Mary's smile froze into a cold glare and her face whitened. Faith thought that if Death were female, she would look something like this.

"You're not humoring me, are you, Faith?"

"Oh no. I really want to know. That's all. I mean, I want to help you do the right thing."

"I hope so." Mary buttered her bread. The rest of her statement was directed to an imaginary audience. "It's not easy. None of this has been easy—bringing you up whole and pure, despite your background, protecting you, while I did what had to be done. If I've been successful, then you should want to help me."

"I do."

"Good. For now, we're not going to do anything different. Do you understand?"

"Yes."

Mary smiled and nodded at her and then they grew quiet again, mainly because Mary fell back into her thoughts. It was scary, because she looked as though she were hearing other voices; but in a way, Faith was also relieved. If Mary asked no more questions, she wouldn't learn what Faith had done and what she planned to do.

Now, sitting by the window, she wondered whether she could really do it. Before she had come up to her room, she had sat with Mary in the living room and listened to some of the religious music. Mary was pleased about that, but Faith was doing it for another reason—she felt herself falling, succumbing to temptation, and hoped that the prayers and the hymns would save her. But when she closed her eyes to recite the words, she saw only Bobby O'Neil's face—that smile, those eyes.

"I'm tired," she told her. "I'm going to sleep early tonight."

"I am, too," Mary said. Faith did hear her follow, shortly after, not even waiting for the end of her programs. It seemed too perfect, as if events were conspiring against her. Was the Devil doing this? She didn't know; she only knew she couldn't pull away from the windowsill; she couldn't close her eyes on such a night.

As if on cue, she heard his whistle. She closed her eyes, pretending she hadn't heard it, pretending it was something she imagined. Her heart began to beat rapidly. He whistled again and she looked back through her room to see if Mary had heard it. She would if he kept it up. Faith thought she had to do something quickly. With that as her rationalization, she brought her leg to the window and stepped out as quietly as she could, moving like someone in a dream.

She had put on her nightgown over her blouse and jeans and gotten under the covers, just in case Mary

126

stepped into her room when she came up from listening to her radio programs. Now, Faith slipped off the nightgown and tossed it back to the bed. It floated through the air with a dreamlike quality. Every action seemed slower, heavier than usual. Was this really happening?

When she stood up on the landing, she saw him below, the moonlight cutting him from the darkness and making his face radiate with what she thought to be a devilish glow. He waved up at her, beckoning in a slow-motion way, reminding her of ephemeral visions—images that dwelled in sleep and haunted daydreams, like the memories of some previous life. She gestured to tell him he must be silent. He understood and remained where he was; not speaking; not whistling; just waiting. She looked back through the window once more. Did she dare? Wasn't it too late to change her mind? No, she could go back and close the window. Would he understand or would he start that whistling again?

She moved to the steps. Every creak of the metal roared in her ears. Mary surely heard it and would be out in a minute. Faith almost wished for that, because that would end it. She would face Mary's anger and be saved. But she was nearly to the bottom of the ladder and Mary hadn't appeared. Bobby stepped forward, as she dropped from the last rung and touched the ground. For her it had been like a descent into hell, but he seemed ecstatic.

"Hi," he whispered. She couldn't speak. "Any problems with your mother?" Faith shook her head. How she was trembling. He took her hand and she was sure he would feel it. If he did, he didn't let on. "Come on." He led her into the darkness and she followed like one drugged.

She looked back when they reached the path that would take them to Brown's Pond. The house looked angry to her; every window reflecting the moonlight

127

was an eye blazing with fury. She felt the building would stretch its shadows toward them to seize her and hold her back. When she hesitated, Bobby O'Neil looked back at the house too, seeing her concern.

"It's OK," he said. "Everything's quiet. Don't worry. It'll be nice. It's a great night," he added. "Look at the stars and the moon."

She nodded. He was right—it was a great night. When they entered the path, though, the darkness closed in around them so quickly, she thought a door had been shut behind her. She didn't speak until they came upon the pond ablaze with moonlight, a sheet of silver spread before them.

"Oh, how beautiful," she said. "I never came down here at night."

"Didn't I tell you? Hey," he said laughing, "you're squeezing my hand so tightly you'll cut off the circulation."

"Oh."

"No, don't let go. Just relax. We're going to enjoy ourselves. There's the boat. Come on," he said and she quickened her pace, the excitement now replacing the fear. He helped her into it and she sat down at the bow. From here she could look back in the direction of The Oaks; but now, even with the bright moonlight, she couldn't see it; the bushes and trees, their branches so thick with leaves, formed an impenetrable wall of dark green. Looking around, she felt as though they had been cut off from the rest of the world and entered some country of the mind where creatures of dreams and nightmares peered out at them. She could no longer distinguish the real from the unreal, and her house and her past were beyond reach.

It was better for her that they were, for if she could look back, she would have seen a shadow move over the windowsill of her bedroom. It had been there ever since she dropped off the fire escape ladder. When she and Bobby entered the path to the pond and disappeared within the darkness, the shadow shifted enough to be visible.

Mary Oaks, her face caught in the moonlight, looked out. Her eyes absorbed the fire in the night sky and turned it back on the darkness. She waited only a moment more and then retreated to her bedroom.

She would pray and ask for guidance, confident that it would come as it always had.

SEVEN

Eddie Morris nearly slowed his patrol car to a crawl as he came to the small hill right before Cy Baum's farmhouse. It was one of the most dangerous sections of any of the country roads he traveled in his jurisdiction, and he always anticipated danger when he approached it. Until a driver was almost to the crest, it was literally impossible to see any oncoming traffic. Someone asleep at the wheel or simply careless could be too far over, and there would be a head-on collision. He had complained to members of the town board about this part of the road, but there always seemed to be a shortage of funds when it came to the back roads. Besides, as usual, it wasn't until one or two people were killed that any real interest was taken in a dangerous spot. He just didn't want to be one of them.

A car accident was practically the only danger he anticipated as a town policeman in Centerville. He had yet to draw his gun from his holster, much less shoot it. Of course, there were occasional drunks or raucous community college students who came down from the campus in Loch Sheldrake, but, for the most part, his patrols were uneventful visits with old-timers, tough talks with teenagers who were careless about the way they drove their cars or their bikes, and investigations of complaints made about dogs.

"Nothing as exciting as an overturned garbage can with a mutt dragging the remains of chicken bones across the road," he would say. His wife, Barbara, would laugh, but she would give him no sympathy.

"Let it stay calm," she told him. "I'd rather have a bored husband than a dead or injured one."

That wasn't the point though, was it? he thought. Lately, he had felt himself on the verge of a midlife crisis, thinking that his problem was something deeper and more comprehensive than mere boredom. He kept it to himself; he wasn't a man who could express his emotions freely. Tight-lipped, monosyllabic—Barbara called him the "Gary Cooper Type," because he believed that what was personal should remain personal. He couldn't stand those television talk shows in which guests would spill out the most intimate details of their private lives—their divorces, their problems with alcohol and drugs, their sexual hang-ups. What ever happened to self-pride? Wasn't it a value anymore?

This was part of the reason why he enjoyed being around old-timers more than he did people a little younger than he was or about the same age. Barbara told him he was born in the wrong age. She called him, "My Miniver Cheevy." She was a high school English teacher, so she could make all these allusions and references. Other men might feel "put down" by so-called "brainy women," but he was proud of her—proud that she was able to manage their home and family while holding down a job. They had three children: Tommy, age fourteen; Carl, age eleven; and Susie, age four, because they both finally decided to try again for a little girl. With each child, Barbara took her year and a half maternity leave. Of course, they were fortunate that his mother-in-law lived near them and was able to handle the children until they were of school age. Even so, they would have placed the children in nursery school or hired a full-time babysitter. Barbara was making a good deal more than he was.

For a while that was hard to accept. He was thirty-eight years old and had been a town policeman for nearly fifteen years. Everyone just assumed that when Sam Cobler retired in a year or so, Eddie would be appointed the new chief of police. His raise in salary then would put him ahead of Barbara, not that it was a major problem anymore. There was never any real competition between them. Again, he believed that was because of old-fashioned values, values they both accepted. The family was a team effort. What was hers was his and vice versa. There was never any such thing as "her money" or "his money"; there was only "their money."

Still, he had been wondering about his life, wondering about the respect he commanded in his community as a local policeman. There was so much degradation of small town law enforcement. They weren't involved with glamorous crime cases or frightening gunfights. They kept traffic running smoothly in the hamlets, kept hoboes and drunks off the streets, helped settle small arguments, patrolled stores to be sure doors were locked, cruised the town highways to remain visible so people would feel they were doing something, and handled relatively minor crimes. Last year there was a stabbing in the hamlet of Hurleyville, but the perpetrator turned himself in immediately afterward, more hysterical than the man he cut.

Five years ago, Sam Cobler, who liked to kibitz with his local cronies in Sol's Luncheonette in Centerville, was playing cards in the afternoon in the back of the store. One of the men playing with them, Jimmy Kaufman, had robbed the bank in Wurtsboro, a town twenty miles away, that morning. Of course, no one at the table knew he was playing with bank money, but the BCI and the State Police tracked him down rather quickly and made the arrest right there in the restaurant, interrupting the game. Naturally, that gave rise to a great deal of humor about the local police.

Now, approaching his forties, the questions Eddie had about his life seemed to be more vigorous in their demand for answers. Did he lack significance? What would it mean even for him to become chief of police, if the whole force were considered to be a bunch of buffoons? Lately, he sensed something belligerent in his older son's questions. "What good is it to arrest some kid who's smoking a joint? That's not going to stop him, Dad."

It was no longer sufficient to reply that he was breaking the law. Tommy was more vocal about his opinions than Eddie ever was at that age. Tommy thought the law was wrong, and if the law was wrong, anyone who enforced it was wrong, too, even if that person was his own father. Can you have respect for yourself if you can't command the respect of your own children?

On quiet spring mornings like this one, doing his patrol along the more rural roads alone, these thoughts and questions would bubble to the surface. Looking out at the trees in full bloom, the colors growing richer, the forests thickening around him, he would think of another poetic line Barbara loved to quote: "The woods are lovely, dark and deep." How nice it would be to escape back to a simpler time when right and wrong seemed clearer, when a man could be assured of who he was and what he lived to do. This longing wasn't something he concocted. The old-timers kept it alive, kept it real with their stories and their memories and their comments about the modern world, a world they increasingly saw as unnecessarily complicated and impersonal.

What was it Maxy Bookbinder, the sixty-eight-year-old town clerk, was trying to tell him yesterday when he used Eddie and his wife as examples of a situation becoming more and more rare? "Do you know what the chances are of a hometown kid graduatin' and comin' back here to work and live? I'll tell you. I did a study coverin' the last five years. Only fourteen percent of the graduatin' high school classes ended up here. Fourteen percent!" Maxy said raising his reddish brown freckled hand in the air to make his point. Although his shock of red hair had thinned considerably, it had remarkably resisted the graying process.

"Well, I had my stint away from home," Eddie told him. "I served in 'Nam. I saw what some of this world was like."

"That's not the point, not the point," Maxy said, lost in his own conclusions. He was a stickler for statistics and spent a good deal of his time preparing various graphs, analyses, and evaluations for the town board. Although most of it was never used for anything significant, Maxy was considered one of the best authorities on the area. People came to him with all sorts of questions, and Eddie himself often asked him things about different families when he had to answer complaints or settle arguments.

Not that he had any difficulties doing it. At six feet three, weighing two hundred and twenty-five pounds, Eddie was an impressive and powerful-looking man. Bob Cohen, one of the two town justices, called him "The Hulk." He didn't mind it, as long as people who called him that didn't think he was all brawn and no brains. Anyway, for a man his size, he was unusually soft-spoken and gentle. He was very fond of little children and had a deep, almost emotional concern for elderly people.

A good part of the reason for that was his closeness to his grandfather, who had been a close friend of Cy Baum's. It was why he enjoyed stopping to talk to the old man now. Invariably, there would be all sorts of references to his grandfather—anecdotes, sayings, funny remembrances.

As soon as he was over the hill, he saw that the old man was out in front of the house with his granddaughter. Eddie had been by before when Cy's granddaughter was visiting. He thought she was a beautiful little girl, a rival for Susie, who some said belonged on magazine covers. He checked his rearview mirror and pulled over. He thought he always looked comical stepping out of his midsize Chevy patrol car. Even though he had the seat all the way back, he was so long legged, that he seemed to unfold forever. It reminded him of the commercial with the basketball star getting out of a Volkswagen.

"Got a visitor, I see," Eddie said, starting across the road. Cy and his granddaughter walked toward him.

"Yep, but she's been a good girl, so you don't have to arrest her today."

"Oh, I'll bet she has. Now let's see . . . your name is . . . I know, Puddles."

"No, it isn't," Gina said and giggled. She took hold of Cy's leg and swung herself behind it.

"It's not Puddles?" Eddie pretended to give it great thought. "Then it must be . . . Gina."

"That's right."

"I knew I'd get it."

"Makin' your usual tour or doin' something special?"

"Little of both. Sam had a complaint from Mrs. Cafton down at Denniston's Ford. She claimed a bear attacked her dog and played havoc with the garbage cans. Don't know how that woman lives all alone out there."

"It wouldn't be a mystery if you ever met her mother. Very independent people. Your grandfather and I once stopped to help her change a flat tire. She already had the car jacked up and told us if she needed our help, she'd call the nursing home."

"True grit, eh?"

"Stubborn was more like it. Was it a bear?"

"I don't think so. Stray dog is what I think. I haven't heard of any bear around here for quite a while now, have you?"

"Saw one two years ago down at Brown's Pond, but ain't heard of any near houses."

"Maybe that's what killed the rabbits, Grandpa."

"No, I don't think so, honey."

"Had some rabbits killed?"

"Yeah, just a vicious prank. One disappeared completely and the other was found with its neck broken right by the cage. I'm keeping the new one in the basement."

"Any ideas who did it?"

"I don't wanna make any accusations. Just leave it for the time being. Suppose you heard what happened to Dick O'Neil's boy."

"No. What happened? Younger or older boy?"

"Younger. Happened two days ago," he said, but he indicated with his eyes that he didn't want to mention it in front of Gina. "Why don't you get the rabbit, Honey, to show Officer Morris."

"Should I?"

"I'd like that," Eddie said. Gina thought a second and then ran toward the basement. Both of them laughed. "So what happened?"

"Stumbled onto a raccoon and got himself badly scratched up."

"Oh, Jesus."

"Yeah. Dick's blaming it on their dog, but if you ask me, the kid was somewhere he shouldn't have been. That's for sure. You leave a coon be and it won't bother you."

"Tough one. Nearly tangled with a bobcat once when I was just a kid. Ugly creatures with their big heads and their slinky, lopsided bodies. Just came upon it in the woods. It looked at me with absolutely no fear. I remember how it took its time to walk off and disappear in the bushes. Told my grandfather and he said really wild animals can sense danger instantly and accurately. Once they know they have nothing to fear, they'll treat you with total disinterest. That's the difference between animals and people. When people realize it, that's when they first take advantage."

"Good advice, but can't figure out how he knew anything about wild animals. He was the noisiest man I ever went hunting with. Talk, talk, talk. I'd say, Pete, you gotta be quiet if you wanna see anything in the woods and he'd promise to be quiet. Not another word, he'd say. Ten minutes later, he'd remember something else and he was off again. Hell, if we saw anything to shoot, it was probably a sick animal, one that was either deaf or stupid."

Eddie laughed. How true all that was. He could see his grandfather now, sitting on the porch, reading or pretending to be engrossed in reading while Eddie worked on his school assignments. Every few minutes, his grandfather would interrupt him to relate another story or comment on something he was reading. Usually, Eddie had to retreat into the house to get his work done.

"How bad was the boy hurt?"

"Arm torn up some. They took him over to the hospital and he had to have a shot. I think it's all this unusually early summer heat. It's got the animals confused and irritable."

"Um," Eddie said. He looked out at the wild bushes and forest as though he were looking for something special. Cy followed his gaze.

"Screech owls have been playin' havoc every night, too."

"You know about the two cases of rabies?"

"Confirmed?"

"Yeah. With a third under suspicion."

"Really? That hasn't happened since . . . "

They both turned to Gina, who was shouting for Cy. She began to cry as soon as she had their attention. Hilda Baum came out on the front porch.

"Now what is it? Oh, hi, Eddie. I didn't know you were here. What's the matter, Gina?"

"The rabbit . . . is gone."

"No. Can't be," Cy said. He looked to Eddie for confirmation, but Eddie only shrugged.

"This whole idea of a pet rabbit has been nothing but trouble," Hilda said. "It's probably loose and hiding under something down there."

"I'll help you find it," Eddie said.

"Stop crying, Gina," Cy said. "We've got a policeman to help us. We'll find him. Did he break loose of his leash?" She nodded. "You mean the leash is still around the post?"

"A part of it is," she said. Her body shook spasmodically. Eddie picked her up and the three of them headed for the basement.

"Watch your head," Cy said. Cy flipped the light switch and went right to the first beam. "I'll be damned," he said, taking it into his hands. "Chewed right through it." He held the leash out to Eddie, who put Gina down and took the leash from him.

"Smart rabbit." Eddie looked around at the cartons and old furniture. It wasn't a cluttered or a messy basement, because Cy Baum was too well-organized a man and hated any kind of disarray. Eddie remembered how neatly laid out his cornfields used to be. Cy anticipated Eddie's question when he saw Eddie look back at the door.

"Couldn't have gotten out last night. I had that closed."

"Maybe it ran out when she opened it."

"Naw, spring closes it. She'da seen it. Let's start

138

here and work ourselves around. That way we might flush it out."

They began on the right. Gina remained in the middle, waiting for her rabbit to show itself. They pulled away nearly every piece of furniture and moved every carton. They checked every possible opening and hiding place, but the rabbit did not appear. Gina's face became sadder and sadder.

"You don't have a hat around here that he could have disappeared into, do you, Cy?"

"Damn." He scratched his head and looked about. "Sure you didn't see it run past ya, Gina?"

"No, Grandpa."

"No lock on that door?" Eddie asked.

"There is, but I don't use it."

"So what do you make of this, Cy?"

"Someone doesn't want my granddaughter to have a pet rabbit. If my daughter-in-law was up here, I'd say it was her," he added to lighten the moment. "What gets me is, how the hell did they know I put this one in the basement? They'd have to be spyin' on me, for Chrissakes."

"And what about the leash?"

"Well, maybe the rabbit chewed through it and afterward someone came in to get it. Had to happen during the night, though."

Eddie nodded and looked around again. Although Cy's explanation sounded plausible, there was something that just didn't feel right. He couldn't explain it, so he didn't even want to bring it up.

"I'll dig around a bit, Cy."

"Yeah. I guess I shoulda called you when the first one was let loose. Arnie wanted to do something about it then. Might as well go down and talk to those Cooper kids. You know how they are. I just didn't think they'd stoop to something like this or have the nerve to sneak into my house."

139

"I'll do that. Don't worry, Gina. If your rabbit's on this road, I'll find it," he said. The little girl nodded, but she didn't look optimistic.

"Damndest thing, ain't it?" Cy said. "Even livin' way out here, I'm not immune to this nonsense. That's what comes of sellin' the land and makin' a damn development."

Eddie laughed. "If you call this a development, what would you call the developments in town?"

"Little cities, that's what. Come on, Honey," he said, taking Gina's hand. "And please don't start crying again. Your grandmother's mad enough at me as it is, because I tried to give you a rabbit for a pet."

Eddie took one more look at the basement and then followed them out. Gina ran into the house and Cy followed him to the patrol car. They both stood there for a moment looking out at the bushes and forest behind the house.

"Looks thicker than ever, doesn't it?" Cy asked. "It don't take long for Nature to come creepin' back once you stop plowin' and clearin' what you have. Never seen things grow so fast and so heavy as they have this spring. It's almost as if something's gone berserk out there."

"What kind of a way for an old-timer like you to talk?"

"Maybe I'm finally realizin' I am an old-timer," Cy said. "Hilda keeps remindin' me I ain't no spring chicken. 'Course, when people do things like this, it makes you feel you've lived too long anyway."

"Hey, nobody lives too long," Eddie said, but the old man was lost in thought. "Cy, I said nobody lives too long."

"Right. OK, Eddie, thanks for your help," Cy said and started for the house. Eddie watched him. He looked old, slumped over, tired. The scene reminded Eddie of his grandfather's last days, how he began to lean over more and more, as though Death were a burden we all carried, one that increased in weight as we drew closer and closer to our end.

"I'll get back to you, Cy," he called. The old man simply raised his hand without looking back and then disappeared within the house.

Eddie looked out at the forest again. He wasn't much of a woodsman, but he was a country boy and knew enough to respect the opinions of old-timers like Cy Baum when it came to reading Nature's signs. Was there something unusual about this spring? The old man seemed almost terrified when he looked out there. Why? What did he see? What did he feel? Eddie thought, if there really were such a thing as a policeman's sixth sense, it had begun to hone in on something . . . something that he had felt in the basement and carried out with him, and now something that he sensed out there.

He started the car and backed into the driveway, so he could turn around and go back to the Coopers. He tried to laugh at his anxious feelings, imagining what Barbara would say if he tried to describe it to her. This was just a prank committed by a couple of wild kids, wasn't it? He hoped so, but he had no idea why he hoped so much.

When Faith awoke in the morning, she stretched and embraced herself sensuously, folding herself into the fetal position and cuddling around her pillow and blanket. The smile on her face revealed the deep, inner satisfaction that permeated her entire being. Never had she felt so alive and happy. It was the morning after and it was beautiful to lie here and remember.

It had been as Bobby had described: moving softly and quietly over the still, silver water, the stars dazzling above them when they reached the center of the pond, and the view unobstructed. For a long while, neither of them spoke. It was as though they both understood that the sound of either of their voices could break the spell. Bobby watched her as he rowed, dipping his oars rhythmically and gently, barely disturbing the water. Although there was a breeze, the night was warm, and the trees, with their rich, new thick leaves, served as protective walls around them.

Because the moon was behind him, Bobby's face was in shadow; but she sensed the intensity of his gaze. A few moments after they had reached the center, Bobby put up the oars and stretched across the seat, letting his feet dangle over the side of the boat. He lay back on his hands and looked up at the sky.

"So what do you think of all this?" he asked.

"It's beautiful. Do you come here often?"

"Whenever it's like this. You've really never been down here at night?"

"I think . . . a long time ago with my father. I must have been very small."

Bobby turned on his side to face her, his head against the palm of his hand, his elbow braced on the seat. Off to the right a screech owl turned the darkness into mystery. The silence fell between them like a curtain. When Bobby spoke again, his voice was softer.

"It's weird to live next to someone so long and know so little about them, don'tcha think?"

"I don't know. No, I guess it isn't," she added quickly. "How about people who live in the city? Sometimes they don't know their neighbors on the same floor in the apartment house."

"It's always been different up here. We're friendly with everyone on the street except . . . "

"Except us."

"Yeah. What does your mother do all day? I can count on my fingers how many times I've seen her."

"She has her work. I don't want to talk about my mother," she said and turned away. His laugh brought her back. "What's so funny?"

"It's not really funny. It's just that you change your moods so fast."

"Do I?"

"Why do you keep to yourself so much?"

"I don't know," she said sadly.

"Because I think you have a lot to offer people."

"I do?"

"Sure. You're bright and pleasant and . . . very pretty."

She didn't say anything, but she felt herself swell up inside. A long, thin cloud crossed the moon and the darkened shadows slid over them. From way off in the distance behind them, they heard the sound of a car horn, reminding them that this natural hideaway was surrounded by the modern world. Even so, the sound died away like some part of the wildlife within the dark forest.

"You mustn't think I'm just giving you a line."

"Why not?"

"I'm not good at that. Actually, I'm pretty shy myself. It took all my nerve to go up your fire escape and talk you into coming out here with me. I was shaking all the time."

"I don't believe you."

"It's true."

"I've seen you with other girls."

"Some girls are easy, because they're so aggressive. They start the conversations, not me. You know how long I've been working on getting up the courage to approach you?"

"No."

"A long time, believe me."

"Sure."

"I can even tell you some of the things you've worn over the past few weeks—that blue skirt with the seam on the side, that one-piece dress with the ruffled sleeves, that locket you wear only on Mondays . . . "

"You have been watching me!"

"I told you. How come you wear it only on Mondays?"

"Superstition. My father gave it to me on a Monday," she added softly.

"It's really the only jewelry you wear, right?"

"Yes." She thought how she had to hide the locket from Mary and put it on after she left the house, taking care to have it off before she returned.

Suddenly, he surprised her by sitting up and taking her hand into his. She didn't resist, but she tightened up and sat up straighter herself.

"I'm not trying to be aggressive or bossy," he said, "but you shouldn't be as shy as you are and you shouldn't lock yourself up in your house after school. You should be out there having some fun with the rest of us, and if it's your mother who . . . "

"I said, don't talk about her," Faith interrupted. Her voice was filled more with fear than with anger.

"OK, OK. Would you get very angry if I tried to kiss you?" he asked.

"What?" He made it sound so simple. She wasn't sure she understood him.

"Just what I said." He leaned forward and then went to his knees, pulling her toward him gently. She let herself slide off the seat, until she was on her knees, too. When his lips touched hers, she began to pull back. He held her shoulders firmly, but softly. She was drawn back to him; drawn back to the electric tingle that she had sampled; drawn back by another part of herself that had come alive in the moment—a part that shut out her mother's voice, a part that made her aware of the stars and the moonlight and the darkness and his strong fingers urging her closer and closer, until their exploratory kiss became a hard, driving search for the secret of their sexuality. She let him bring his chest to her breasts; she enjoyed the feel of his arms around her and the way he moved his lips off hers and traveled down her chin, caressing her neck. It was only when she felt her body loosen completely, all resistance wane, that she experienced any panic; but when she pulled away, he remained there patiently until she came forward again, this time pressing her lips into his and turning her body comfortably against his, so he could hold her securely.

They remained like that for a while, cheek to cheek, him holding her, the boat drifting. His forearm grazed her breast, but, surprising herself, she didn't jerk away.

"I've never kissed a boy like that."

"Well, you couldn't tell."

"Really?"

"Really," he said.

"It's the truth."

He laughed, and she tightened up defensively in his arms.

"I believe you. All I'm saying is there's nothing awkward or ungraceful about you. You are just what I thought you were."

"And what's that?" She sat up.

"As fresh and as beautiful and as new as each night sky."

"I don't know, Bobby O'Neil," she said "you don't sound like a very shy person to me." He laughed again.

"For your information, you are the first girl I have ever taken out on this rowboat, daytime or night-time."

"I'm not sure I can believe that."

"It's true." He leaned forward and kissed the tip of her nose. Then they kissed again, a long, sensuous, deep kiss that made her feel as though the boat were spinning. She loosened her grip on him, letting her arms fall to her sides. He brought the palm of his hand across her breast and she stirred, turning herself into him. Then they heard a splash.

145

They both sat up quickly and peered into the darkness to the right, but they could see nothing.

"What was that?"

"I don't know. Some animal, I imagine. A deer or a . . ."

"A bear?"

"I don't think so."

"We'd better get back, anyway. I can't stay out much longer. It's too dangerous."

"Dangerous? What would she do if she found out?"

"I don't want . . . "

"I know, I know . . . you don't want to talk about your mother. OK," he said, taking up the oars again and getting into position.

"Let me help," she said, sitting beside him. She took the other oar and began. They laughed when their coordination wasn't always perfect, but they brought the boat back to shore rather quickly. He helped her out and secured the boat. Just after they started back up the path, she paused to look over the pond once again. "It was beautiful," she said. He thought she made it sound as though this were the last time she'd ever see it.

"We'll come back."

"Yes."

He took her hand and they walked up to The Oaks. They kissed at the bottom of the fire escape, and he waited there until she was up to her landing. She waved and then went through her opened window into her room. After she was gone, he started for home, feeling elated and invigorated. He paused only once, because he heard something behind him. Studying the darkness, he could see nothing; but he felt a presence. It made him think of his brother, Billy, and that angered him because it changed his mood. It was enough of a change to quicken his pace and turn the warm darkness into something frightening. When he reached his house, he put that feeling out of his mind

146

and thought about Faith, until he was in bed and sleep finally overtook him.

In her bed Faith lay awake for what seemed like hours. Every part of her had become so sensitive, so aroused. She relived Bobby's kisses, tying the excitement of them to the pleasure of his words and the thrill of his touch. She tossed and turned so much, she thought she would never fall asleep. It finally came, surprising her, taking the thread of one of her fantasies and turning it into a dream that carried her into a restful repose.

After she had enjoyed the luxury of lying there awake in the morning, she rose quickly with the sound of Mary's footsteps. Her mother was particularly loud this morning, as she went past her room and down the stairs. But Faith was determined not to be depressed by anything today. She was anxious to get dressed, have her breakfast, and get on that school bus, where she knew Bobby would be waiting for her.

At breakfast, Mary was unusually quiet. She sat reading a copy of *The Torch,* one of her religious journals, and behaved as though she were sulking. Faith eyed her cautiously.

"I'm going to have to stay after school today," Faith said. Mary raised her eyebrows first and then looked over the paper at her. "I have to go to the library and do some research for my term paper in English."

"Don't you have time during the regular school day?"

"Not today. I have gym and music. I'll take the late bus and walk from town." Faith knew that Mary understood the late bus didn't bring students to their homes, but just took them to central locations.

"Maybe I can pick you up," Mary said. Faith felt that she was studying her face for a reaction.

"Oh, that would be nice if you can, but if you can't . . . "

"I'll see. I have some errands. If I'm not there when you arrive in town, start walking."

"OK."

"Whatever you do, don't take a ride with strangers."

"I won't."

"Even some of these neighbors are questionable," Mary added. "Not that they'd offer you a ride, I imagine."

"Oh, some of them do."

"Really? Who?" she asked quickly.

"Mr. Baum and Mrs. Cooper have stopped for me in the past."

"Busybodies, both of them. Probably poked you full of personal questions."

"No, not really. Mrs. Cooper asked how you were, that's all. Mr. Baum didn't talk about anything but the weather."

"Even so, be careful."

"All right." She stood up. "I'll fix the garbage before I go down to the bus. Heard skunks in it last night."

"Last night? When?"

"Early. Before you came up."

Mary simply nodded and went back to her paper, but Faith thought there was definitely something different about her today. She looked sneaky, almost as if she were anxious for Faith to leave, so she could plan something. Faith wondered about the baby again. She wished Mary had gotten up first and left the kitchen, so she could have tried to reach him through the floor.

"I'm going," she called from the door, but Mary didn't reply. No warnings, no commands, just silence.

Faith stepped out and closed the door softly behind her. The porch had a fake foundation. In it they kept their rakes and shovels and other tools, some of which hadn't been taken out since her father's death. She pulled out the rake and a small shovel and went around

148

to the side where the garbage cans were, so she could gather up the loose material that the animals had scattered. They had two cans. One was on its side and one was upright with its lid on.

She stopped and studied it—there was garbage strewn about the upright one. Had Mary been out to clean up? That didn't make sense, since there was still much litter remaining. She shrugged and went forward, uprighting the other can and scooping up what she could. After it was refilled, there was still a good deal of garbage left. She raked some of it onto the shovel and then took the lid off the first can. She lifted the pile of litter with the shovel and held it over the container; but she never dropped it within, for she caught the movement inside and leaned over to look.

When she saw the rabbit, she nearly screamed.

Eddie Morris left the Coopers convinced that the Cooper kids had nothing to do with Cy Baum's problem. Florence Cooper was the only one at home, but Eddie knew her well, and knew that she was quite candid when it came to her children. She had the look of a person who hated deceptions—her brown eyes always locked tightly on the individual to whom she was speaking. She often came to the point with a sharpness that bordered on downright cruelty.

"My boys are hell raisers, Eddie," she told him. "I'm the first to admit it. When the teachers call me from school to complain, I don't put up any arguments. I know what they're going through; I go through it here! But," she continued, changing the tone of her voice, "they're not vicious kids. They wouldn't deliberately hurt anyone's animals. Why Buddie won't even go hunting with Grant, and he gets all riled up when Grant bags a deer and brings it home to butcher."

"Yeah, well, this might have started out as a prank and ended up something else. Sometimes kids don't

149

know what they're getting themselves into. I've seen it dozens of times."

"Last night you say?"

"Yeah. Had to be during the night."

"Leaves them out, Eddie. I had them both upstairs doin' their homework as soon as they finished dinner. We got some bad news from the school. Both of them are failing two subjects just because they don't do their homework. Grant's already taken away their biking privileges."

"If you say they were home all night, that's good enough for me, Flo. Appreciate it."

"I feel sorry for Cy Baum. Wish I could solve it for him."

"Me too. Give my regards to Grant," he said and left. He thought about stopping back at Cy's house to let him know it wasn't the Coopers, but decided that wasn't much of a result. Not having a good lead might make him and Hilda more frightened, too. He decided to go on. It stood to reason that whatever happened, it happened within the neighborhood; so he thought he would visit each house.

He hesitated at The Oaks, almost deciding to pass it up. He knew as much about Mary Oaks as anyone in the community, and he had known Tom Oaks well. He had the misfortune to have been on duty the night Tom was killed. He still had a vivid recollection of him and Bill Campton going up to the house to tell Mary Oaks Tom had had a fatal car accident.

They had flipped a coin to decide which one of them would do the actual talking. It fell to him. When the little girl opened the door, he looked down at her wide-eyed face and went dumb. Bill had to ask for Mary, who came up rather quickly behind her. Eddie had the feeling she had been waiting in the shadows. He thought she already looked like a wife in mourning. She wore a black dress, her face was pale, and she carried a Bible. Her voice was strange, too, because she sounded like someone in a trance. The little girl stepped away as soon as Mary came forward. It was obvious she knew her place.

"What is it?" she asked. Was she looking at them or beyond them? He almost turned around to see if there were anyone behind them . . . maybe Tom's ghost. He was so unnerved he heard his voice quiver.

"There's been a bad accident, Mary," he said. She said nothing, but her cold, expressionless eyes made him feel like someone standing in ice water. "Tom went off the road," he added. "That bad turn . . . there's been so many accidents there . . . "

"Is he dead?" She was impatient and would permit no preliminaries, no easing into it.

"Yes. I'm sorry, Mary. We're . . . "

"Was he alone?" Eddie couldn't help but look away. He met Bill's gaze and they both looked down. "Both dead?" He nodded, looking up to express a deeper sympathy, even though in his heart he couldn't blame Tom for his unfaithfulness. He wondered who could be faithful to such a woman. Even so, he wanted to tell her that they would do what they could to keep things discreet, but she didn't appear concerned. She looked relieved, as though they had confirmed something she already knew.

"He's at the hospital if you want to . . . "

"Thank you," she said and closed the door. Just like that, she left them standing there, hats in hand, melting on the porch. He remembered the little girl in the background listening, embracing herself tightly, looking small and frightened. He wanted to go in there and take her in his arms. Somehow he knew she wouldn't get much comfort, and he regretted that he would be part of what would surely be a recurring nightmare for her. But Bill nudged him.

"Let's go," he said. "Let's get out of here. She gives me the creeps."

He remembered thinking that Bill was right. Since

that time he could never look at Mary Oaks without experiencing that same cold feeling, that heavy sense of dread. Later, of course, everyone buzzed about the fact that she didn't give Tom a funeral, that she buried him secretly. His friends were outraged. Two of them, Jimmy Kuhn and Fred Boyles, wanted to hire a priest and hold their own funeral service at the grave site, but they talked themselves out of it.

Now, as he looked at the big house, he realized he hadn't been here since the day he brought Mary the terrible news. Of course, every time he passed it, he thought about Tom and the accident; but parking the car in the driveway and getting out to approach that door was a great deal more intense.

The house had been degenerating continually over the years. He remembered it as a beautiful building, an impressive structure, a testament to the quality of workmanship that once went into things. But now, with much of its siding faded and chipped, with its shutters and door in need of paint, with the grounds unkempt and the hedges untrimmed, The Oaks looked forlorn, tired, and neglected, a symbol of a dying age. It was the home of skeletons and shadows and the weird Mary Oaks.

How dark the house looked to him, even in the daytime. All the shades and curtains were drawn on all the windows. Everything appeared shut tight. Anyone walking up to the porch would wonder if the place had been deserted. He hesitated and looked about. Why did he come here, anyway? Mary and her daughter lived alone. They wouldn't know anything about pranks.

Wait a minute. What's wrong with you, Eddie Morris? he asked himself. Are you trying to find reasons not to knock on that door? What about the possibility that pranks might have been pulled on them? Be a policeman. Look for patterns.

He nearly laughed at himself and then started forward again, walking up the narrow sidewalk to the front steps. He was almost there when something off to the left caught his attention. It was just a slight movement in the tall grass, where the spotted lawn, filled with weeds and patches of dirt, met the wild undergrowth. He stopped again and studied the area. There was another movement and then another. He stepped toward it. Could it be . . . another movement and then . . .

The rabbit hopped freely over the lawn, dragging its torn leash behind it.

EiGHT

As Mary worked, she thought of Faith's betrayal as a different sort of betrayal. It was deeper and perhaps even everlasting. Yes, it was the Devil's victory. But she would do what she could to snatch it from him, just as God had done in John Milton's famous epic *Paradise Lost;* the Devil returned to hell after causing the fall of man in Eden and found all his followers had been turned into snakes. She remembered how good she felt after reading that. God had had the last laugh, after all.

Nevertheless, she couldn't conceal her disappointment and pain over Faith's actions. Faith, her darling Faith. Look at what they had endured together. Look at how much Faith had resembled her when she was Faith's age. All her prayers and her promises, all the care she had taken to be sure Faith was well protected and spiritually strong seemed to have gone wrong; yet how could it be her fault? She couldn't be with Faith all the time, helping to make decisions and resist temptations. God wouldn't blame her. Hadn't He answered her questions? Hadn't He told her what to do?

She looked around Tom's room. It was fitting that this would be the place. The Devil had been defeated here. She saw that the key was still in the lock in the door. She knew that Tom had taken to locking his door at night, because he had grown afraid of her—afraid that she would come to him in the middle of the night, when he was in one of his drunken stupors after whoring around, and kill him. Why else would he have done it? She had considered it and asked God about it, but He had given her no answer. It wasn't until Tom's accident that she understood why—He had had His own plans for Tom.

Now, though, this room and the door that locked would come into some valuable use. She had left it much the same as it had been—the dresser and the night table dusty, the rug stained and unvacuumed, towels strewn about. Why clean it? It was his pigsty, a perfect home for a man like him. Of course, she would change things now. Cleanliness was important and some of the things would only be distractions to someone placed in meditation.

She stripped the bed, rolling the sheet and blanket into a ball. She opened the window and beat the mattress, and then remade the bed using Faith's own linens. She cleared the dresser and the table and dusted and polished everything. Then she brought in the vacuum cleaner and did the rug. She even had plans to scrub down the walls, but before doing that, she went to the pantry to get the hammer, nails, and boards. She wanted to nail both of the windows shut, blocking out any outside view. But the doorbell rang just as she started.

She stopped to listen. They still had that hand-cranked bell whose ring reverberated with amazing volume throughout the house. It rang again. Who could be there? She rarely had callers. Putting everything aside carefully, she started down just as the bell rang for the third time. Whoever it was was impatient and was sure she was at home. When she reached the entrance way, she looked out a window just to the side of the front door and saw the police car. The sight of it made her shudder. For a few moments, she couldn't move. Then there was a loud knock.

She opened the door and faced Eddie Morris. Despite the passage of time, confronting him nearly took her breath away. It was the worst kind of déjà vu. She half expected the same words.

"I'm sorry to bother you, Mary," he began. She had been so stunned by his appearance that she had nearly failed to notice the rabbit in his arms. It was so still, it was more like a toy.

"What is it?"

"Been tracing down a prank. Cy Baum bought a coupla rabbits for his granddaughter, for pets, you see."

"So?"

"He bought 'em one at a time. One was set free and one was killed. This one was stolen right out of his basement last night." He held the rabbit higher to verify his statements, but Mary didn't change her expression.

"What does any of this have to do with me?"

"Well, I was checking the neighborhood, looking to see if anyone else had been bothered, when I . . . I was on my way to speak to you, when I saw the rabbit by the side of your house. See, it's Cy's; it still has the leash." He lifted the leash for emphasis.

"That's very nice," she said, starting to close the door. "I'm happy for him."

"Yeah, but I was wondering how it got all the way over here. It's a ways and . . . "

She held the door half open and stared out at him for a moment. Although he was uncomfortable looking intensely at her, he took note of the dramatic changes in her face and body. Seeing her walking on the streets or driving in her car, he hadn't realized the differences. Her face was drawn and sallow and her bone structure so evident, it was as though her skin were transparent. She looked like someone being tormented from within, pulled and tightened by unseen forces that lived off her like parasites. Although her eyes still reflected some

156

strength, he had the terrible feeling they were reporting back to someone else. Her face had become a mask. He thought of science fiction stories, body snatchers, invaders from other planets. It gave him the chills and made him conscious of his own vulnerability. Despite how much he wanted to, he couldn't throw off the fears.

"Are you suggesting I took it?"

"Oh no. I thought you might have seen some kids about or . . . "

"No one. This all sounds very silly to me."

"Uh huh." He looked to the side. "I suppose it could have made its way over here. If you're sure you haven't seen anything suspicious and you haven't had any pranks pulled on you . . . "

"I'm sure."

"Thanks," he said just before she closed the door.

After she shut it, she stood there listening to him walk off the porch. Even though she had presented a strong and cold appearance, she couldn't help but tremble now. Images were returning—a younger Eddie Morris, another cop hovering nervously beside him, her sense of dread and her awareness of the power of God, and then that great light behind them before they spoke. No one but her could see it. It was the tip of God's finger piercing the night, comforting her with His vision. It gave her the strength she needed.

She stepped away from the door and peered through the side window. Eddie Morris was walking slowly toward his patrol car, petting the rabbit and looking back and around. He stopped once and stared at the house. She didn't move from the window until he got into his car and drove off.

Ridiculous, the whole thing, she thought. It showed her how trivial her neighbors were. Pranks, pet rabbits . . .

She started back upstairs to finish her work, but

stopped at the bottom of the stairway to listen. What was that sound under the floorboards? A distinct rubbing or clawing. He was at it again, spying on the upstairs. She had known about it for some time now, but she hadn't taken any serious action. Maybe it was time she should. She took the padlock key out of the pocket of her housecoat and went to the basement door. After she opened it, she listened. Sure enough, there was the sound of his scurrying about, his looking for a hiding place. He knows he's doing something wrong, she thought. She put on the light and descended.

Odors came up at her again, odors that were new. She had smelled them before, but she hadn't thought about them until now. Through the years, she had grown accustomed to every scent down here. What was different now? She wasn't sure, but she knew it was something obvious. At the bottom of the stairs, she paused and looked about. Nothing seemed visibly different and yet she sensed a change. What was it?

"IMP," she called. "WHERE ARE YOU?" She panned the basement floor, turning slowly until she saw him cowering against the far wall. With his body squeezed so tightly and protectively in a crouch, he looked even more deformed than usual. His head looked enormous today and he was dirtier than ever, much dirtier than he often was between the days that she bathed him.

She approached him slowly, sensing something more aggressive about the way he moved and held his arms up. He grimaced; his teeth, although small, looking threatening. He slid along the floor, moving in anticipation. This angered her, but she realized she hadn't brought her strap along and she didn't want to lay her hands on his dirty body. Diseases, she thought, maybe that's what she smelled.

"Stay away from the roof," she said slowly and as

ominously as she could. She pointed upward and he understood. She could see the comprehension in his face. To her, his face was always distorted, but today, she thought she saw Tom's features more clearly. Perhaps it was that same combination of hate and fear in the eyes. She stepped closer to him and when her shadow reached him, he cowered more meekly and began to whimper in anticipation of a blow.

For a few moments she hesitated over him, undecided about what she wanted to do. Then she remembered the work that had to be completed upstairs. She looked at the breakfast tray and saw that he had eaten everything. His appetite had grown considerably. Lately, he left nothing on the tray. She picked it up and then turned back to him.

"Stay away from the roof," she repeated, pointing again. He had his arms crossed over his face, peering out over them, his look of hate now stronger than his look of fear. She started back toward the stairs, but paused when she realized that scent again. There was definitely something different. But what? She heard him move behind an old dresser. It took her mind off the thought and she started up the stairs.

She completed nailing the boards over the windows and then gathered everything together. After she brought things downstairs, she went back up and put a Bible on the bed. Then she took the key out of the lock and tried locking the door from the outside. It worked. She was satisfied that things would be as they should be. Despite her success in making these arrangements, she was still quite sad. It was depressing to think that it had come to this.

When she went downstairs to relax, she sat in her soft chair and reminisced. She thought about her mother and she remembered how the two of them, alone in the house, would talk for hours in her mother's room. Of course, her mother did most of the talking, doing a great deal of reminiscing herself. The sicker she became, the more vivid and revealing she was, especially about her sinful brother, Mary's uncle Billy, who finally left home and was never heard from again. The worst Uncle Billy story that her mother told was the last one about him that Mary would tolerate.

"He was always a no-good, boozing up with older boys before he was even in high school."

"I thought you said he never finished high school," Mary had said.

"He didn't; he was in trouble so much—stealing from parking meters, shoplifting. He and two of his friends even broke into a department store after it closed. He spent a night in jail before he was sixteen. Everyone thought it would do him some good, but it didn't. Maybe they should have kept him there longer to contemplate his sins. Maybe they should have kept him in solitary confinement so he could be alone with just the voice of God and his own conscience. He never went to church unless my father dragged him, and when he was there, he was usually unruly."

Mary had to admit there was something fascinating about the Uncle Billy stories. Despite her realization that he was wicked, she wanted to hear about him. He became a mythical character, perhaps the Devil incarnate. But when her mother told her about the day he attacked her, she became so revolted by any reference to him, she pressed every memory deep into her mind, hoping to wipe away all thoughts of him. She burned his pictures and couldn't understand afterward why her mother was angry about that.

One day when she was half-sedated, she told her the terrible Uncle Billy story. It seemed to spill out of her mind like hot milk boiling over the pot. She spoke in a hypnotic trance, her mind intensely locked in on the past. Mary felt like an intruder, an eavesdropper, but she couldn't pull herself away.

"I was sick," she said, "and they had given me these pills to help me sleep . . . tiny little pinkish pills. I laughed. These can't make me sleep; they're too tiny. Take them, my mother said. Just take them. She left me. She had to go to work and my father wasn't home yet. I was fifteen. Everyone said I was going to be a beautiful girl, despite my illnesses. I was so groggy."

She looked like she was about to cry. Mary took her limp hand into hers.

"Go to sleep now, Mother. Don't talk anymore."

"I could barely raise my head from the pillow," her mother said, ignoring Mary's advice. "But I heard him come to the door. He had been drinking down at the railroad station with Ron Toomey and the Clayton brothers. Unwashed, low-class friends . . . What do you want, Billy? I asked him. I could open my eyes, but he looked fuzzy. I saw him smiling. Go away, I said. Ma says leave me sleep. He laughed and came closer. You always have to sleep, he said. You're lazy, but shrewd, he said. Me, I thought. Me? How could he of all people call me lazy? He pulled the blanket off me."

Mary was frightened. Her mother's face took on a twisted grimace. This story was too painful. Her mother started to sit up as though she were reliving it. Mary stroked her arm and tried to get her to relax.

"Don't talk anymore. You've got to sleep now. Don't remember things," she said, but it was as though her mother couldn't hear her.

"His hands . . . his hands were on me. I said, Billy, what are you doing? But I couldn't lift my arms . . . sleepy, groggy. He was laughing, pulling my night-gown up."

"Ma, don't talk no more."

"Touching me . . . I thought it was a dream. Soon it would stop, but he didn't stop . . . "

"Ma!"

"Hands on my legs, fingers poking, pushing. His

161

laughter, then his hands on my breasts. Billy, my brother Billy . . . drunk, incestuous . . ."

Mary had her hands over her ears. She wanted to scream. She went into a crouch and felt sick herself. Her mother went on and on, revealing the disgusting details. Finally, Mary ran from the room. Even now, years later, remembering that day, she couldn't help but feel revulsion and nausea.

Afterward, there were those redundant nightmares—Uncle Billy coming back, discovering her, raping her. That was why she burned the pictures. She wanted no reminders of his face; no images. Gradually she overcame them, until they were replaced by nightmares of her own origin. Uncle Billy merged with all the other shadowy figures of evil.

When her mother realized what she had told her, they prayed. They prayed even for Uncle Billy, for his soul, and for those he might have harmed. Her mother was apologetic, too.

"It's not a pretty story," she said, "and I wanted so to give you only pretty things."

Her mother, her body so weak and vulnerable, her soul so strong and beautiful. Please God, she prayed, take something from me and give it to her. Make her strong enough to enjoy what she has. But it wasn't meant to be.

That was why, when her mother's death finally came, Mary did not cry. She turned from the grave strengthened by an inner knowledge, a truth the others didn't have. She felt their eyes on her; she knew what they were thinking. Her face was too radiant; her eyes were too clear. They thought her Madonna smile was insensitive. But she thought they were hypocrites. They claimed to believe in an afterlife, but mourned the entrance into it. They had no contact with God, or they would have been happy that He had released her mother from the imprisonment of her weak and sickly body and made her angelic.

162

She could remember walking independently while the others gathered around her father. She was so strong then. Why didn't Faith have that same spiritual strength? Would she ever have it, God? She listened for His response; she closed her eyes; she let herself relax even more, and she waited. God would help her. Upstairs the room was ready. It was only a matter of time.

What was it her mother had said . . . if only they had left Uncle Billy in a form of solitary confinement so he could be alone with the voice of God and his own conscience.

She wiped some tears from her cheeks and she hummed the tune of a hymn her mother and she had sung together often. Then she began to sing it, certain that there was another voice in the room. It filled her with renewed spiritual joy. She was ready for whatever was to come.

"Hi," Bobby said, moving over quickly to make room for Faith on his bus seat. She had boarded the bus slowly, still moving in a daze, confused and frightened by her discovery of the rabbit in the garbage can. What did it mean? she wondered. Who put it there? Bobby misinterpreted her pensive look. "Got into trouble last night?" he asked sadly.

"What?"

"When you got back into your room?"

"Oh. No, no, that was all right. No problem." She sat down and smoothed the front of her skirt before placing her books on her lap.

"You look really upset."

She nodded, still thinking. Then she turned to him. In the back of the bus, the Cooper kids were throwing paper balls at each other. Willie Rosen chastised them, but they didn't seem concerned. He shifted into gear and pulled away, occasionally looking at them angrily through his rearview mirror.

"Before I came down for the bus," she began, "I had to fix our garbage cans. Once in a while, skunks or stray dogs get into the bags and pull the cans over, spilling everything around."

"Oh, yeah," Bobby said, thinking that was the whole problem, "we have that trouble, too, sometimes. My father thinks Captain does it, but now that he's tied up . . . "

"One of the cans was still covered, but its garbage obviously had been spilled. I scooped it up, but when I took off the lid to put some of it back inside, I found a rabbit."

"Dead?"

"No, a living, breathing rabbit with a collar and a leash."

"A live rabbit?"

"Someone's pet."

"And it was in your garbage can with the lid over it?"

"Uh huh."

"Someone's idiotic idea of a prank," he said.

"Think so?"

"What else could it be? Wait a minute," he added quickly and turned around. "Excuse me." He stood up and moved past her. She watched him go to the back of the bus, where the Cooper kids continued to horse around. He grabbed both of them by the back of their necks and both began to howl. Willie Rosen laughed.

"That's it, quiet 'em down," he called. Bobby sat them down on the long, rear seat, still holding on to both of them securely. He spoke to them in low, but threatening, tones. Faith waited with interest, now that she understood his purpose. Before the bus reached the village, where they would pick up most of the remaining students who rode this run to school, Bobby returned to his seat.

"Was it them?"

164

He didn't reply right away. She could see he was in deep thought, and that made her more uneasy.

"I don't think so," he said. "I had them pretty scared. They've done some wild things, but . . . "

"Then who?"

"It could have been anyone, I suppose. You know, just snuck up there and did it," he added, but he didn't sound very convincing. "What did you do with it?"

"I didn't want my mother to find out. She gets very upset when she thinks people have been around our property doing things. We had a lot of trouble last Halloween, if you remember."

"Um. So what did you do?"

"I just turned it loose in the bushes."

"Maybe someone was riding by and decided to get rid of it."

"But we're well off the road."

"Yeah. Jes . . . I mean, heck, I don't know. It's weird. I'd question my brat brother about it, if it weren't for the fact that I know he's terrified of going out alone now. He won't wander from our property."

"Because of the raccoon?"

"I guess so," he said. He sounded very indecisive and suddenly looked as pensive as she did when she first came on the bus.

"What do you mean?"

"He keeps telling me it wasn't a raccoon."

"What does he call it?" she asked, as the bus stopped at the corner to take on the town kids. There was a surge of noise and excitement, and for the moment, Bobby's attention was pulled away from her by other students who greeted him. After things got settled and the bus started away again, he leaned close to her, practically touching her ear with his lips.

"He still calls it an E.T., a little creature that looks human but . . . "

"But what?"

"But doesn't. I don't know. He's a kid. Forget

165

about it. Whoever put the rabbit in the can is a nut. What if you hadn't seen it? It would have been emptied into the garbage truck and you wouldn't have known about it. So I don't know what the point of the prank is."

"Me neither," she said. "But that's what worries me," she added, barely loud enough for him to hear.

He tried to get her mind off it. They talked about many other things. They made all sorts of plans for different rendezvous to be made throughout the school day—meeting at his locker between these two periods; meeting at her locker between those. They knew they'd meet at lunch and decided where they would sit in the cafeteria.

All of this excited her and changed the face of the world for her. Passing through the halls, meeting him for even a moment, seeing him across the corridors— every moment of it turned the usually mundane day into an event. Each little thing they did together, no matter how small, carried great significance. Her ordinary locker, with its dull orange color and its scratched surface, suddenly became wonderful to touch and be near. Instead of walking with her head down, her mind lost in her own deep thoughts, she looked up, stood straight, her eyes bright and alive, her ears attuned to every sound. She could see that other students noticed the changes in her. Some of them looked at her in puzzlement; others smiled and nodded. She finally felt noticed, accepted, even resurrected.

But when she entered her classes and there was no possibility of her seeing him or him seeing her, she retreated to quieter, more pensive thoughts. Invariably, during each class, her mind turned back to the events of the morning. She thought about the rabbit and she thought about her conversation with Bobby concerning it. Something was trying to make its way to the forefront of her consciousness all morning. Memories and images came back to her; words, isolated and apparently insignificant, were heard again. What did it all mean? What was the theory that was trying to be born? She sensed there were real clues, clues in words, clues in sights and sounds. Clues to what?

It wasn't until English class, when Mr. Baker started a discussion about modern-day heroes, that something Bobby had said repeated itself in her thoughts. In the course of his lecture-discussion, Mr. Baker mentioned E.T.

She thought about Bobby's little brother, and when she recalled the way Bobby described his little brother's monster attacker, she suddenly saw a frightening possibility. It came to her with such a shock, she nearly stood up at her desk. She was sure she uttered a subdued groan, because some of the students around her turned her way and Mr. Baker said, "What's that, Faith?"

"Nothing," she said quickly. She must have looked terrible, because he and most of the class stared at her. It was only for a long moment, but to her it seemed as though they would never turn away. They finally did and Mr. Baker went on. She was left to follow the thread of her thoughts.

After that period's bell rang, she got up slowly. It was time to go to lunch to meet Bobby, but her new surge of energy and excitement had waned. She looked like her old self again, moving in a trancelike manner, ignoring everyone around her, looking through people instead of at them, hearing nothing but the sounds of her own thoughts. She was in such a daze that she actually sat down at the wrong table in the cafeteria, leaving Bobby alone and perplexed in the corner. He had to come up to her.

"Hey," he said.

"What?"

"What are you doing? I thought we were going to sit back there where we could be more alone."

"Oh. Oh, I forgot."

"Forgot?" His half smile of confusion widened and he shook his head. "Talk about dizzy dames. You wanna sit here?"

"No," she said quickly. "Let's go back there." She picked up her tray and followed him back.

"You all right?" he asked.

She looked at him. Her heart began to pound. For the first time in her life she wondered if she could trust another human being beside her mother. The very thought of it made her flush with fear. Bobby's face reflected his sincere concern. He took her hand quickly.

"God, you feel ice cold."

"I'm all right," she said.

"Says who? What is it?"

She looked at him again, studied his warm, concerned eyes, looked at his soft, inviting lips, and wondered what it would be like to throw herself into his strong arms, to rely on and confide in someone else, someone her own age. He could see her hesitation, but he could sense her longing as well.

"Come on," he said. "Something's really wrong. I want to help. Does it have anything to do with that rabbit you found this morning? You're still thinking about that, aren't you?"

"I . . ."

"Yeah?"

She turned away and looked down at her tray. Some of his friends called to him, but he ignored them. She felt his closeness, the demand of his eyes, but her warm feelings for him were suddenly clouded by images of her mother and the memories of their prayer sessions, especially that first ritual when they had sworn secrecy to each other and prayed for God's guidance. How could she turn away from all that now? Yet she felt a need to and she wanted to; she wanted to be exposed, in someone else's hands. What she wanted was relief, relief from responsibility. It was so confusing.

"I've got to think," she said. She turned away again, shaking her head. Other students came to their table. Bobby was as cordial as he could be, but Faith ignored them. Their appearance sobered her, however. She caught her breath and regained her composure.

"Faith."

"It's all right," she said, sounding more like her stronger self again.

He turned his body toward her, blocking the others from her view and her from theirs. His face was so close, his eyes so intent. She felt the excitement again; she had to resist the temptation to draw closer to him.

"If you can't trust me, you can't love me," he said. "Ever." He sounded so sad about it that she felt like crying.

"Give me a chance. Things are happening so fast."

"OK. When?"

"Tonight. Come back to me tonight. My balcony," she added and smiled. It brought a smile to his face, too, and for the moment, her crisis was over.

Eddie Morris had put the rabbit beside him on the front seat and driven directly to Cy Baum's house. Of course, the little girl was ecstatic. Cy was surprised because he had written the animal off. Even Hilda was happy about it, despite her disapproval of the whole thing. Eddie felt good about bringing some sunlight back into their home. Hilda and Cy invited him in for coffee and he sat at their kitchen table to explain how he found the rabbit.

Eddie was eager to relax here for a while. The Baums' kitchen reminded him of his own when he was young. The delicious and tempting aromas of food in preparation filled the air. Regardless of the great use of and the activity in the kitchen, it looked immaculate. The old stove was as shiny as the day Cy Baum had it installed. There was a homey warmth to the room, a sense of family. He couldn't describe it in exact terms, but he sensed an air of something real here. Prepackaged, push-buttoned dinners to be eaten in front of a television set while the family consumed in silence just didn't exist for these old-timers. What's more, Hilda's friendly, warm smile brightened by her grandmother eyes was a welcome contrast to the cold, deathlike stare of the pale Mary Oaks.

"So what did she tell you?" Cy asked, after Eddie explained how he had gone to the front door of The Oaks.

"She said she saw no one, heard no one. Claimed she hadn't been victimized in any way by pranks or the like. Made me feel stupid for asking her."

"I hardly see her nowadays," Hilda said. She put a plate of freshly baked soft rolls on the table. Eddie eyed them almost lustfully. Next to them was a jar of the homemade jam Hilda had made from the blueberries last year.

"My wife says if I don't lose some weight . . . "

"Never mind," Hilda said, "you need your strength, too."

"Yeah, that's right," Eddie said, smiling. He reached for a roll and stabbed the jam with a butter knife.

"Strange, though," Cy said. He was slumped down in his seat and looked as though he were talking to himself. He leaned his head against his hand and stared ahead at the shelves of spices hung on the wall above the counter. "I can see a rabbit makin' its way over there, maybe; but I can't figure how it got out of that basement."

"Gina must've not seen it go out, Cy," Hilda said.

"And it made a beeline right over to The Oaks? Naw, it got out last night."

"What else can we think?" Eddie said. "Why would anyone just bring it over there and leave it?"

"No sense to it. Yet," Cy said, sitting up straighter, "we do have the problem of the other two rabbits, don't we? The one didn't unlatch itself, and the other didn't break its own neck."

Eddie chewed thoughtfully and drank some coffee. They heard Gina giggle in the living room.

"If that animal messes in this house, Cy Baum . . . "

"I know, I know. Gina," he called, "you'd better take him down to the basement."

"All right, Grandpa."

"What's Mary's daughter like?" Eddie asked. "I don't think I'd recognize her if I saw her."

"We haven't seen her much ourselves," Hilda said. "Keeps to herself in that big house."

"What Hilda means is Mary keeps her in that big house. I can't help but think that somehow that woman's responsible for all this."

"Cy!"

"Well maybe she thinks it's some kind of a sin to own a rabbit. How do I know? He found the animal over there, didn't he?"

"That's no proof."

Eddie thought about another roll, but forced himself to consider Barbara's warnings about his weight. She had gotten him to give up smoking last year, and she hounded him continually about his bad eating habits.

"Why don't you take a few with you, Eddie?" Hilda said, seeing where his attention had gone.

"Thank you, but no, Hilda. If I took them into the car with me, they'd be eaten before I reached the station." Cy laughed and for a few minutes they talked about other things. Cy related the tale of the time Eddie's grandfather ate woodchuck.

"Did it by accident. It was his own darn fault. We had been over to Sam Cohen's playin' a game of hearts, you know, and he had this black fella, Henry, who worked on his chicken farm. Maybe you remember him—a big, bulky man, strong as an ox."

"I think I do."

"The woodchuck was Henry's. He had killed it and prepared it and left it in Sam's refrigerator that afternoon. Anyway, Sam steps out to do something and Pete goes and rips off a chunk, thinking it was some kind of roast. He had eaten a good portion of it by the time Sam returned. What a laugh that was. Good beef, your grandfather says. Hot damn, Sam says, you're eatin' Henry's woodchuck. I went into hysterics and your grandfather nearly heaved up all he ate."

"Wait a minute," Hilda said, her expression turning serious, "do you suppose somebody wanted to eat the rabbits?"

"Mary Oaks?" Eddie offered.

"Naw," Cy said. Then his skeptical look strengthened. "I don't think they're hard up at all. Heard she was left a bundle when Tom died."

"I suppose he's right," Hilda said. "Look at what's happening to me, thinking such thoughts. You and that damn rabbit," she said, remembering her reason to be angry.

"How is this my fault? Can't a person have anything anymore?" Cy went into a sulk, and Eddie smiled to himself.

"Well," he said, "I'll keep trying to get to the bottom of things." He slapped his knee and stood up. "What are you going to do with the rabbit tonight?"

Cy looked at Hilda.

"Not upstairs, Cy Baum."

"I'll just lock the basement door securely," he said. Eddie nodded.

"Thanks for the coffee and roll, Hilda."

"You're welcome to take a few more."

"I'd better not. I'll be by again shortly, just to check on things," he added.

"Appreciate it," Cy said, following him to the door. When he was sufficiently beyond Hilda's hearing, he took Eddie's arm. "What do you really make of all this?" he asked.

"You haven't seen anyone strange in the area?"

"Not a soul."

"I was thinking about that Oaks girl," Eddie confessed. "Growing up in that weird house."

"With that woman. I know. Thought of it myself."

"I'll see what I can dig up. Call me if anything else happens, no matter how simple it seems."

"Will do. Thanks again," Cy said. He watched Eddie leave and then closed the door.

Eddie slowed down when he reached The Oaks' driveway again. He felt certain that the answer to the mystery, whatever it was, would be found up there. Then he thought, what would the chief say if he knew he was spending all his time tracking down the rabbit snatcher? He could just imagine his sarcasm.

"Maybe I'll assign a detective to it, Morris. Do you have the rabbit's paw prints? Should I call in the BCI, or do you think we can handle this ourselves?"

No, Eddie thought, I'm not even going to tell him about this . . . at least not until there's something more to it. It could have been only a prank by a goofy girl. Strange prank, though, he thought. He couldn't shake off the feeling there was more to it.

He looked back through his rearview mirror to watch Wildwood Drive weave out of his vision. It disappeared like some kind of a dream. Why did he feel as though he had just passed through a kind of nether world? It was just the effect that weird Mary Oaks and that house with its shadows and vacant windows had on him.

Ridiculous, he thought, and chastised himself for not taking a few more of Hilda Baum's homemade rolls.

NINE

For the entire trip to Centerville on the late school bus, Faith was pensive. Her deep thoughts were born out of an overwhelming fear that had been intensifying gradually throughout the latter part of the school day. She felt like one sinking into an icy pool, her body growing weaker by the moment. As she grappled with her thoughts, her isolation from the people around her became more and more severe. Other students bumped into her; younger students shouted and laughed around her. She was even hit with a glob of chewing gum, but she didn't feel it or turn around to see who had thrown it. She was oblivious to everything but her own terrifying images, for in her mind she was creating the scenario that frightened her more than anything she could recently recall.

The baby had gotten out. How? What would Mary do when she discovered it? Had she discovered it? It struck Faith as curious that he was vicious enough to attack Bobby's little brother. But then she realized that she didn't really know what he was like; she hadn't had that much contact with him. And maybe (and this was perhaps more important) he was as evil as Mary claimed he was.

She tried to envision him, to recall his physical features. Her glimpses of him were so few and far between. She knew he moved like a monkey and expected that down there in the basement he had become some kind of a creature, but to venture out and attack people and steal things from the neighbors . . . what kind of intelligence did he have? How did he get along and know where to go and how to go?

She thought about her communications with him through the floor. Something that she had seen as warm and humane, even exciting, now seemed horrifying. Was the baby reaching out for desperately needed human contact or was the breath she had felt through the boards the Devil's own hot gasps designed to draw her down into the depths of darkness? She studied the palms of her hands where the baby's fingers had grazed her skin. Was her mind playing tricks on her? They seemed singed, discolored. She rubbed them together like Lady Macbeth and then, becoming self-conscious, she looked about to see if anyone had noticed her strange behavior.

Her heartbeat quickened. She pressed herself against the side of the bus and gazed down at the monotonous macadam liquefying before her, as the bus increased its speed on the straightaway approaching the village. Perhaps she already had been corrupted and her affections and desires for Bobby O'Neil were symptoms. What should she do? Should she tell Mary what she thought and knew? Or should she try to discover the truth herself and do something about it? Could she do it by herself?

The question of confiding in Bobby returned. He couldn't be evil. The feelings they had for each other were too sincere. The only way she could overcome this terrible paranoia was to have faith in someone else. Together they could investigate and determine. But what would it mean to betray Mary? What would Bobby think of her, if he knew she had kept this terrible secret all these years? Could he be expected to understand? Did he believe in the ever-present existence of a conscious Evil?

She was more confused than ever. Thinking things out like this didn't help; it only made matters worse. The bus had become stifling. When it pulled up to the curb, she practically launched herself from her seat and bulldozed her way past the other kids getting ready to disembark. She looked around quickly, expecting Mary to be waiting for her. She was surprised and grateful that she wasn't there. She wanted the extra time to walk and to think.

As if under a hypnotic spell, she found herself stopping automatically at the auto dump. She hesitated. Frank and one of his workers were tearing parts of an engine out of a wreck. Usually, they paid little or no attention to her, but now they stared. After a few moments, she heard Frank's indistinct mumbling and then their laughter. When they went back to their work, she entered the car graveyard, moving magnetically toward her father's automobile, unsure herself as to what she hoped to accomplish.

She stood looking at the car. Once again her mind played tricks on her, for to her the car looked different—cleaner, newer, almost as it was before the terrible accident. She drew closer. There was something unusual here, a sense of another presence. She half expected her father to suddenly appear in the front seat. He'd be smiling and looking out at her and beckoning her to come closer. Was it him or was it the Devil disguised as him? Was one of her nightmares about to come true?

She moved forward, but she trembled as she did so. She embraced her school books, holding them tightly to her body, and stood by the door, staring in through the cracked side window. Slowly she reached down for the door handle, and when her hand found it, she thought it felt hotter than ever. Yet she couldn't release it; her fingers were glued to the metal. She had barely any strength, but the door seemed to open on its own. Taking a deep breath, like one about to go under water, she slid in behind the steering wheel as she had done many times before.

For a few moments she simply sat there in a trance. Then she put her school books beside her on the seat and took the steering wheel in her hands. The spiritual energy in the car traveled up through the column into the steering wheel and into her hands. It permeated her body, moving like electricity, firing her up for new visions. She was set for a truly supernatural experience. Perhaps wisdom and answers would come to her and she wouldn't feel as alone and afraid.

She sat back, closing her eyes, her hands holding the steering wheel as firmly as one in the midst of an accident. All that she heard was the sound of a fly buzzing by the passenger side window, and then . . . she felt the hand on her neck.

"GET OUT!" Mary screamed. She tore the door open to reach in and grab Faith's arm. "GET OUT!" She pulled her roughly, sending her to the ground. Then, seizing Faith's hair, she dragged her until Faith got to her feet. Mary's first blow caught her on the right side of her head. Faith raised her arms to protect herself and Mary shoved her forward toward their car, which had been parked secretly behind other wrecks just across the way. "GET IN!" Mary commanded as soon as she opened the door. Faith covered her head with her hands and Mary pushed her onto the front seat. The tears were streaming down her face now. Mary, in a rage, went around the front of the automobile and took her seat behind the wheel. Before Faith could utter anything in her own defense, Mary swung her right hand around and caught her directly on the mouth. The blow stung and brought blood where her lips met her teeth.

Faith brought her knees up against her body and

178

embraced herself. She pressed her body tightly between the door and the seat and cried most of the way home. She couldn't think of anything to say in her own defense and she was shocked that Mary had discovered her in the dump. How long had she known? Was she ever there before? If so, why didn't she let on until now? Once again, Faith was both impressed and frightened by her mother's powers. For the present she could only hope for the rage to lessen.

As soon as they pulled into the driveway and stopped, Faith got out of the car and hurried for the front door, hoping for the sanctity of her own room. But Mary was right behind her, slapping at her and pulling at her hair. She screamed and pleaded and fell over the front steps.

"Get up!" Mary said, her voice in a kind of hiss. Never had Faith seen her this wild. She struggled to her feet, tripped again, struggled up, and lunged at the front door. Inside, Mary took hold of her wrist and spun her around. "WHY DID YOU GO THERE? WHY DID YOU DO IT?"

"I don't know; I don't know. Please . . . "

Mary brought her face very close to Faith's. When Faith tried to look away, Mary seized her chin in her hand and forced her to look at her. Mary's eyes were wild; her teeth were clenched. She was pressing them so hard against one another, it made the veins in her temples bulge. The corners of her mouth were white, and her eyes grew wider and wider, until they seemed to consume her face with the fire of their anger. Faith subdued her sobs, but she was unable to swallow. The pain that had built in her chest and throat was excruciating.

"And the Devil that deceived them was cast into the lake of fire and brimstone, where the beast and the false prophet are, and shall be tormented day and night for ever and ever," Mary whispered.

"Yes," Faith said. "Yes, yes." She nodded emphati-

cally, hoping to calm her mother with her assent, but
Mary's anger didn't lessen. Her grip on Faith's wrist
tightened enough to cause pain. Faith was amazed at
Mary's strength. From where did it come in such a
small and fragile body? Surely it was spiritual. And
Faith had defied the spirit! She felt doomed.

"You were intimate. You let him touch you and
know you."

At first Faith couldn't speak. She simply shook her
head. Mary's grip tightened even more as Faith
stepped back.

"No," Faith said. She knew about Bobby, too!

"You lied and betrayed me."

"No, no, I didn't betray you. Listen to me. Listen . . ."

"You must pray. Pray for salvation."

"I will. I promise."

For a moment Mary's expression relaxed. Faith felt
hopeful. She took a deep breath and when Mary
released her wrist, she rubbed it and kept her head
down.

"You must go upstairs now," Mary said. It was said
very matter-of-factly. There was no hint of a threat
and no anger. Faith looked up suspiciously, because
Mary's face had suddenly turned considerably softer;
she looked more concerned than angered.

"OK," Faith said.

"And you must pray and fast and seek redemption."

Faith bit her lower lip gently and nodded. Mary's
swollen shoulders relaxed. The redness left her face
and her eyes cooled. It was then that Faith realized she
had left her school books back in her father's wrecked
car. She wanted to say something about it, but she was
far too frightened of bringing up the subject. What she
thought was she would go up to her room and pretend
to pray for an hour or so, as she had done many times
before when Mary was angry with her, and then come

down to a much calmer, more reasonable Mary. But for now she knew that it would be best to remain silent, so she turned and started up the stairs. Surprisingly, however, Mary was right behind her, almost breathing down her neck. She quickened her pace toward her room.

"No," Mary said when Faith reached the doorway and started to turn in. "Keep walking."

"Keep walking?"

"KEEP WALKING!" Mary shouted.

"OK, OK," Faith said, afraid the wild rage would return. She continued down the hall. When they passed Mary's room and the bathroom, she slowed her pace. They were moving into the darker part of the house, a section shut up. Even Mary kept out of it.

"Keep going," Mary said when she hesitated again. Faith felt as though they had crossed a boundary. Her heart began to beat fast. The door to the room her father used had been driven into, was opened, and the light was on. "Here," Mary said when they reached it.

"But . . ."

"This is where you must go. This is where the Devil is to be defeated. I have been told. You must do what I say."

"I don't want to," she said. She started to back up, but Mary blocked her.

"You must. The Devil's keeping you from wanting to go in there. Fight him," she whispered.

"No." She stepped back. "Please. Listen to me first."

"Go inside," Mary commanded, taking her wrist again. She pulled her toward the door. Faith shook her head, but Mary's strength was overwhelming. She drove her forward until she was in the doorway. Then she pushed her into the room.

The sight of the boarded windows, her own bed-spread and pillow, the Bible on the bed, the cleared dressers and tables frightened her, because she realized that Mary had prepared this as a kind of prison for her. Then another realization quickly came to her—this was similar to what Mary had done with the baby. Remembering him at this moment reminded her of her frightening theory. She turned to tell Mary about it, for now it was more important than ever that Mary knew what kind of dangers existed.

But Mary didn't wait. She stepped back quickly and closed the door. Faith rushed at it and tugged on the knob just as Mary turned the key in the lock. The click sounded like a bullet to Faith. She went into a panic and began pounding hard on the heavy, old wooden door, but her hands quickly became sore and began to sting.

"WAIT . . . LISTEN . . . MOTHER, I'VE GOT TO TELL YOU SOMETHING . . . PLEASE." She listened in anticipation, but she could barely hear Mary's departing footsteps.

"Oh no," Faith said, turning around to study the room. She went to a boarded window and tugged on one of the planks, but the nails had been driven in firmly. The windows were securely blocked. She turned in circles, looking for some avenue of escape, some way of communicating with the outside, but there was nothing but the Bible.

She ran back to the door in a frenzy and pulled and pulled on the knob, but the door barely shook. Expending all her strength and crying hysterically, Faith sunk to the floor and collapsed in her own embrace. Her body shook with her now silent sobs. She didn't have even the strength to cry. It had all happened too fast; realizing the truth about the baby, going to the wreck, Mary's surprising discovery, and now this—trapped in her father's old room, a room she had been afraid of for so long. What did Mary mean by "the Devil could be beaten here"? What was she going to do? How long would she leave her here?

"Ma," she called in a weakened voice. "Ma, please. Listen to me. You've got to listen. It's about the baby . . . Imp . . . please, you've got to hear me. Ma . . . "

There was nothing but silence. She clutched her body tighter and leaned against the closed door. The silence seemed to get deeper. Finally, exhausted and defeated, she stood up and went to the bed. She pushed the Bible aside and sprawled out on her stomach, clutching the pillow to her as a young girl would clutch her favorite doll. She closed her eyes and swallowed hard. She didn't want to stay in this room; there were ghosts in this room. One thing she would never do was turn off the light.

After a while she turned on her back and looked around. Even the old walls seemed threatening with their faded and cracked paint. She sat up and wiped her cheeks and then looked down at the Bible. There seemed to be nothing else to do, no other way to protect herself. She grasped it firmly in her hands. Just then she thought she heard something, so she looked up quickly and listened hard.

"Ma? Is that you?"

Nothing. The dead silence was ominous. She took a deep breath and then put the Bible in her lap and opened the cover. Hovering over it intensely, she lowered herself mentally into the pages and drew the words around her like a protective wall. For the time being, she would do what Mary wanted her to do.

When Eddie Morris drove up to his own home after work, he felt an unusually vivid sense of pride and happiness. He simply sat in his car for a while and stared at his four-bedroom ranch-style home with its modest but tasteful landscaping: the dozen or so spruce trees he and Barbara had planted together one weekend fifteen years ago, the rock garden he had built off to the right, and the poured cement patio that he and Chester Trustman had made one Sunday afternoon, about a month after the house itself was constructed. He still had plans to put a cast-iron railing around that patio and plant new hedges this spring. Barbara was the real gardener, though. Her poppies, reacting to the unusually warm spring, had burst into full bloom, sprinkling the front of the house with bright colors.

What a sharp contrast all of this presented when compared to the frontage before The Oaks. It wasn't just the well-manicured lawn and hedges or the freshly whitewashed siding and newly painted shutters. There was an air of life about his house, a mood of optimism, and a feeling of contentment and security. He always looked forward to going home, but today he seemed relieved because of it. He anticipated his children with their own excitement and even welcomed the advent of some of Tommy's teenage problems. He looked at his watch. There was still a good hour before Barbara would serve supper. Maybe he would get Tommy to go down to the basement with him and lift weights. He felt like having some father-son companionship.

He wasn't going to analyze any of this; but, throughout the day, certain images had lingered on the surface of his mind, and he knew that it was because of those feelings and thoughts that he was so eager to enter his home and close the door on the world outside. He was even haunted by an odor. As ridiculous as it might seem to someone else, he was sure he had caught the scent of Death when he visited The Oaks, and that scent remained with him all day. He hardly ate his lunch because of it.

Being a policeman and a wild game hunter, he had smelled it many times. Caked blood, battered flesh, the carcasses of animals, and the bodies of traffic accident victims all produced that same revolting putrescence. Once he came upon it, whether it happened in the evening or early in the morning, it lingered about him. One of the first things he did after such experiences was take a long and soapy shower. Even so, it usually took him a while to get the scent from his mind. Today, although he had seen nothing dead and had handled no fatal accidents, he carried such an impression of death in his mind, that he thought he detected the odor everywhere, even in George's Luncheonette. It was only now, when he pulled up to the brightness of his own home, that the images diminished. He was glad of that.

He hated bringing his work home with him. Instead, he enjoyed listening to Barbara's school stories. It didn't take much to get her going and he so relished sitting back and watching her dramatically relate something "outrageous" that one of her students had done or one of her fellow teachers had said. Barbara had been a teacher for some time now, and despite the radical changes in the job and in the nature of the students, she still had a new teacher's idealism and enthusiasm. He didn't know whether to term it naiveté or faith, but she always gave the child the benefit of the doubt. He was reminded of the movie, *Boys Town* and Spencer Tracy. "There's no such thing as a bad boy."

"There's always a reason why one of them acts up," Barbara said. "If you knew some of their home lives . . ."

"I know some." He usually didn't interrupt her when she went on and on, at least not until she got very excited and her face turned red with emotion. Then he would simply have one of his laughing smiles on his face and she would stop abruptly in the middle of a sentence. Her hands would go to her hips and she would stamp her foot.

"You're teasing me again, Edward Allen Morris."

"No, honest." He quickly cleared the smile off his face and tried to look attentive, but she saw through him every time. Sometimes she threw a dish towel at him and swore she would never discuss her school problems with him again. Sometimes she ignored him and went on until one of the children distracted her.

Once, he half seriously said, "What about those kids who are pure evil and would be in trouble no matter what their home lives were?"

"I don't believe there's any such thing, Eddie. You'd have to believe in the existence of the Devil."

"Sometimes . . . I do," he said, but he said it too softly for her to hear.

Now, as he sat there in his car, he thought about that conversation again. Toward the end of the day, driven partly by curiosity and partly by this unexplainable sixth sense, his "policeman's sense," he had decided to go back to Wildwood Drive and visit the O'Neils. He knew Dick O'Neil all his life, Dick having been only two years ahead of him in school. When he arrived there, Dick hadn't yet returned from work, but Cindy seemed sincerely grateful that he had taken the time to stop by.

"I just heard today what had happened to your little boy," he told her, "while I was investigating another matter on this road."

"Come on in, Eddie." She stepped back to make way for him. He took off his hat and entered the house. He had been there only a few times before, back when he was in high school, but he remembered Dick O'Neil's father, a giant of a man with wrists as thick as most men's forearms. He recalled being at Slat's Garage in Centerville one afternoon when John O'Neil and Gary Slat had a contest to see who could hold a twelve pound, short sledge hammer straight out the longest. John won by a good ten seconds more. Eddie was already fourteen, but neither he nor any of his friends could hold it out for more than a second or two. Most couldn't even hold it straight out.

"Been a while since I was here," he said, looking around. "I always admired this house." Cindy smiled.

"Dick's great grandfather and grandfather built it."

"I know. Solid," he said. Little Billy O'Neil appeared in the living room doorway just off to the right. "Hello there. How're you doing?" Eddie asked, noting how the boy's arm bulged from the bandages under his shirt. Billy didn't say anything. He just eyed him curiously for a moment and then ran through the hallway to the stairs so he could go up to his room.

"Billy!" Cindy shook her head. "He hasn't been the same since . . . "

"Oh, it takes time to get over something like that. I remember when this stray cat scratched me. I was stupid enough to go for it. It got infected and I had to go to the doctor. Been a little timid about cats ever since." Cindy nodded, but he felt she wasn't in complete agreement.

"Come on in; come on in. Can I get you a cup of coffee or . . . "

"No thanks, Cindy. I was just wondering . . . did Dick confirm what he originally believed happened?"

"Confirm? Oh. Well, he didn't go out there looking for the animal. There are so many of them, anyway, but the doctor seemed to think that what he thought was probably what happened."

"Your older boy . . . "

"Bobby?"

"Yeah, he wasn't with Billy at the time?"

"No. He's not home from school yet, anyway. He had to run some errands for Dick. They're building a deck for the Millers."

"Nice feeling when your son works right beside you. So," he said, not sure of where he was going with his questions, "Billy was out by himself that day?"

"Yeah, but he won't go anywhere alone now," she said sadly.

"Understandable. I tell you, those raccoons . . . "

"He won't let go of his story," she said quickly, as

187

though she just had to get it out. "And he's been having nightmares. I have to leave the light on in his room."

"His story? A lot different from what Dick thinks, is it?" She nearly laughed and then a thought occurred to her.

"You know," she said, "maybe if you spoke to him, being a policeman and all, maybe he would . . . "

"Sure, be glad to," he said.

"Thanks." She went to the bottom of the stairway and called up to Billy. He came to the top of the stairs slowly and looked down at them. Eddie didn't know the boy, but he did note what he thought to be an unusual timidity. He looked pale and small, like a child who was constantly beaten. "Officer Morris wants to talk to you, Billy. Come on down."

"No, I don't want to," he said and turned and ran back to his room.

"Billy!"

"Hold it, Cindy," Eddie said. "Let me see what I can do." He started up the stairs.

"First room on the left," she said.

When he reached Billy's doorway, he paused and looked in. Billy was sitting on his bed fingering some toy soldiers. Eddie knocked on the doorjamb.

"Can I come in?" he asked. Billy shrugged and continued to look down at his toy soldiers. Eddie walked in and looked around the room. "Nice room," he said. "Oh, you've got an Atari, huh? My son Carl's got that other one, what's it called . . . "

"Intellivision?"

"Yeah, I think that's it. You have Naval War?"

"No."

"I like that one, but I don't get to use it much," Eddie said and put on a look of disgust. Billy smiled. Eddie walked to the window across from the bed and looked down at the O'Neils' backyard. He could see The Oaks looming across the field. It looked gray and

188

quiet, yet somehow ominous as well. Then he saw the O'Neils' dog chained beside its doghouse. "Oh, so there's your dog."

"Captain," Billy said.

"Captain, huh? Nice dog."

"My father says we got to keep him chained up on account of . . . on account of what happened."

"He does, huh? Well, I'm sure he doesn't want any more problems."

"Captain doesn't want to be chained up."

"Maybe it's for his own good, though. This time of the year, they go off chasing so many animals, especially raccoons. Some dogs just have it in them to go after coons. I had a dog like that once."

"It wasn't a coon," Billy said. He said it so defiantly that Eddie understood the boy was tired of repeating his tale.

"Oh, it wasn't?"

"No." Billy looked back at his toy soldiers.

"Yeah, well you know when people are in a dangerous situation, they often get confused. I see it all the time in police work, you know," he said and Billy looked up with interest. "Like when someone sees a bad accident or maybe a fight . . . things often get mixed up. It takes time and careful investigation to straighten it all up."

"I'm not mixed up," Billy said, "because I saw it before."

"Before? Before what?"

"Before he hurt me," he said, holding up his arm for emphasis. "He was out there and Captain was barking at him and I looked out the window and saw him."

"Saw who?"

Billy snapped his mouth closed and looked down again. Cindy O'Neil had come to the bedroom doorway and stood just outside, trying to be inconspicuous.

"If it's something unusual, maybe I should know. I

189

have to keep the police department on alert, you know."

Billy looked up and searched Eddie's face for sincerity. Eddie kept his look as stern as he could.

"It was an E.T.," Billy said. For a moment Eddie continued to stare at him.

"An E.T.?"

"Like in the movie."

"Oh. Oh, yeah, yeah. Why don't you describe him to me?" Eddie said and took a small note pad out of his back pocket. Billy's eyes widened when Eddie clicked his pen and sat on the little chair across from him. "Now remember what I told you about people getting confused, so give me only what you're sure you remember."

"OK," Billy said. His eyes grew smaller as he focused on his memory. Eddie was both amused and impressed with the boy's determination. "He was only about up to here on me," Billy said, pointing to his chest. "But his hair was down to his shoulders. He had big eyes and a funny nose that moved like a rabbit's."

"Rabbit's?" Eddie said, looking up.

"Uh huh." Then Billy smiled. "He wasn't wearing any clothes either."

"What did he do to you?"

Billy stopped smiling and pressed his lower lip under his teeth. His eyes took on the inner terror as he ran his left hand softly over his right arm.

"He . . . he grabbed me and scratched me with his fingers."

"His fingers?"

"Uh huh."

"Was there any hair on his arms?"

"Nope."

"Did he make any noise?"

"Noise?"

"When he scratched you. Like a bark or a growl or . . ."

"He screamed like a baby," Billy said quickly. "Is he gonna come back here?"

Eddie shook his head. "No, no. Why do you think he grabbed your arm?" Billy looked guilty. "Did you do something to him?"

"I just reached toward him."

"Oh." Eddie shot a glance toward the doorway. "Did you tell your parents that?" Billy shook his head. "So you must have scared him, huh?"

"I don't know. I kept telling him I wanted to be friends."

"Yeah, but maybe he hadn't seen anything like you before. Don't you think that might be it?"

"Maybe," Billy said. "Maybe he went back to space, huh?" he asked hopefully.

"Oh I'm sure that's what he did. Maybe he had gotten lost in the first place and his parents found him. I wouldn't worry about him anymore. He's probably telling stories about you."

Billy started to smile, but then remembered something else.

"Captain still barks a lot at night."

"There are a lot of things for him to bark at, especially this time of the year." Eddie closed his notebook. "That's why your father is right about keeping him close to the house."

Billy nodded and Eddie stood up. He walked over to him and put his hand on the little boy's head.

"There's nothing to worry about, Champ. You're safe now. I'll report this to all the other policemen and they'll be on the lookout anyway, OK?"

"Uh huh."

"Tell me one more thing, Billy. You didn't see any pet rabbits around, did you? I mean, one with a leash or a collar?"

191

"Pet rabbits? No. I saw rabbits, though."

"OK. Best thing now is for you to forget it, but just to make you feel safe when you're outside . . . " Eddie snapped the whistle off his belt chain and handed it to Billy. "This is an official police whistle. If you see anything that scares you, just blow it, and anyone who hears it will know."

"Thanks," Billy said, eyeing it like it was the most valuable gift he had ever received.

"I'll be seeing you, OK?"

"OK."

"Don't go blowing that in the house now."

"I won't." He thought for a moment. "Maybe I should go outside and test it."

"Maybe you should," Eddie said and walked out. Cindy greeted him in the hall.

"That was very nice, Eddie. I'm sure it's going to help," she said. The words were no sooner out of her mouth when Billy ran by. "Button your jacket," she called as he went down the stairs. They laughed.

"He had quite a scare. I'm sure that's why he came up with such a story. The way he described the scream makes me think Dick's right. Those raccoons can sound like little babies."

"Sure." They stopped at the doorway. "Why did you ask him about pet rabbits?"

"Oh, that's what I was checking on earlier today. Cy Baum had a problem with pet rabbits . . . someone stealing them, hurting them, that sort of thing."

"Terrible."

"Yeah. OK." He stepped out.

"Thanks again," she said.

He got into the car and drove off, gazing only perfunctorily at The Oaks as he passed it on the way home. Even so, the image of it set against a darkening gray sky lingered in his mind now as he remained in his vehicle in his driveway.

Barbara opened the front door of the house and

stepped toward him. He turned and looked at her almost as though he were looking through her.

"What are you going to do?" she asked. "Sit in your car until supper?"

"What?" He smiled at himself and got out. "Watchin' me, huh?"

"Carl pointed you out. He said Dad's just sitting in his car for the longest time." Her face turned to concern as he approached. "Trouble?"

"I don't know. Probably not. I'll tell you about it later," he said and put his arm around her waist. Then he kissed her, the kiss lasting a little longer than usual. When they parted, she looked at him askance.

"There's something bothering you, Eddie Morris."

"I'm hungry, that's all. What's for supper since you're using it to tempt me inside?"

"I am not, even though it happens to be one of your favorite gourmet meals. I just got into the mood," she explained. He stopped at the doorway.

"What?"

"Rabbit," she said.

Cy Baum checked his basement door again. The original lock that had been sufficient all these years had suddenly looked puny to him and to Hilda, so he went downtown to Mac's hardware store and bought a hasp and a padlock. Naturally, there was a card game going on in the rear of the store. When it was interrupted so that Mac could get up to serve him, all of Mac's cronies became interested in what Cy wanted and why. There's no need for a newspaper in this hamlet, he thought. His story set off a whole slew of "I remembers," and it was nearly a half hour before he got out of there.

He didn't like having to double up on his door locks. It made him feel like those old people he saw on the television news. Some of them had four or five locks on their apartment doors in the city; some had taken to having watchdogs and installing alarm systems. "It's a helluva way to grow old," he said and he felt thankful that he still lived in an area where such crimes against the elderly were practically nonexistent. He couldn't remember ever feeling insecure in his own home.

Now, here he was testing the firmness of two locks on his basement door. He looked back at Gina and the rabbit and shook his head. Once again, with a new leash, the rabbit was tied securely to the post. Gina had placed a small plate of lettuce in front of him and stood by watching him nibble peacefully on his food. The animal looked content. Perhaps the bizarre incidents were over, Cy thought.

"You think Daddy's going to let me take him back with us, Grandpa?"

"I think your grandmother's going to convince him of that," Cy said and laughed. "OK," he said. "I think it's time we went back upstairs now. You've got to wash up for supper. He'll be all right."

Gina nodded, knelt down, and stroked the rabbit a few times. Then she turned and headed up the stairway. Cy went to the leash and tested it one more time. His eyesight wasn't spectacular anymore, but it was remarkably good for a man of his age. He never suffered from cataracts or glaucoma, and he hadn't even taken to wearing reading glasses until he hit sixty-five. That's why he often wondered why Arnie had such bad vision. He blamed it on Hilda's side of the family. She did have a younger brother who was terribly nearsighted.

Anyway, it was probably because of the angle he was at or the way the light reflected off the floor, but suddenly, he saw something he hadn't seen before—the outline of a footprint in a dusty area. Of course, he thought his eyes were playing tricks on him, so he took out his handkerchief and wiped them. Gina had left the basement door opened upstairs, so he could hear her and Hilda setting the table for dinner. Gina was telling Hilda how she helped her mother with the housework whenever the maid failed to show.

Cy put his handkerchief back into his pocket and then knelt down beside the post and the rabbit to study the print on the floor. There was no doubt about it—it looked like a tiny human foot. It was too small to be Gina's. And yet, maybe it wasn't a human foot, he thought; maybe it was a monkey's. Could someone in the area have a pet monkey that got loose?

He decided he wouldn't mention it to Hilda, but he would call Eddie Morris in the morning and have him come up to look at it, too. Hilda wouldn't sleep tonight if he told her what he found, he thought. Even he would have trouble sleeping. He stood up and looked around the basement. Nothing else was disturbed; they had checked every nook and cranny. It was safe and secure from whatever was out there.

To be sure, though, he went back to the cellar door and tested it one more time. It didn't budge and there was no way for anything to slip through. Just before he flicked the light switch, he looked back at the floor by the post and shook his head. What a crazy thing. What did it all mean?

He thought about the story Eddie Morris had told them when he brought back the rabbit—how he had found it and how Mary Oaks had reacted. He thought about the Oaks girl he rarely saw and he thought about the strange, deep darkness that was always around The Oaks when he went by it during his walks.

He had no real proof and no real reason to make any conclusions, but he thought, if this situation ever got solved, somehow it would have something to do with that crazy Oaks woman.

"I've got a mind to go over there and talk to her myself," he muttered, "and see what she might tell me."

"But then why would she talk to me, if she didn't talk to a policeman?"

Hilda interrupted the dialogue he was having with himself when she called him up for supper.

Even so, he might just go over there, he thought. He might just do it.

TEN

The rain began slowly in a mist and then increased and thickened into what was to become an all-night downpour. Although he couldn't see it, because there were no windows in the basement, he could hear it against the upper walls of the house. He didn't know it as rain; he had yet to see and experience rain. But he knew it through his other senses. The dampness crept through the walls as always and cloaked him in a garment of cold air, penetrating his skin and reaching down into his muscles and flesh to make his bones shudder. He curled up in his box and drew the raggedy blanket over him as he waited for his supper. His built-in clock told him it was nearly time for the creature to appear with his food.

Sure enough, it was only a little while longer before he heard her moving toward the basement door above him. He honed in on her footsteps, and his image of her was so vivid, he could practically see her through the ceiling. He heard the click of the padlock and the door open. The light from upstairs unraveled down the stairs and settled over the wall and floor at the base of the steps. He widened his eyes expectantly and waited. When she snapped on the cellar light, the brightness was a shock to him and, for a few moments, he blinked rapidly and shaded his face from the abrupt illumination. He heard her start down. By the way she stamped her feet on the steps, he knew she was going to be more vicious and meaner than usual.

When she made the turn at the foot of the stairs and started in his direction, he noticed that she looked quite different. Her hair was loose and strands curled into the air as though they were electrified. Under the sharp light, the contrast between her face and her hair was that much greater. It had the effect of making her skin even whiter, washing away every blemish, every color. She looked vapid and chalky like a faded manikin.

He saw that the strap of punishment was tied loosely around her waist, the two ends of it dangling like the heads of dead snakes. Her arms were extended stiffly, so she could hold the tray of food forward and away from her body. She acted as though she were carrying something contaminated. There was a small, lit candle on the tray. She hadn't done that for a long time, and he was even more afraid because of it.

She held her head stiffly as she held her arms. Her eyes were locked in that hateful gaze that combined fear and anger. When she moved into a shadow, the tiny candlelight cast a sickly yellow sheen over her face, making her look thinner and more skeletonlike. Her sallow cheeks were concave, which resulted in puffing out her lips and making her mouth look swollen. All of her features were exaggerated to him. The sharper bone structure caused her eyes to become even deeper and darker. Her entire demeanor terrified him.

He began to whimper before she was close. He embraced himself even more protectively and tightened his fetal position, squeezing his legs so hard against his stomach, that they brought pain into his abdomen. At first, it was as though she didn't see him; it was as though she were looking through him or beyond him. Her gaze was frozen and her head unmoving. She was carrying herself like a blind woman or someone locked in a hypnotic trance. He did not know these things; he simply sensed her changes instinctively and reacted to them. The only image of comparison that he had was that of a stick, hard and straight.

As soon as she knelt down beside him to place the tray on the floor, he held his breath and tightened his fingers into tiny fists, pressing his long nails into his own palms so hard, he actually brought blood to the surfaces. Finally, she seemed to notice him. She reached forward mechanically and took a fistful of his hair into her hand, jerking his head up and forward so abruptly, she nearly tore his neck. He started to scream, but swallowed it quickly with the pain. He knew that such a reaction could only make her more violent.

With her other hand, she lifted the candle in its holder and brought it dangerously near his face. He could feel the small heat threatening to singe his skin. She used the tiny light to search his face and what she apparently saw, satisfied her. The wry smile took form and she nodded slightly. He wanted to take a deep breath, but he was afraid to make the slightest movement.

"Demon," she said, "Thou shalt see no victory in my house." Her smile widened. "Glory to God in the highest . . . "

He continued to do nothing, but she held him firmly. For a moment the memory of the little boy's bleeding arm came to him. He remembered his feeling of power afterward and he thought of reaching out to do the same thing to her arm; but his fear of her was so powerful, he couldn't budge. Instead, he hung there limply in her grasp and waited for her to release him. It seemed as though she never would, because she continued to glare at him and use the candle to search his face for some clue, some reaction. He barely moved his lips, but his tongue pressed forward, almost as if it

199

had a mind of its own, and the tip of it emerged like the tip of a snake's tongue. That seemed to satisfy her, for she smiled and nodded more emphatically.

She placed the candle back on the tray and quenched its flame with her hand. That amazed him, because fire was something he had always feared and she suffered no pain. When she released him, he fell back to the floor of his box quickly, but his relief was short-lived. She stood up and untied the strap of punishment from her waist.

He cringed and pressed his back against the rear of the makeshift bed, when she folded the belt and stood over him, dangling it ominously. He closed his eyes in anticipation of the blows, but they did not come. When he opened them again, she was looking upward, her head back so hard, that her Adam's apple thinned and whitened her skin to the point of tearing it.

Looking up at her, he thought that she began to swell—her shoulders rose and her body seemed to stretch toward the ceiling. In his eyes she had grown gigantic. Suddenly, she raised her arms and clasped her hands above her head, and then, after a quick series of gasps, she chanted, "Amen, Amen, Amen."

After that, she lowered her arms to her sides slowly and deflated, until she appeared her normal size to him again. The belt dangled loosely beside her. Then she jerked her head to the side and up, as though she heard something. Without so much as looking down at him one more time, she turned and walked back to the stairway. He heard her go up the steps slowly, her ascent much softer than her descent. After a few more moments, the light switch was thrown to off, the basement door was closed, and the padlock was locked. Despite her soft gait, he still heard her footsteps above him. But they disappeared so quickly, it was as though she stepped onto the air. Then, all was quiet, except for the terrible beating of his heart and the tiny sound of his own puppylike whimper.

Although the food was there, he had lost all appetite. The dampness had depressed him, and her terrifying appearance had so tightened his stomach and twisted his insides, that he felt weak and nauseous. He waited for himself to calm down. Also, he wanted to be certain she was not coming back. Satisfied he was somewhat safe, he rose slowly to a sitting position. His eyes, now used to the dark again, made out shapes and objects quickly. He could think only of escape and crawled out of his box to go to the wall.

He worked methodically and extra quietly to remove the rocks and create his opening. The breeze carried some of the rain into him, but despite that and despite the thick darkness, a darkness that was even blacker than his own, he wasn't dissuaded. The odor of the damp earth and wet grasses was not unpleasant to him, but the feel of the cooler, rain-soaked ground was somewhat shocking to his feet and hands. He hesitated at the house. The rain was driving at him because of the wind, and he was quickly soaked. Even with his good night vision, he was unable to make out the familiar pathways, so, like any other wild creature of the bush, he relied on his power of scent to lead him.

Without any real foresight or understanding of the significances in things, he could not envision that his trip would be in vain, that the little girl would not be outside, and that he wouldn't be able to see her. All he could think of was her beautiful, soft hair and her happy laugh. Confident that he had the power to bring her to him, he went quickly to the garbage can to retrieve the rabbit, so he could bring it back to her.

A skunk was there, feeding off some scraps that Faith had not picked up in the morning. When it heard him, it arched its back and studied him with suspicion. For the moment it seemed satisfied that he was no threat. Indeed, he had no interest in it or anything that would interfere with his plan. It took a few steps back and continued to eye him carefully, as he went to the first can. When he lifted the lid off and pulled himself to a standing position, the skunk arched its back again and prepared to douse him. He reached into the can blindly, searching for the rabbit, but all he felt was garbage. Frustrated, he turned the can on its side abruptly, its contents spilling out again, cans rattling, bottles shattering. The action and the noise frightened the skunk, so it shot a stream in his direction. Most of it hit the can, but some splattered onto his face and upper body.

The stench was beyond belief. It drove him back on all fours, scampering for safety and whining like a stricken dog. The skunk trotted off into the darkness and all was quiet for a few moments. He rubbed his face and shoulders where he had been hit by the odorous liquid, but that only spread the stench to his hands and every other place he touched himself. After inhaling it directly a little longer, he began to dry-heave, squatting there in the wet darkness. The acid taste in his throat burned him. Instinctively, he knew to roll himself over and over in the wet grass. The odor never left him, but it became tolerable. At that point he went back to look for the rabbit.

He thought that he had checked the wrong can, so he turned the other one over with the same result. Surveying the mess, the reality of the rabbit's being gone occurred to him. He sat there like a cat that had lost its kittens and whined and moaned in frustration. The rabbit was important to his plan and now, with it gone and the rain coming down harder, all the world was as dark and as cold as it seemed. He didn't know how to deal with this disappointment, so he sat there for the longest time, pawing the ground around him and whimpering like a child who has been denied a toy. When his tantrum subsided, he swallowed his sobs and crawled forward, still determined to salvage something from this terrible night.

It vaguely occurred to him that the rabbit might have escaped and gone back to the basement of the other house. He began to picture the girl down there with it. That picture with all its possibilities drove him forward, and he ignored the rain, the mud, the thorny bushes that caught him. He went onward, deeper into the darkness, sniffing and moaning like some hybrid creature born from the marriage of the rain and the darkness. The downpour swept over him in invisible, cold, wet sheets, washing away the mud and dulling the odor of skunk. Out of shelter in the field, it was difficult for him to see. His eyes were opened in slits and his long strands of black hair stuck to his shoulders and neck like charcoaled lines. His naked body slipped in and out of the dark places, his toes digging deeply and firmly into the wet earth.

Sometimes he slid like a snake; sometimes he crept like a bobcat, moving so quietly, it was as though he crawled on a shelf of air. He never paused in his pursuit of his vision, until the house came into full view, its well-lighted and warm-looking windows tempting him like the promise of pleasure and happiness he sought so desperately. Then and only then did he stop to wipe the mud and water from his face. His breathing quickened with his anticipation of excitement. He turned his head slightly to see if he could catch the sound of the little girl's voice, but the rain was relentless. He would have to get closer.

When he entered the lighted part of the lawn that glowed from the illumination of the windows, he emerged from the darkness like a bright jewel cast on a sheet of black velvet. His wet skin shone, his eyes glowed, and his naked little form wove itself in and out of the shadows like a string of radiation, glowing with beauty and danger, and tying the pockets of darkness together into a fabric of mystery and terror.

He was at the house. Not the storm nor the blackened world nor the frustrations of travel had prevented him from getting here. Satisfied and even more determined, he made his way toward the basement door to fulfill his expectations. He was a spoiled child who would tolerate no more denials.

But denial came when the basement door would not budge. He remembered how he had opened it before and he went through the process again and again, each time with no success. His frustration turned into anger. He tugged and pulled and finally clawed at the door, but all to no avail. Despondent and dejected, he sat on the steps while the rain came down on him, pounding his body with a ferocity that had begun to frighten him.

He scampered back to find shelter under Cy Baum's rear porch. A sudden streak of lightning brought a high-pitched scream out of him, which frightened him almost as much as the thunder that followed. He tore away enough of the wooden webbed porch skirt to be able to shove his body through it and settle himself securely within. Now shivering, he embraced himself and squatted on the hard-packed earth. Gradually feeling more protected, he calmed down until he loosened the grip he had around himself and relaxed in a sitting position.

He heard something scurry only a few feet beside him and he caught sight of a field mouse. Simply because of his frustration and anger, he lunged forward and seized it just before it escaped through the wooden webbing.

He held the squirming creature firmly in his hands, really uncertain about what he would do with it. For now he enjoyed its struggle and his power over it. In the inky darkness, he was unable to make out many details about it. He pressed its tiny legs firmly against its torso and put his thumb under its head, pushing the head back as far as it would go. He could feel its little heartbeat and, for the moment, he was filled with the wonder of life and curiosity about its source. The harder he squeezed, the more frantic the mouse became and the faster its heart beat.

Before he snapped its neck, he envisioned the big creature standing over him, her strap raised ominously. For a few seconds he saw himself the way she saw him—as small and as helpless as the mouse, his heart beating just as rapidly. The image made him clench his teeth and, without even thinking, he pushed the mouse's head back too far, until there was a tiny click. As soon as that happened, the animal became limp in his hand. When he took his thumb from its head, the head slumped over his fingers.

Its stillness and limpness annoyed him now, so he cast it deeper into the depths of the back porch's foundation. Then he sat there and listened to the rain tap on the wooden slats above him and the roof runoff trickle down the gutter beside the porch. As he looked out at the darkness, he realized now that the girl would not come out of the house; and, since he was unable to get into the basement, he would not hear her footsteps or have even that small contact with her.

His sadness made him aware of his fatigue and he lowered his body to the hard-packed cool earth. The rain continued to pound monotonously on the porch floor above him. He could see the trees silhouetted against the darker and deeper blackness. They moved in a way that frightened him, their leafy branches turning and twisting reluctantly in the wind. He felt some kind of a struggle going on around him, and he was hypnotized by the awkward movements of the trees and the constant sound of the rain. He became drowsy.

When he closed his eyes, it never occurred to him that he might fall asleep here. That kind of foresight was beyond him. Like any of the other small creatures that were around him, he acted on impulse and lived for the moment. And, for the moment, he was tired; so he folded his hands beneath his head and curled his body up tightly. He whimpered and shuddered and sniffed the damp, cool earth. The odor of the skunk still lingered over him. He turned his face into his arms to avoid it. He missed his raggedy blanket, but he thought so hard about it, that he imagined it was over him.

It was only a few more moments before he fell into a deep sleep.

When Faith awoke in her father's room, she was confused. It took her a moment to remember where she was and how she had gotten there. She sat up quickly and looked at the boarded windows and the locked door. How long had she slept? Was it still afternoon or was it night? She had no watch, so she slipped off the bed and went to one of the boarded windows to peer through a crack. There was no light; darkness had fallen, and, from the sound of things, it was raining hard. She brushed her hair back and walked to the door, listening first and then trying the knob. She turned it slowly and pulled, but the door wouldn't budge. It was still locked.

Oh God, she thought, looking about the room again, how long is she going to keep me here? She stood there, undecided as to what to do next. She was thirsty and she had to go to the bathroom. Bringing herself close to the crack between the door and the jamb, she called for Mary, softly at first and then louder and louder, until she sounded close to hysterical.

"Mom? Mary? Can you hear me? Please. Mom. MOTHER! Please. MOTHER!"

She tugged on the knob and pounded on the door. Then she waited to see if what she had done would bring any reaction. But there wasn't the slightest sound from without. Nothing. All she heard was her own heavy breathing. She thought she sounded like a terminally ill patient in her last hours.

The room looked so small and so tightly closed. She could feel panic setting in. She tried to ignore it by forcing herself to think of other things, but it was almost impossible to do so. What was it Mary had told her before she locked her in here . . . prayer and fast; prayer and fast? Mary meant it, but for how long? Would it last throughout the night? Throughout another day? Mary had often confined her to the house, but never to only a single, locked room. And she always had things to do . . . things to read, the radio, her few games and toys.

Now, she thought, she could appreciate what the baby was going through locked in the basement all this time. Yet, the baby had no comparisons. He had never known any other world. That is, until now. The thought reminded her of her original purpose when she had come home from school. Mary didn't understand; Mary had to give her a chance to talk and explain what she thought.

She turned back to the door and immediately raised her voice.

"MOTHER. I HAVE TO TELL YOU SOMETHING IMPORTANT. PLEASE, LISTEN TO ME!"

Not a sound. She had been deserted. For all she knew, Mary was listening to one of her programs or sleeping in the easy chair below. She looked around again. She had to urinate and the ache in her groin from holding it in was intensifying. Then she spotted the old chamber pot just under the foot of the bed. Mary had made provisions. God, Faith thought, that meant she really was going to keep her in here for a while.

She went forward and took out the pot, using it as she assumed her great grandparents and grandparents had. The two outhouses were still standing behind the house, and Mary had explained to her why they needed chamber pots. Even so, she felt a little self-conscious and silly about it. But, the relief was good and necessary. Afterward, she pushed the pot under the bed more completely, so she wouldn't have to think about it.

What was she going to do in here? She began to pace about the room like a caged animal, stopping every once in a while to listen for Mary. Finally, she decided to look for something, anything she could use to break out of the room. She went to the dresser and looked into the drawers, but they were all completely empty. There was absolutely nothing in the closet, not a hanger, not even any real dust. Mary must have been cleaning this room from time to time, she thought. But why? Did she know she was going to use it for this purpose someday?

She went back to the windows and ran her hands gently over the boards. She tried getting the tips of her fingers between them and the walls, but the nails had been driven in too tightly and held the wood firmly against the window casings. When she turned and panned the small room again, she realized she really had nothing but the Bible, her bed, and the chamber pot. What was she going to do?

Feeling more of a sense of anger now, she got on her hands and knees and began pounding the floor. Mary would have to hear that, she thought. She did it until her hands grew sore and numb again, the redness running down the sides and over the wrists. Then she took off her shoes and used the heels as a tool to continue the noise. The longer she did it without any success, the more frantic and angrier she became. At one point, she threw her shoes at the door and crumpled up in tears. All of it brought nothing. Mary was shut away where either she couldn't or wouldn't hear her.

She began to shake from the frustration. This was

208

like being tied down. She couldn't stand the closeness; she felt stifled. It was getting hard to breathe. She realized most of this came from her imagination, but she couldn't help it, and she could no longer hold back the growing sense of panic.

Still on her knees, she clasped her hands in prayer. With her head down, her eyes closed, she began.

"Oh God," she said, "Mary's God, please help me. Make her let me out. I'll be a good girl. I will. Please. Have mercy."

After she uttered the words, she waited in anticipation, almost as if she expected God would answer her directly or the door would simply fly open. But there was only that silence, that terribly deep, haunting silence.

She stood up slowly, a sense of great defeat pervading, and backed up to the bed. She sat there in a daze, waiting. Minutes passed, but she did not move. She didn't cry and she didn't speak. When she raised her head and looked around again, the realization that she was in her father's old room became more intense. Up until now, she had been somewhat successful in keeping that fact subdued, but she felt that she was losing control of everything, especially her once imprisoned fears.

This room was always out of bounds for her. When she was a little girl, she thought it was a place of great heat. Mary made her think so. "The Devil's been there many times," she told her, "and any place that the Devil's been often is scalding to a good person. If you walked in there barefooted, your soles would burn, and if you ever slept in there, you would be visited by demons and ghoulish things. Sometimes," she added, bringing her face close and lowering her voice to that tone and volume that made her words even more frightening, "I hear them. I wake in the night and I hear them. They dance around your father's drunken body," she said.

As Faith grew older, she thought the images Mary drew up were wild and crazy, but she had been successful. No matter how much her father wanted her to come to him in that room, she resisted. Even Mary wouldn't go into it in those days, and that impressed Faith.

Why did she lock her in it now, then? Did she think her old stories still held true? I have taken off my shoes, yet my feet don't burn and the floor isn't hot, she thought. Is that because I am a sinner?

An idea came to her. It was as wild as some of Mary's ideas, but maybe it would work; maybe it would bring Mary to the room and get her to open the door.

She went back to the door and listened. As far as she could tell, the radio wasn't going. Mary was either asleep or praying. There had to be a good chance she would hear her, even if she didn't want to. It was worth a try, at least.

"MOTHER," she screamed, "PLEASE. IT'S HOT! MY FEET ARE BURNING. I'M BEING SCALDED. OH! MOTHER. I CAN'T STAND ON THE FLOOR. THE WALLS ARE GLOWING."

She paused to hear Mary come up the stairs, but what happened instead shocked her.

Mary whispered through the door. Mary had been there all the time, waiting and listening, practically holding her breath, so that Faith would not know it. Her response came immediately. There was no doubt about it. She had heard everything.

"You must pray," she said. "Pray until God hears you. Pray to his glory and mercy."

"Mother, Mother. Oh Mother, please, listen to me. Listen."

"Pray," Mary said. "I want to hear you pray. I won't listen to anything else, until you pray."

"Mother . . . " Faith paused for a moment and pulled her head back from the door. What was she doing . . . talking to her mother through a crack? This was what Faith had been doing with the baby. She thought she felt her mother's breath, too. The comparison was too shocking. It left her speechless for a few seconds. Then she came back at Mary with a flood of words.

"Mother, it's the baby. I have something terrible to tell you. I've got to get out of here. We're in danger. It's important. Please, let me out. Please." Faith held back her concrete thoughts. She believed that the only way to get her mother to open that door was to appeal to her curiosity. She waited in hope, but Mary was relentless and trapped in her own train of thought.

"Our Father who art in heaven . . . "

"Mother!"

"Hallowed be Thy name. Thy kingdom come. Thy will . . . "

"MOTHER!" she screamed. She attacked the door in an hysterical rage, pounding at it, kicking at it with her shoeless feet, forgetting the pain, until it became excruciating. Then she slammed at the door with her arms and her body and then banged her head against it, behaving like someone in the throes of an epileptic fit. The outburst exhausted her again and she crumpled to the floor, sliding down the door until she was completely seated, her arms bruised, her knuckles bleeding, and her toes sending up such pain, she felt certain she had broken one or two. She tried to catch her breath.

Mary was squatting down on the other side. All throughout Faith's outburst, she had been reciting the Lord's Prayer. She continued it.

"Our Father who art in heaven, hallowed be Thy name . . . "

Faith groaned.

"Thy kingdom come; Thy will be done . . . "

Sliding, rather than crawling, Faith pulled and pushed herself from the door and made her way back to the bed. When she got herself back onto it, she lay back and stared up at the ceiling. Pain telegraphed from all parts of her body. Her moans did nothing to bring relief. It was painful even to cry. She turned over to bury her face in the pillow to smother her sobs. But she could still hear Mary's whispering through the door, so she took the pillow and placed it over her head, pulling the sides down over her ears and pressing hard against them. It was as though Mary could look through the door and see her doing it, however, because she raised her voice at that moment. Over and over she recited the Lord's Prayer.

Finally, Faith either passed out or fell asleep, because when she opened her eyes again, Mary's voice was gone and all was back to that deep, haunting silence. She lay there in a daze, feeling helpless and alone. It was at that moment that she remembered Bobby was going to come to her tonight.

Bobby! His name sounded like the anthem of hope. Maybe he would come; maybe he would search for her until he found her. Maybe she would be saved after all. That thought was all she had to fight the heavy silence and the faces of bad dreams that hovered in every corner of her father's old room.

ELEVEN

Eddie Morris put his feet up on the hassock and sat back on the couch in the den. Tommy and Carl were playing video tennis, and Eddie stared at the television set as though hypnotized by the small, glowing ball bouncing back and forth over the two-dimensional court. Susie was seated beside them, her legs folded neatly under her body. She cradled the new Barbie doll they had bought for her fourth birthday two weeks ago. Although she had no mother-infant relationship in the house to emulate, she was a good example of the impact television had on the preschool-age mind. Her mimicry included lines about diapers, baby powders, and oils that she had heard while watching commercials. Whenever the boys' voices rose after a particularly close play, she would look up; otherwise, her attention was fixed on her doll.

Barbara lingered in the kitchen. No words were yet exchanged between her and Eddie about dinner, yet he knew that she was let down by his less than enthusiastic reaction to her gourmet meal. He ate lethargically and he didn't ask for seconds. Even consumption of the homemade apple pie seemed forced. Of course, the children were unaffected by it all, hardly aware of Eddie's subdued mood. When it was over, Barbara moved about mechanically, insisting that no one remain behind to help her clean up.

As Eddie sat there watching the boys play their video game, he was reminded of Billy O'Neil. There was something in that boy's face, some look that haunted him now. It was as though Billy had seen something or learned something before his time to learn it. Eddie remembered a similar look on Vietnamese children who had been exposed to the gruesomeness of war. Sometimes he thought of them as freakish and distorted, a new kind of humanity—old people placed in the bodies of children. Eddie kept telling himself that Billy's look was a result of great fear, just as the Vietnamese children were weaned on death and destruction and reflected that in their faces. Why couldn't he just ascribe Billy's situation to a terrible, freakish accident and leave it at that? He thought that if events had been reversed, he probably could.

But first there was that strange situation with Cy Baum's pet rabbits, and then his meeting with Mary Oaks and his discovery of that rabbit. This was the preface to his interview with Billy and it left an air of eerie uncertainty about everything on the country road.

If the kid didn't live next to The Oaks, he thought, I probably wouldn't have given this a second thought. But what was there to think about now? What could there be? A little boy's wild story about some extraterrestrial creature?

Barbara's entrance interrupted his thoughts.

"Don't you boys have any homework tonight?"

"In a minute, Mom," Carl said.

"Not in a minute. Now. You do this after you do your homework, not before it," she snapped.

"Let's go, boys," Eddie said. He slapped his hands together, and the boys groaned and shut down their game. Susie took the clue from the discipline and announced that it was time for her doll to go to sleep.

All three children left the den obediently, with Barbara standing back, her arms folded across her chest. She looked like a prison matron.

"You're tough," Eddie chided kiddingly, but she didn't smile.

"Someone's got to do it," she said and began clearing away the toy parts.

"I'm sorry about not being much of a ball of fire tonight," he said. She didn't turn around.

"Are you going to tell me what it's all about or . . . "

"The trouble is I don't know myself what it's all about. Whenever I think of explaining it to somebody, I feel silly."

"I'm not somebody, Eddie. I've come home and told you a lot of stuff that wouldn't be much to anyone else, but because you're my husband, I don't feel embarrassed about making too much of little things. If we can't share our little aggravations . . . "

"Oh, it's not a question of that," he said. "I'd love to share my aggravations with you." The way he said it made her smile. "I mean . . . see, I don't know what I mean."

"Just start at the beginning and let me be the judge," she said and took a seat beside him on the couch.

"All right," he said. "I was coming back from doing a morning patrol, just routine stuff, when I stopped at Cy Baum's. He was out there with his granddaughter, and Cy and I . . . well . . . "

"I understand. Go ahead."

"He was telling me about these pet rabbits he bought for her. He bought them one at a time. The first one was mysteriously freed from its cage outside. It disappeared, so he bought her a second. It was freed and its neck was broken."

"Oh, how terrible. A prank?"

"At first, I thought so."

"What do you mean, at first?"

"Well, he buys her a third, and this time he puts it

safely in the basement. Or, at least, he thought it was safe. She went down to get it while I was there and came back to report it was gone. We investigated and found the leash chewed through, the rabbit gone. The door wasn't locked so . . . ''

"Chewed through?"

"Yeah. Very unusual for a rabbit to do something like that."

"And open the door to leave. Smart rabbit."

"Right. Anyway, the first suspects we come up with are the Cooper kids, who live nearby."

"Terrors, both of them. Mildred Wilson has them in her class, and she's close to murdering them."

"But I've concluded they didn't do any of it."

"Oh."

"Cy mentioned Mary Oaks' daughter."

"I had her in a class last year."

"Really?" He paused. "Tell me about her."

"Not much to tell. She was very shy, terribly withdrawn. I don't think she has one friend. None of the other kids seems to take to her. She did good, neat work most of the time. A polite girl, no trouble, but . . . ''

"But what?"

"I don't know. I guess I would describe her as someone who seems constantly afraid. Her mother never came to parents' night. I've never met her."

"I have. Knew her a long time ago, too. Religious zealot. A fanatical missionary . . . drove Tom Oaks into adultery."

"Oh come on, Eddie."

"I mean it. Everyone says so. Anyhow, I go to see her to see if anything's been happening around her place."

"And?"

"This is one of those parts I can't explain. She's not belligerent exactly, she's . . . she's . . . ''

"What?"

"She's like someone in another world who resented being made to pay attention to this one. I don't know. Sounds stupid no matter how I put it. Anyway, the main thing is I find the missing rabbit, leash and all, there."

"In her house?"

"No, right nearby. I suppose it was possible for the rabbit to make it all the way over there, but . . . "

"But very unlikely?"

"Yes. I showed her the rabbit and told her about it."

"What she do?"

"She made me feel . . . silly, but when I continued to look at her, I felt . . . " He paused again, but she knew to wait it out. "I don't want to say 'afraid' . . . "

"What did she do?" Barbara's voice was almost a whisper.

"Nothing really. But her eyes . . . they were so glazed. For a moment I felt as though I was standing before a vampire. I actually got this chill."

"What happened?"

"Nothing. I left and brought the rabbit back."

"They must have been grateful."

"The kid was ecstatic. Cy talked about the Oaks girl. That's why I asked you about her."

"Oh." Barbara became thoughtful. "That's really not proof of anything, though," she said, thinking aloud.

"I know. But that's not all."

"Tell me," she said, impatient with his hesitation.

"Well, another crazy thing happened on that road. Dick O'Neil's little boy was attacked by a coon."

"I heard about that today. Carl was talking about it, too."

"So, before I came home tonight, I stopped at the O'Neils' and talked to the kid." He paused again.

"So?"

"He told me he was attacked by an E.T."

"An E.T.?"

"A creature from outer space. You know . . . "

"Oh, Eddie."

"Yeah, yeah. I'm not telling you I believed him, but there was something about the way the kid stuck to his guns . . . and he tells me he had seen it before."

Barbara's smile froze and her eyes showed the excitement and the fear of one wild possibility after another emerging from the depths of her imagination.

"Could it be that the Oaks girl stole the rabbits and then attacked him . . . maybe while she was in some disguise?"

"I don't know. You see why I hesitated to tell you any of this, though, don't you? There's nothing really concrete," he said, but Barbara wasn't listening. She was off on her own trend of thought.

"Faith Oaks is the kind of child that you read about . . . introverted, paranoid . . . a loner. She has no girlfriends and no boyfriends."

"Not true, Mom," Tommy Morris said, standing in the den doorway. He had overheard the last part of his parents' conversation.

"Tommy! I've told you a hundred times not to listen in on our conversations."

"I wasn't. I was just coming in to ask you to help me with something in math."

"All right," Eddie said. "What did you mean by 'not true'?"

"I heard Mom say Faith Oaks had no boyfriend. She's been going with Bobby O'Neil. Some jerks have been writing things about Bobby and Faith all over the bathrooms. . . ."

"She's going with Bobby O'Neil?" Barbara asked, a half smile on her face. "He's quite an outgoing young man. Popular, too, isn't he?"

"Yeah. That's why everyone's talking about it."

"Bobby O'Neil," Eddie said, as though he had just heard it. "Billy's older brother?"

"Uh huh."

"Doesn't add anything, does it, Eddie?"

"Huh? No, I suppose not. It just . . . "

"Confuses it more."

"Yeah."

"Anyway," she said, taking his hand, "I can understand why my rabbit dinner didn't exactly impress you tonight. You've had rabbit on the brain."

"Rabbit on the brain?" Tommy said. They both looked at him and laughed. His look of humor turned to puzzlement.

"Let's see your homework," Barbara said. "What's Sebastian Topper assigned tonight?" Just as he came over to sit beside her, the phone rang.

"I'll get it," Eddie said, rising. He answered it in the kitchen. It was Cy Baum.

"Didn't want to disturb you at home," he said. "I was going to call you tomorrow, but I thought to myself just now that you might be off or doin' something else, so . . . "

"No problem, Cy. What's up?"

"Oh, that rabbit thing again."

"What?"

"I was down there before, tying the rabbit up good this time and making sure the door was locked and all . . . helluva way to live now . . . but, what's got to be done, got to be done," he said. Eddie thought he might drift off to an entire series of digressions.

"What about the rabbit?"

"Anyway, I was tying him up when I see something on the floor. It was something we didn't see before. Maybe because of the light. I know there's not much light down there with no windows and all, but windows in the basement weren't practical in those days. Still not, if you ask me. Heat loss is all they are."

"What did you see?"

"Can't really describe it so as to make any sense. Wanted your opinion of it."

"Well, what's it look like?"

"Look like?" He paused so long, Eddie thought he might have hung up. "It looks like a baby's foot."

"Baby?"

"Well, a really small child. The print ain't perfect, but it's clear enough for my old eyes. I've seen prints and I've seen prints. This one looks human."

"I'll come over to see it. I'll be there in a little while."

"Tonight, you mean?"

"Sure."

"Well . . . "

"Problems?"

"I didn't tell Hilda nothin' about it, Eddie. I don't want her worryin', you understand."

"Sure."

"Tell you what. I'll go down and unlock the basement door. You just come around and go right to it without knocking on the front door, OK? I'll leave the light on and meet you down there. She's going upstairs in a little while anyway."

"Fine. Figure on twenty minutes."

"Thanks."

Eddie hung up and went for his jacket. He poked his head into the den just before leaving.

"Who was it?"

"Cy Baum. I've got to make a run over there and look at something. Shouldn't be long."

"Having to do with what we discussed?"

"Uh huh." She came to him. "I don't know what it is," he said in a low voice so Tommy wouldn't hear. "Some print of some kind." She held his arm and her face took on a deep seriousness.

"Maybe you should tell someone else about all this now, Eddie. Haven't you told the chief anything?"

"Not yet," he said. "We'll see." He kissed her and walked out. She stood there looking at the closed door for a moment. This will all come to nothing, she told

220

herself, and she tried to ignore the heavy sense of foreboding that crept through her body immediately after Eddie kissed her and was gone. It was as though he had infected her with his inexplicable fear.

She went back to the den and attacked Tommy's homework with an enthusiasm that surprised him. He didn't know what made her do it, but he was happy about it, because his math couldn't have been made any clearer.

Bobby O'Neil opened the back door of his house and stepped onto the porch. He wasn't sure whether or not the rain had really let up some. It sounded as though it had, but he recognized that he wanted it to diminish so he could make his way to Faith and meet with her as he had promised. He had had bad feelings all afternoon and he was anxious to get over there to find out what was really on her mind.

So that his parents wouldn't know he was leaving, he had practically tiptoed his way to the back of the house, pausing only when Billy called him to show him the whistle Eddie Morris had given him. Bobby tried to show a greal deal of interest and excitement in it so Billy would be happy, but he was intent on one thing only—getting over to see Faith.

"You wanna play Moon Raiders on the video game?" Billy asked him.

"Not tonight. I gotta do something."

"What?"

"Something. I'll play with you tomorrow. I'll get you a new game tomorrow," he added quickly.

"Really?"

"Sure. Just leave me alone for a while now, OK?"

"OK. I want Naval War."

"Fine, fine. Naval War."

"Where are you going?"

"Shh. I don't want to cause a ruckus. Just forget about me for now."

"OK," his little brother said, "but if you go outside, be careful. Captain was barking a lot."

"Right. Thanks." He patted Billy on the head and went to the back porch, where he now stood contemplating the rain. He'd get soaked for sure, he thought, and then he remembered his father's volunteer fireman's rain outfit that was kept in the garage. Without any more hesitation, he lunged off the porch and ran to the garage. It was still coming down hard, no matter what he wanted to think. He flipped on the lights and went to the back of the garage, where he found his father's things hanging on hooks. Anyone else would think this was kinda silly, he thought, but he was determined.

He put on the high rubbery pants and high boots. Then he found the jacket and the water-resistant cape, and draped it over himself. He pulled the rain hat over his head, tugging it down the sides of his face. Now, he considered himself well protected. I'm probably quite a sight, he thought, and laughed to himself imagining how Faith would react when she saw this monsterlike creature emerge from the rainy darkness.

After he put the garage light out, he checked to see if he had attracted his parents' attention. All was quiet, except for the continuous sound of the rain drumming on the garage roof and tapping on the trees and grass. Just before he ran out, he realized it would not be wise to go into the darkness without a flashlight. So he went back in, not bothering to put on the lights again, and found it where he knew it to be. He tested it, shining the beam at the door. Satisfied and proud of himself for being so resourceful, he headed out of the garage and toward The Oaks.

The rain did begin to slow. The lightning and thunder were gone and the steady downpour thinned and lightened even as he made his way across the field. This, too, encouraged him and he became even more optimistic. He was glad he had remembered the flash-light, for the darkness was so thick, he would have had trouble finding the paths. With the light, he was able to move as quickly as ever; breaking out in the clearing near the big house without any trouble. He paused to look up at Faith's room and was surprised to see it was dark. For a moment he thought he was too early, but when he directed the light at his watch, he saw that he was even a little late. What did this mean? Did she want him to stay away or had she told her mother she was going to sleep and now waited for him in the dark?

He thought for a moment and then decided to risk something. He directed the flashlight's beam up the building until it reached her window. As soon as it hit the glass, he turned the light off and waited. Then he flicked it on and off again, doing this two or three times. He was just about ready to give up and go home when the bedroom light went on and then off, repeating his kind of signal.

"Hot dog," he said. Filled with excitement, this being an even greater adventure than he had dreamed, he went forward toward the fire escape ladder and the landing just outside Faith's bedroom window.

Mary had been on her way down the hall, coming from the room in which she had imprisoned Faith so she could pray and fast for redemption, when she saw the light flash on the wall. She stopped and waited and then it came again. It came right through Faith's window and out her opened door. Almost immediately, Mary knew what it meant. She went into Faith's room and looked out the window at the blinking flash-light, catching a momentary glimpse of Bobby O'Neil below. As soon as she did, she didn't waste a moment.

She went to Faith's light switch by the doorway and flicked it on and off, imagining that to be the kind of signal that Faith might have planned for him. Then she rushed out of the room and down the stairs to the kitchen, where she had her pot of water boiling for tea. She turned up the flame to bring it to an instant boil and then took the handle with her pot holders and carried the water back to the stairway. She was as careful as she could be not to spill a drop. The steam rose from the boiling water as she rushed back into Faith's room.

She set the pot down by the window and slowly opened it and the screen. The rain had slowed to a drizzle and the metal landing and fire escape ladder glistened from the small amount of light that spilled out of the house. Looking down through the grate floor, she could see Bobby O'Neil making his way up the ladder, his flashlight in his right hand giving him enough illumination so he could make his way. She thought the outfit he wore made him look like something evil, something that had come from the darkness.

As quietly as she could, she stepped out onto the landing and reached back for the pot of still steaming water. She crawled to the edge of the landing and peered over. Bobby was more than halfway up the ladder by now.

He heard something above him and directed the light toward the landing. There was still enough rain to pepper his eyes enough to blur his vision, but he was almost certain that someone was out on the landing. Why would Faith come out in the rain? he wondered. He paused, took a few more steps up, and directed his light as best he could.

Just at that moment, Mary rose on the landing. The shock of seeing her come out of the shadows was enough, but the fact that she had been crouched down, hiding from him, terrified him. He realized that she had given him the signal with the room light, but he didn't have too much time to think about why. He stood frozen, his left hand clinging to the thin banister of the fire escape, his right hand holding the flashlight up and out.

224

"DEVIL," she cried; "BE GONE!" she shouted, and with that, she cast the boiling water down at him. Two things saved him from getting his face scalded: his quick reflexes and the wide brim on his father's rain hat. Most of the water hit the hat, but when he dipped his head to get the maximum protection, some of the water hit the back of his neck. It burned like a finger of fire, tracing its way down his back. That, combined with her wild shout, caused him to lose his grip on the banister. He turned on the rung and his feet slipped off the wet metal step. As he began to fall, he dropped the flashlight and it went crashing into the darkness below. He slid down a half dozen rungs, bouncing and scraping his legs and his hands before catching a grip on the fire escape to break the impact of his fall. Even so, he landed awkwardly on his right foot and he felt his ankle twist. Pain shot up his leg, even before his torso hit the ground.

It was a dazing concussion, but he was able to roll over and absorb the main part of the impact with his buttocks. For a moment he simply lay there in the rain and the dark, his heart beating like mad, in expectation of other pains. To his joy he realized he had broken nothing and had survived the fall. But when he tried to stand, he felt the sprain in his ankle. He was sure it wasn't broken, but he knew he had a bad twist.

Above him, he heard Mary Oaks slam the window down. He listened to see if she had any other plans for additional attacks on him, but there was silence. Grateful for that, he pulled himself into a straighter standing position and looked about for the flashlight. Since there was no illumination, he imagined it had been smashed and the lens and lamp had been damaged. Surveying the situation, he decided it was best for him to head down the driveway to the road instead of going back through the field. He would make his way home as quickly as he could.

As if on cue, the rain intensified again. He tucked his

chin in and pulled the cap down as far as he could and limped forward. It was rough going, but he was nearly halfway home when the car headlights appeared. As the vehicle drew closer, it slowed down. He imagined that was because he made for some sight in the rain and the darkness; but when the car was nearly on him, he saw that it was a police car. It stopped only a few feet from him and Eddie Morris opened his window to call out.

"Hey." He directed his side spotlight on Bobby, who raised his hand to block out the bright light. "What are you doing out in this rain? Who are you?"

"My name's O'Neil."

"Dick O'Neil's boy?"

"Yessir."

"Well, get in," Eddie said. He leaned over to open the passenger's door. Bobby went around the car and got in beside him. "What the hell are you doing out here now?"

"I was . . . was visiting someone."

"In the rain? Don't you even have a flashlight?" Eddie looked closer at Bobby. "What'dja do, fall down or somethin'?"

"I . . . yeah. I fell."

"You were over to The Oaks?" Eddie asked. Bobby hesitated. "Your name's Bobby, right?"

"Yessir."

"Seein' the Oaks girl?" Eddie asked him. Bobby nodded slightly. When he turned his hand, the scraped left palm was exposed. "What the hell happened to you? Where'd you fall? Anyone else get hurt?"

"Nossir."

"So?" Eddie said. He waited, but Bobby wasn't forthcoming. "How did this happen?"

"I fell down a ladder."

"Ladder. You were on a ladder in this weather?"

"Fire escape."

226

"Oh. Oh, I see," Eddie said. He started to smile. "Sneaking around then, huh?"

"Kinda."

Eddie laughed.

"I saw your little brother today. Gave him a whistle."

"I know. He's really proud of it."

"What do you make of his story?"

"What story?"

"About what happened to him. You know, that whole thing about an E.T.?"

"I don't know," Bobby said. He turned away and Eddie leaned forward.

"Hey, you have a little scratch on the left side of your forehead, too." Bobby reached up and touched it. "How the hell did you fall off a fire escape?"

"Lost my grip. You going to tell my father?"

"Not if you don't want me to. Unless you were committing a burglary or something."

Bobby thought for a moment. Mary Oaks could very well claim something like that. What if she had already called his home and made such an accusation?

"I was going to see Faith Oaks," Bobby said. "We planned to meet on the fire escape landing right outside her bedroom window."

"In the rain?"

"Well . . . we had to discuss some serious things. It was lettin' up some and . . . "

"Never mind trying to explain. Kids in love don't feel the cold or the wet. So what happened?"

"Her mother was waiting there instead. She surprised me."

"What'dya mean?" Eddie was very interested now, but he tried to control his enthusiasm so as not to frighten Bobby. There was a long pause, during which Bobby reached back and felt the back of his neck. "Did she do something to chase you away?"

"Yeah. She threw boiling hot water down on me while I was on the ladder. She waited until I was quite a ways up. I lost my grip and fell."

"Shit."

"Yeah. If she says I was trying to break in, it's a lie," Bobby said quickly. "I swear, I was just going over to see Faith."

"Take it easy. We don't know she's going to say anything yet. I'd better get you home. Did she burn you?"

"A little on the neck. Do you have to come in with me?"

"No, I won't go in. Not unless she does make a complaint. But my advice to you and your girlfriend is meet someplace else."

"Fat chance of that now," Bobby said. Eddie drove on to the Oaks driveway to turn around. He paused for a moment and looked up at the house. Only one window was lit and that was rather dim. In the rainy darkness, the large old building looked eerie and frightening.

"You been in that place?"

"Not really."

Eddie grunted and backed up quickly. When they reached the O'Neil driveway, Bobby opened his door before Eddie had come to a full stop. He wanted to run to the garage and get everything put away, but the moment he put his foot down, he knew he'd have to limp.

"Sure you're all right?"

"Yessir."

"Take care," Eddie said. Bobby waved. Eddie watched him for a moment and then shook his head. "Boiling water. Holy shit," he mumbled and then realized he'd be late for his rendezvous with Cy Baum in his basement. As he drove on, he thought that his initial instincts about all this were being reinforced. He

228

was beginning to get a bad feeling about the conclusions, whatever they might be.

Mary was concerned. Although she felt strong and confident, she also felt heavily put upon. The Devil was coming at her from every direction. Shut in the basement, he hovered just under the floor, breathing and peering through every crack. She kept him contained, but he was always there, a reminder of the evil that had touched her.

Now he had touched her daughter, as well. But she had countered by imprisoning her in holy words and prayer. Her spirit would be cleansed and she would be purified once again.

Finally, he had come from the outside in the guise of that boy, assaulting her "castle of perseverance." She had driven him back into the darkness from whence he had arisen. She was victorious on every front. Glory to God in the highest.

After she shut Faith's bedroom window, she decided to go back to her and speak to her through the locked door. Faith should know how strong are the good and the faithful and with what righteous might the hand of God could fall. When she got there, she stood by the door listening. Faith heard her approach.

"Mother? Is that you?"

"Why aren't you praying? You must pray."

"Mother, please." Faith came off the bed and stood against the door. She turned the handle. "Let me out."

"You have nothing to fear anymore. I have driven him away."

"Driven him? Driven who? Please, Mother, just listen to me."

"He that came out of the night. He had come for you, but I was there and I was prepared."

Faith waited, her head against the door. Was Mary being literal or figurative? Who did she mean? Bobby?

"Mother?"

"He was climbing up to your room," she said, now more in whisper. "Coming to take you, to spoil you, to turn you into a thing of the night like him. But I was waiting and I baptized him in the name of the Father and the Son and the Holy Ghost," she said and she laughed.

"Mother . . . you don't mean . . . what did you do?"

"Pray. Read the Scriptures. John, Chapter III. Get it. I want to hear you read."

"Mother, please."

"Read. Behold what manner of love the Father hath bestowed upon us . . . "

"Mother, listen to me. Listen, listen. It's about the baby in the basement . . . " Faith thought the only way to reach her now was to tell her what she thought, but Mary wouldn't listen. She raised her voice.

"WHOSOEVER COMMITTETH SIN TRANS-GRESSETH ALSO THE LAW: FOR SIN IS THE TRANSGRESSION OF THE LAW."

"MOTHER! I THINK HE'S OUT. I THINK THE BABY'S BEEN OUT. DON'T YOU UNDER-STAND? PLEASE. OPEN THE DOOR. WE HAVE TROUBLE . . . HE HURT SOMEONE . . . BOB-BY'S LITTLE BROTHER. MOTHER!"

Faith waited, but she heard nothing.

"Mother?"

She pressed her ear hard against the door. She thought she heard Mary's breathing.

"Mother," she said in a loud whisper.

And then she heard her footsteps, going away, going toward the stairs, descending . . . into silence.

Twelve

At the sound of a car door closing, he stirred and peered through the rain and the darkness. He saw the gray shape of a big creature. He thought it was running toward him, so he backed even further into the depths of the under-porch; but when the light spilled up from the opened cellar doorway, he saw that the creature was going to go down the steps and into the house.

As soon as the creature disappeared, he edged his way out from under and moved quickly over the wet earth, until he reached the basement landing and could look down. The door was slightly open and there was enough light escaping to attract his curiosity. Was the little girl there now? Could he slip through that entrance way and find her?

He came around and paused on the first step. His heartbeat quickened as he considered the possibility. Moving his feet inch by inch, a very cautious little creature, he reached the second step. Then the loud sound of the voices within sent him scurrying up and away to cloak himself in the darkness. There he waited and listened, but the big creature did not reappear. Still, his courage had been damaged.

Indecisive, he remained there, not retreating to the under-porch and not going back to risk descent into the basement. He was oblivious to the rain and the chill, because his attention was so fixed on the action in the cellar. He half-expected and half-hoped that the girl would emerge. Although the voices below were muffled, he could tell when they were near the door. He was as patient as a cat.

But the thin ray of light over the basement steps stirred his imagination and memory. The sliver of illumination reminded him of the big creature's strap. In his mind it had a life of its own. Like a snake, it could come out, slithering up those steps, looking for him. To his thinking, the strap would be found in any cellar. His vision was so vivid, that he actually retreated a few steps in anticipation.

When the cellar door opened completely, he was so terrified of the possibility, that he scurried back to the under-porch, where he curled up protectively, hugged himself, and shut his eyes. When he opened them again, the light was gone, but he thought the big gray figure was still there in the darkness. After a moment more, he caught its silhouette and saw it go away. Relieved, he loosened the grip on himself and relaxed. He closed his eyes, unable to fight back the fatigue. But just before he drifted off, he envisioned himself going down those steps again. This time staying there until he found the girl.

Cy Baum was at the basement door when Eddie parked his car and came running to the house. Eddie couldn't remember a night as dark as this one. He kept his voice low, figuring they were still supposed to keep this rendezvous a secret from Hilda.

"Raining like hell," Cy said. "The heavens just opened up."

"Yeah." Eddie shook some of the water off and lowered his hood. He looked at the rabbit squatting by the pole. "So, let's see what you've got."

"Didn't mean to get you out on a night like this. It coulda waited, I suppose."

"No problem. Quicker we get to the bottom of this, the better we'll all feel."

"That's for damn sure."

He followed Cy to the beam and knelt to look at the print on the floor. Cy handed him a flashlight, but the increased illumination washed out the detail.

"What'dya think?"

"Just this one?"

"Well, I didn't check out the whole floor, but . . . "

Without offering any comment, Eddie paced about slowly. He knelt down every once in a while and studied what caught his eye.

"Another one here," he said. "And here." He examined one more closely and measured it with his long fingers and big hand. "It looks human, all right," he finally said.

"That's what I thought. That's what I thought!" Cy repeated with excitement. Eddie stood up and looked at the old man. His face softened, as he felt a mixture of frustration and humor.

"It's no mystery though, is it, Cy?"

"What'dya mean? Sure it is. That's a real little kid. That's a . . . "

"It's probably Gina's print."

"Huh?"

"Your granddaughter. It must be about her size foot, don'tcha think?"

For a moment Cy just looked at him. Then he shook his head.

"No, can't be Gina's."

"Why not?" Eddie smiled.

"Well she . . . this is made by someone barefoot."

"So?"

"She never comes down here barefoot, Eddie."

"How do you know that?"

"I didn't put the rabbit down here until late yesterday afternoon and she was wearing shoes the whole time."

"She came down after or . . . "

"No, we came down together all the time. And in the morning she didn't come down until I sent her in. You were here then. We had gone out to put a bag of garbage in the can and then we were going to get the rabbit when you pulled up."

"Cy, it has . . . "

"I'm tellin' you, Eddie. It ain't her footprints."

Eddie took a deep breath and knelt down beside one of the prints again. There wasn't much detail, but he did notice that the toes looked stilted or curved. The tips of them were awfully close to the sole of the foot. Or paw. Or whatever the hell it was. What the hell was it, if it wasn't his granddaughter's foot? The old man had to be wrong, but Eddie thought it was probably best to humor him about this.

"What kind of animal out here makes a print that close to a human's?"

"Nothin' I know. I imagine a monkey's is, but I don't know anyone who has a monkey, do you?"

"If anyone did, how would it get in and out of here, anyway?" Eddie asked and regretted it immediately.

"Gotta have more brains than a monkey then, don't it?"

"Look, Cy, we've got to be sure. Tomorrow morning some time, get Gina aside and ask her about it. See if she didn't come down here some time when you were unaware of it."

"The kid hangs around me all day and night."

"I realize that, but she was probably so excited about the rabbit . . . kids are like that, Cy. Believe me. I'm talking from experience."

"Um," he said, but Eddie could see that there wasn't the slightest agreement in Cy's face.

"Nobody around here's got kids this small on the loose, do they? I mean, the Cooper kids are . . . "

"Too big, for sure. Those prints are Gina's size and she's just a little more'n four."

"That's why she came to mind first," Eddie said. Cy nodded.

"Too bad the rabbit can't talk," he said. He sighed deeply. "I'd invite you up, but Hilda would know I called you and she'd . . ."

"No, no. I got to get home. Tell you what," Eddie said, seeing the old man was still quite perturbed, "I'll stop by in the morning some time and talk to Gina myself. Sometimes kids tell things faster to other people, especially cops. I stopped over and talked to the O'Neil kid and was able to get him calmed down some."

"Oh?"

"Yeah. Couldn't shake him from this story he had about this little creature, this . . ." He paused and looked down at one of the prints.

"What's that?"

"Huh? Oh, nothing really. My idea OK with you?"

"Fine, fine. Thanks. Appreciate your efforts."

"No problem," Eddie said, as he pulled his hood up again. "See you tomorrow," he added and went to the door. Cy came up behind him and waited until he went out. Eddie heard him snap the locks closed as soon as the door was shut.

He paused on the cement stairway and looked into the inky darkness. If the chief could tap in on his thoughts now, he mused, he'd have him put away, if he didn't fire him outright. His whole family had gone to see E.T. It was like a national event, for Chrissakes. Now he tried to conjure up the memory of that little creature. Cy was so sure of himself about those prints not being Gina's. Billy was so definite about his story, positive that it wasn't a raccoon.

Something stirred in the darkness to the right. He peered into it as hard as he could, but it was too dark to make out anything. He should have grabbed his flashlight before running from the car to the house, but he didn't want to go parading around here now, anyway. He'd just frighten Hilda. Late morning was time enough. It would have to be.

He ran back to the car and headed away. Damn, he thought. Most of the year I ride over this road as nonchalantly as possible, and now it's become a street of mystery. Remembering the blind spot in the road, he took his time and then hurried on through the darkness and the rain.

Mary undid the lock on the basement door and opened it, her fingers moving mechanically, her every motion slow and deliberate. She flicked on the cellar lights and waited, but she heard no scurrying, no rush for safety; so she began her descent. About halfway down, just as before, she detected the scents of different but familiar things. She had forgotten about that, but now it came back to her.

When she made the turn at the bottom of the stairway, she reached into her housecoat pocket and pulled out the flashlight. She could see that his box was empty and she expected he was hiding. He had to be. She began to walk toward the box and then stopped, because of the sound coming from her right.

Slowly, she turned toward it, bringing the beam of the flashlight up from the floor to the wall. When she saw it, she gasped and pressed her left hand against her mouth. She bit down on her fingers and stared ahead, keeping the light on the gaping hole in the fieldstone wall. Through it she could make out part of the lawn; she could hear the rain, and she could even see drops in the air.

"Devil," she whispered and walked to the wall, where she examined the opening and found the pile of rocks on the floor. She peered through the hole, shining her light about to see if she could catch sight of him out there. But there was no sign of any movement.

The first thing she thought was that it wasn't her

fault. How could she have anticipated this? This field-stone wall had stood for decades. Sure, stones could become loose, but to pull them out so neatly and create this opening . . . how long had he been doing it? She had never seen this any other time, but the odors . . . they were the scents of things from the outside. He must have put the rocks back after each escape and each return. How conniving and deceiving.

For Mary, this reinforced everything she believed. He was a thing of evil, endowed with a sly, wicked intelligence. She was glad now that she had kept Faith away from him. She was only sorry that she hadn't chained him to the wall. This was the result of being too merciful. Hadn't she often had nightmares about him, seeing him come upstairs, oozing through doors, twisting and turning his distorted body, until he was in her bedroom, threatening to touch her . . . to touch her like Uncle Billy touched her mother. She always awoke in a sweat when that happened.

She peered out of the hole again. Should she put the rocks back and shut him out there? Where had he gone? What was he doing? Faith said something about his hurting the O'Neil boy. Did others know about him? Was that why the policeman came to her to talk about stolen rabbits? No, there would be a bigger uproar if others had seen him. There had to be.

She decided to leave the hole as it was, so that he could come back into the basement. And when he did, she would chain him to the wall. She would put a collar and a leash on him, just like the collar and the leash that was on that rabbit in the policeman's arms. First, she'd beat him, though. That was important.

It was getting later and later, and with the rain coming down as hard as it was, he'd have to come back soon, she thought. She went back up the stairs and flicked off the basement light. Then she returned to the darkness and took a position in the corner across from the opening in the wall. She would let him get back in and put the rocks in place again. Then she would grab him.

It truly amazed her how intelligent he was. She had never considered him anything but a contaminated, distorted little creature. She didn't think of him as a baby or a child; she called him "Imp," because in her mind he was a little thing of evil, ugly and malformed like some aborted fetus that came to life. She refused to see anything of herself in him. Often, during the pregnancy, when she felt him move within her, she prayed for his death. She thought of him as something parasitical, draining her goodness, sucking her soul. All she could do was trust in God and be prepared for the tasks that had to be done.

She recalled the terrible agony of the delivery, how she had spent hours and hours of labor down here in the dark. She remembered squatting like a peasant in the field to drop him, and she never forgot the piercing scream that came from the deepest part of her soul when she realized he was alive, squirming below her, demanding her attention, calling on her almost immediately, and forcing her to face the reality of his existence.

Waiting now in the darkness, she had feelings similar to those she had had that terrible night. He was going to appear in that hole, coming in from the darkness. Did he meet with the Devil, his father, out there? How dare he escape from where she had kept him? How dare he be born?

The rain continued to fall. Waiting here in the darkness in the bowels of the house, she understood why she believed that evil was an ever-present part of this world, lingering in the shadows, hovering in the darkest parts of people's minds. She didn't like staying in his world long. Lately, she had liked it less and less, bringing his food down quickly and leaving quickly. That was probably why she had failed to notice what was happening. She realized she had even skipped one of his bath dates.

But being here, draped in the shadows and the dampness, hearing nothing but the scurrying and the slithering of rodents and vermin, she found herself having to fight off horrible images and vicious thoughts. It was as though she had planted herself in the perfect environment for the nurturing of sin. Now sin was trying to emerge even within her.

She saw herself strangling him, squeezing his little neck until his eyes bulged and his tongue hung out. She saw herself smash him with a piece of pipe, and felt his skull crumple. She saw him plead for mercy and she heard herself laugh as she smothered him under a pillow. She killed him in dozens of different ways while she sat there in his darkness. She was ashamed of these thoughts and she blamed it on being near his things, near his evil.

She concentrated on Scripture as a way of fighting back, struggling to find the right words, the right thoughts and images. As she stared through the darkness at that hole in the wall, she began to see an aura of light around it. It grew brighter and brighter until the vision began to form in the blackness. She didn't move; she didn't gasp; she didn't show any outward signs of fear. She had seen this image before and she had invoked the power of God to drive it away. She would do it again.

"And I beheld another beast coming up out of the earth; and he had two horns like a lamb, and he spake as a dragon," she whispered.

He was smiling at her now, looking in and smiling.

But she did not turn away nor did she cower. She faced him directly.

And so he began to retreat. The light dimmed and the darkness swept itself back in and over the hole.

He was gone and she was still the stronger. She was

safe. She could wait as long as she had to and be ready when the time came.

The first rays of sunlight came through Gina's window and nudged her eyelids. They flickered and opened. Her awareness came quickly, because in her last dream she had seen herself getting up to go down to check on her rabbit. After what had happened to the other two and what almost had happened to this one, she wanted to be certain it was still there. She drew her blanket off her quickly and lowered herself to the floor, moving as silently as she could, because she realized her grandparents would want her to wait. She listened for any signs of them and then went to the door of her room. It wasn't closed completely, so she simply pulled it open enough for her to slip through.

Dressed only in the new cotton nightshirt Grandpa Cy had bought her, she practically tiptoed in her bare feet over the hallway carpet. It was only when she took hold of the stairway banister that the sleeping house complained: the steps squeaked. She paused to see if her grandparents had heard her, but all she heard was the water dripping from the sink faucet in the upstairs bathroom. It was that quiet. Confident she would be successful then, she continued on down the stairs and moved quickly to the basement doorway. She had a little trouble turning the knob and getting the door open, because it stuck on the jamb; but once she had, she slipped in.

She had forgotten that it would be very dark in the basement, but there was enough light from upstairs to illuminate the basement light switch. She flipped it on and began her descent, not minding the feel of the hardwood steps on her bare feet or the feel of the cold cement floor below. Once she was there, she hurried over to the basement beam and rejoiced in the discovery that the rabbit was still there. He had messed just to the right of where he was sitting, but she ignored that and took him into her arms. Then, in a low voice, she greeted him and, while she petted him, described to him all the plans she had for herself and for him that day.

Cy had been the first to hear the basement door open. He was attuned to every sound in the building, having built, rebuilt, and remodeled a large portion of it. He knew the creaks in the structure, the metallic moans in the pipes, and the places where the wind would whistle through crevices. It wasn't so much that he had good hearing for a man of his age, but rather that he felt the vibrations through the walls and the floorboards and the very legs of his bed. He wasn't a late riser anyway and he had been close to full consciousness when Gina had made the stairs squeak. For him the sound of the basement door being tugged might just as well have been a pot clanging to the floor. He sat up immediately.

"What is it?" Hilda asked. She opened her eyes immediately when he sat up in bed.

"Nothing. I have to check something."

"What time is it?" She looked at the table clock. "My God, what do we have, cows to milk?"

Instead of answering her, he pulled on his pants. He always slept in a flannel nightshirt, no matter what the weather, and now he simply tucked it in like an ordinary shirt. He slipped into his shoes and started out.

"Be right back," he mumbled.

"It's not Gina, is it?" Hilda called as he went into the hall.

"I'll see," he said. "Don't get up."

"Don't get up? Don't get up? I'm up. What good is saying don't get up?"

He hurried down the stairs and paused when he saw that the basement door was opened and the light was on. After all that had happened, he couldn't help but feel some sense of foreboding. It had to be Gina, he thought. Who else?

241

"Gina?" he called from the top of the basement steps.

"Yes, Grandpa?"

"What are you doin' down here so early, Honey?" he asked her and breathed relief. He went down the steps quickly.

"I was checking on Mr. Rabbit."

"Oh my. But it's so early," he said. He scrubbed his hair with both his hands and stared down at her. "And you're in your bare feet," he said, quickly realizing the significance. "You could get a cold and your feet will be dirty. Grandma's goin' to be madder than a penned bull in heat."

"What's going on down there, Cy?" Hilda was at the basement doorway.

"Oops. See," he said. He took the rabbit from her gently and set it down. Then he picked her up. "Nothing, Hilda. It was Gina checking on the rabbit."

"That rabbit again?"

"Go back to sleep. I'll take care of it," he said and began wiping the soles of Gina's feet vigorously.

"I thought he wasn't going to be here again," Gina said. "I wanted to see."

"But I locked the door good. See," he said pointing to the extra lock. "He can't get out and no one can get in."

"But he had to get out. He had to go to the bathroom."

"I see that. That's another thing that'll make your grandmother happy today. We'll get dressed and take him out for a walk. I don't think either of us is going to go back to sleep anyway. Tell me," he said, as he started back to the stairs, "did you do this before—come down here in your bare feet without telling me?"

"Nope."

"You don't have to lie now. I'm not going to be mad."

"Can we give the rabbit a carrot now, Grandpa?"

242

"We can if you'll tell me the truth."

"What is going on, Cy?" Hilda was still there.

"She was nervous about the rabbit and went down to check on him. I'll take care of it."

"Well I might as well get dressed and start thinking about breakfast. In your bare feet, Gina? Oh, you'll have to wash them before she puts anything on, Cy."

"I intend to. Don't make it into a federal offense, Grandma."

"I'll give you a federal offense. Lucky you didn't buy her a horse."

"A horse!" Gina said.

"When you're bigger," Cy said. "We'd better wash your feet now and get you dressed," he said, eye to eye with Hilda. She turned and went up to her room. "Tell me when you went down there before, Gina. You did, didn't you?"

"No, Grandpa. I was sleeping."

"Some time yesterday, maybe?"

Gina didn't respond. She was confused. The excitement concerning the other rabbits, the disappearance and recovery of this one, the dreams—all of it entangled time and place. Cy didn't push her, but he began to give credence to the possibility that Eddie Morris had been right. It certainly helped explain things and made him feel a lot more relaxed. He was glad now that he hadn't alerted Hilda to the mystery of the strange prints on the basement floor.

He hurried on to wash Gina's feet and get her dressed. They'd take the rabbit out before breakfast and then come in to eat a hearty one. He felt more energetic than usual today and mentally ran a list of chores he'd like to accomplish. He could see the rain had passed and there was a lot of blue sky. It was good his granddaughter got him up early. Why waste a nice day. Best part of the day was the morning. He always believed that and old age wasn't going to change it.

"All right," he said. "Now let's clean up these

rabbit paws," he added, tickling her. The sound of Gina's giggle washed away his feelings of gloom and doom. He was grateful for it.

He slept past the first rays of sunlight, but when he opened his eyes, he saw a doe and her fawn on the lawn, grazing not twenty feet from where he had slept under the back porch. He stirred and sat up, wiping the sleep from his eyes. For a long moment, he was confused. This was the first time in his life he had ever fallen asleep and awoken someplace other than his basement. That, plus the total brightness of a new day, made for a fresh, new experience. He looked about in dazed wonderment.

Everything appeared different in the daytime. He hadn't fully realized the structure of the porch when he crawled under it. He had simply slipped into the available shelter and had no concept of its width and length. He looked about for his box; he felt so certain he had slept in it, and he was surprised that neither it nor his raggedy blanket was here. He touched the wooden board behind him and found himself fascinated with the texture and the length. Then he spotted the field mouse he had killed. That memory returned, but it was more like the resurrection of a dream than the remembrance of an actual event.

He felt the grime on his lips and face and rubbed it off. Most of his body was streaked from mud and grass stains. Like a monkey he picked out some of the dirt that was between his toes and wiped off his legs and stomach. His movements attracted the doe and she raised her head to stare at him. After a beat the fawn did the same. He looked out at them with almost as much curiosity. When he shifted his body and went to all fours, the doe turned and trotted back into the bushes, her fawn following obediently. He watched them go and then he slid through the opening in the wooden grate.

Once out from under the porch, he squatted again and looked about. The full realization of where he was came back to him now, and seeing the house, the cement steps, and the basement door in bright sunlight made it all much more exciting and interesting. He scampered toward the steps, keeping himself close to the house. He paused when he heard the sound of voices, because he was sure one voice was the little girl's. He remained there on all fours, his head tilted toward the house as he listened. When her voice died away, he moved about in small circles like a confused and panicked little puppy. Then he went around the back of the house to the other side and listened again.

He was too excited to think about the fact that he hadn't returned to his own basement world, that he had left the hole opened in the wall back there, and that the big creature would discover his absence and what he had done. At this point, these kinds of realizations were beyond him, anyway. His mind could center on one thing only—seeing and being with the little girl. He wasn't even concerned with his thirst or his hunger.

When he didn't hear the little girl on this side of the house, he returned to where he had heard her. This time, though, he heard other voices first and that frightened him. He returned to the back porch and slipped in under it to wait and to listen. On his knees, his face up against the grate, he peered out in anticipation. He had no concept of time and no awareness of patience, but he had an infant's monomaniacal intensity and determination. She would soon appear. He had an instinctive certainty about it. He concentrated on that basement door. He willed it to open and he willed her to appear.

When she did so, he was disappointed that the big creature was with her, but he was ecstatic that what he had expected to happen had happened. There she was, just as he had dreamed.

·Gina carried the rabbit in her arms up the cement steps and put it down on the grass, holding firmly to the end of the leash. Cy stood beside her, his hands on his hips, looking out over the right front lawn toward the peaks of the small mountain range just visible over the line of trees. He was surprised at the warmth of the morning breeze and remarked to himself how unusually mild this spring had been. Behind him in the house, he could hear Hilda starting her preparations for breakfast. Thoughts of eggs, Hilda's biscuits, and coffee heartened him. It was good to be alive and healthy enough to appreciate the full blooming of another spring.

He put his hand on Gina's head and stroked her hair as she carried on a conversation with her rabbit. It looked up at her meekly and then began to hop along the lawn. As soon as the slack went out of the leash, she giggled and followed it.

Cy was about to say something when Hilda threw open a window behind him and stuck out her head.

"It's this damn plug on the coffeepot again. I nearly got electrocuted. Threw a circuit breaker. Everything's off in the kitchen."

"Oh, I thought I fixed that."

"Apparently, you were so busy with rabbits that you forgot."

"I'll flip on the breaker. Don't do anything until I come up from the basement."

"You don't have to worry about that," she said and closed the window.

"I'll be right out, Honey," he said. "Just stay around here."

Gina didn't respond. She was too busy following the rabbit in a circle. Cy went back into the basement. The moment the door closed behind him, the imp emerged from the porch. His chance had finally come.

Thirteen

Because she didn't see him immediately, he made a short cry that sounded more like a whine than anything else. When she turned and looked his way, he stood up and attempted an imitation of her happy sound. She froze in position and her mouth opened wide. The rabbit continued to hop, coming around completely and heading in his direction. In a state of amazement, she relaxed her hold on the leash and it flew out of her hand. That snapped her out of her daze, but when she reached forward to take back the leash, the rabbit picked up speed and the leash slipped beyond her fingers.

"Mr. Rabbit," she called, but she couldn't take her eyes off him, especially because of the way he waddled in her direction. His hair was as long as hers or longer and his eyes were blocked by the strands that fell over his forehead. He had to brush them away in order to get a clear view of her. Although his skin was actually lighter than hers, the streaks of dirt along his legs and over his stomach and chest made him look darker. "Where are your clothes?" she demanded. Then she laughed.

He stopped and slapped his hands together. It was an automatic reaction, but it brought a laugh from her. That was what he liked to hear.

"You have to wear clothes," she said; and then,

remembering what her father would say, she added, "Your watchamacallit's hanging out." She laughed the way everyone in her family laughed whenever he said that.

Of course, he didn't understand why she was pointing at him, but because that, too, brought laughter, he imitated the action and pointed at her.

"I'm going to tell my grandpa," she said, nodding emphatically. He nodded just as emphatically. Mimicking her as exactly as possible became the most important thing and took all his concentration. He didn't see the rabbit go by and was surprised when she screamed and pointed to it disappearing in the bushes behind the house. "MR. RABBIT!" She ran past him, but the rabbit disappeared quickly. He followed at her heels and stopped when she stopped.

He was right beside her now and reached up slowly to touch her hair. The tips of his fingers grazed the strands and the result was as exciting as he had imagined. He was going to grasp and pull some when she turned on him.

"It's your fault," she said. "You've got to get Mr. Rabbit back for me or I'll tell my grandpa. Go ahead," she commanded and pointed to the bushes. At first, he couldn't take his eyes off her face, but when she pumped her arm, he looked in the direction her finger pointed. He understood that her gesture had to do with the rabbit, but he wasn't sure what.

He could be like the rabbit, he thought, and got back to all fours. She lowered her arm and cocked her head to the right, this half smile on her face.

"What are you doing?"

When he hopped, she laughed. That made him very happy, so he hopped again and again, looking back at her the whole time. He didn't watch how he was going and he landed awkwardly, doing a partial somersault to catch his balance. That made her laugh harder and clap her hands. He liked the way her face squinted and her body shook with glee.

He tilted his head and thought about it. Then he did the somersault again. Soon she was running alongside him. Her laugh fueled him and he became even more reckless and daring with his gymnastics, tripping and rolling. They were around to the back of the house before Gina realized how far they had gone. When he stopped in a sitting position, her laughter wound down and she remembered her rabbit.

"Mr. Rabbit," she said again and took a step toward the undergrowth, but she had forgotten exactly where the rabbit had entered the bushes. It all looked the same to her. She brought her hands to her cheeks. "Oh, no."

The sad look on her face drew him to his feet again. When he straightened up completely, he was about an inch shorter than she was, but his long arms, thicker neck, and muscular legs made him look much bigger than her. She wasn't afraid or intimidated by him; she was only concerned about her rabbit.

"It's your fault," she snapped. Her tone of anger brought a scowl to his face. "You're dirty," she said, "and you need a haircut. Ugh, you smell," she added and pinched her nose. He thought that was amusing so he did the same thing. "I don't smell," she said and stamped her foot. He was confused. Nothing was making her laugh anymore and she still had that mean voice.

They both heard something move in the bushes and turned to it. Neither of them could see anything, but he sensed one of those funny-looking crawling creatures that burrowed in the earth.

"It's my rabbit," she said. She took a few steps in, parting some branches to see. One caught her hair. "Ow," she said and he shot forward to free her of it. When he did so, he touched her, but she didn't seem to notice. Instead, she continued on into the tall grass and the bushes. He remained a few feet behind her.

"Mr. Rabbit. Mr. Rabbit," she called and knelt down to look under the heavy vegetation. He got on all fours and scurried by her. "Get my rabbit," she commanded and he went even faster. He liked this; this was his kind of play.

She followed as best she could, catching her dress on limbs, freeing herself, stumbling over rocks and through the thick clumps of hardwood trees, wild berry bushes, and weeds. It wasn't long before they reached the forest. As he went along, he paused to be sure she was following him. He could go much faster, but he kept his pace slow enough so that she wouldn't lose sight of him.

When they reached a clearing in the woods, he squatted by two large rocks and she stopped and put her hands on her hips again, taking on an angry demeanor. She cast herself as her mother making demands on her.

"I want my rabbit," she said. He rubbed his face and hopped about. "NO," she snapped. "I want the real rabbit." He stopped jumping and stared at her. Again they heard something move and this time they turned to see the doe he had seen earlier. It sauntered through the forest. When the fawn appeared, Gina came forward. "Oh," she said. "Look how pretty."

He liked the softness in her voice and understood that the sight of the small deer had brought it on. In an instant he made a decision and shot forward over the rocks toward the small deer. He leaped and barely missed catching the fawn. Gina ran up behind him as quickly as she could to see.

When he turned in disappointment, she laughed at him. He had stepped into a pool of mud and caked his legs and inner thighs with it. He looked down at himself when she pointed, but he didn't understand the source of her hilarity.

"You've got to take a bath," she chanted. "You've got to take a bath. You're going to get a spanking," she added, her hands on her hips again. He sloshed his way out of the pool of mud and sat on some dry, high ground. "I've got to find Mr. Rabbit and go back," she said. When she started back, he jumped up and screamed a high-pitched sound that was closer to the cry of a frightened cat than anything else. She stopped and looked back at him.

"Why don't you talk?" she said. "Are you still a baby?" she sang. He tried to repeat the sound of laughter, but without her immediate model, it didn't come out right. "I don't think you're funny. You look silly. I'm telling," she said and started away again; but then they both saw a rabbit. It wasn't hers, but it was enough to hold her attention and keep her from leaving the forest. He scrambled off after it. "Wait," she called. "That's not my rabbit."

Reluctantly, she walked on behind the small boulders and went deeper into the forest. She could see him moving quickly over the rocks and fallen trees. She ran as fast as she could, tripping once and coming close to hurting herself. When she looked up, she was surprised to see him standing just ahead of her in another clearing. He had the rabbit in his arms.

"You caught him! You caught him!" She started toward him, but he turned. "Wait," she called and followed him, as he did his half walk, half hop further and further into the woods. She stopped once and looked back, realizing she had lost her way. Before panic could set in, though, she heard him ahead and saw him sitting on a very big boulder, the rabbit clutched in his lap. "Stay there," she commanded. "I don't want to walk anymore. It's wet and I don't like it." He didn't understand what she wanted, but he didn't move. When she reached the boulder, he held the rabbit out as an offering.

She contemplated the climb. He had simply dug his

hardened toes against the boulder and scurried up, but her slippery-soled shoes wouldn't permit. She made a vain effort to get some sort of footing and then took off her shoes and tried to wedge her feet into a crevice. She was able to get enough of a toehold to get herself started. After a moment, she found that she couldn't go further up and she couldn't go back down. She hovered there precariously and reached out for his help.

When he saw her hand before him, he got overly excited and grasped it too quickly. His long nails dug into her dainty skin and she screamed. Instantly, he released her and she lost her balance, falling backwards onto the ground. She wasn't hurt, but the shock of the fall frightened her, so she began to cry.

The sound amazed him. He had made something like it from time to time, but it never quite came out like this. He tilted his head and studied her. At first, he didn't know what else to do. Then he slid off the rock and squatted beside her, putting the rabbit into her arms. That brought her sobs to a slow halt. She ended with a series of small gasps, her body shuddering, and then she began to pet the rabbit with her free hand.

"It's your fault," she said glaring at him. "You're stupid. Why didn't your mother cut your fingernails? And they're dirty, too. Ugh."

She turned her attention to the rabbit and he was free to study her face. He felt like placing the tips of his fingers on her cheeks and tracing the thin lines her tears had drawn down to her chin. When her nose twitched the way the rabbit's did, he nearly found the way to laugh again. Strands of her golden hair lay over her shoulder and back. He had to touch it, but he did it so gently and she was so involved with the rabbit, that she didn't notice until he tugged on it.

"Stop it," she said and leaned away from him. Seated so close to him, she was able to see how dirty and strange he really was. There was something wild

252

in his eyes and in the way he held his head. His tongue worked over his lips nervously. He reminded her of the neighbor's collie back home.

When she pulled back from him, his hand remained in the air. Now the fingers were folded like a bird's claw. They opened and closed threateningly.

"Here," she said, holding the rabbit out to him. "This isn't Mr. Rabbit."

He looked at it and then looked at her, but he didn't reach for it. The rabbit squirmed and she released it, but as soon as it hit the ground, he slammed his fist down on it, catching it on the back of the neck. Stunned, it fell forward.

"Bad," she said. "That's bad." She stood up quickly. The rabbit struggled to its feet and began to hop away slowly. He watched it and then looked up at her. Because she didn't seem to care, he didn't go after it. "I'm going back," she said. "I don't like you. You're dirty and stupid. Ugh," she said and picked up her shoes. She was so anxious to get away from him now, that she didn't want to take the time to put them on.

But she wasn't more than ten feet before she realized she was confused about direction. Every avenue in the forest looked similar. When she turned to look back at him, she saw he was in that half stand, half crouch position, eyeing her curiously, but unmoving. He had to go back, too, she thought.

"Go home," she said, hoping to tag along. But he didn't move. She waited a moment and then went to her left, moving carefully and determinedly through the forest. After small rocks pierced her socked feet, she had to pause to put on her shoes. When she looked up again, he was right beside her. She was amazed at how quiet he could be. "I want my grandpa," she said.

Her sad look troubled him. He could think of only one way to help her—the embrace and the hum. He reached out and took her around the waist. His action was so sudden and his grasp so firm, she had no chance to resist. He pulled her back and they both fell into a sitting position. But before he could try the hum, she screamed.

That and her subsequent crying frightened him. He released her, and as soon as he did so, she stood up and ran in a southwesterly direction, almost directly opposite to the Baum homestead. She didn't look back; she continued to sob, wipe away the tears, and run. She fell twice, once flying forward over a rotting birch tree. The decayed wood crumpled under her and little red ants came out instantly. This made her even more hysterical and she ran on wildly. The deeper the forest became, the faster she went. Her sobs turned to desperate cries.

"Grandpa. Grandpa. GRANDPA!"

The silence that followed fanned her terror and panic. Nothing looked familiar; nothing looked right. The stillness of the trees and the long, deep shadows of their heavy foliage made it seem as though she had fallen into a nightmare. It was a world in which no one heard or saw her.

Exhausted from her running and crying, she slowed into a fast walk. As she went forward, she actually felt the drop in temperature caused by the shade of the heavy pine trees and the far-reaching, entwining branches of old maples and oaks. The sun, somewhere behind her, played peekaboo. This was the home of the perennial bogeyman. She had to find someone or some safe haven soon.

Still stunned by her radical change in mood, he followed her, but kept a wider distance between them. He heard her screams and her cries. Once he thought to imitate the sound and actually tried to vocalize the word "grandpa," but it came out in a distorted "grrannaaa." Confused and curious about everything, he went into his cavemanlike crouch and scampered off to her right flank, moving into a parallel position from where he could observe her more closely. He saw her fall and heard her shrill cries, but he kept his distance.

Her pace slowed and her crying subsided when she came to the foot of the mountain and a short wall of large rocks and small caves. Here in this untouched and rarely traveled part of the forest, she paused, and with her limited capabilities, contemplated her situation. She was lost, bruised, and afraid, and there didn't seem to be anyone who could help her. Yet, this area of the woods was different enough to calm her.

The woods were always dark and dank here, even in the fall, when the leaves were gone and the skeletonlike trees had a diminished effect. However, the forest was so thick it became a wall around the rocks. A mountain spring contributed to the wetness. It came out just above the rocks and moved in a web over the stones, finding crevices and holes and creating a cold and continuous stream which escaped by running down the walls of the caves and dripping through every available orifice. As a result, the earth around the rocks took on a dark black color, mixing the richness of dead leaves into the soil. For nocturnal creatures, this was home. Nature had provided a place for them and they flocked to it instinctively and claimed it for their own. Other creatures of the forest seemed to understand this and didn't visit the area.

The cave that was closest to Gina and most accessible to her had an opening about three-quarters the height of the average doorway. Because of the square shape of the rock, the cave reminded Gina of her child-size dollhouse at home. Often when she was upset or angry, she would withdraw to it and choose only her dolls for company. Within this make-believe world, she could create anything to make her happy and shut out anything that didn't. Frightened, confused, and alone, she saw the cave as a kind of sanctuary from the hard reality of the moment. She would rest there and think nice things. Soon her grandfather would come to take her back.

As soon as it was obvious to him that she was headed for the cave, he closed in on her, his own curiosity whetted. He had seen openings like this before, but he had always eschewed them. For one thing, they reminded him of being in his own basement; and when he was out, he wanted to avoid that kind of experience, unless there was something valuable to seek, such as the little girl's rabbit or the little girl herself.

For another thing, he had a wild animal's instinctive fear of openings in the ground and in the rocks. He could sense that they usually housed other creatures, and he had a primitive understanding of territoriality. He knew what it was to violate another creature's space. Animals had shown their teeth and their claws whenever he got too close.

His natural alarms went off as the girl drew closer and closer to the opening. He felt a need to stop her, so he released a high-pitched scream. The rocks became resonators and his sound echoed between them, entered the openings, and came ricocheting out. She was surprised by it, but instead of being frightened, she became angry. She put her hands on her hips and turned around.

"Go away," she commanded. "Go away."

He stared up at her, his head arched back, his hands clenched. His legs were slightly bent at the knees, making him look as though he were about to spring. She didn't wait for him to do anything; she turned away and continued on to the cave. He scampered up behind her and paused when she entered. His mouth went into the shape of an O and he pawed at his upper right thigh nervously. When the little girl disappeared from view, he rushed in after her.

Because of the position of the sun, the cave was fairly well illuminated. It was a little less than twenty feet deep and cone-shaped, narrowing down to nothing more than a crawl space after ten feet or so. The jagged walls seemed to have small shelves chiseled out of them. Water trickled over the far right wall and formed a puddle in the corner. Random patterns of moss clung to the lower portions of both the right and left walls.

Gina did not see the row of bats along the left wall and the clump of them that dangled from the low, rear ceiling. Each one looked like a large black wart clinging to the face of the stone. With their wings draped around their bodies like cloaks, they were still and unthreatening. Having been out most of the night, they had come back into the cave only hours ago. A half dozen or more of them were in the last stages of hydrophobia. Their rabid condition had made them irritable and extra sensitive to any disturbances. Their sleep was no longer peaceful: they twitched, lost their grips, and recaptured their holds on the rocks. Whenever they moved, their tiny bulldoglike heads jerked back and then came forward slowly, as though animated by a dream. Their mouths opened spasmodically, showing their long, pointed teeth in a kind of wry smile. Their eyes seemed sewn closed. The thumbs at the front edge of their wings were bent inward, concealing the nails at their ends.

A smaller boulder just inside the cave was a makeshift seat for Gina. She settled on it with her back to the cave entrance and rested her head against her opened hands, her elbows propped on her knees. She stared down at the cave floor and listened absentmindedly to the trickle of water that dripped down the wall. When he came to the cave's entrance, he blocked the sunlight. Once again, she turned on him.

"You can't come in," she said. "Go away."

He didn't move. He peered in beyond her and studied the darkness. His nocturnal eyes picked up the little black mounds along the cave walls. He had seen

257

them before, and although he had not captured one or confronted one, his tiny heart had speeded up whenever one flew close to him.

Gina was impatient with his disobedience. Back home no one could come into her dollhouse unless she said so. This, plus her frustration and unhappiness, was too much to tolerate. She had seen her mother lose her temper many times and she knew what it was to be dramatic about it. She stood up with her arms folded across her body and stamped her foot. When he took another step forward, she screamed.

Although her voice was small, the high-pitched hysterics exploded in the narrow and compact enclosure. The hard walls amplified her shouts and sent them bouncing back and forth with ten times the original volume.

The rabid bats were the first to be jolted out of their sleep. Ordinarily, they had a keen sense of hearing, enabling them to perform the natural sonar wonder that made them one of nature's most technically accurate creatures. But the virulent strains of rabies had intensified their senses so that their ears reported the most insignificant sounds. Their instant reaction to the disturbance was translated into only one desire— escape. But when they twittered to locate the opening of the cave, they found themselves blocked first by Gina and then by him. This put them into a frenzy and with little room to manipulate, they turned instinctively to attack.

As soon as the bats flew off the walls, he put up his arms. Gina spun around and screamed. She tripped over the boulder and fell backward. Some of the healthier bats made their way out between her and him. One of the rabid ones swooped down to follow suit. Confused, its hearing now distorted, it flew too closely to her hair and its claws caught on some strands. Her screams became so high-pitched, they were nearly inaudible.

Instantly, he reached forward and grasped the entangled bat, but before he crushed it, it nipped him on the right forefinger. While he bent down to help her, three other rabid bats landed on his back, two right on his neck just below the base of the brain. They nipped wildly and frantically, and thin lines of blood appeared immediately.

He stood up and bellowed in pain, turning and twisting to throw them off. His arms turned in windmill fashion, until he slammed his body against the outside rock wall, crushing one and throwing the other two off. As soon as they hit the ground, they lifted and flew away.

With her on the floor of the cave and him out of the opening, the remaining bats made their escape. The moment that the twittering and the sound of their wings flapping was gone, she lowered her arms from her eyes. He was crawling about outside, moaning and crying, the noise so guttural and horrible, that it added to her terror. She rose to her feet and started out of the cave.

As soon as she emerged, he turned toward her, moaning and holding his arms out in search of sympathy. Her eyes widened and she backed away. Then she turned to flee, but he ran alongside her, crying and whimpering. She stopped and spun around to push him away. When she started away again, he reached out and seized her skirt, pulling her so hard and so abruptly that she lost her footing and flew forward. She smacked the side of her head on a small boulder the size of a basketball and rolled over on her back.

He stood crouching beside her, his arms hanging limply, his torso moving up and down with the heavy, quick rhythm of his breathing. He didn't understand. Her eyes were closed and she did not move. The pain from the back of his neck drove him to his knees. He reached forward and touched her face as gently as he could, but she didn't stir. When he looked around, the forest seemed to be closing in around him. He pulled his head back and looked up at the tops of the trees until he could see the sky, and then he released a cry so deep from the depths of his being, that even he thought it came from another creature, one too horrible to imagine.

When Cy Baum came out of his house and saw that his granddaughter was not where he had left her, he had a terrible sinking feeling, even though it was very possible she had simply gone around back or to the other side. His immediate sense of panic weakened him and he could barely raise his voice or take a step. He felt his face grow pale and cold, so he took two deep breaths to regain his composure. Then he called.

And then he went around the back; and then he went around to the other side; and then he came to the front, all the while moving like an old stone savage, his steps deliberate and awkward, his shoulders hunched up. His shouts grew louder, his voice more intense. It finally brought Hilda to the front door.

"Cy? What is it?"

"Is she in there?" Her facial expression told him the answer. He went back to the basement. When he was confronted with the dark, empty room, his panic became unleashed. He stumbled up the cement steps, bruising his left hand when he reached out to keep himself from falling on the stone. Hilda was waiting on the front porch steps.

"What is it?"

"She's gone," he said. He was breathing hard now.

"Gone?" Hilda grimaced as though the word were ridiculous. "Did you look out back?"

"She's not there."

Hilda brought her hands to her throat. She shook her head in disbelief and began calling, herself. She came down the steps and went around the house. He followed some distance behind, calling and shouting whenever she left a gap. They stopped when they reached the basement door again.

"What does this mean, Cy? Where could she be? She wouldn't go far from the house."

"And the rabbit's gone, too," he said, but she didn't understand why that was significant.

"The rabbit? Who cares about that damn rabbit?"

"Huh? No, I mean . . . let's check inside once more. She might have slipped in behind us or . . . "

"And not hear us doin' all this calling?" Skeptically, Hilda followed him in. They called and called and checked all the rooms and bathrooms. Then they confronted each other, the panic, the fear, and the sorrow equally painted on their faces.

"I'll phone Eddie Morris," he said.

"Hurry," she said.

He fumbled twice with the dial, impatient with his own clumsy, thick fingers. It wasn't until he made the connection and the phone began to ring that he felt any sense of hope at all. He got his words out quickly.

"I'll be right there," Eddie said. "Don't panic," he added, as much for himself as for Cy. He had already begun to wonder if he hadn't made a terrible mistake by not doing what Barbara had suggested, by not telling the chief about the strange events that had occurred on Wildwood Drive.

He reported a missing child, called for some backup, and headed out as fast as he could, his lights blinking and his siren, the anthem of danger and trouble, flowing freely from the patrol car as he rushed over the country roads.

FOURTEEN

At first Faith was unaware of the morning. She had fallen asleep on and off and now, when she opened her eyes, it occurred to her that she might have passed away the night. The room light had been left on continuously, but she figured out how she could test the time. She rose from the bed and flipped off the light. Light penetrated the boarded windows. It was indeed another day. Why hadn't Mary come to wake her?

She put on the lights again and listened. The stillness was frighteningly complete. There wasn't even a creak in the house. She hoped Mary was outside her door again, but when she put her ear to the crack between it and the jamb, she heard nothing.

"Mother?" She waited and listened. Then she went to her knees and put her ear to the floor, desperately trying to pick up the vibrations of movement downstairs. There were none—no pans rattling, no dishes clinking, no radio, no footsteps; just deep, empty silence. Had Mary left the house?

Faith used the chamber pot again and then sat thinking on the bed. Surely Mary would bring her water . . . something. It couldn't last much longer; it couldn't. She wouldn't want to keep me out of school, she hoped, but that hope was weakened when she considered Mary's priorities. Mary wanted her to do well in school, but she also thought there were too many temptations there. And now with what she knew and thought about Bobby O'Neil . . . she might never want me to go back to school again, Faith thought. She knew Mary was capable of such radical decisions, especially if the decision had come to her through some kind of divine communication.

It was hard not to succumb to panic now. She was trapped and she felt helpless. She went back to the boarded windows and pressed the tips of her fingers hard against the sides of the slabs, pulling and tugging at them. But she couldn't get enough of a grip to work them away from the window casing, and the tips of her fingers became raw with the effort. She went back to the door and tried sliding her fingers between it and the floor to get some kind of grip and pull it open. She succeeded in getting the tops of her fingers through, but this gave her no advantage, and her efforts barely shook the heavy wooden portal.

Growing increasingly frustrated, she felt so closed in that she thought it was affecting her breathing. The panic continued to build in her. She slammed her fist into the wall and screamed, but when she waited silently afterward, she heard nothing. She stood up and kicked the wall. She did it again and again and again. Small indentations formed in the faded wallpaper, but the inch and a half Sheetrock backing didn't crumble.

She made her hands into fists and went to the windows again, this time pounding the boards that Mary had nailed to the casings; but they barely rattled. Tired, she sat on the bed and stared blankly at the wall across from her. She had cried herself out; she couldn't produce any more tears and her throat ached from the screaming.

She lay back on the bed and looked up at the ceiling. The silence was having a different effect on her now. Twice she thought she heard voices. She yelled, but all that came in return was her own echo. When she heard the voices again, she seriously thought they might be spirits trapped in the walls, trapped in the structure, trapped in the history of The Oaks.

She began to hallucinate.

Faces from the past came in and out of focus on the ceiling. A younger Mary smiled and spoke softly to her. She was saying nice things about her hair and her eyes and she was singing pretty little hymns. Her father, handsome and young, untouched by the inner turmoils that would eventually destroy him, told her stories. She could even hear herself as a little girl, laughing.

She remembered her father's cousin from Philadelphia who had come to visit them only once. She and her husband brought their little girl, who was two years younger than Faith. Even so, they had a good time together for the short time they stayed at The Oaks. Even in the early days, there weren't many times when she had friends over here; and after a while, there were none. There was a doll she and her little cousin both loved, and she had kept it all these years, preserved in her closet, a memory of a time when she shared make-believe and felt a child's happiness. Her cousin and she never wrote each other; they never called; they never communicated. Whatever happened that weekend was enough to drive her relatives away for good. Mary wouldn't even talk about them, especially after the accident. All her father's relatives died with him that day as far as Mary was concerned.

As she lay there thinking, she increasingly began to see herself as a younger child. Images and memories rolled by, faces and things juxtaposed with no apparent logic. It was the free flow of memory, as though her entrapment had lowered the dike and permitted the escape of anything warm, touching, and significant—all that had been dammed up in the recesses of her mind.

She moved from these memories to thoughts that Mary would have forbidden—sexual thoughts, erotic images, fantasies that had begun to recur with more urgency each time. She closed her eyes and imagined Bobby O'Neil climbing up the outside wall, as he had climbed up her fire escape. She saw him open the window and pound out the boards Mary had nailed to it. She saw him crawl in and come to her here on this bed.

As she sat up, he took her in his arms and they kissed a long, passionate kiss that brought a delightful weakness into her. He knelt down before her like her knight and put his head in her lap. She stroked him and stroked him until he looked up at her with those deep blue-green eyes. He was asking her, calling to her, softly demanding.

"Yes," she thought. "Yes, yes . . ."

He sat back as she began to unbutton her blouse. When she unfastened her bra and her breasts shook freely, he stood up and took her hands into his. She stood before him and they kissed again, this time his lips moving off hers and down over her cheeks to her neck and shoulders. She lifted her breasts to him and the tip of his tongue grazed her nipples. She moaned and felt his fingers travel down her stomach to unfasten her jeans. As they slipped down her legs, she sat back on the bed. In a few moments he was beside her, his own shirt and pants off. They embraced; they caressed and murmured their love for each other, and then they became completely naked and moved under the blanket.

To her, the eroticism was another form of prayer. In it she found hope and warmth. She wanted to give herself up to it as completely as she would give herself up to God, no matter how terrible a sin that might be.

These thoughts took her mind away from any regrets. In fact, the entire erotic image became her act of defiance. In it, through it, she would strike back at Mary for what she had done to her.

Yes, she thought, this is right . . . yes, yes . . .

She moved harder, faster. She ran her hands over her body, fumbling with her clothing, until she aroused herself to a pitch of excitement. It was better than anything she had done before and when the climax came, she exploded with deliberately loud moans.

Perhaps Mary would hear her. She didn't care; she wanted it. Good, she thought, good, good, good.

When it was over, she lay still in anticipation.

But God didn't punish her and Mary didn't come. There was only that deep, heavy, and now frightening silence.

Cy and Hilda were waiting on the front lawn when Eddie arrived. He grabbed his megaphone and joined them quickly. Their expressions of fright were somewhat lessened when he appeared. He only hoped he could do something for them and do it quickly. Before he spoke to them, he remembered his training—act cool, professional, and deliberately casual. It would calm them.

"So, what do we have?"

"She's gone, Eddie. She's gone," Cy said. Now, in this bright sunlight, under this tension, he looked every minute his age. Time had caught up with him swiftly, almost instantaneously. It reminded Eddie of the Edgar Allan Poe short story, *The Strange Case of M. Valdimar,* the story of a man hypnotized at the point of death and kept that way until he was awakened to degenerate right before the hypnotist's eyes. Eddie was afraid Cy would crumple and become dust in the course of a few moments.

Hilda looked a little more in control.

266

"He left her out here for a few minutes when he went into the house to fix a circuit breaker. By the time he returned, she was gone. We've gone around the house and out back, calling and calling; and we've checked every nook and cranny inside. She's nowhere to be found."

"She was with the rabbit," Cy said, eye to eye with Eddie. He nodded.

"Why do you keep talking about that rabbit?"

"Oh God," Cy said. He buried his face in his hands.

"Hey, take it easy. Take it easy. We'll find her. She wandered off, that's all."

"I just can't imagine her doing that," Hilda said, shaking her head.

"All right," Eddie said. "I'll start in the back. Help's on the way, only minutes behind me."

"Should I call Arnie?"

"No, not yet," Eddie said quickly. "Let's not panic everyone. This could be something very simple."

"I pray to God."

Eddie started for the backyard and Cy followed closely behind. When he came to the edge of the lawn, he brought his megaphone to his mouth and called.

Out front, Chief Sam Cobler arrived in a patrol car driven by Officer Burt Rosen. Cobler, a lifelong resident of the area, knew all the permanent residents, so Hilda went right into her story. Then they all joined Eddie and Cy in the back.

"Well?"

"Nothing, Chief. We'll have to fan out and search."

"All right. If we don't find her in fifteen minutes, I'll have them ring the fire siren in town and bring up some volunteers."

"Oh, God," Hilda said.

"I'll go in with you," Cy said.

"No," Eddie said. "You better wait here in case she calls from another direction."

Cy looked disappointed, but he remained behind as the three policemen went into the forest. Periodically, Eddie called through the megaphone.

The noise and the amplification of Eddie's voice turned the imp away from Gina's limp form. He scurried deep into the bushes and crouched low to the ground, forcing himself to hold down his moans of pain by biting his lower lip and squeezing his body tightly. After a few moments he saw Eddie appear.

When Eddie spotted the little girl, he lunged forward, crashing through the saplings. He was at her side in seconds. He put the megaphone down quickly and checked her pulse. He lifted her head gently and turned it to study the bruise just above her left temple. It looked like a nasty scrape. He saw the small boulder nearby and imagined what had happened. Then he raised the megaphone to his lips and announced that he had found the child.

As he carried Gina back through the forest, she began to regain consciousness. He tried to reassure her, but he had never seen such a look of terror on a child's face.

"She's all right," he called, as soon as Hilda and Cy caught sight of him. Nevertheless, Hilda began to cry.

"Grandma."

Hilda took her into her arms quickly and hugged her. Cy stood by, his eyes watering.

"Looks like she took a fall in there," Eddie said. Burt and Sam came out behind him.

"What did you do? Why did you go in there?" Hilda asked her and tried wiping away some of the streaks of dirt formed by her tears.

"My rabbit . . . " She pointed to the forest.

"Is that what you did? You went into the woods for your rabbit?" Eddie asked. His wide smile captured her attention.

"Look at her," Hilda said. "Oh, she needs a bath

and hot milk, and your hair, Gina . . . we've got to shampoo."

At the mention of her hair, Gina began to cry again. She touched her head to be sure nothing was still there.

"A bird went into my hair, but he took it out." They all looked at Eddie, but he shook his head.

"Who did?" Hilda asked. "Eddie?"

"No, that bad boy. He made me lose my rabbit. He made me. Make him get it back, Grandpa. Make him."

"Bad boy?" Cy turned to Eddie.

"Call the station," Sam Cobler told Rosen, "and tell them all is well up here."

"What do you mean, Gina?" Eddie asked, stepping closer to her. "There was a boy here?" She nodded. "Was he bigger than you?" She shook her head. "He wasn't?"

"He smelled," she said.

"I'll bet," Sam Cobler said. Gina stared at him. She was momentarily taken with the way his rubbery lips moved around the cigar.

"I better get her cleaned up," Hilda said. "Talk to her later. And forget that rabbit," she added, her eyes wide as she looked at Cy.

"All right. All right."

They watched her take the child back to the house. Eddie looked back at the woods and Sam Cobler lit the cigar.

"What do you make of that bird in the hair stuff?" Eddie asked, not looking at either of them.

"Kids imagine things when they're lost," Cobler said. "I'll bet she has an imaginary friend, too, right Cy?"

"She never said nothing about one before."

"Well . . . birds in the hair, smelly little boys . . . "

"Only kind of bird that might get caught in your hair is a bat," Cy said. "But it'd hafta be trapped and disoriented. Never could stomach them. Got one caught down my chimney last year and killed it with a broom."

"There shouldn't have been any kids around here now. School's in session," Eddie said, mostly to himself. "Maybe I'd better take a little walk in there and look around."

"Don't get lost yourself," Cobler said. Eddie turned and looked at him as though first realizing his boss was still there.

"I've got to talk to you, Chief. There have been a few odd things going on around here."

"Why should this place be any different from the rest of the township," Cobler said dryly. "Maybe you oughta take the child over to your doctor, Cy, just to have her checked out. Not a bad precaution after something like this."

"I will."

"After you come back from your nature hike, see what else you can do for them, Eddie. I'll be at the station all morning and we can talk there."

"OK, Chief." He and Cy watched Cobler walk off.

"What do you expect to find in there, Eddie?"

"I dunno. Bats could be anywhere in there, I guess, huh?"

"Oh sure. In trees, in caves. Big rocks southwest of here," he added, pointing. "Perfect spot for them. But why do you want to look for bats?" He paused for a moment until the thought connection was actually visible in his face. "You don't suspect rabies?"

"We've got to check out everything, Cy. You make sure she hasn't been bitten by anything." Cy turned and looked at the house.

"Oh my God."

"I'd like to know what she meant by 'little boy,' too. As soon as I return, we'll both talk to her some more."

"Right, right," he said. The shakiness had returned to his legs. He wiped his forehead with the palm of his

270

right hand and blew a long puff of air. Eddie reached out and patted him on the shoulder.

"Stay calm. I'll be back as fast as I can. Southwest, you said?"

"What? Oh, yeah, yeah, but that's some distance in. I can't imagine her . . . " He shook his head, but Eddie had already entered the bushes. "She must've imagined it," Cy muttered, picking up on Sam Cobler's theory. It was the most hopeful one and Cy thought Sam should know about these things. He turned and started for the house, stopped, and looked back. He wanted to say something else and get some more reassurance from Eddie, but Eddie was already too far in for any more conversation.

With long, quick strides, he moved through the forest. Occasionally, he used the megaphone he was still carrying to push away branches. As he traveled, he thought about his own daughter and how he had first felt when Cy called to tell him Gina and the rabbit were missing. On the way up to the Baums, he tried to envision Gina, but he continually saw Susie in his mind instead. He had the same confused vision when he spotted the little girl lying in the woods.

What did she mean by "little boy"? he asked himself again. He thought so intensely that he was sure he had said it aloud. Could one of those Cooper kids have cut school and come up here? He'd have to check that out, too.

After a while, he stopped traveling and stood quietly to get his bearing in the woods. He wanted to be sure he was traveling in the southwesterly direction. For a moment it was relatively silent in the forest, but then he heard something scurrying through the heavy foliage directly to his right. He listened and thought about deer. However, deer are usually quieter, he concluded. An idea came to him and he raised the megaphone to his lips.

"ALL RIGHT," he called. "WHOEVER IS IN THERE, STOP. THIS IS THE POLICE. I REPEAT, STOP." He lowered the megaphone and listened. Now it was very quiet. He started in the direction of the sounds and, almost immediately, they began again. "STOP!" he called. I could be yelling at a raccoon or a woodchuck, for all I know, he thought. The sounds grew more distant and soon were gone altogether. He waited a moment and then headed back in the direction of the caves.

When he arrived there, he immediately agreed with Cy—they were a perfect location for bats. He approached the rocks cautiously and stopped about six feet from the entrance of the first cave. He studied the opening and the grounds, looking for some evidence that Gina had indeed been this far into the woods. He couldn't imagine why she would ever go into a cave, but he took another step forward. It was then that he spotted the bat on the ground.

He went to it quickly and turned it over with the toe of his boot. It was obviously dead. He took out his handkerchief to wrap around the bat. He thought it would be wise to bring back a specimen for lab tests. While he was in a kneeling position, he saw what looked to be blood stains on the rock wall. He reached forward and touched them with his fingers. Because of the dampness and the coolness, the blood had not dried completely. It came off on the tips of his fingers.

"I hope this isn't hers," he muttered and then he thought, who else's could it be?

He turned around quickly and studied the forest around him. Everything was unnaturally still to him. It was as though Nature were waiting for him to make some kind of a discovery. He stood up in a crouch and peered into the cave entrance.

The bats that had been frightened out earlier, had returned. Even the rabid ones had been able to sense that their hole was safe again. They didn't like being out in the daylight long and the shadows they had located for the time being were nowhere as comfortable and as satisfactory as their cave. Only moments after they had reentered their darkness, they were asleep. Eddie could see them lining the walls. He whistled to himself and began a very slow and careful retreat. He saw another dead bat on the floor of the cave, but he made no effort to retrieve it. He had seen enough and gathered enough bad news for the Baums.

Clutching the dead bat in his handkerchief and the megaphone at his side, he jogged through the forest, his heart heavy, his mind reeling from confusion and anger. He looked off to the right from where he had heard the sounds of something moving. The only thing to do now, he thought, was to see if there were someone with Gina, find him, and learn from him what actually happened out there. Now, he felt a desperate urgency about it.

By the time he got back to the house, Gina had been bathed and her hair brushed out. The little girl looked revived and secure again. There was a small Band-Aid over her bruise.

"You two look like you lost your best friend," Hilda said, looking from Cy to Eddie and back to Cy. "She's all right." Cy looked to the floor to avoid Hilda's eyes. "What is it?"

"I went back into the forest," Eddie said. "I think the bird in her hair she was talking about was a bat."

"Oh no."

"I've one of them in the patrol car. Gonna take it in for lab tests, but there was some . . . some blood. Did any of her scratches look like a bite?"

Cy looked up quickly, waiting for her answer.

"Oh, I don't think so, Eddie. They're all surface scratches."

"Did you check her head?" Cy asked.

"Scrubbed it thoroughly. I didn't find anything."

273

"You'll have to take her over to the doctor and get a full examination," Eddie said. Hilda nodded.

"Now I'd better call Arnie and Bea."

"I think that would be wise," Eddie said. He turned to Gina, who sat obediently on the couch and stared up at them. "Well," he said, "maybe Gina and I can have a little talk now."

"Did you find my rabbit?"

"No," Eddie said, sitting beside her.

"He took it."

"Who?"

"That bad boy. I'll bet he took it. Get it back, Grandpa. I don't want him to have it. He's . . . ugh."

"Tell me about this bad boy, Gina. Was he taller than you?" She shook her head. "Was he fat?" She smiled and shook her head again. "Um, what color was his hair?"

"Dirty." She paused and her grimace turned to a laugh. "He wasn't wearing any clothes."

"What!" Hilda said.

"Did he tell you his name, Gina?"

"He couldn't talk. He made noises."

"Oh forgodsakes," Hilda said. "What is she talking about?"

"Was his hair long?"

"Uh huh." She nodded for emphasis. "It was over his eyes, too. He needs a bath, Grandma."

"Sounds like it. Who is she talking about, Cy?" Cy shrugged and shook his head.

"He didn't have a name then?" Eddie asked. Gina imitated her grandfather's shrug. "Did you ever see him before today?"

"Nope."

"But you went to the caves in the woods with him?" She nodded. "And there you saw the bats, the little black birds?" Her face reflected the memory of terror. "And one got into your hair?" She nodded again. "You were in the cave then?"

"Oh Gina, how could you do such a thing?" Hilda asked when she nodded. Gina's face began to crumple.

"That's OK. You're all right now. Don't cry. Just tell us again what happened and what the little boy did."

"A bird went into my hair and he grabbed it."

"Did any bite you?" Eddie asked. The three of them held their breaths. She shook her head. "Or even scratch you?" She shook her head. "Are you sure?"

"Uh huh."

"What happened then?"

"He pushed me down."

"The little boy? Where is he now?"

She shrugged and turned to Cy.

"Can we go back and look for the rabbit, Grandpa?"

"Oh, God," Hilda said. "Did you ever?"

"Children have a way of rebounding quickly," Eddie said, standing. "I think you'd better take her to your doctor, though, just to be sure about all this."

"We will."

Eddie started away, stopped, and thought a moment, and then turned back to Gina.

"Gina, did you ever see E.T.?" She nodded emphatically. "This littly boy, did he make you think of . . . " Before he could finish his question, her eyes widened and she nodded rapidly again.

"What the hell . . . " Cy took a step toward him. "What are you thinking of, Eddie?"

"I'm not sure. But I know one thing."

"What's that?"

"I'm gonna have a helluva time explaining all this to Sam Cobler," he said. "Talk to you later," he added and left.

As Eddie expected, the chief was not only skeptical about any relationship between events, he was downright amused by Eddie's seriousness. Eddie described the killing of the rabbits, Billy O'Neil's violent confrontation with "something" in the fields, the entrance

275

into Cy's basement, the strange footprints, and finally Gina's tale of the dirty, naked little boy.

"And you think all of this was done by some extra-terrestrial creature?"

"I didn't say that."

"Not in so many words. Look, almost anything could have killed those rabbits . . . "

"By opening a hasp on the cage first?"

"Maybe he forgot and left it opened."

"Twice?"

"All right, so it was a dumb prank. You, yourself, said the kid could have made those prints in the basement. Both those kids were in a state of panic. Their imaginations ran wild, that's all."

"There's one other thing," Eddie said and proceeded to describe his meeting with Mary Oaks and how he met Bobby O'Neil walking home in the rain.

"So what? I know about Mary Oaks. First off, you said the kid was climbing up her fire escape. He's lucky she didn't shoot him. She's a religious loon, hangs out with that crazy pastor from Neversink, but there's no crime in that." Sam took his feet off the desk and sat forward, his cigar plugged into the corner of his mouth. "Eddie, things have been somewhat dull around here, I know, but . . . "

"Maybe you're right," Eddie said quickly.

"Sure I'm right. That little girl went through quite an experience, bats and all. She's hallucinating. I mean, what else could it be? You know all the people in that area and all the kids. Any fit the description she gave you?" Cobler twisted the cigar with his tongue and lips and then smiled.

"No, of course not."

"So?"

"Yeah. I just wanted to have someone else hear it all and make a conclusion."

"Like anything, when you get too involved, you get a little blind to what's real and what's not. Check on the girl and make a couple extra passes down Wild-wood Drive the next few days. After a while, it'll all pass. It always does," Cobler said. Eddie nodded and got up. "In the meantime, the bat'll be checked out for us. That was real good police work, Eddie, real good. There's no doubt in my mind who's goin' to sit behind this desk after I retire."

"Thanks, Chief."

Eddie called the Baums later that afternoon and learned that the doctor believed none of Gina's wounds was made by anything but twigs and branches. He had gone over her body thoroughly and concluded there were no teeth marks, only scratches. Her scalp was clean.

"Thank God there weren't any real wounds," Cy said. "All surface stuff. My son's comin' up late this afternoon to get her, though. His wife wants to take her to their own doctor and . . ."

"The bat analysis came back positive, Cy. It did have rabies."

"Oh."

"I contacted the conservation department. We're going into the cave tomorrow morning and extermi-nate what's left."

"Good idea."

"So it may not be a bad idea for their doctor to reevaluate."

"No, no, you're right." Cy's voice became weak and trailed off.

"I can take a ride up and talk to Arnie, if you'd like."

"No, that's OK."

"I'll be in that area anyway. I want one more discussion with the O'Neil boy who was attacked by . . . by whatever."

"Chief wants that?"

"No, not exactly," Eddie said.

After he hung up, he finished his patrol, making

Wildwood Drive his last stop. Bobby O'Neil greeted him at the door when he drove up. From the way he looked when Eddie stepped out of the car, Eddie assumed he had been watching for him, expecting him. Eddie reassured him immediately.

"I'm here to talk to your little brother again," he said.

"Oh, for a moment I thought . . . " He looked behind him in the house. "Faith didn't come to school today. I think it was my fault. She's probably being punished."

"Well you guys'll hafta work that out. Just stay off of their fire escape. Billy around?"

"Yeah, I'll get him."

"Who is it, Bobby?"

"It's Officer Morris, Mom. He wants to see Billy again."

"Oh, Dick, go see."

"Hey, Eddie." Dick O'Neil came out from the kitchen and met him in the foyer. They shook hands quickly. "What's up? Thanks for what you did with Billy."

"It was nothing. How's it going?"

"Busy for a change."

"I know what you mean."

Billy appeared at the top of the stairway. When he saw Eddie, his eyes lit up and he hurried down, Bobby walking slowly behind him.

"Hi."

"What'dya say, partner? Get a chance to use your whistle yet?"

"Has he? He's been blowin' it all afternoon," Bobby said. Eddie smiled and rubbed Billy's head.

"Come on into the living room, Eddie," Dick said. He led everyone in.

"This won't take long. I just wanted to talk to Billy for a moment." He paused and looked at Dick

O'Neil's smiling face. "About his experience in the field. We had another sort of incident on the road."

"Oh?"

"Yeah. Cy Baum's granddaughter got lost in the woods this morning."

"What!" Cindy came in from the hallway.

"We found her, though. She's all right. Just a little scratched up. However, we located some rabid bats in the process."

"Damn," Dick said. "Now I'm glad I had that dog tied."

"Yeah. Don't let him loose for a while."

"No chance of that," Dick said.

"But Billy wasn't attacked by any bats," Cindy said. She turned to him for confirmation.

"No. It was an E.T.," Billy said.

"Billy!"

"That's all right," Eddie said. "I want to hear about that."

"Huh?"

"Go ahead," Eddie said, ignoring Dick for the moment. "Tell me about the E.T. again. You said he had no clothes, right?"

"Yeah."

"And he didn't say any words, nothing at all?"

"No. Just a scream."

"Tell me about his hair again."

"It was long, down to his shoulders and some of it covered his eyes."

"What is this, Eddie? You're not saying there's any truth to his story, are ya?" Dick asked.

"Billy, think hard now. Did he look like a little boy?"

Billy eyed his mother and father for a second and then smiled.

"I saw his pee shooter," he said.

"What the hell's going on, Ed?"

"Cy's granddaughter gave me the same kind of description. Something like that was in the woods with her, she says."

"Well, what the hell kind of a story is that?" Dick asked.

"I don't know. Both kids were in a panic and both could have done some imagining, but why should both come up with the same wild tale?"

Everyone looked down at Billy for a moment.

"If he comes again," he said, "I'm gonna blow the whistle." He took it out of his pocket to demonstrate, but Cindy stopped him.

"What about those bats?" Dick asked.

"Going in tomorrow morning with the conservation men to exterminate them. They're holed up in some caves behind the Baums'."

"I know those caves," Bobby said.

"You stay away from them," Cindy said quickly. "In fact, you stay out of the woods altogether until Eddie says it's safe."

"I'll let you know how we make out tomorrow," Eddie said. "OK, thanks. See ya, Billy." He started for the door. Dick followed him out.

"What are you going to do with this story?"

"I don't know. The chief doesn't think there's anything to do. Maybe he's right. Talk to you tomorrow."

"Right," Dick said. "Let me know if there's anything I can do to help."

Eddie stopped at the Baums', but Arnie had been there already and taken Gina home. Both Hilda and Cy looked distraught. They sat lethargically in their living room.

"My daughter-in-law made him leave right away once I called back and told them about the bats."

"Can't blame her, Cy."

"No, but she'll blame us. If only I hadn't left her out there when I went in to fix that breaker."

"Can't blame yourself for that. You didn't leave her alone that long."

"Long enough to do the damage. I guess we are too old for lookin' after little ones."

"Stop it, Cy," Hilda said.

"Well, it's true."

"Depends on what happened out there, Cy," Eddie said. "Even a younger person might not have prevented it. You can't anticipate everything."

"Maybe," he said, but he didn't look convinced. "How did the chief react to all you told him?"

"He didn't. He might be the smartest of all of us. Well, see you in the morning."

"I'd like to go with you."

"Oh no, Cy."

"She's right, Cy."

"Just like to see them creatures destroyed, that's all."

"I'll let you look at the bodies. Why should you go traipsin' through the forest?"

"You listen, Cy Baum. You're not as young as . . . "

"As I think. I know, I know."

Eddie stared at both of them for a moment. The heaviness of the scene depressed him. It reminded him of the sitting room in the Baker Nursing Home in Liberty—old people just staring into space, eyes glassy, hypnotized by the emptiness of their lives and the monotonous highway that led them only to their deaths. In this moment he hated whatever it was that had done this to them, and he wished that he had something concrete to attack.

Even if it were some extraterrestrial creature.

FifTEEN

Mary's determination was so intense that she didn't leave the basement even though she had grown tired. She fought sleep for as long as she could, and even when she dozed, she woke up periodically, searching the darkness and listening to be sure he hadn't entered while she wasn't awake.

The night seemed to take forever and when morning came and he was not back, she was surprised. She suspected, though, that he would come in just before she usually brought him his breakfast, so she continued to wait.

The little illumination that came through the hole in the wall transformed the basement into a dreamy, surrealistic world. The shadows elongated; their shapes twisted and turned in bizarre configurations. Particles of dust caught in the tiny rays of light seemed in perpetual motion. Mary felt lightheaded and ethereal herself. She was like someone caught between the real and the unreal worlds, floating on gray-black clouds, waiting . . . waiting.

She heard him only moments before he began his reentry.

He had been in a frenzy, charging through the forest and the undergrowth, driven on by the stinging pain that radiated from the bat bites. The only thing that gave him pause was Eddie Morris shouting through his megaphone. He heard it, listened, and then ran from it. Everything in the forest was frightening to him now. The girl was gone and he had been hurt. That made him wild. He neglected well-traveled paths and tore through the fields, tripping on roots and vines, scratching himself, bruising his feet and his calves. The more he hurt himself, the more panicky he became. He could think of only one solution—get to the safety of his box, the warmth of his raggedy blanket, the soothing comfort of his own hum and embrace. In fact, he longed for it, longed for what had been distasteful to him once he had discovered the outside world—his basement.

He never thought about the big creature or about being discovered. He had lost all sense of time and he had forgotten how long he had been out. In his flight he came across other animals, friendly animals, but he felt threatened by them, so he growled at them and showed his teeth. Some ran from him; some looked at him curiously, but stayed their distance. It seemed to him it was taking him too long to get back and that made him even more irritable. He struck at branches and vines, attacking the wilds that had once been so beautiful and exciting. But all the world was gray now; everything was of one color, one texture. Nothing attracted his interest; he no longer had the impish curiosity.

It wasn't until he saw the house before him that he felt any sense of calm, but even that didn't slow him down. His hair was filled with stickers and twigs; his body was covered with dirt and pieces of leaves. There was a long scratch from the right corner of his mouth nearly to the tip of his ear. Blood had appeared on his left foot, caking over the toes. But he noticed none of this. It was as though he had begun to crawl out of himself and leave his body like a shell on the ground behind him.

He whimpered and went forward, the house looming above him, growing, growing. He saw it as a living thing about to swallow him, but he welcomed that. He wanted to escape the outside world now, and he wasn't capable of seeing the irony in such a desire. When he came upon his hole in the wall, he finally paused, feeling safe. It would only be a matter of moments and he'd be secure in his box.

He wiped his face. The bites on his back felt like the candles the big creature often brought with her when she came down to feed or bathe him. In fact, he spun around, half expecting her to be there, touching the base of his brain with the tiny fire. Of course, there was nothing, nothing but the pain. He tried to reach back and touch it, but he was too muscular and tight for such a contortion. There would be no relief, until he got into his box.

He approached the hole. Only then did he consider the possibility of the big creature discovering him. For a moment that vision left him undecided. He sniffed at the opening. He couldn't be sure, but he thought he sensed her.

What was the alternative? He looked back at the wild bushes and the forest. They were no longer as attractive to him as they had been and the little girl wasn't friendly. He would have to chance it, chance facing the big creature and her anger. The thought of that had a new and quite unexpected effect on him. Perhaps it came from the radiating pain in his neck, pain that was now traveling over his shoulders and sending fingers of heat into his head. The effect was to make him angry and to make him show it. He heard himself growl. He felt his body tighten in anticipation of his defiance. His fingers stiffened into claws and he ground his teeth together until his gums hurt. Then, he began to enter the hole.

She saw him lowering himself in, finding his footing on the fieldstone wall. She waited until he touched the floor of the basement and then she moved forward out of the darkness. By the time he heard her behind him and turned, she had raised her hand, clutching the strap. He brought his arms up just in time to block most of the first blow. But a piece of the strap caught him on the right temple. Because of the surprise, it stung more than usual.

"SATAN!" she screamed. She struck him again and again. He tried to escape the blows, but he didn't flee to a corner or the safety of the old furniture piled against the wall. Instead he went in a circle around her, moving faster and faster. Her blows began to miss, because turning quickly to strike him made her dizzy. "DEVIL, DEVIL, DEVIL . . . "

Whenever one of her blows did catch him on the back or on the head, he reached forward angrily and swiped at her legs, scratching her with his long, sharp fingernails. She kicked him, hitting him in the ribs and turning him over. She swung again, this time striking his face and his chest. He screamed his distorted high-pitched cry and scampered toward an old dresser against the rear wall.

But she followed him, striking harder than ever, each blow coming down full force. Some hit the bat bites, making the pain so excruciating he could barely crawl; but finally he squeezed under the dresser. Her anger intensified when she couldn't get at him. So she grabbed onto the heavy, old furniture and literally moved it off him. Exposed once again, he went to the wall. His only hope now was height.

Her blows had begun to tear at his flesh. The welts were antagonized, bleeding. He grasped a protruding stone and dug his now swollen feet into a groove. Like a monkey, he scampered straight up the wall, until he could hook his hand around a beam and swing himself into an opening between the ceiling and the wall of the basement. She paused only to contemplate how she could continue whipping him. He pulled himself in as far as he could, when she snapped the belt above her head at him. But she couldn't reach him.

Unsatisfied, yet still determined to punish him further, she pulled the old dresser close to the wall and crawled up on it. The layer of dust on the shiny veneer made it slippery, but she was too intent to notice. From this height she struck him easily. He pressed himself back, now growling freely and showing his teeth. He no longer had control of his reactions. She reached back to hit him straight on, but he would not suffer any more pain.

He leaped out at her, clawing her face with his fingernails as he dropped to the floor. His unexpected aggressiveness took her by surprise and she lost her footing on the dresser. Her feet flew out from under her and she went crashing down, the base of her spine hitting the edge of the dresser and her upper torso slapping over it, smashing the back of her head against the thick, solid oak. Her spine snapped and she flipped over completely, landing in a folded position, face down.

He was at her again, this time surprised at how easily he could push her over onto her side. But a stream of blood rolled out of her mouth and he backed away immediately. Her eyes were still open and she glared at him with a glazed, hateful look. Her arm extended toward him slowly. When her hand opened, he slapped at it, gouging the palm. The fingers closed instinctively and she was still.

He waited, his growling diminishing. The hateful belt lay a few feet from him. He took it up and then flung it across the basement. He looked for her reaction. She didn't move, but he still didn't trust her. He waited and watched her closely. Nearly a half hour passed before he ventured forward in tiny, careful movements, expecting her to be up and at him in a moment.

His body was tensed, ready for flight, but she didn't move or turn toward him. He circled away from her, studying her constantly. Once he thought her fingers twitched, but after he waited, growling again, nothing happened.

He reached his box, and still staring at her, crawled into it. Once there, he lay back facing her. He was like that for a little more than an hour before fatigue and pain finally drove him into sleep. His eyes closed and he fell into a restless slumber filled with wild sounds and horrible faces. He dreamed of bats and snakes and the big creature's belt. He tossed and turned until he woke himself with his contortions.

It took him a few moments to reorientate himself. After he did, he remembered where the big creature had fallen and looked in that direction. He was surprised she was still there, just as quiet and as unmoving as before. Gradually, his curiosity overcame his fears and he crawled out of the box. He moved toward her in short, quick steps, crouching and crawling and sniffing the air.

When he was an arm's length from her, he whimpered and waited in anticipation of one of her blows, but nothing happened. He sensed something different about her now. The small pool of blood that had formed on the ground by the side of her face had begun to sink into the hard earth. The red line from the corner of her mouth lost its brightness and didn't drip any longer. Her mouth was slightly opened, the tips of her teeth visible. He thought he saw her tongue just under her upper lip. Her eyes were opened and she looked upward.

He sniffed the air between them and then reached forward slowly . . . slowly . . . the tips of his fingers nearly there. He thought she moved and pulled his arm back instantly, springing a few feet backwards at the same time; but apparently, she hadn't.

It took him almost as long to approach her the second time as it did the first. Once he was in arm's reach again, he did the same slow extension of his arm until his fingers were inches from her face. Then, in a burst of courage and curiosity, he touched her. What he felt caused him to pull his hand back as quickly as if he had touched fire.

He paused to understand it. Then to confirm what he sensed, he reached out and touched her again. This time he permitted his fingers to linger and travel down her face. When she didn't move, he was certain. He sat back and stared at her. His whimpering and growling ceased. He waited, undecided about what to do next. The pain in his neck and head had intensified terribly. He could feel it moving over the tops of his eyes.

He embraced himself and rocked, but even the humming didn't sound right, so he stopped and touched her again. Then he crawled back to his box.

She was as the little creatures he had squeezed too hard, but even so, he didn't feel safe closing his eyes in her presence. She was spoiling the power of the box. It gave him no relief and did not ease his pain. He couldn't be sure she wouldn't get up again and hit him with the strap. She was the big creature; he couldn't think of her as anything else.

He was confused and irritable. The headache had become more intense and now made it impossible for him to sleep. His limbs seemed uncontrollable. He kept extending them and pulling them back. He turned and twisted and moaned. The box just wasn't comfortable. It was no good here anymore, no good . . .

He looked to the hole again. Everything ached, but he had to get up and get out. He moved over the floor slowly now, not because he wanted to be careful, but because the pain running down his back and through his legs made it difficult for him to go fast. He paused at the wall and looked back at her. She didn't rise to prevent him from leaving. He looked about the basement sadly. Everything about it seemed so different to him now. He didn't understand, but he felt betrayed. He got his footing on the wall and then put his head back and released a long, piercing howl of pain and confusion.

With the sound echoing behind him, he slipped through the hole like a shadow and was gone.

He had lost all sense of direction and moved in a senseless circle, zigzagging and crisscrossing his way through the field. The sunlight brought pain to his eyes, but it was the tightness in his throat that held most of his attention. The aches and the restlessness kept him moving, as though his only hope lay in motion. There was a small pool of stagnant water just beyond the bushes to his right, but the mere thought of drinking produced such contractions in his throat that he began to gag. He crawled as fast as he could to get away from the sight of the liquid.

Finally, he found a cool spot under a large maple tree. He lay there gasping, too tired to react to his drawing limbs. He closed his eyes, but that didn't diminish the pain in them. A swelling had begun at the base of his brain, and the whole area was supersensitive, so that if he just grazed it against something, it sent knives down his neck and caused him to cry out.

Gradually, the afternoon sun draped longer and wider shadows over the landscape. The first star appeared, and then the lights of a house some distance to his left went on. He struggled to his feet again, steadying himself against the tree, and looked out at the house. For a few moments he simply stared at it as though he were drunk on the sight. All different kinds of unrelated images and thoughts passed before him in a staticlike jumble.

He suddenly felt clothed in a warm glow and started forward, not stopping until he heard the dog bark.

Upstairs, Billy O'Neil opened his window and looked out. Captain was straining at the chain, going up on his hind legs and driving his body forward, until the chain and the collar pulled him back with equal force. His bark was high pitched and hysterical. Billy didn't want to call down to his parents. He took the whistle out of his pocket instead and blew and blew and blew, as hard as he could. The noise only aggravated the dog more and he lunged at the air. The chain loosened and snapped, loosened and snapped.

Downstairs, Bobby and his father finally heard the racket. Bobby lowered the volume on the television set so they could listen more clearly. Cindy joined them in the hallway.

"What the hell's going on now?" Dick said. He rushed to the back door. Billy continued to blow his whistle. Just as Dick O'Neil stepped onto the back porch, Captain's chain snapped loose from the tree. Instantly, the dog dove into the bushes and was gone.

"Damn! Get my shotgun," Dick commanded and Bobby hurried back into the house. "Stop that damn whistling!" he screamed. Billy pulled himself back inside and hurried down the steps, just as Bobby brought his father the gun.

"Where are you going, Dick?" Cindy asked.

"The dog's loose, dammit."

"But it's getting too dark to shoot anything," she said, as he went down the steps. "Dick, those bats . . . they're out by now!"

He paused at the doghouse and looked out over the fields. He heard Captain barking and charging through the brush. Dick took a few steps in and then stopped. He couldn't see anything to shoot at and he didn't want to go running after that dog. Cindy came up behind him.

"Dick, come back. It's no use. Come back. We'll call Eddie Morris."

"Shit," he said. "How the hell did that chain break

loose?" He spun around looking for Bobby. "Didn't you see it was loose?"

"It wasn't, Dad."

"Damn. That animal comes back, we'll have to take him to a vet and keep him tied. Damn."

"Come back inside, Dick. Please. I don't like this," Cindy said. She searched the darkening night sky for signs of bats. The dog's barking became more distant.

"Aaa, maybe he'll get lost for good," Dick said and turned back. The three of them returned to the house. Billy was waiting in the doorway.

"I blew my whistle," he said excitedly. "I blew my whistle and it worked. It kept him away!"

"Kept who away?" Cindy asked.

"E.T.," Billy said. "I saw him again."

The three stared down at him. Then both Bobby and his father looked back over the fields. Neither saw anything.

"This is scaring me, Dick. Call Eddie Morris. Please."

"All right, all right." The dog's barking now came from the woods. "I hope he gets whatever he's chasing, so we'll find out what it is once and for all," he said.

They went inside, but Billy and Bobby waited by the doorway and listened to Captain pursuing in a frenzy.

The animal had crossed the field rather quickly, the dragging chain not holding him up. But when he reached the forest in pursuit of his prey, his chain became tangled in some stumps and the resulting tug snapped him back so hard, he fell to the earth. He struggled to his feet and continued to bark and pull, but the chain was too entangled for him to simply break loose. The prey was getting further and further away.

Of course, he had fled from the dog as quickly as he could, but there was no question now that with his slowed, painful movements, he would have been caught if the dog had not snarled himself on the stumps. He went back into the fields, creating as much distance as he could between himself and the barking, yelping animal. Exhausted from the flight and the pain, he finally collapsed in a gully not far from The Oaks.

His body felt as though it were on fire, so he drew the cool night air around him and welcomed the chill of the earth beneath him. Unaware of how close he was to the safety of his own basement, he curled up, put his thumb in his mouth, and fell into something that resembled a state of unconsciousness more than it did sleep. But it didn't last long.

He awoke in a piercing, ghoulish scream that ripped through the night. Red ants had found him, crawled over his body, and begun to bite on his tender skin. He jumped up and flailed about wildly, slapping at his arms and legs and stamping his feet until most of the ants were brushed away. Then he crashed through the bushes and fled to the edge of the forest. There, he rested a moment, taking hold of a tree and looking about with yellowed, frightened, and confused eyes. Nothing looked familiar; nothing looked friendly.

He turned and went further in, moving trancelike, his awkward gait slowed, his head lowered in fatigue and defeat. Finally he stopped near a large rock. First, he leaned against it, breathing hard, his tongue out, his eyelids drooping. After a moment he tried to get some footing on the boulder, but his feet didn't work right and his toes didn't grip as they always had. He clawed at the stone to pull himself up, but he was no more successful at that. Frustrated, he went around the rock and placed himself against the pocket of it. On this side the rock had something of a ledge, which served him as a roof.

He rubbed his legs and arms again, and felt a great thirst and then a great pain in his throat. It was better to close his eyes and try to forget. He couldn't remember much anyway, and there was an increasingly loud buzzing in his ears. He slapped at them and put his palms over them, but nothing seemed to help. He wanted to do something else to make himself feel better, but he couldn't recall what that something else was.

He had a vision of another like himself, but he couldn't put all the parts together. There was long hair, but it was a different color from his. There were sounds, but the sounds were nothing like the sounds he made. The vague memory of laughter threaded through his confusion. He attempted to catch it mentally a few times, but every time he put all his concentration to it, it evaporated.

He felt a need to reach out for something or someone, but when he extended his arms, he couldn't even imagine what it was he sought. So he slumped back against the rock. He was too tired to react to the jagged surface digging into his skin. Instead, he let his head fall against his right shoulder, his drooping arms at his sides. His hands, palms up, opened and closed spasmodically.

He could see his legs in the darkness and for a moment he thought them to be two long, thick snakes moving about him. He made some kind of sound at them. At least he felt the sound come from him, come from somewhere in the center of his chest. And then he closed his eyes.

There was more illumination behind his lids—colors and flashing lights in lightning streaks. He opened and closed his eyes many times because the brightness disturbed his rest. When sleep came again, it felt like a heavy, wet sheet covering him with the weight of darkness and the damp odor of his own dirty flesh. In his crazed nightmares, he gnawed on his own lower lip.

Things of the night stirred around him. Animals that sensed him, even in their sleep, started in fear, instinctively hearing the bad vibrations, and moved away.

After a while nothing was too close to him. But he didn't know anything of his solitude. He was a part of the rock, hard and grainy, practically inanimate, stirring and jumping convulsively as he fell down the twisted, nightmarish tunnel dug by his infected and sick body.

He was spinning and falling and all he grasped to stop it turned into oozing mucus. The world was filled with sores, abrasions, and bruises. The sky was inflamed and the cry he heard was the primeval cry of the race being born in fire and brimstone, the flesh of every embryo turning instantly into ashes and smoke. He was thrown back through time, back over the genetic highway, until he settled into a mass of bubbling protoplasm waiting to be born again.

The morning sunlight would cut through the trees and slice him like a hot knife.

"OK, Sam Spade," Sam Cobler said, "you went and did it."

"What?" Eddie looked back at Barbara who stood a few feet behind him in the kitchen. "What's up, Chief?"

"Nothing much, except you've got one of those families up on Wildwood Drive a little hysterical."

"Which family?"

"Just got a call from Dick O'Neil. His wife's terrified. Seems their dog broke loose and went after E.T."

"I don't understand, Chief."

"Oh, that's a twist. I was beginning to think you were the only one who did. That kid of theirs, Billy, said he saw your creature again and the dog's out in the woods barking his head off. Dick wants to go after it; his wife's screaming about rabid bats, and his little boy is blowing a police whistle to scare away creatures from outer space. You were up there again today asking questions?"

"Well, I just thought . . . "

"All right, all right. Look, Ralph's up in Loch Sheldrake checking on a brawl in Groman's Tavern. I got Bob and Willie on an ambulance call. You're going on overtime. Get up there and settle the problem, will ya. And forgodsakes, don't get anyone else on that street hysterical, will ya."

"OK, Chief. I'll take care of it."

"Call in when you're finished," Cobler said and hung up.

"What is it, Eddie?"

"I don't know," he said, going for his jacket. "I might have botched things up. I probably should have left things alone instead of letting my instincts dictate my actions."

"Your instincts have been pretty reliable in the past, Eddie."

"Yeah." He thought for a moment. "I don't know about this time, though," he said and then kissed her on the cheek.

When he reached the O'Neils', things had not calmed down much. The dog was still barking wildly from the woods. The O'Neil boys were at the back door and Cindy was seated at the kitchen table, a cup of coffee between her hands. Dick O'Neil paced about angrily.

"She won't let me go out there," he said. "It sounds like the damn dog is caught. He ran off draggin' his chain behind him, the stupid mutt."

"Tell him everything, Dick. Tell him what Billy said."

"Oh, Billy, Billy. The kid's got a wild imagination," Dick O'Neil said and then focused on Eddie. "I'm sorry, Eddie, but I don't think you're coming here today and asking him about that boy creature helped the situation."

"Maybe not," Eddie said. "I didn't mean to cause problems."

"Oh, he was just doing his job," Cindy said.

295

"Don't worry about the dog. I'll go out there and get him," Eddie said.

"Well, I'm comin' along."

"Dick!"

"Dammit, Cindy, I'm not a little boy."

"I didn't say you were."

"I'll get my flashlight and meet you in the back-yard," Eddie said. He went out to his patrol car and then walked around the house. Billy and Bobby came out on the porch.

"I saw it again," Billy said. "I did."

"The dog went wild," Bobby said.

"It could have been anything, boys. Let's not jump to conclusions," Eddie said. Dick O'Neil appeared with his flashlight.

"But I blew the whistle," Billy said.

"And that probably scared the hell out of the mutt, too," Dick said. "You guys get back inside and don't worry your mother. Women," he said, joining Eddie and starting for the bushes.

"Well, you can't blame her. You're right, though," Eddie said, looking toward the forest. "The dog sounds caught. Barking from one spot."

"It's not that bad here. Let me lead," Dick said and they went on across the field.

Although there was no moon, the sky seemed ablaze with stars because of the cloudless sky. The spaces between the dog's barks grew shorter, as it sensed their coming. When Eddie looked back, he could see Cindy and the two boys silhouetted in the back porch door. The darkness around him, the heavy foliage and undergrowth, and the reverberations of the dog's barking created an ominous atmosphere. He couldn't help but think about the mysterious creature both children described. When he did so, he turned almost hypnotically to the left and looked out at the dark, brooding house that was inky against the starlit sky. The Oaks looked deserted. He suddenly felt that the illumination

296

cast by his flashlight was sorely inadequate. They were at the mercy of shadows.

"There he is!" Dick said and ran toward the dog. Eddie followed quickly. It was obvious Captain was eager to see his master. He jumped all over Dick, licking his hands and face and making it difficult for him to loosen the twisted, entangled chain. Eddie stood by and looked out over the field toward The Oaks. "What a mess."

"Need help?"

"No, I got it," he said and after a few more moments, he freed the chain. Almost immediately, the dog started toward The Oaks. "What the . . ." Dick leaped forward and caught hold of the chain again. "The crazy mutt."

"Something's still out there," Eddie said. "Near The Oaks." The dog began barking again.

"Look at him. If I let him, he'd get lost and tangled out there again."

"Better get him back. Cindy's nervous."

"Yeah. QUIET!" Dick commanded. He pulled the dog closer to him and forced it to sit. It did so, but it continued to growl. "This time I'll cement him to the tree." He shortened and tightened his grip on the chain so he could have better control of the dog and started for home. Eddie didn't follow. "Ain't you comin'?"

"What? Oh, no, no, I think I'll just walk over to The Oaks and have a look about. Something might be about to disturb them."

"Disturb Mary Oaks? I doubt it. All right. I'll see you back at my place."

"Right."

Eddie watched Dick and the dog go and then he started toward The Oaks, shining his light before him and making his way through the bushes carefully and slowly, watching both sides as he moved and listening as hard as he could. What was it? he wondered. What was out here? Was it just a wild animal, a raccoon, like

Dick and the chief thought? He fought back any fantastic proposals his imagination tried to present to him, but as he drew closer to The Oaks and the dark building loomed higher and wider, it was difficult not to think of terrible things.

He suddenly realized that there didn't seem to be a light on anywhere in the house. No one home? They couldn't go to sleep this early, could they? he wondered. Something scurried to his right and he spun around with the flashlight. He wove the beam in and out of the bushes, over the earth and through the saplings. A pair of eyes stared out at him, but when he took a few steps toward it, whatever it was turned and was swallowed by the darkness. He heard a screech owl way off to his right, probably a half a mile or so in, and then he looked longingly for a moment toward the O'Neils', where Dick was just arriving and the voices of the boys could be heard in their excitement.

Directing the beam to the house, he ran the light up the rear wall and down by the corners of the building. How lonely it must be to live in such a place, he thought, and once again considered the kind of person Mary Oaks was. He would at least have to go around to the front and knock on the door. If he were lucky, no one would be home and he could forget about all this for now.

He stepped onto what were once the back lawns and manicured grounds. Tall grass and weeds grew wildly about the old wooden benches and tables. He saw the remnants of what was once a beautifully hand-built pond constructed with fieldstones. Now the stagnant water looked oily and the hearty weeds practically grew into it. He was sure it was just his imagination, but there was a pervasive odor of decay about the place.

He started around toward the front, running the beam of light before him and over the building. All the windows on this side were as dark as the ones in the rear. He had quickened his pace in the hope of getting this over with quickly when he saw it. It stopped him in his tracks and he held his flashlight on it—a small, but significantly gaping hole in the fieldstone foundation wall. What an odd thing. What could be its purpose? Slowly, he approached it. He knelt down before it and turned his flashlight in.

The basement smelled dank and sour and the darkness was so complete, it was like looking into a black curtain. He started the light at the foot of the stairway to the left and cut a line through the thick darkness along the floor, over old furniture. He stopped when he spotted an oddly shaped box. There were bowls beside it and a shredded blanket draped over one side of it. It looked like it had a piece of a mattress or a small cushion on the floor of it. He continued his investigation, running the light over the back wall and around to more furniture, the water heater and the oil burner, and then . . .

He stopped.

First he saw the hand and then the arm and then the entire body of Mary Oaks. From this angle, he couldn't tell that her eyes were opened.

"HEY!" he shouted. His voice echoed through the basement and came back at him, as though there were five duplicates of him within, but she didn't stir.

A cold chill threaded its way up his spine and settled at the base of his brain. He turned abruptly and looked behind him into the darkness. When he looked back, his hand shook and the light danced over Mary Oaks' torso. He paused a moment longer, the realization settling over him.

"MRS. OAKS!" Again, there was no movement. Since he couldn't fit through the hole to get to her, he stood up and hurried around to the front of the house.

His instincts were right after all.

SIXTEEN

Eddie Morris pounded on the front door of The Oaks and waited. No lights went on and no sounds were made. He shouted, pounded again, stepped back, and contemplated the front windows, and then put his shoulder to the door. The Oaks' front door was an antique. More than one traveler with an eye to valuable old things remarked about it in passing. It was nearly a half foot wider and a foot taller than the average modern door. It was made of thick oak wood and the front of it was handcarved. The years had weathered it, but age had only made it stronger. Eddie thought he might as well have tried to move a solid wall.

He went to the nearest front window on his right. The windows were the old six-panel type, so when he broke one panel with his flashlight, he was only able to get his hand in to search for the window lock. He couldn't reach it, so he broke all the frames and then kicked in the narrow wooden crossbars. Now he was able to step through it carefully. He came down in what he thought to be a sitting room. The furniture was barely visible, until he put on his flashlight and looked about.

"HELLO!" he called, hoping to get some reaction from Mary Oaks' daughter. Hearing nothing, he continued on through the room and out to the hallway. He explored everything around him, looking into other rooms, shining his beam down to the kitchen and coming back to find what he thought must be the basement door. He was surprised at the hasp and open lock that dangled from it. Did they think someone might enter the house from the basement?

As soon as he stepped in, he found the light switch and turned it on. He paused for a moment to think about the odors and the dim glow of the inadequate ceiling fixture. What the hell is going on? he wondered and started down the steps slowly. When he reached the bottom and turned around, he held the light in the direction of Mary Oaks' body. He went to her quickly and knelt down beside her. The moment he took her hand into his, he knew she was dead.

He let her body fall over completely so she'd be on her back and shined the light on her face. Her eyes were still wide opened, a look of total surprise and horror locked into them. He searched for wounds and found the stain of blood down the side of her mouth. Other than that, there was nothing on her body to indicate what had happened.

He stood up and looked around. When the light of his flashlight fell on the dresser, he saw what looked to be footprints in the heavy layer of dust. For a moment he studied that and then directed the light up the wall. He traced the beams all around the basement, but he saw nothing. Puzzled, he remembered the box.

The blanket was absolutely disgusting. It reeked of urine and other odors. There were the remains of some food in the dishes and bowls beside the box and traces of food in the box itself. Did they have some kind of pet down here? he wondered and looked for any signs of an animal. There were no bones, no boxes of dog or cat food. The body of a dead rodent just to the right caught his eye. He looked at it and ran the light up into the far corner, where he saw what looked to be other dead things—decayed bodies of field mice, small rats, even a snake.

301

Damn, he thought, looking back at Mary Oaks' body. Must've been an accident. She fell off that dresser somehow. Better call it in, he thought, and went back up the stairs. When he got to the kitchen, he thought about Mary Oaks' daughter again. Perhaps she was out. She certainly would have heard him shouting and walking through the house.

He picked up the receiver of the wall phone and called the station. Sam Cobler answered the phone himself. As soon as he said hello, Eddie went into a detailed description of events.

"No sign of foul play?"

"Looks like she fell off a dresser. I found her footprints on the top of it in the dust. Imagine she hit her head. The daughter's not around, so you'd better put out a call on that."

"OK, we'll send up an ambulance. I'll be there in twenty minutes. That's one helluva street."

"You don't have to remind me," Eddie said.

After he hung up, he unzipped his jacket and looked about the kitchen. He poured himself a glass of water and leaned back against the sink, staring ahead down the corridor. It was then that he heard the slight tap, tap, tap, coming from somewhere above him, deeper in the house. He listened as hard as he could for a few seconds. Then he put the glass down quietly and moved out of the kitchen. When he reached the stairway, he stopped and listened again, but now he didn't hear anything. Even so, he directed his flashlight up into the darkness and followed the beam to the second level. Once there, he located a light switch and illuminated the corridor. He listened again. This time he was sure—there was a distinct tapping coming from further in; so he headed toward it.

The periods of hallucination and hysteria had begun to merge in Faith. She had taken to crawling around the floor of the room and stopping randomly at a spot.

302

There she would sit and sing and talk to herself until the urge to move came on her again. She wouldn't cry out or call. Her mouth had become so dry, that her lips cracked and her tongue felt hard and brittle like old leaves.

In her nervousness she had pulled and tugged on her clothing and hair. Her blouse was torn at the collar and unbuttoned, some of the buttons having been ripped off. Her hair, wild and disheveled, puffed out around her head as if filled with static electricity. The palms of her hands and her knees were raw from the crawling. When she sat back against the wall, she held her hands on her lap, as though they were on fire, keeping the fingers opened and bent, the palms up. She stared forward, her eyes glassy and empty, her face bland. She looked like someone beyond pain, now in a stage of numbness and on the border of unconsciousness.

Occasionally, her hands would drop to the floor. When that happened, she would form her small, soft fists and pound with slow, methodical up and down motions devoid of much enthusiasm. It was this sound that Eddie Morris had first heard. The house carried it through its structure, amplifying it slightly in the ceiling beams.

Even so, she didn't hear Eddie's footsteps or realize he was just outside the door. He stopped and listened again. This time he heard her shuffling about and moaning, so he directed his light on the door. He went to it and knocked.

To her it was like thunder. She stopped her movements and sat back. He knocked again and called. She stood up and leaned against the wall to steady herself. Before she went to the door, she cupped her hands and brushed back her hair.

"Hello?"

"Daddy?" she said.

Eddie heard her and tried the handle. He saw that

the door was locked and the key was gone. He rattled the knob and knocked once more. She turned the knob from the inside.

"It's the police," he said. "Can you open this door?"

"I'm locked in here, Daddy. I've got to get out to tell Mary about the baby. Hurry."

"It's the police, Officer Morris," Eddie said, pressing his face to the door. "I'm going to force this door open. Step back." He waited a moment and again tried to open one of The Oaks doors by slamming his shoulder against it. Like the front door, it barely budged. "Dammit. Hold on," he said and turned about to look for something to pry it open.

He remembered seeing some tools in the kitchen, so he hurried back downstairs and got a hammer and a long screwdriver. When he returned, he listened again before he started and heard some soft sobbing. "Hold on," he called and worked the screwdriver in between the door and the jamb near the lock. He pounded it with his hammer and then began to pry and pull. The tooth of the lock came undone and the door flew open.

The sight stopped him cold. Faith hadn't realized how many times she had scratched her face. She looked like a caged animal that had turned on itself. Her torn clothing, the wild hair, the crazed look in her eyes, and the terrible odors in the room all made him step back.

"What the hell happened?" he asked.

"She doesn't know," Faith said in a loud whisper. "We've got to tell her."

"Look," he said. "I don't know what's going on here, but there's been an accident in the basement."

"Yes." She nodded her head quickly. "In the basement . . . he's been getting out."

"Huh? Do you know something about what happened down there?"

"We've got to tell Mary," she said, pronouncing each word very distinctly. "Now."

"OK. Just take it easy. Come on," he said, "let's get you into the bathroom first where you can clean up. All right?" He went to reach for her and she screamed. She embraced herself and cringed. His arm froze in the air. For a few seconds he didn't move a muscle. "Take it easy," he said. She pressed herself back against the wall and glared at him. "Jeez," he muttered. "Listen, I'm not going to hurt you. Relax. I'll get you help. Don't you want to come out and get a drink or something? How long have you been in here?" he asked her and recalled Bobby O'Neil telling him Faith wasn't in school today. "Huh?" She shook her head.

"Your name's Faith, right?" he said smiling. "I'm Eddie Morris. You know my wife. She's one of your teachers—Mrs. Morris." She simply stared at him. "Is there someone you'd like me to call? Someone who can come to stay with you?"

"Where's Mary?"

"Mary? Mary's . . . er . . . Mary got hurt in the basement. That's why you should come out."

"Hurt? He hurt her? He hurt her, too? Oh, God . . ." She brought her hands to her cheeks.

"Who? Who hurt her? Did you see someone hurt her or threaten her?"

"The Devil," she whispered.

"Huh?"

"He *is* the Devil. She was right. I've got to tell her before it's too late."

She moved around the room, edging toward the door, eyeing him closely as she did so.

"I'm not going to hurt you," he said, stepping back to make her feel more secure. The moment he did so, she ran by him out the door and down the corridor to the stairway. He took another look around the room, at the boarded windows and the bed with the Bible on it, and shook his head. "This is really something," he muttered and went out to see where the crazed teenager had gone.

By the time he reached the bottom of the stairs, she was on her way to the basement. He heard her pounding down the old wooden steps. He wondered if he should call in to tell the chief to bring Myra Goodman up with him so there would be a woman to help out. But then he thought, Myra wasn't working tonight; that's why the chief answered the phone himself.

He followed Faith into the basement, deciding it wasn't good to leave her alone down there, even for a few moments. She was already in an hysterical state. Who knew what this sight would do to her? Why was she locked in that room, anyway? he wondered as he went down to her.

He found her kneeling by Mary's body, holding her hand and talking to her.

"You were right. You were right all along," she said. "Now we've got to go and find him. He's out there. Come on, Mary. Come on." She waited a moment and then said, "Mother . . . you were right. Mother . . . "

He knelt beside her, afraid to touch her for fear of how she would react. She looked at him and then she looked back at Mary. Through the hole in the fieldstone wall, he could hear the siren of the ambulance in the distance.

"She's been hurt badly," he said as softly as he could. "Looks like she took a bad fall. She was standing on this dresser, I think. I imagine she was trying to get to something up there," he said and gestured toward the ceiling. Faith followed his gesture and then stood up quickly, glaring at the ceiling. She backed up and held her arms extended as though to protect herself.

"MAYBE HE'S UP THERE!" she screamed. "HE'S UP THERE!"

306

"What? Who?" Eddie stood up quickly and ran the light over the ceiling. "What's up there? Tell me."

"The baby," she said.

"Baby? What baby? How could a baby be up there?" he asked incredulously, but directed the beam into the dark corners anyway.

"He crawls. He climbs. He calls to me through the floor," she said in that loud whispering voice. "He blows through the boards and touches my hand. He touches my hand!"

"There was a baby down here?" Eddie looked at the box and the raggedy blanket. "Living down here? Whose baby?"

"Mary!" Faith said, kneeling beside the body again. She took Mary's hand. "Get up. You've got to get up!"

"She's not going to get up, Honey," Eddie said gently. "Please, talk to me. What baby?"

His kind tone, his soft expression, and his height and size reminded her of her father when she was young. She wished she could be that young again and there could be some sunlight on the house. She closed her eyes and waited for the magic. It could come. If you wanted it hard enough, it could come.

"Daddy," she whispered.

"I'm listening," he said. If she wanted to call him Daddy, that was all right. As long as it led to her explaining things. "What baby are you talking about, Faith? Whose baby was down here?"

"Mary's baby," she said, looking down at her mother. "My . . . broth . . . brother."

"What? Your mother had a baby? How old is the baby? Was it a boy?" he added quickly.

"Yes."

"How many years old is he?"

"He's a little more than four," she said. She spoke like someone under hypnosis.

"And she kept him . . ." Eddie looked around

307

again. Then he looked at the hole in the wall. "He got out? He's been getting out. That's it, isn't it? That's it," he said. "Incredible. Why did she do this? Has he always been kept down here? My God, he has, hasn't he?" he said before she could respond.

He heard the ambulance pulling up to The Oaks.

"Let's go upstairs," he said, reaching out for her this time. "You need some medical treatment, Honey. Come on."

"I'm afraid," she said.

"No. Don't be. I'll go up with you. Come on."

"Promise?"

"Sure."

"And take me for rides again and be with us . . ."

"I will." He brought her to her feet. She looked down at Mary sadly and shook her head.

"Mary's asleep. Mary's with God," she said and then she smiled. Even though it was a good smile, it gave him the chills to see it. "That's all she ever wanted anyway," she said.

He led her away and up the stairs, turning back only once to look at the box and the hole in the fieldstone wall.

He told the paramedics to take care of her first. There wasn't much for them to do with Mary Oaks. He waited out front for Sam Cobler to arrive and then he took him through the old house and the mystery it had hidden.

SEVENTEEN

The barking dogs woke him. He hadn't really slept much during the night and he had dozed off only minutes before he heard them. Although they were far off and held on leashes, he thought they were dangerously close. He had lost his sense of perspective. Things that were solid looked liquid. Colors merged and faded. His hands and his feet seemed far away and growing farther and farther.

He forced himself into a standing position. Somewhere in the back of his brain, the last vestiges of sensible thoughts were emerging. He didn't like where he was; he didn't like the sounds coming from his right, and he was very uncomfortable.

He grunted and moved forward, feeling as though he were floating. The bottom part of his body was numb. He had to look down to be sure he was touching the ground. He could see the house, and he had enough consciousness left to know that he wanted to go to it. Despite his eagerness, he moved like one treading water. Gradually, he quickened his pace until he almost charged out of the bush. As he hurried along, he heard a strange, high-pitched cry and realized it was coming from him.

The dogs, chasing his scent, followed his earlier zigzagged journey and led Eddie Morris and two other patrolmen off to the left. He heard the barking diminish and felt a little safer, but he didn't slow down. When he reached the house, he went to all fours and crawled to the opening. There was a police car parked in the front and two policemen standing beside it, but he didn't see it or them and they didn't hear or see him.

Breathing hard now, he struggled to get himself through the hole. He missed his footing on the stones, as he lowered himself through, and slid all the way to the basement floor, scraping his legs and stomach. He lay there for a few minutes, gasping and clawing the floor. Athough he felt pain, he didn't cry. His throat was much too constricted and the heaviness in his chest made it difficult to do much more than inhale and exhale.

He didn't think of Mary anymore. Indeed, he didn't even remember that he had left her lying there, not far from where he himself lay now. Something triggered his memory, finally, and he turned and headed for the box. When he got there, he was disappointed that his blanket was gone, but he was much too tired and too weak to do anything about it. Instead, he slipped in and curled up as comfortably as he could.

Another memory returned and he embraced himself. He felt his eyes growing heavier and heavier. It was good to close them and close out as much light as possible. Something nudged at him and he opened his eyes again to discover that he was jerking his legs up against his stomach. This convulsion frightened him, so he started to do his hum. He couldn't control the volume and length of it, but it gave him some pleasure and some sense of security.

The convulsions grew more intense. It became impossible to hold the embrace on himself. His arms began moving on their own and his head started to bob spasmodically. He bit his tongue a few times and tasted the blood. His eyes rolled and he foamed at the mouth, nearly choking on his own sputum.

Then, just as suddenly as the convulsions had begun, they stopped. He felt a warm glow come over him and he settled into himself. He felt as though he were shrinking. The sides of the box grew larger, taller. He struggled to stop it, but he continued to diminish. The only thing that would slow it down was closing his eyes.

When he did so, a sound struggled to emerge from deep within. It wasn't a familiar sound. At least, he couldn't recall making it often. But when it came, he welcomed it. It made him extend his arms into the air above him. He wanted something very much. It was the touch of something, something like himself, something warm and secure, something that would end his fear.

But when he opened his eyes, he saw that there was nothing there. He brought his hands back to his body in disappointment and stroked himself softly. He tried for the hum, but even that was gone now. Gradually, his arms settled beside him on the bottom of the box. His closed eyes wouldn't open and he felt a great, all-pervasive fatigue. He whimpered once and then surrendered to it.

He didn't think of death and dying; he thought of something very cold crawling over his body. When it reached his face, he turned to it and, like a baby seeking its mother's breast, he moved his lips and swallowed.

They found him with his eyes sewn closed, his lips pursed, and his arms holding his twisted little body.

Epilogue

Cy Baum stepped out on his front porch and took a deep breath. Hilda was right. It had cooled down and gone back to being a normal spring. Perhaps the summer wouldn't be as unbearable as he had first thought.

He looked up at the night sky. It was mostly overcast, although he didn't think it was going to rain. He would take the walk after all, he thought, and started down the front steps.

Arnie had called and he had told him about the destruction of the bats. Then Hilda got on and told him about the Oaks baby. Cy didn't want her to tell him, but Hilda said they'd find out, because it would be in all the newspapers anyway. She was probably right. He was just afraid that somehow this would all be translated into his seeing his grandchildren less and less.

The farm, the land, the whole area had taken on a new meaning because of what had happened. Even he felt it. He wondered if this feeling would pass. Would the trees and the forest ever be as beautiful? Could they take short walks in the woods? How would he and Hilda feel sitting out here nights this summer? Would the darkness be threatening?

Just as he reached the road, he heard Hilda open the front door behind him.

"Where are you going?"

"Just for my usual walk."

"Be careful," she said. "Are you dressed warm enough?"

"Yeah, sure."

She lingered in the doorway. In the distance the roof of The Oaks was visible just over the tops of trees. He thought about it, dark and brooding. Years from now, the Oaks girl might come back to it. Or perhaps she would be unable to return. Perhaps it housed too many unpleasant memories for her.

He heard Hilda close the door. He took a few more steps into the darkness and then he stopped.

He always believed that the dead left something of themselves behind. His father and his father's father were in this land, in his house, and in him. What part of Mary Oaks was left in that house? More importantly, what part was left in her daughter?

Maybe she would come back. Maybe she would have to, because she was drawn to it by things she could never understand or control. What really makes us the way we are? he wondered.

Eddie Morris told him it looked pathetic in the box.

Pathetic and frightening, he said. Like something gone wild in Nature. Like something of ourselves that we would like to forget.

He heard a screech owl in the darkness. It sounded too much like a child. He felt the cool breeze wrap itself around him and he decided to turn back to the house, back to the light and the warmth.

It was too late to take a long walk in the darkness. He would leave that for another time.

Behind him, The Oaks remained draped in the shadows of the night. Someone had slapped a thin board up against the hole in the foundation. It rattled against the stone as though something inside were trying to get out.

Then the breeze changed direction and the rattling stopped.

All was quiet, as though everything in Nature paused to take a breath before going on again.